Never Dead Enough

Book 3 of *The Dead Among Us*

No matter how dead the dead are, they're just never dead enough.

by

J. L. Doty

TELEMACHUS PRESS

Never Dead Enough, **Book 3 of** *The Dead Among Us*

Cover designed by Telemachus Press, LLC

Cover art:
Copyright © iStock/82137475/KatarzynaBialasiewicz
Copyright © iStock/46900354
Copyright © iStock/46852058
Copyright © Thinkstockphoto/100549058/Hemera

Published by Telemachus Press, LLC
http://www.telemachuspress.com

Visit the author's website:
http://www.jldoty.com

Follow the author on Twitter:
http://www.twitter.com/@JL_Doty

ISBN: 978–1–945330–27–8 (eBook)
ISBN: 978–1–953757–07–4 (Paperback)
ISBN: 978–1–953757–18–0 (Paperback)

Version 2022.11.16

KEpuz!po!KJNEFTLUPQ:
Formatted using eTools for Writers 3.8.8, Nov 29 2022, 18:05:38
Copyright © 2013-2016 by J. L. Doty

Printed in the United States of America

10 9 8 7 6 5 4 3 2 1

Never Dead Enough

Book 3 of *The Dead Among Us*

Prologue:
A Typically Unusual Day

PAUL PAUSED FOR a moment in the lobby of the office building on Market Street, and looked at his reflection in one of the floor-to-ceiling windows separating him from the sidewalk outside. For just an instant he thought he saw a blood-red glare flash from his eyes, but the moment ended quickly, though the red flare reminded him of the chicken-headed, snake-legged monster he and Katherine had encountered in the Netherworld, and he wondered about that.

He took one last look at his image in the window. His tie was straight, suit neatly pressed; perhaps a bit more formal than day-to-day attire, but he didn't know this Mierfendoplay fellow, didn't know why he'd asked to see Paul, so he wanted to err on the side of proper and conservative.

He turned away from the window, headed for the elevators, got one right away and stepped into it. He pressed the button for the forty-fourth floor.

"Suite 4401," Mierfendoplay's secretary had told him on the phone. For some reason that struck a familiar chord in Paul's memory, but he couldn't quite recall exactly what or where, so he shrugged it off.

When the elevator doors opened it was obvious suite 4401 occupied the entire forty-fourth floor. There was no hallway leading to other suites; the elevator opened directly into a large and luxurious lobby for Mierfendoplay's firm. Behind a darkly wooded desk sat a receptionist that could've made it into any modeling agency in the world. As Paul approached her she smiled.

"I'm Paul Conklin. I have an appointment with Mr. Mierfendoplay."

Her smile widened, she leaned forward and spoke in a confidential tone. "*He's* a she, and yes, Mr. Conklin, Mierfendoplay is expecting you. Please have a seat"—she waved her hand at a couch against one wall—"and I'll let her know you're here."

Paul sat down, picked up a magazine and leafed through it, not really paying attention to anything on its pages. He didn't have to wait more than a minute or two before the door to an inner office opened and a woman stepped out. She made the runway-model receptionist look plain.

Paul rose up from the couch as she stepped through the door and he realized she stood well over six feet tall—had a couple inches on him—wore a dark business suit with a pencil skirt cut just above her knees, with long legs that ended in what looked like expensive shoes. Beneath a suit coat cut to emphasize her figure, she wore a white blouse Paul thought might be made of silk. She'd left two or three buttons undone, exposing a bit of cleavage, and Paul tried not to stare, for she was incredibly beautiful. She wore her coal-black hair cut chin-length, and her face had a slight Asian cast to it. A piece of him thought he should be surprised at her blood-red skin—blood red face, arms, legs, chest, cleavage—but that thought fluttered away as soon as it came, because, of course, her blood-red skin seemed quite normal.

"Paul Conklin?" she asked politely, speaking in a deep and resonant contralto. She stuck out her hand. "I'm Mierfendoplay."

"It's nice to meet you, Ms. Mierfendoplay," Paul said, shaking her hand. Paul looked into her eyes, and for a moment he thought they were amber, like the eyes of a cat, with vertically slit pupils. But when he blinked and looked again her pupils were quite normal and round, though her eyes were a striking hazel that complemented her bright red skin.

"It's just Mierfendoplay," she said. "No *Ms.*"

As she turned and led him into her office, Paul couldn't escape the feeling he'd done this before. She pointed him to a comfortable chair facing a desk the size of an aircraft carrier. He waited until she sat down behind the desk before seating himself.

"I must confess," Paul said, "I'm not sure why you want to see me."

"Hmmm!" she said. "That you wonder at that speaks volumes for your potential."

Paul spoke without considering his words. "That's a rather obscure response. It sounds like something Dayandalous would say."

Dayandalous, Paul wondered. Where had that name come from?

Her eyes widened in surprise, and for an instant they flared red through vertically slit pupils, but the instant passed. "It was Dayandalous who told me I should meet you. He said you would surprise me, pleasantly so, and you have. I haven't been surprised that way in centuries."

Paul wanted to ask her what she meant by *centuries*, but as he opened his mouth to speak the thought fluttered away, and he couldn't recall what he'd been about to say.

At his hesitation, she asked, "Is there something on your mind?"

"Um . . ." he said, realizing he sounded like a dim-witted fool, ". . . I was going to ask you something, but the thought slipped my mind."

Her eyebrows rose. "That too is impressive."

"How so?"

"Not only should the thought have slipped your mind, but the fact that the thought slipped your mind should have also slipped your mind." She leaned forward intently. "Dayandalous finds that quite interesting, as do I."

There was that name again: Dayandalous. "Why do you and he always speak in riddles? And why do I feel like I know who you're talking about, and yet I've never met anyone by that name?"

Paul had walked into the room with a dozen questions on his mind, and during their conversation the number had grown considerably. But as he tried to order his thoughts, to pick the first question to ask, his concerns dissipated and all his questions became irrelevant.

Mierfendoplay stood. "Well thank you for coming in, Paul."

Paul also stood, because that was what he was supposed to do. He was certain of it. Mierfendoplay escorted him back to the elevators, personally called an elevator for him, and kept up a polite and charming banter while they waited for it.

When the elevator doors swished open, Paul stepped through them and turned to face Mierfendoplay. She smiled, and just as the doors closed she said, "Be wary of the Egyptian, Paul."

That was an odd thing to say. As the elevator plunged downward he tried to recall if he knew any Egyptians. He'd lost touch with most of his friends after Suzanna and Cloe had been murdered by Simuth, but as he considered them all, he certainly didn't know any . . .

Any what?

In the back of Paul's thoughts he kept thinking there was something he'd forgotten, and it wasn't until he stepped into the lobby on the ground floor that he realized he hadn't learned anything about Mierfendoplay's reason for wanting to meet him.

He turned around, went back to the elevators and called one, thinking he could at least ask the receptionist a few polite questions. When the elevator arrived he stepped into it, and was going to press the button for the forty-fourth floor, but there was no such button. He stood there for a moment staring at the buttons, and they ended at thirty-eight. Perhaps one of the other elevators went all the way to the top. There were six of them, and he patiently waited for each, but not one went beyond the thirty-eighth floor. He searched the lobby, thinking he'd taken a wrong turn and would find another bank of elevators, but that wasn't the case either.

Paul asked the security guard in the lobby, "How do I get to the forty-fourth floor?"

The guard's eyes narrowed and he looked at Paul oddly. For some reason Paul's question had angered the man. "We've been through this before, buddy. There's no forty-fourth floor in this building. The top floor is thirty-eight."

"But I was just on the forty-fourth floor." Paul decided to mention the name of the woman he'd just spoken to up there, but he couldn't remember anything about her.

The guard's eyes narrowed further, and he spoke as if talking to a dimwitted child. "I said no forty-fourth floor. If you have business on the forty-fourth floor, then you got the wrong building."

Paul glanced around the lobby and again saw his reflection in the window, but now a young girl stood next to him. She looked to be about eight years old, wore a gray pinafore over a pale-blue dress, with white knee-high stockings and shiny black shoes, her blond hair in pigtails. He quickly scanned the lobby, but he and the security guard were alone.

The guard ushered Paul out onto the sidewalk. Paul stood there for a moment, then turned back to the building and looked at it carefully. It was like any of a dozen other buildings on Market Street, and for the life of him he couldn't remember why he'd wasted his time coming there.

••••

Standing on the top of the steps in front of his building, Paul fumbled in his pocket for his keys.

"Meow."

He looked down and found a little cat nestled against his ankles, probably female because of her smallish size, with a random pattern of black-and-white blotches covering her from head to tail. He'd heard such cats were called tuxedoes because of their coloring.

"Meow."

He squatted down and scratched her beneath the chin, wondering if she belonged to someone in the building. She appeared healthy and well groomed, nothing like the feral cats he occasionally spotted on the city streets. One smear of black fur started in the middle of her upper lip and extended to the left, like half of a Hitler mustache.

"You're a cute one," he said, as she pressed her chin forcefully against his fingernails, clearly enjoying his attention, purring and grumbling in her throat.

He wondered if he should bring her in, in case she did belong to someone in the building and had gone missing. But he really didn't have time to care for a pet, so with a bit of regret he stood and unlocked the front door of the building. As he stepped through it, a little black-and-white streak shot between his legs and disappeared up the stairs. She probably did belong to someone in the building, and would wait at the door to her owner's apartment.

He closed the front door of the apartment building, and checked to be sure it was locked. He heard her meow from somewhere up the stairs, and when he turned around he spotted her standing on the landing above him. As he took the first step she shot out of sight farther up the stairs.

When he got to his own floor she stood on the landing half a floor above him and meowed piteously. "Go on and find your owner," he said.

He turned, retrieved his keys, opened his apartment door, and the little black-and-white lightning bolt shot between his legs a second time. She ran across the living room, jumped onto the back of the couch and stretched sensuously. "Meow," she said in a very satisfied tone.

He crossed the room, reached down and scratched her behind the ears. She arched her back, again enjoying his attention. When he picked her up she purred.

"Sorry, little girl," he said. "I'd love to keep you, but you probably have an owner somewhere, and in any case, I can't take responsibility for a pet."

He carried her to the door, opened it, and gently placed her on the floor in the hall. But the instant he released her, she streaked between his legs again back into his apartment.

She hid behind his couch, refused to come out, and when he tried to reach for her she gave him a self-assured, "Meow." When he moved the couch away from the wall she shot past him into the bedroom and hid under his bed. He spent a good half hour trying to corner her, but every time he got close she proved to be too fast for him and he couldn't get his hands on her. He finally gave up.

"Okay," he said. "I guess I don't have much choice, guess you're going to spend the night."

He retrieved a small bowl from the kitchen, poured a little milk into it and put it on the floor. She sauntered over to it, clearly confident he was never going to get his hands on her. She sat down in front of it and lapped up the milk.

"What'll I call you?" he asked her. "Though I guess it really doesn't matter, since you're going to have to go as soon as your owner turns up."

He considered putting a little poster in the foyer on the ground floor, something about *found a stray, black-and-white, female cat.* He'd provide his phone number so her owner could call and retrieve her.

She looked up from the milk and said, "I don't have an owner. Nobody owns *me*. And the name's Madge."

Paul started and stepped back a pace. "You— You— You talked!"

She lifted a paw, licked it with a little pink tongue, looked at him and said, "Meow."

"No! No! You spoke English."

She rolled her eyes. "Of course I spoke English. You wouldn't understand me if I spoke Chinese."

"But— But— You're a cat."

"Well," she said. "About that. This form is . . . convenient. And I love hunting, killing and eating little mouses. It reminds me of the time I killed— No, best to save that story for when we know each other a little better."

Paul couldn't keep his voice from rising a couple octaves, "But you're a cat."

"No I'm not. I'm your familiar."

Paul sat down on his couch and buried his face in his hands. He must be imagining all of this. He was certain of it. Somehow he'd adopted a cat, and he was lost in another hallucination.

"You're not hallucinating. And you didn't adopt me, I adopted you."

••••

He'd taken a small bachelor apartment in the Castro District, then transferred the car registration to the state of California. He'd been so careful for so long that caution and attention to the little details came almost without thought. Texas plates could make him stand out in San Francisco, a minor issue easily overlooked by someone less thorough than him, but just the kind of thing a passerby might notice. Constant diligence regarding seemingly trivial matters ensured that his activities never came to the attention of the local practitioners, though, in Dallas, *he* and *she* had changed that. He would make them pay for that.

As twilight settled over the city he drove down the street, careful not to exceed the speed limit by more than a few miles per hour. Prostitutes were plentiful in the Tenderloin District, but he needed the right kind. He'd learned to stay away from Larkin Street, where most of the working girls were actually transgender. And then there were other streets where the girls were predominantly black. Black, or Asian, or any race, for that matter, would satisfy his master's need to grow Its power, but only Caucasian girls could be a true Alice.

He drove slowly down the street, rejecting several possibilities. One girl was considerably overweight, which wasn't Alice. Another wore clunky boots and goth clothing, and when he got close and saw all the piercings, he knew nothing could turn her into an Alice. He turned a corner wondering if he'd ever find the right girl, and then he spotted her. She was white, probably female—which he'd have to confirm—small, with a petite figure, and blond hair.

Yes, the voice said. *She's perfect.*

He slowed the car a bit, and as he got closer she looked his way. Her eyes tracked him carefully, but as he slowed further and approached her he saw more details, and she had an emaciated look about her, with dark circles under her eyes. She wore a tight skirt that ended well above mid-thigh, and he noticed a small tear in her dark, fish-net stockings. It was not a strategically placed tear like some of the girls chose to wear. Up close she was far from perfect.

"She's not Alice," he said.

But she'll have to do.

"Why can't we just find another Alice, a young, pretty one?"

Because that would alert them to our presence.

He understood that. It was the little things that kept him alive. It was the little things that could get him killed.

He stopped the car next to the curb in front of her and pressed the button for the passenger side window. As it rolled down she leaned forward and her halter top billowed outward, giving him a clear view of small breasts; he had no doubt she'd done that intentionally. Now that he saw her face clearly, he figured she was in her mid-twenties. She sniffed as if she had a runny nose from a cold, though it was more likely she had damaged her nasal passages by snorting any number of illegal substances. Her left hand also shook with a slight palsy, though she controlled it well enough.

"Hi," she said. "Looking for some fun?"

His voice trembled when he spoke. "How much?" He wasn't really going to pay her, but he had to go through the motions of asking.

"You gotta say it," she said, "so I know you ain't a cop. Gotta cross the line so if you are one, it's entrapment."

"How much for a fuck?" He wasn't going to fuck her either, but he had to properly play his role as a john and at least pretend.

Her face showed no emotion. "Hundred bucks. Half before I get in the car, half when we're done."

"Are you a real girl? I'm not paying for a trannie."

She grinned. "Don't worry, honey, I got a real pussy for you."

He looked up and down the street, saw a few more girls milling about, didn't see any police, wasn't sure he'd know what to look for if they were undercover, or something like that.

"And you don't gotta worry about that either," she said. "When the cops are around we know it. And they ain't hassling us tonight."

He reached into his pocket, pulled out a small roll of ten-dollar bills. He touched a finger to his tongue and put a little saliva on it, then peeled the top bill off the roll; the saliva was an important ingredient. He held the ten out to her. She wouldn't know he wasn't giving her the full fifty until she had the bill in her hands, but once her fingers touched it, it wouldn't matter.

She took the bill and that was the last thing needed to trigger the spell. Her eyes widened for a moment, and for the first time he noticed they were blue, which was very Alice. Her face slackened, her fingers relaxed and she dropped the bill onto the front seat. He reached over and retrieved it as she stepped back from the car. Then he put it in gear and slowly drove away. She'd wait a few minutes, then follow at a leisurely pace, not even aware she was doing his bidding. No one, especially none of the other hookers on the street, would see her get into his car. No one would identify him as the last person to see her alive.

He pulled into the parking structure on O'Farrell Street. It was late, and the monthly permit parkers had all gone home. He had no trouble finding a slot and parked his car on the ground floor; how convenient. He got out, locked the car and walked out onto the sidewalk. He strolled casually for two blocks, then turned into the alley. It was dark and unlit, and he found her waiting half-way down it in the darker shadows behind some dumpsters. Perfect!

"Please," she said.

She had no control over her actions, but it was imperative that she feel the terror, that she experience every second as his master devoured her soul.

"Please," she said again.

"Silence," he hissed, "not a sound."

He liked it when they pleaded, but he couldn't afford the possibility someone might overhear her, or that she might cry out when the time came.

He bent down next to one of the dumpsters and retrieved the charm he'd left under one corner. It was mated to the spell he'd woven into the ten-dollar bill, and had led her to this spot.

He pressed her against the wall of the alley, pulled on surgical gloves and retrieved the syringe from his pocket. "Hold out your left arm."

She did so obediently. He looked into her eyes, and savored the terror he saw there.

The syringe contained a designer drug he'd concocted using his considerable arcane abilities. If the authorities tested it, they'd find it produced a mild buzz for about fifteen minutes, after which it was most unpleasantly lethal. But this young girl would be dead from a much more horrible cause long before that.

He removed the protective cap on the needle and tossed it aside, then retrieved another spelled charm from his pocket. He spit on it, pressed it against the vein on the inside of her arm, and lightly pressed the needle against it. In the dark the spell caused her vein to swell nicely, then guided the needle into it. He injected about half the syringe into her arm, then clamped the syringe to her arm with his hand so it wouldn't fall out.

She stood there with her mouth open trying to speak or utter some cry, but he'd commanded her to silence, and his spells controlled her completely. He caressed her cheek and she shivered. Tears streamed down her face as he leaned forward, cupped the back of her head in one hand and tilted her head back. He opened his mouth and covered hers with his. Then he exhaled, and as he leaned away from her a black shadowy stain extended from his mouth to hers, flowing from him to her and entering her soul.

For just an instant she looked at him with blood-red, goat-slitted eyes. Then a spasm shook her and she stiffened. Because of his spell she couldn't struggle, thrash or cry out, and that disappointed him. She stood there in catatonic rigidity for the longest time, then she died, and her death washed over him, filled him with sorrow. It would have been wonderful if she'd been more of an Alice.

He let her slump to the ground, the needle still in her arm. The authorities would find her and conclude she had died from an overdose. When they examined the syringe, they'd learn it was a new designer drug they hadn't seen before. In any case, there'd be no injuries or trauma, and she was a drug-addict prostitute, so the medical examiner probably wouldn't even perform an autopsy.

There was one last detail that must be attended to if he wanted to ensure no practitioners detected demon scent on the corpse. His master gained even greater strength by leaving a remnant of itself in a victim's soul, but they'd learned in Dallas how dangerous that could be. "You can't stay with her," he said.

Nothing happened for the longest moment. Then she twitched, and the oily black cloud slowly emerged from her eyes, ears, nose and mouth. A wisp of it even emerged from her crotch. He inhaled and took all of it into his soul. He'd never taken it back before, never felt such intimate contact with violent death, and he loved it. He also sensed his master's increased strength.

Yes, the voice said. *I am stronger now, but not strong enough. A few more like this one and we'll be ready to hunt the young wizard and his woman.*

1

A Difficult Boundary

PAUL GOT UP early and searched his apartment carefully; no sign of Madge, so he concluded she was just another hallucination. He thought it might be best if he didn't mention her to anyone.

He stripped, hopped in the shower, soaped down, rinsed, and when he pulled the shower curtain aside he froze at the sight of the little cat. She'd climbed up onto the lip of the toilet bowl with her paws balanced there, her tail and butt in the air, her head hidden beneath the rim. He heard the sound of her tongue lapping up water. He stood there dripping wet and watched as she lifted her head above the edge of the toilet and licked her lips with a satisfied look on her face.

He was hallucinating again. "You . . . uh . . ." he said. "Um . . . you shouldn't . . . do that."

"Why not?"

"It's . . . uh . . . not sanitary."

She rolled her eyes. "Paul, I'm a cat. I'm always subject to the proclivities of the form I've taken."

"The form you've taken. Um . . . you said that before."

She shook her head sadly. "You're not making a good impression with the stuttering, the hesitation, and the *uhs* and the *ums*. You need to be more forceful. I mean, like, how are you ever going to score with that pretty young McGowan girl?"

"Score?" he asked, unable to keep his voice down. "Score? I'm not trying to score. You sound like a pubescent high-school boy."

She hopped down from the rim of the toilet, and as she sauntered out of the bathroom, she said over her shoulder, "I'm just trying to help you get laid." She paused and turned her head around to look at him, turned her head the way only a cat could. "Though I heard you had quite a time of it with that Belinda slut."

Paul grabbed a towel and started drying off. "But . . . I . . ."

She walked out of sight into the living room. "You're stuttering again. Way not cool."

By the time Paul had dried off, got his underwear on and followed her, Madge had disappeared. He searched the apartment and found no sign of her. She'd probably found a little hiding place he'd never uncover, but then again, since he was hallucinating, his mind could certainly make her disappear and reappear at will, though, apparently, not at *his* will. In any case, he had an appointment to meet old man McGowan, and he didn't have any more time to waste.

He combed his hair, shaved, gulped down a bowl of cereal, bushed his teeth and threw on his clothes, then ran down the stairs to the ground floor. But as he closed the front door of his apartment building, and paused to make sure it was locked, he glanced through the small window in the door and saw her sitting on the first landing, licking a paw. He hadn't let her out of the apartment, and he was certain she hadn't streaked between his legs as he walked through the door, so she was definitely a hallucination.

As he stood there, staring through that window at her, she slowly morphed into Alice in Wonderland, standing there in her pinafore, knee-high socks and black shoes. But there was something decidedly wrong about her.

The piercing cry of a hunting hawk interrupted his thoughts. He started, spun around and dropped into a crouch, expecting to find the seven-foot-tall crazy woman with haunted eyes charging at him, ready to chop him in two with that big sword of hers. It was a busy San Francisco morning, so the street was far from empty, but there were no nut-cases close at hand. Then again, it was San Francisco, so the coefficient of whackos-per-city-block was probably quite high, but at least there were no heavily armed Faerie crazies in gray leathers and dreadlocks.

As he walked toward the Powell Street cable car terminal he tried to recall if he'd ever heard the cry of a hawk in the city before. Red-tailed hawks were quite common in California, and surely there must be some in and around the city parks. But before his recent misadventures, if he had heard such a sound, he'd probably not paid it the least bit of attention. Most likely it had just been part of the constant din of the city. He'd never again be able to simply ignore the cry of a hawk.

••••

Most tourists in San Francisco think of the cable cars as a fun ride and must-do attraction, and probably don't realize they can be a practical means of transportation as well, though because of the open nature of the cars, weather is often a factor. As an urban resident, Paul knew the city's bus and BART routes well, but for certain destinations, a cable-car ride would do the job nicely, and Cloe had loved the cable cars. Just for fun, she, Paul and Suzanna had used them quite frequently when they weren't crowded.

Paul could take the Powell-Hyde Line up Powell Street, over Nob Hill and down to Fisherman's Wharf, all the way across the city, though that worked well only when the cars weren't packed with tourists. In October, when the crowds of visitors had thinned out some, and especially in the early morning hours, Paul had no trouble getting a seat. And as the car clanked and rattled its way up Powell Street, he couldn't put aside the memory of Alice, and the image he'd seen while standing on the front steps of his apartment building.

She'd worn the classic white pinafore over a blue dress that ended just below the knees, white knee-high stockings and glossy, black, round-toed shoes; very Walt Disney—somewhere he'd heard the shoes were called Mary Janes. But the girl in his delusional image had been older—maybe late twenties—and she'd appeared sickly, with dark circles under her eyes; and gaunt, with a wasted look about her as if she hadn't eaten a decent meal in a long time. He kept thinking *drug-addict prostitute*, and it bothered him that he would imagine Alice in Wonderland that way. He wondered about that all the way down Hyde Street to the end of the cable-car line near Fisherman's Wharf.

The walk to the National Cemetery was almost two miles, and while the autumn morning had a bit of a chill to it, the sky was clear and the sun warmed him. It would have been an enjoyable hike if he could have put Alice out of his mind. The images in his thoughts kept alternating between the hooker-addict, and little Monica Clarkson, a victim of the demon, serial killer in Dallas. He recalled her lifeless body lying on a steel gurney in the Medical Examiner's Office in McKinney, Texas. What did an emaciated prostitute have to do with that poor little girl?

McGowan was waiting for him at the entrance to the National Cemetery. "How you doing, kid?"

The old man sported his local-college-professor look: tweed sport-coat, brown slacks, pale-blue shirt and conservative tie. Paul decided not to tell him about his hallucinations; he'd keep to himself things like Madge the cat, the Alices, and the seven-foot-tall crazy woman from Faerie.

"So you want to learn to use a boundary," McGowan said. "You know, when it comes to Mortals, you're pretty unique in your ability to just step into and back out of Faerie. Why waste your time with a boundary?"

Paul shrugged. "Because I'm not sure what I'm doing, and sometimes it doesn't work."

"It doesn't work?" McGowan asked. "How so?"

Since killing Simuth and avenging Suzanna's and Cloe's murders, he'd experimented a bit. "I tried to go to Faerie from my apartment a couple of times, just as a test, but nothing happened. It didn't work no matter how hard I tried."

McGowan frowned and gave him a questioning look. "That's odd."

"Ya, I'm missing something, and I don't know what. And you and Colleen told me the halls of Sidhe aren't necessarily real. What if the place I want to go to isn't really there when I try to step into it? And I just can't seem to get the *stepping-back-out* part right. I keep reappearing here in the middle of the air in an odd position, and it hurts like hell when I slam into the ground, probably break my neck the next time."

"Ya," McGowan said, nodding and grinning. "You made a real mess of my office the last time."

McGowan slapped him on the back and said, "Come on. Let's go give this a try."

They walked past a stone bench then turned toward the edge of the cemetery. Some months earlier Paul had run into Katherine seated on that same bench, and the leprechauns Jim'Jiminie and Boo'Diddle had used the cemetery's boundary to take them to Faerie for their meeting with the triple goddess. The Morrigan had turned out to be another nut-case from Faerie, but with a three-way split personality: an old crone, a beautiful young maiden, and a naked, skeletal corpse, all three of them loony as hell. To test them she'd set them loose with the Unseelie Hunt on their trail, and then the seven-foot tall crazy woman had shot Paul with *les flèche du coeur*, the heart arrow with blood-red fletching and a coal-black shaft that wasn't supposed to miss its target. It occurred to Paul he had to be a nut-case himself to even consider going back to Faerie, because the place was filled with nothing but crazies.

A gravel strewn walking path lined the edge of the cemetery, with rows of grave markers on one side and trees lining the other. McGowan stopped and examined it carefully. "The perimeter of a cemetery," he said, "the boundary between life and death. The little people were right, a very powerful symbol."

"Symbols are important, huh?" Paul asked.

McGowan looked at him pointedly and said, "Very. Think of something like the Golden Gate Bridge, or the Statue of Liberty. Think of all the immigrants over the past couple of centuries who've looked at one or the other for the first time and thought to themselves, 'Now I've made it.' Think of all the tourists who visit those symbols, or locals who see them every day. If those images stir even the slightest emotion, good or bad, it adds to the power of the symbol, and it accumulates."

"You mean like ley lines?"

"No, it's not the kind of power we can tap directly to create a spell."

"Then how do we tap it?"

"We don't. We just let it influence us. But we have to make it influence us in the right way. Where do you want to go in Faerie?"

Paul had thought about that a lot. He wanted to talk to Anogh, the Summer Knight, and to Cadilus, Magreth's High Chancellor, but he didn't want to simply stumble into the Seelie Court. And he didn't want to ask McGowan to contact them for him. He was running on instinct, and the Old Wizard would have all sorts of questions Paul couldn't answer. "The non-aligned territories," he said.

"Good choice," McGowan said. "Nobody there will try to kill you—well . . . at least not too many of them will. Can you picture the place you want to go?"

"Ya," Paul said. He recalled standing with Katherine beside two leprechauns on a hillside above a green and verdant countryside of low rolling hills, watching smoke curl upward lazily from the chimneys of a dozen quaint little huts as a pink sun burned off a low morning mist. He described it carefully to McGowan, finishing with, "Yes, I can picture it rather vividly."

"Good," the old man said. "That's the first part of the equation."

He pointed along the length of the cemetery's edge. "We're going to walk along that boundary, and as we do so you have to consider the probability that you exist here on the Mortal Plane, and the probability that you exist there in Faerie."

He lowered his arm and turned to face Paul. "This is the hard part for us mortals. Deep down in the lizard part of our brain we fundamentally believe that we're either here or there, and not a mixture of the two. But you're going to have to overcome that kind of thinking. Start out knowing there's one-hundred percent probability you exist here, and zero percent there, and slowly change that. You have to create a slow, steady decrease of the probability in one, while creating an increase in the other. Got it?"

Paul wasn't sure he did *get it*. "I just have to think of it that way, huh?"

McGowan grimaced. "It is a little more complicated than that, but I don't think I can explain exactly how. You're just going to have to try."

The old man turned back to the boundary, and Paul stepped up beside him.

"Okay," McGowan said. "Just a slow, steady pace."

They walked at a few steps per second, and Paul tried counting down from one hundred percent. But when they reached the end of the cemetery, clearly nothing had happened: no verdant countryside, no little huts, and no pink sky.

McGowan turned around. "We'll try again, try walking back the other way. But first, tell me what you did."

Paul shrugged. "I tried to count down from one-hundred."

McGowan shook his head. "No, it's not a precise thing like that. You have to *believe* the probability here is declining, and the probability there is increasing. And between here and there you have to get to a point where you're a bit here, but not fully here, and a bit there, but not fully there."

Paul was not in the least confident he could come up with such convoluted thinking. They tried once more, and when they reached the other end of the cemetery, again nothing. After two more tries, McGowan said, "Let's try something else. Stop thinking of your destination, and I'll take us to one I know of. And you try to get a sense of what I'm doing."

Again they walked down the gravel strewn path, and the Old Wizard took them to an old, abandoned stone structure somewhere in the non-aligned territories. Paul sensed only that shift in reality along a spiral track he'd sensed before, but nothing beyond that. McGowan took them back to the Mortal Plane, Paul tried four more times, and still nothing.

"Let's call it a day," the old man said. "You'll just have to keep trying. Why don't you come back to my place and we'll grab some dinner?"

"Sounds good," Paul said.

McGowan pulled out his cell phone and speed-dialed a number. "Colleen," he said, "glad I caught you. Paul and I are on our way, should be there in about half an hour. You'll join us for dinner, won't you?"

He listened to her response, then said, "Great. See you in a bit."

••••

Jim'Jiminie watched McGowan and Paul walk away from the cemetery's boundary. Standing beside him was Boo'Diddle and Dan'Dandio, a younger version of the two older leprechauns.

Dan'Dandio asked, "Why didn't you let the young wizard cross over?"

Jim'Jiminie said, "Faerie is too dangerous a place for the young man without the young woman at his side. Together they influence the fates. Alone, he is merely a powerful wizard."

"But you let the Old Wizard bring them over."

"Sure enough we did, young fellow," Boo'Diddle said, "but they didn't stay long, and it would have been obvious if we'd tried to block the old man. And the Young Mage is safe with such a strong practitioner at his side."

Jim'Jiminie added, "And I'm not sure we could have blocked the Old Wizard. He's very powerful."

Dan'Dandio said, "So is the young man."

Boo'Diddle shrugged. "But inexperienced."

Jim'Jiminie stroked his beard as he watched the two men leave the cemetery. "If he's trying to cross over, we'll have to keep a closer eye on him."

"Sure," Boo'Diddle said. "That we do. And the young woman too."

2

The Search Begins

HIS BIGGEST PROBLEM was locating the young wizard and witch. From their disastrous encounters in Dallas, his master had acquired their arcane scents. He didn't fully understand the various senses at his master's command, but while a powerful practitioner might mask his capabilities from other mortals, a demon could apparently still pick up some sort of trail and follow it like bloodhounds tracking an escaped prisoner in a movie. His master also assured him the scent of each wizard or witch was unique. There were some limitations, for they could track them only when they had a reasonably fresh trail to follow, and in a city the size of San Francisco he couldn't simply count on stumbling across such a trace.

He knew what they looked like, had seen them that day outside the little Mexican boy's house, taking leave of the boy's father and grandmother. He'd followed their chauffeur-driven limousine back to Highland Park and the mansion of the wealthy, black witch. At that point he'd had to commit to a very dangerous course of action.

He'd rushed home and hurriedly prepared a spell that was difficult for most mortals, but one the Sidhe used quite regularly when on the Mortal Plane. He wasn't confident he could have done it alone, but with the help of his powerful master he'd prepared a potent glamour that would divert an onlooker's eyes from him or his car. A shadow spell would have been much easier, but a large shadow on the street in broad daylight, where no shadow should be, would attract its own attention. The glamour would simply compel an onlooker's eyes to slide off him and find something of interest nearby, not true invisibility, but close enough.

He'd caught a few winks of sleep that night, then in the early morning hours rushed back to Highland Park. He'd parked his car a few blocks away from the witch's mansion where he could keep an eye on the front gate. It was dangerous to just sit there, even with the charm protecting him from the chance curiosity of a neighbor, and if he'd had to do so for more than a day or two, he'd have abandoned the plan. But his luck held; a few hours after sunrise on the first day of watching the place, the front gate of the mansion had slid open and the limousine emerged. He followed it all the way out of the city to Dallas/Fort Worth International, watched the older wizard and witch, accompanied by the younger wizard and witch, step out of the limo onto the curb near the departure gates. As he drove past them they got in line to check their luggage with the skycaps outside.

He'd taken careful note of the airline, then parked his car and hurried back to the ticketing counter. He'd bought an airplane ticket he didn't intend to use, then picked up the trail of their arcane scent and used the ticket to follow it through security. The trail was quite fresh, and he'd had no trouble following it to their departure gate. He got there with time to spare, and careful to mask his arcane abilities from detection, took a nearby seat. While waiting he heard the older witch call the older wizard *Walter*, and the younger witch called him *father*, and he heard the old fellow say something about getting back to San Francisco. An hour later he watched them board a non-stop to the city by the bay.

A senior wizard named Walter something-or-other, with a very pretty daughter, in San Francisco. But where in San Francisco? They could be anywhere from the wine country north of the bay, to a good distance down the peninsula, or even in the east bay. That was the question he must now answer, and the best way to do so would be to tap into the local community of practitioners.

He had to be careful though. His master was powerful beyond imagining, and even though It had not physically manifested on the Mortal Plane, if he came across a true practitioner and they viewed his aura, they'd see the contamination of the demon there. So the demon temporarily withdrew, which left a painful sense of loss in his soul. He also crafted a charm that should hide any residual corruption still visible in his aura. It could be subverted with the right spells or charms, but it should work under a casual *viewing*, as long as the practitioner doing so didn't put any serious effort into it.

He started with bookshops that catered to the occult, and also canvassed local fortune tellers and psychic mediums. Most were scam artists, or delusional old hippies with no real talent. One place was just a front for a travel bureau trying to sell him airline tickets to Sedona, Arizona, plus several nights in an expensive spa where he could experience the healing properties of the Crystal Vortex. He spoke to several psychic mediums on the phone, telling them he'd just moved to the area for a new job and needed a reading and a little career guidance. A few had some potential, so he made appointments to see them. The first had no real talent whatsoever, though she was quite sincere and truly believed in her abilities and the crap she told him. The second had no more talent than the first, and was a flat-out scam artist. He wanted to kill her on general principal, but leaving a trail of bodies would be foolish in the extreme. He'd saved Miss Labella's Tarot and Psychic Reading Service for last, because instinct told him she had the greatest potential.

Miss Labella was an attractive woman of average height who appeared to be in her mid-forties. She had black hair, dark-brown eyes, and wore a simple dress with a fair amount of exposed cleavage, which probably helped her distract her male clients. Most importantly, when he walked into her reading parlor he sensed immediately that she was a true practitioner, though of middle-grade capability, nothing compared to his own abilities. He also sensed the protective wards she'd installed in the room. They were strong enough to handle a mundane assault, or the arcane assault of most practitioners. No wonder she'd agreed to meet alone with a stranger with whom she'd had only a single phone conversation. He also sensed that he could defeat those wards easily with the help of his master, if it came to that.

"Mr. Jardine," she said, using the phony name he'd given her. "It's a pleasure to meet you."

She'd furnished the room with a round table at which two chairs faced one another from opposite sides. The walls were covered with Persian rugs, giving the place a dark and mysterious atmosphere. Even though she was a true practitioner, to make a living at this she probably had to play the role of the fortune teller to the hilt; give people what they expected, as it were.

They shook hands, and she indicated one of the chairs at the table. "Please, make yourself comfortable."

As they sat down facing one another, she placed a large, milky-white crystal in front of her on the table. It was about the length of her longest finger, and twice as wide, with sharp planes and angles and a creamy translucence that prevented it from being truly transparent. He sensed the power she'd fed into it and realized she'd turned the crystal into some sort of tool to aid her. He was glad she hadn't opted for the cliché of a clear, round crystal ball.

She smiled and said, "On the phone you told me you're concerned about your new job. Tell me a little about it."

He'd carefully concocted the story that he'd just moved to the city for a new job, with a make-believe boss and a few coworkers. He described them now, including phony physical descriptions and various personality traits. And while he spoke, she constantly fingered the crystal, which did concern him a bit.

"I don't believe you're being completely honest with me," she said, and his gut clenched with concern. She continued, "But that's understandable for a first reading. As we get to know one another better, and you come to trust me, I hope you'll be more forthcoming."

He relaxed, his fear dissipating with her words. She lifted the crystal and pressed it to her breast as her eyes focused at a great distance—what some referred to as a thousand-yard stare—the characteristic look of a practitioner examining someone's aura. But then her eyes widened and she gasped.

"Demon spawn!" she said, sliding her chair back from the table. The magically enhanced crystal must have helped her see through the effects of his charm.

She triggered her wards at the same moment he summoned his master by saying, "Abrasax."

His master swept into his soul, and the force of her wards bounced off him with no effect. He exhaled, and the oily black cloud of his master's corruption emerged from his mouth and enveloped her completely. "Don't let her cry out," he said as she stiffened, her body going rigid, her mouth open for a scream that never came. In an instant the cloud plunged down her throat and into her soul, and since there was no time to savor the death, his master took her life quickly.

He left her there, slumped at the table. With no physical trauma to the body, like the others, the authorities would attribute her death to *no known causes*. Her demise did provide the added benefit of strengthening his master.

••••

Seated in McGowan's study, Colleen switched off her cell phone and put it in her purse. She lifted the old grimoire off the small side table next to her, and opened it to the page she'd been reading before the old man's call had come in. It was a diary she'd found in a bookstore that specialized in old and rare tomes, and she'd immediately recognized that it was authentic. But it was only about a hundred years old, and the practitioner who had penned the notes contained within it had been of limited talent. Her initial excitement had quickly waned as she realized she already knew all his spells and incantations.

The old man's study was just off the hall near the house's front entrance, so when someone opened the front door, she heard the lock click and the creak of the hinges. Katherine called out, "Hello. Anyone home?"

Colleen called back, "I'm in your father's study, dear."

As Katherine stepped into the study Colleen stood and they hugged. She was glad to see the young woman had fully recovered from her misadventures in Faerie a few months ago.

"Your father just called," Colleen said. "He'll be here shortly and we're going to get some dinner. You'll join us won't you?"

Katherine smiled and said, "Of course. It'll be fun. Let's try someplace new."

"I'd like that too. Oh, and Paul's with your father. We'll make it a foursome."

Katherine started and frowned, an odd reaction. "Paul?" she asked, and her earlier calm demeanor shifted to fright. She tried to hide it, but did so poorly. She looked at her watch. "You know . . . I forgot I have an evening appointment with one of my patients. I really can't stay."

It was such an obvious lie that Colleen asked, "But surely you can cancel it?"

"No. No, I can't."

Katherine turned and walked hurriedly out into the hall.

Colleen followed her. "What's wrong?"

"I have to run," Katherine said as she opened the front door and stepped through it. And just like that she was gone, rushing away in an almost desperate panic.

Now that was odd, Colleen thought. There was no reason Katherine should have reacted that way. Yes, she and the young man had been through quite a bit under Simuth's thumb in Faerie. And Paul's pragmatic brutality in killing the Winter Knight had stunned them all. But once the dust had settled their relationship had seemed to strengthen. No, something was very wrong here.

••••

Paul, Colleen and McGowan had dinner at a nice place on Powell Street just off Union Square, though he would have enjoyed it much more if Katherine had been there. They said their goodbyes outside the restaurant, and since it was a warm night he decided to walk back to his apartment.

When he turned down Market Street a shimmer in the air at the edge of his vision caught his attention. He looked that way, but saw nothing unusual; it had been no more than a fleeting glimpse in the glow of a streetlight. A year ago he would have shrugged it off, thought nothing of it and continued on his way. But recent experience had taught him to be wary of little inconsequential things like a shimmer in the night air.

He headed west on Market, and as he got farther from Union Square the crowds thinned out a little. He spotted the shimmer again not far behind him, and that confirmed his suspicions.

He abruptly turned right on Fourth, and now out of sight of whoever—whatever—followed him, he jogged down the street about twenty paces, then slipped into the shadow of an alley. With his lack of experience in such matters, he concentrated hard to mask his arcane abilities and call forth his *sight*. As his vision shifted, the pedestrians on the sidewalk glowed, the colors of their auras enveloping them. He reached inside his coat and rested his hand on the butt of the nine-millimeter.

When a being stepped in front of the entrance to the alley exhibiting only an aura without a person attached, he knew he had his invisible follower. He was still a novice at interpreting auras, but there was no question he was about to confront a member of the Summer Court.

Paul said, "Why is a Seelie mage following me?"

To his credit, the mage didn't jump or start, but simply halted and turned slowly to face Paul. The shimmer in the air grew more pronounced for a second, then a handsome young man appeared. Like all of them he was inhumanly beautiful, and he had pointed ears.

The Sidhe shrugged and nodded his head. "Young Mage," he said, addressing Paul with the title they had adopted for him. "Anogh warned me you would be more . . . alert than I realized."

Paul knew he'd get nothing but evasion and dissembling from the Seelie mage, so he wasn't going to fall into the trap of pressing him on the matter. But the fellow's presence did offer him an opportunity he'd hoped for. He said, "Please deliver a message to the Summer Knight for me."

The Sidhe tilted his head, raised an eyebrow and said, "A message?"

Paul had thought long and hard about this. "Yes," he said. "Tell him I wish to speak with him, at his convenience. Tell him I wish to call in the boon Magreth offered me."

The Seelie mage closed his eyes and bowed his head. Paul felt a little shift in reality, and the fellow disappeared in a sparkle of fairy dust.

3

The Search Succeeds

LOCATED IN THE Haight-Ashbury district, *Alternate Earth Books* claimed to have the largest collection of occult reading on the west coast, and that all employees were skilled practitioners of the psychic arts and advisors in the paranormal. It advertised itself as a place where *renowned experts and seekers of spiritual guidance gathered in a metaphysical environment of wisdom and healing.* Besides books, it sold psychic crystals, living stones, rare and antique artifacts, tribal fetishes, occult art, tie-dyed clothing, incense, fragrant soaps, paranormally enhanced chocolates, medical marijuana in decorative vials and a variety of flavors, espresso, cappuccino, coffee and donuts. He wasn't sure what living stones were, and didn't really care, so he wasn't about to ask. And as for paranormally enhanced chocolate . . .

When he opened the front door it triggered the tinkle of a small bell. He paused just within the entrance and surveyed the place, which appeared to have little order or structure in the way the various items for sale had been displayed. He meandered slowly through the store glancing at titles, saw one that might be of mild interest and picked it up. He leafed through its pages, not really paying any attention to its contents, frustrated that his attempts to locate anyone in the local community of practitioners had met with so little success. He'd monitored the obituaries in the newspapers, and apparently Miss Labella had a history of mild heart problems, so her death had been attributed to heart failure. That was one thing he didn't have to worry about.

"Can I help you?" a pleasant voice said from behind him.

He turned and found himself facing a sixtyish woman wearing a tie-dyed dress, too much makeup, a few too many years, and a few too many pounds. He smiled and said, "I've always had an interest in occult literature."

She returned his smile in a flirtatious way, probably thought of herself as an attractive cougar since he was easily twenty years her junior. "Really", she said. "We have an extensive collection. Did you have anything specific in mind?"

He looked at the book in his hands and shrugged indifferently, then returned it to the haphazard pile on the table in front of him. "I collect old grimoires, but only if they're *true* antiques." That was actually the truth.

Her eyes brightened. "We keep those in the back. Many of them are somewhat fragile, so we don't want just anyone handling them. Come with me."

She turned toward the back of the store and he followed her as she walked with a little extra sway in her hips. She led him into a back room to a shelf where the books were all leather bound and carefully racked. She selected one, pulled it off the shelf and handed it to him. "Perhaps this might interest you."

To his surprise, it was truly an old book, and not a fake, though of no arcane value.

"I haven't seen you in here before," she said. "What brought you to our store?"

Now for the lie that had, as yet, produced no results. "A recommendation from an acquaintance."

"Who might that be?"

"Walter ah . . . ," he said. "Can't remember the fellow's last name, but he's definitely interested in the occult." He gave her a brief description of the older wizard he'd seen in the front yard of the little Mexican boy's house. He added, "I believe he has a daughter who's rather attractive, and also concerned with the paranormal, though I've never met her."

"Oh, you must mean Walter McGowan." She leaned close, winked knowingly and gave him a conspiratorial look, as if they were collaborators in some secret cabal. "He's a very powerful wizard, you know."

"No, I didn't know."

"He comes in here all the time. You're a friend of his?"

The last thing he wanted was her telling a senior wizard about him. "No. I don't know him at all well, only met him briefly, once, some time ago. I doubt he'd even remember me."

It took a while to extricate himself from the old hippie. Once out on the street, he paused to consider his next move. He now had a family name to go with the given name, though it had come from a mundane mortal so he couldn't be sure this McGowan fellow was the senior wizard he sought. He would still follow up on the information.

He returned to his apartment, fired up his computer and quickly learned it wasn't going to be as simple as looking up the old man's phone listing. Like any practitioner the fellow probably cherished his privacy and anonymity, so he almost certainly had an unlisted number.

The old hippie at the bookstore had said McGowan came there *all the time*. If that was true, the next time he did so, he'd leave an arcane scent trail his master could follow, as long as it wasn't too old. He decided to return to *Alternate Earth Books* every day just after closing time and let his master sniff around the sidewalk outside. He'd just have to be patient. He had no need to hurry.

••••

As Cadilus entered the queen's private audience chamber, Magreth was obviously in a good mood. No primordial Sidhe spirits fluttered about her head, obscuring her brilliant red hair with their shadows, and flames did not hide the emerald-green of her magnificent eyes.

"Leave us," she said to the courtiers attending her. "I wish to speak with the High Chancellor alone."

The attendants simply vanished.

"Cadilus," she said, extending her hand.

He crossed the few paces separating them, bowed and kissed the ring on her betrothal finger.

As he straightened she said, "Tell me of the Young Mage and the Old Wizard's daughter. Have you confirmed what we suspected?"

Cadilus nodded. "Yes, Your Majesty. There is now no question that the two together are far more powerful than the sum of their individual abilities."

"Which makes them quite dominant," she said, "and potentially, a considerable danger to us."

"Exactly, Your Majesty."

She turned away from him to face the wall behind her, and a set of French doors appeared where a moment before there had been only unrelieved stone. She threw the doors open and stepped out onto a balcony overlooking the countryside of Faerie.

"Come join me," she said, patting the stone rail in front and to one side of her.

He followed and stopped beside her.

"And how well have you progressed in keeping them apart?"

"That has gone well, Your Majesty."

She cocked her head slightly. "But you told me you could not penetrate the wards the Old Wizard has placed about his home."

Cadilus nodded. "That has proven problematic regarding the young man. Now that he is apprenticed to the old fellow he spends a considerable amount of time there, and my assistants can only reach him when he leaves the premises. Unfortunately, any progress they then make weakens rapidly when he returns."

"And the young woman?"

Cadilus allowed a satisfied smile to cross his lips. "There, we have been much more successful, Your Majesty. She is close to her father, but, unlike the young man, there is no need to enter his home on a daily basis and remain there for hours at a time. They see each other regularly, but they're just as likely to meet at some café for lunch where his wards do not hinder us."

"But might he sense your interference if he's there right next to her?"

"It's very subtly done, Your Majesty. We cast only minor compulsion spells but strengthen them by nudging the possibilities in the direction we desire. And as you know, we Sidhe are quite adept at that, much more so than our mortal rivals. And the young woman doesn't feel anything dramatic like fear or danger. At this point, if she thinks for any reason she'll be in the young man's presence, she merely believes there is an important reason she must be elsewhere. That's different from thinking she must be away from him. That might arouse suspicion."

With her gaze still focused outward on the countryside beneath them, she said, "Excellent, my dear Cadilus. Excellent!"

"There is another factor to consider," he added.

"And that is?"

"If she does enter his presence, we have a narrow window of time in which to separate them. As we've discussed, together they are quite powerful, and the fates quickly dilute the artificial sense she has that she must be elsewhere. For that reason I am having both of them watched day and night."

"Interesting!" she said, turning her head and looking at him. "Perhaps we should consult the Summer Knight in this."

That pleased Cadilus, because Anogh always offered clear, level-headed advice. "A most wise decision, Your Majesty. During the centuries of his absence, we lost the habit of involving him in these matters."

She smiled. "Exactly."

••••

Anogh sensed Magreth's summons, and with a whim and a thought the Summer Knight stepped into the queen's private audience chamber. As he dropped to one knee before her and bowed, he noticed High Chancellor Cadilus standing to one side. "Your Majesty," he said. "You summoned me."

"Rise, Sir Knight," she said.

Anogh stood and looked into the queen's emerald-green eyes. She smiled at him and said, "It brings us great joy to have you restored to us, my dear Anogh."

Anogh lowered his eyes. "To look upon you once more, Your Majesty, the joy is all mine."

"Then look upon me freely."

Anogh looked again into her eyes. He had once loved the long-dead Taal'mara, the Winter Princess murdered by her own father, King Ag. But any Seelie mage loved his queen above all others. "How may I serve you?"

She looked toward Cadilus. "The High Chancellor and I were discussing the Young Mage. We believe he is connected to the Old Wizard's daughter in some way."

"That he is," Anogh said.

Her eyes darkened and she regarded him carefully. "Why are you so certain?"

He shrugged. "The Morrigan summoned me in a dream, though, at the time, I knew not why."

Cadilus's frown mirrored the queen's.

She said, "Tell me more of this."

"Before we were even aware of the Young Mage's existence, I felt compelled to be on a particular street corner in the Old Wizard's city, on a particular day, at a particular time, and the compulsion tasted unquestionably of the Triple Goddess. I was waiting there when the ghost of a pretty young woman walked past me, paused, looked at me directly and smiled in the oddest way."

The shadows of primordial Sidhe spirits coalesced and fluttered about Magreth's head. As yet, there were only a few of them. "Who was this young woman?"

"I didn't know it at the time, Your Majesty, but before her death she had been the Young Mage's wife. That day her ghost continued on down the street, and the young man himself came a moment later, following her, though, just as I knew nothing of her, at the time I had no inkling of his identity as well. I followed, watched her lead him to a store where mortal women buy expensive shoes, and inside he encountered the Old Wizard's daughter. It appeared to be a chance meeting, though the ghost's intent was quite clear. I believe it was the first time he and the young witch met, even if only briefly."

Magreth gasped and backed a step, her eyes flashed with flame, and hundreds of Sidhe spirits coalesced in every corner of the room. They darted toward her and fluttered about her like a flock of frightened starlings.

"There was no coincidence in this," she asked, her voice trembling, "no chance meeting, no vague and ill-defined connection?"

Anogh glanced at Cadilus, and the look on the High Chancellor's face mirrored that on Magreth's. The Summer Knight shook his head, and could not hide his consternation. "No, Your Majesty. I think it quite clear the Triple Goddess created the connection between the two of them for her own purposes, created it quite overtly."

"And we," Cadilus said, "have tried to thwart that connection."

Anogh shook his head. "Forgive me, Your Majesty, but I think that is ill advised."

Because of the flames there was no longer even a hint of green in her eyes as she shook her head. "No, Sir Knight. We cannot allow the Triple Goddess a free hand in this."

She turned to Cadilus. "Do not slacken your efforts."

The High Chancellor nodded. "As you wish, Your Majesty."

The flames disappeared as Magreth's eyes narrowed in thought. "And it occurs to me you men have been thinking too much like men."

Cadilus's eyebrows rose as he asked, "How so, Your Majesty?"

Her lips curled upward in a calculating smile. "There are always multiple dimensions to these problems. While you continue your efforts to keep them apart, one of our witches—one of our most beautiful, young witches—will distract the young man, give him a reason to willingly focus his attention away from the Old Wizard's daughter. One does not necessarily need the arcane arts to turn a man's heart."

Cadilus nodded. "An excellent idea."

Anogh added, "And a much less dangerous course of action since it's not in direct opposition to the Morrigan. Who were you thinking of?"

"Si'entha," Magreth said. "No mortal man can resist her."

"Aye," Anogh said, feeling a bit sorry for the young man. "She certainly has destroyed her share of them, hasn't she?"

••••

Alternate Earth Books closed at 8:00 in the evening on weeknights, and 6:00 on weekends, and after they shut the doors the employees left in a matter of minutes. He always walked down the sidewalk about half an hour after that, just so the old hippie didn't notice the pattern of him being there every night. She had claimed McGowan came there *all the time*, when in fact he and his master had now returned every night for more than two weeks, and nothing. But that night, as he strolled past the front of the store, his master breathed a sigh of relief into his soul.

He was here. There is no question, a powerful old wizard. And he's the one we seek.

He'd never before needed to have his master guide him this way, and it took some practice and a few false starts. The trail led to a parking space on the street about a block from the bookstore, then down the middle of the street. He returned to his own car and drove back to the parking space where his master again picked up the trail. He found it difficult following his master's instructions, because he frequently didn't know he needed to turn until it was too late. Several times he had to circle around the block and pick up the trail again, or change lanes quickly to make the turn.

At one point an SFPD motorcycle cop pulled him over. "You're driving a little erratically," the officer said. "Had anything to drink?"

"No, officer," he said. "Nothing at all. I'm just new to the city and having a little trouble navigating the streets."

The cop had him step out of the car and questioned him further, though he didn't make him do any of the obvious sobriety tests. Once satisfied he hadn't been drinking, the cop let him go with a warning. After that, if he missed a turn, he carefully circled back to pick up the trail again; no more quick lane changes.

Following the old wizard's arcane scent he slowly worked his way to the downtown area and up Nob Hill. The trail ended at one of those classic, San Francisco, early-twentieth-century, wood-frame houses. It had a single-car garage on the downhill side of the ground floor, with a front door next to it, and four stories of bay windows above that.

He drove to a nearby garage and parked his car, then walked back to the house. Out on the sidewalk his master immediately picked up the scents of the druid and the necromancer, but not the young witch. Out of curiosity, he followed the scent of the necromancer. It led him down Nob Hill, past Union Square, and along Market Street. It ended a few blocks south of there at a nondescript apartment building.

He walked up the steps to the door at the front of the building and stood there pondering his next move. His master needed to gain more strength before they could do anything, but when the time was right he wondered if he should go after the necromancer first, now that he knew where he lived.

No, the voice said. *Safer to isolate the witch first, then go after the necromancer.*

"As you wish," he said. But he still needed to know the patterns of the young man's behavior. To take a powerful practitioner without leaving a trail, it was imperative he know the fellow's habits, his routine.

He turned away from the door and walked down the steps to the sidewalk. He glanced up the street, and to his surprise saw a young man walking his way that he recognized. He'd seen him in the front yard of the little Mexican's boy's house in Dallas that day: the necromancer. What an amazing development!

He turned that way and walked up the sidewalk toward the fellow.

No, his master said. *It's too dangerous.*

He ignored It and continued walking. He and the young wizard passed each other going in opposite directions, and the necromancer didn't flinch in the least. Yes, when it came time to take him, it would be easy. But first, the witch.

He now knew where the senior wizard lived, and he could reasonably assume the man would meet up with his daughter at some point. It would be much too dangerous to attempt to follow such a powerful wizard, so he'd have to wait until the young witch came to her father's house and pick up her scent there. With cunning and patience he'd learn the location of the daughter's home. But his master was still too weak to possess her, so he'd have to give equal time to hunting down more Alice prostitutes. He hated the Alice prostitutes.

4

The Caorthannach

KATHERINE PAUSED IN front of the building on Market Street. There was nothing remarkable about it, a lot of glass windows rising up thirty or forty stories.

Yesterday she'd received a call from Ms. Kellmarishmae, Amalgamated Healthcare's CEO. The woman asked Katherine if she would come to their offices on Market Street. Katherine had never heard of Amalgamated Healthcare, thought it might be a scam of some kind, so she'd been reluctant to commit to anything, had told the woman she'd check her schedule and get back to her.

She called a friend in administration at one of the downtown hospitals, and at first he said he too had never heard of Amalgamated Healthcare. But on the phone he hesitated, then said, "No, wait a minute. There've been some rumors circulating, a new outfit, lot of venture capital money behind them, some of the biggest firms in Silicon Valley. Word on the street has it they're making takeover offers to some of the largest healthcare networks, and are willing to go hostile if necessary." With some doubts, Katherine had called the woman back and made an appointment, though for the life of her she couldn't imagine why they wanted to speak to her.

Standing there on the sidewalk, she turned toward the main entrance of the building. But as she did so she caught a momentary glimpse of her reflection in one of the tall, street-level windows and she hesitated, looked again. There had been something odd about her appearance, but now her image seemed quite ordinary. She'd chosen to wear a DKNY suit, though she'd picked one not at all conservative in its cut. The skirt ended well above her knees, she wore four-inch heels, and she'd chosen a blouse with a plunging neckline and a little exposed cleavage. She'd be damned if she would dress as conservatively as she did for her clients.

She closed her eyes, had difficulty recalling what had bothered her about her reflection, something about a pale-blue dress and white, knee-high stockings. She opened her eyes again. The street was busy with pedestrians. She must have seen a young girl's reflection in the window as she walked past, though glancing up and down the street, she saw no sign of the girl now.

In the lobby she nodded politely at the guard as she passed him headed for the elevators. She caught a glimpse of his reflection in one of the windows and noticed him checking her out from behind. She took a little satisfaction in that, though it occurred to her she would have enjoyed it more if it had been Paul ogling her that way.

She got an elevator right away and stepped into it. "Suite 4401," Ms. Kellmarishmae had told her on the phone. She pressed the button for the forty-fourth floor, and when the elevator doors opened it was obvious suite 4401 occupied the entire floor. Behind a darkly wooded desk sat a receptionist that made Katherine feel plain. She smiled when she saw Katherine.

"I'm Dr. Katherine McGowan. I have an appointment with Ms. Kellmarishmae."

The receptionist's smile widened. "She's expecting you, Dr. McGowan. Please have a seat"—she waved her hand at a couch against one wall—"and I'll let her know you're here."

Katherine had barely sat down when the door to an inner office opened and a woman stepped out who took Katherine's breath away. Katherine rose up off the couch and realized the woman stood well over six feet tall—literally towered over her. A big lump of jealousy welled up in her throat as she realized the woman wore about five thousand dollars' worth of dress. If she had to guess she'd say Donna Karan, the couture line, not the DKNY line Katherine could afford. The dress ended at mid-calf, with a high neck-line and no sleeves, and the dark-brown color of the material nicely offset the bright, lemon-yellow of the woman's skin.

"Dr. McGowan?" she asked politely, sticking out her hand. "I'm Kellmarishmae."

"It's nice to meet you, Ms. Kellmarishmae," Katherine said, shaking her hand. Katherine looked into her eyes, and for a moment she thought they were amber, like the eyes of a cat, with vertically slit pupils. But when she blinked and looked again the woman's pupils were quite normal and round, though her eyes were a striking green that complemented her yellow skin.

"It's just Kellmarishmae," she said. "It's not our custom to use honorifics."

There were two other people waiting in the woman's office, a man and a woman, both, like Kellmarishmae, well over six feet tall; Katherine felt like a child among towering basketball players. But it was their attire that drew her attention, because she stood in a room with about fifteen-thousand dollars' worth of clothing. The fellow with coal-black skin wore Armani or something close to it. Kellmarishmae introduced him as Dayandalous. She introduced the woman with blood-red skin as Mierfendoplay, and Katherine's best guess on her outfit was Dolce & Gabbana.

Kellmarishmae pointed Katherine to a comfortable chair facing a desk the size of her bedroom. Katherine and Kellmarishmae both sat down while Dayandalous and Mierfendoplay remained standing.

"I must confess," Katherine said, "I'm not sure why you want to see me. I've never before been involved with corporate health networks."

"We're curious," Kellmarishmae said, "and we may have a little advice for you."

Katherine said, "That sounds rather vague."

Dayandalous and Kellmarishmae shared a look, and there was something familiar about the man. Katherine spoke without considering her words. "Dayandalous, have we met before?"

He nodded and smiled, all three of them shared a look, and in that moment, looking at the man's coal-black skin, for some reason Katherine thought of a sword.

One of Dayandalous's eyebrows lifted as if he could read her mind. He said, "You and the young man are a surprise to us all."

Mierfendoplay added, "And you mustn't avoid him so."

"I'm not," Katherine said, though she knew it was a lie.

"You may lie to yourself," Kellmarishmae said, "but not to us."

What was this, Katherine wondered. *Some sort of intervention?* She wanted this interview ended right now, and wanted out of that room this instant.

Mierfendoplay said, "We're making her uncomfortable, and that's unkind. We need her strong and confident."

Katherine stood, not in the least intimidated by the three of them. "If you don't mind, I'd like to go."

Dayandalous said, "That's better."

Kellmarishmae stood, walked around her desk and said, "I'll escort you out." She opened the office door and held it for Katherine.

Katherine said, "Thank you," and stepped out into the reception area.

At the bank of elevators Kellmarishmae pressed the down button, then turned to Katherine. "You and he are stronger together. Divided, you can be defeated, and everyone will suffer."

Katherine wanted the damn elevator to get there now. They stood there for a few seconds in uncomfortable silence. When the doors finally opened Katherine immediately stepped into the elevator and turned to face Kellmarishmae. The woman reached out and blocked the doors with her hand, preventing them from closing. She leaned forward and smiled pleasantly. "By the way, my dear, you were wrong about Dolce & Gabbana, but you were right about Donna Karan. I like Donna Karan as much as you do." She glanced down at the expensive dress she wore, then looked back at Katherine. "Would you like one?"

In that moment Katherine couldn't recall what had bothered her so about the woman. She said, "I . . . uh . . . can't accept—"

"Oh posh!" the woman said. "Of course you can."

She released the doors and they swished closed.

In the back of Katherine's thoughts she kept thinking there was something she'd forgotten, and it wasn't until she stepped into the lobby on the ground floor that she realized she hadn't learned anything about the reason Kellmarishmae had wanted to see her.

She turned around, went back to the elevators and called one, thinking she might at least ask the receptionist a few polite questions. When the elevator arrived she stepped into it, and was going to press the button for the forty-fourth floor, but there was no such button. She stood there for a moment staring at the buttons, and they ended at thirty-eight. Perhaps one of the other elevators went all the way to the top. There were six elevators, and she patiently waited for each, but not one went beyond the thirty-eighth floor. She searched the lobby, thinking she'd taken a wrong turn and there was another bank of elevators, but that wasn't the case either.

Katherine asked the security guard in the lobby, "How do I get to the forty-fourth floor?"

The guard's eyes narrowed and he looked at her oddly. For some reason her question had angered him. "There's no forty-fourth floor in this building. Why do I have to keep telling people that? The top floor is thirty-eight."

"But I was just on the forty-fourth floor." Katherine decided to mention the name of the woman she'd just spoken to up there, but she couldn't remember anything about her.

The guard's eyes narrowed further, and he spoke as if talking to a dimwitted child. "I said no forty-fourth floor. Do you nut-cases come in pairs?"

The guard ushered Katherine out onto the sidewalk. She stood there for a moment, then turned back to the building and looked at it carefully. It was like any of a dozen other buildings on Market Street, and for the life of her she couldn't remember why she'd wasted her time coming there.

The day was almost over so she caught a cab home. She decided to change into something more comfortable before making dinner. She walked into her closet, removed the DKNY suit, carefully folded it and draped it over a hanger. She glanced up and noticed a cedar box on the shelf above, the kind in which one might store a piece of expensive clothing.

She lifted if off the shelf, placed it on her bed and opened it. Inside lay a navy-blue dress, carefully folded with padding to prevent wrinkles. When she lifted it out of the box she knew immediately it was cashmere. Moving cautiously, she unfolded it, noticed the label read Donna Karan, not DKNY. She held it up against her, and it looked to be a perfect fit. It ended at mid-calf, and had a moderately high neckline with long sleeves, though the back plunged to her waist, and even a little bit beyond. It was a beautiful piece of clothing, but not something she could ordinarily afford. She'd managed to get it . . .

For some reason she couldn't recall how she'd acquired the thing. But she didn't really care. She thought Paul would like her in it; from behind the plunging back would drive him nuts.

••••

Vasily Karpov watched Vladimir and Alexei fidget as reality shifted and the walls of the Unseelie King's personal audience chamber materialized about them. "Stand still," he snapped at them.

They both froze fearfully.

Alexei, who young Conklin called Joe Stalin, asked in heavy Russian, "What did we do wrong, Mr. Karpov?"

He did look like a young Joe Stalin, dark bushy mustache, square face and bristly hair. Alexei was Karpov's big, dumb bear, though he reminded himself they were *both* idiots. The bear just excelled at stupidity. Karpov gave him a withering look, and he lowered his eyes.

Karpov turned to Vladimir and said, "You need to pay more attention to your appearance."

The Slav had high cheekbones pitted with acne scars, and long, straight, greasy blond hair that hung lankly down to his shoulders. He took his cue from Alexei, lowered his eyes and said nothing. The Slav was smarter than the bear, but not by much.

"Vasily, my dear friend."

Karpov turned toward the sound of the Winter King's voice. Ag lay sprawled on a snow-white chaise lounge. He wore a white, silk, ruffled shirt and white breeches tucked into shiny, knee-high black boots. His long, coal-black hair drifted on a slight breeze that was anything but natural. Lying next to him, a young Sidhe witch of incredible beauty wore a diaphanous gown of translucent silk through which the dark areolas of her breasts were quite visible. The front of her gown was slit down its full length. Ag slid it open, fully exposing one of her breasts. He reached down and put a hand in her crotch, began stroking her as he licked one of her nipples. She growled like an animal as Vladimir and Alexei looked on with undisguised hunger, their eyes following Ag's antics with jealous desire.

Karpov said, "Your Majesty."

Ag ignored him, continued to fondle the young witch and bit the nipple. She grew more excited with each second, but then Ag abruptly stopped, stood and licked his fingertips. The young witch glared at him angrily.

"Vasily," he said. "Come. You and I must talk in private"—he glanced at Vladimir and Alexei—"while your two young men finish what I started."

He looked down at the young witch and she grinned lasciviously, while Vladimir and Alexei's eyes widened.

Ag told the two young men, "I've prepared her for you, a gift for two loyal retainers of my dear friend."

Karpov said, "No beguilement. Yes, give them pleasure, but don't turn their minds."

Ag turned to the witch and said, "You heard the wizard. He is a guest in my house, so be careful to obey his instructions."

She smiled and the gown opened even further as if moved by a magical breeze. "I need no beguilement to satisfy these two young men. But I do require they satisfy me as well."

Karpov glanced at his two thugs, and from the looks on their faces knew they'd be her obedient puppies. Still, he told them, "You do not *force* her to do anything, only what she is willing." He didn't care about the young witch, would normally not care what the two idiots did to her. But he had to be certain they didn't do anything to which she might object because here, in the Unseelie Court, he couldn't afford any complications.

Ag leaned close to him and said, "Trust me, she's definitely up to the task. She'll be quite a challenge for them. In fact, she can easily handle an army of your young men in a single night. You need not concern yourself with her, though your two young men will be utterly useless for a few days."

The two were useless most days, if there wasn't any killing for them to do, but Karpov kept that thought to himself.

"Come," Ag said, and Karpov followed him. The woman and the two young men began grunting and rutting before they'd even left the room.

Ag led him to another room furnished more like a private office. As he closed the door, cutting off the sounds of the threesome's foreplay, Ag said, "Thank you for coming, Vasily."

Karpov regarded him carefully. "We have much to discuss about our mutual problem."

Ag poured two of glasses of Sidhe wine and handed one to Karpov. "Yes, the Young Mage. How do we eliminate him?"

"I don't know," Karpov said, swirling the wine in his glass. Ordinarily he preferred something stronger, like Vodka or Bourbon, but even he could be tempted by Faerie wine. He took a sip, and it tasted of a spring day after a cleansing rainfall. If he could figure out how they did that, he'd make a fortune on the Mortal Plane.

"I can't take direct action against him," Karpov said, sniffing the bouquet of the wine. "He's not a rogue, and his apprenticeship to the old man guarantees him quite a bit of protection. Otherwise, I'd simply send a group of strong wizards with mortal weapons to kill him. A bullet in the back of the head is quite final even for the most powerful practitioner. But that would set all of my mortal colleagues against me."

He looked at the wine in his glass and said, "Is there nothing you can do, Your Majesty?"

Ag shook his head. "My hands are as tied as yours when it comes to direct intervention. With the non-aligned fey maintaining we were the aggressors when he murdered Simuth . . ." Ag shrugged and didn't finish the thought.

"There might be a way," Karpov said. "If only we could count on the young man to be as stupid as my Slav or my bear."

Ag perked up. "How so?"

"The most important rule for mortal practitioners is that you don't bring anything dangerous to the Mortal Plane, you don't draw attention to the arcane arts. If he were foolish enough to bring a demon over, even if by accident, then I could act. I've toyed with the idea of bringing one over and blaming it on him, but that's a chancy gambit I'd rather use only as a last resort."

"Hmm!" Ag said.

His tone drew Karpov's attention, and he asked, "What are you thinking?"

Ag smiled and nodded at some pleasant thought. "Does it have to be a demon? Does it have to come from the Netherworld?"

"What do you have in mind?"

"What if the young man brought over a very dangerous creature from Faerie and it caused quite a bit of destruction, even took a few lives? And if we're lucky, it might even take his."

Karpov considered that carefully. "That could work, but how do we frame him for it?"

"I think I can send it from here. But you'll have to make sure it arrives where and when it can be blamed on him."

"What is this creature?"

Ag's smile turned quite menacing. "The Caorthannach. Your legends have it that your St. Patrick destroyed it, when in fact he only banished it from the Mortal Plane. But before I can proceed, I'll have to consult with some of my most powerful mages. Let's return to this discussion after I've had time to do that."

Ag put his wine glass down on a table. "Come, let's retrieve your two young men."

Back in Ag's private audience chamber both Alexei and Vladimir lay naked and sprawled on the floor, their eyes glazed, a dazed look of satisfaction on their faces. The witch stood over them, naked, holding the remnants of her gown in one hand trailing it on the floor. Her breasts glistened with sweat and saliva, and only she knew what else. When Karpov and Ag entered the room she turned toward them. As they approached, Karpov noticed she had a number of bite marks on her thighs, belly and breasts.

"They were adequate," she said, "but just barely."

5

The Witch Found

TO FIND THE young witch's trail, he used the same strategy with the old wizard's house he'd employed with the bookstore, with one variation. The bookstore was located in a busy commercial area in the Upper Haight. Shoppers and tourists crowded the street in front of it throughout the day and well into the evening. McGowan's house was situated in a residential neighborhood near the top of Nob Hill, and saw only small amounts of foot traffic. He dare not walk down the sidewalk in front of the place at night when he'd likely be the only pedestrian on the street. Something like that might draw someone's attention. The little things were always important.

Through experimentation he quickly learned that early in the morning on weekdays there were always other pedestrians on their way to work. He joined them, and pretended to be just another resident hurrying to his job, though he quickly noticed that if he walked past the house at the same time each morning, he soon recognized the other pedestrians from previous mornings. He didn't like the idea that they might recognize him, so each day he varied his timing over a period of several hours.

In that way he walked past the old man's house each morning, hoping to catch the arcane scent of his daughter. Of course, McGowan's scent was almost always present, and frequently that of the druid and the young wizard. But his master had a stronger sense of the young witch's arcane scent because she and the necromancer had confronted It directly in Dallas, whereas her father had always been on the periphery.

His diligence paid off, and one morning he picked up the young woman's trail. He followed it to a parking structure, retrieved his own car from the garage on O'Farrell Street, and from there followed it to another parking garage. But a sign on the street read, *No daily parking, monthly and yearly permits only*. He parked elsewhere and returned to the garage on foot. He found her car on the fourth floor; her arcane scent permeated it nicely.

From there he followed her trail to an office building, and saw the name of Dr. Katherine McGowan on the directory in the lobby. She had some sort of medical practice in the building.

He returned to the garage where she'd parked her car, and noted a bus stop across the street. It was a busy, public avenue with a constant stream of pedestrians walking up and down the sidewalks. He could linger at the bus stop for hours without appearing suspicious. He'd watch her for several days to determine her routine, then come back another day, prepared to follow her at the end of her workday.

••••

In late afternoon, standing on the front steps of his apartment building and holding two bags of groceries, Paul fumbled in his pocket for his keys.

"Young Mage."

Paul recognized Anogh's voice immediately. He turned to face the Summer Knight, who stood on the sidewalk below him, though just a few seconds before there'd been nothing there. "Lord Anogh," he said, trying not to marvel at the Sidhe's beauty, and almost regretting that he wasn't gay.

Anogh's lips curled upward into a slight grin, as if he could read Paul's thoughts. "You wished to speak with me."

"Yes, about Magreth's offer of a boon."

"Such an offer is a rare honor. I hope you've thought carefully about it."

"I have," Paul said, though he'd have trouble explaining his decision to anyone. It wasn't based on a carefully considered train of logic, or on need or desire, but on an instinct that gnawed continually at his gut. "I want you to teach me how to fight with a sword." Now that he'd said it, it sounded as ridiculous as he'd thought it would.

Anogh's eyes widened, and Paul realized he'd surprised the Summer Knight, a rare occurrence indeed. "A sword," the Sidhe said. "A most unusual request. Why learn the sword?"

Paul had known that question would arise, but since he didn't exactly know the answer, he'd come up with a handy lie. "Since guns and gunpowder don't work in Faerie, I want to be able to defend myself when I'm there."

Anogh's eyes narrowed and he considered Paul in silence for several seconds. Then he shook his head and said, "No. You're wiser than that. And you defended yourself rather nicely with cold iron against that Unseelie witch and her four warriors . . ."

Paul recalled the attack by the Winter Court spies while being tested at the Summer Court. He'd hurt the witch and three of her colleagues, but still ended up with the blade of a silver rapier protruding from his chest.

"But I'll not press you on the matter," Anogh continued. "A boon was offered, and a boon will be given. Swords it will be, but the lessons will take place in Faerie. I'll come for you at your convenience."

"But how will you know when it's convenient?"

Anogh smiled and said, "I always know such things."

He disappeared in a cloud of gray smoke that dissipated slowly in the chill air of the October day.

••••

Paul had begun to suspect Katherine was avoiding him, and throughout the day, as McGowan grilled him on a battery of complex spells, his thoughts kept returning to her. He proved to be an exceedingly poor student that day and was glad when the old man said, "Let's call it a day. You're way off your game today, kid. What's wrong?"

Paul shrugged it off and said, "Nothing, just preoccupied."

Colleen gave him a knowing look. He wondered what she knew to give him a *knowing* look.

On his way home he stopped at a gym and got in a good workout, which helped relieve some of the tension. The sky was just beginning to darken as he climbed the steps to his apartment. When he opened the door he saw no sign of Madge the cat, but since she was just a hallucination, he didn't doubt she could disappear whenever she desired.

He paused at the table in his kitchen, wondering what he might scrape up for dinner. Maybe he'd head down to Jessie's, the pub owned by the two gay fellows, get a burger and a beer.

His cell phone rang. He fumbled it out of his coat pocket, saw on the phone's display that the call was from Colleen. He took the call and said, "Hi, Colleen, it's Paul."

"Hi Paul," she said, and oddly enough, she was whispering. "Katherine's just arrived, should be here for another hour or so. Perhaps you'd like to join us."

The whispering confirmed Paul's suspicions. "She's avoiding me, and that's why you're whispering, isn't it?"

"Yes, she is."

"Why?"

Colleen let out an exasperated sigh. "I don't know, but there's something about it that feels wrong."

"What are you saying?"

"I don't know exactly. Just instinct."

He wanted to get Katherine alone without the druid and her father present, and he didn't want Colleen stalling her to keep her there indefinitely hoping he'd show up. "I'm sorry," he lied, "I can't make it. I'm all the way over in the east bay."

"Oh, that's a shame."

Paul hung up and shoved the phone back into his coat pocket. When he turned around he spotted Madge the cat sitting on the couch, licking a paw and staring at him, a look of disdain on her face. "Disdain," he said. "How do you do that? Cats don't have looks like that on their faces."

She stopped licking her paw, raised one eyebrow and said, "Meow."

Paul shook his head and ignored her. He hurried out the door of his fourth-floor walkup, and headed down the stairs. But on the second floor landing he came upon a young girl in jeans, sneakers, a windbreaker and a baseball cap, a long, loose ponytail of brownish-blond hair hanging out the back of the cap down past her shoulders. She was leaning over a large box and panting heavily. She glanced up as he came down the stairs, and gave him a pleading look.

He stopped just above her and asked, "What's wrong?"

"I just moved in," she said, nodding toward the box. "Got a new TV, but it's heavier than I thought. I'm afraid I bit off more than I can chew. I can't believe I made it this far."

Paul looked at his watch, desperately wanted to get to McGowan's place before Katherine left. But it would be downright rude to refuse to help the girl. "Where's your apartment?"

"Third floor," she said, looking hopeful.

"Okay, but I've got to make it fast."

"Thank you so much," she said, breathing a sigh.

The box was a little heavy, though mostly just awkward because of its size, but nothing Paul couldn't handle with a few grunts as he took the steps one at a time. Her apartment was down the hall a bit, and she already had the door open when he got to the third floor. She waved to him and called out, "This way."

The box was wide enough that he was forced to walk sideways down the hall. He put the box down gently in the middle of her living room and said, "Can you handle it from here?"

"Yes, thank you" she said, extending her hand. "I'm Eileen Cleary."

He stuck his hand out, saying, "Paul Conklin."

As they shook hands he really took notice of her for the first time: dishwater blond hair, blue eyes, and much prettier than he'd thought. Somehow he'd gotten the impression she was younger, but now he realized she was closer to his own age, and quite attractive.

She gave him a glowing smile, an inviting smile. "Can I offer you a beer to say thanks?"

He almost took her up on it, and for a moment wondered if she was offering him a lot more than a beer, but he didn't want to go there. "Sorry," he said, having trouble convincing himself he was making the right decision. "I have an appointment, and I'm in a hurry. If you don't mind I'll take a rain-check."

She released his hand, saying, "Any time you want to collect, just holler."

Again, she seemed to be offering far more than a beer, but then he was probably just being a dumb-shit guy and letting his ego read more into her words than she really meant. He forced himself to look away from her and walk to the door. When he opened it he found Madge sitting in the middle of the hall, licking a paw and giving him that look. He hadn't let the cat out of his apartment, but such limitations didn't apply to a hallucination.

"Oh," Eileen said. "What a gorgeous little kitty."

She walked past him and reached down, but before she touched the cat, Madge streaked out of sight down the hall.

So much for the hallucination theory, Paul thought. He now couldn't deny that she was a real cat, but the talking part was certainly a hallucination.

He stepped out into the hall, and as Eileen closed the door she said, "Don't forget. I owe you that beer."

As he hit the stairs he had a little trouble putting her out of his mind, and it took him a block or two of walking before Katherine returned to the forefront of his thoughts.

••••

Eileen Cleary closed the door to her small apartment, turned and walked into the kitchen. She retrieved a copper bowl from her pantry, filled it half-way with water, then placed it on the small table in the kitchenette. She pulled out a chair, sat down and looked at her reflection in the water. She cleared her mind, focused on the face she saw there and mentally reshaped the image. With a thought she shortened the dishwater blond hair, darkened it and added a little salt-and-pepper gray at the temples, then arranged it into the style a male, British diplomat might wear. She adjusted the tops of the ears so they were pointed, and modified the nose into an aristocratic arc, then restructured the overall shape of the face. When she was done she nodded her head and said, "Lord Cadilus. Greetings."

The image in the scrying bowl nodded in return and said, "Lady Si'entha, were you successful? Did you get him into your bed?"

"No, of course not. Not yet."

"Then you failed."

She shook her head slightly. "Not at all. He met a pretty, young woman and felt attracted to her. I encouraged him with just a hint of beguilement, though only the faintest touch. With a little patience, I'll make that attraction grow, and with each meeting his thoughts will turn more and more to me, and less and less to her."

The skin between Cadilus's eyebrows furrowed. "We've had greater access to the young woman and our control of her has progressed nicely, but the Young Mage has proven problematic. Can't you move any faster, perhaps use more beguilement or compulsion?"

"No," she said. "Don't forget he was tested in our own court and proved quite capable of resisting our natural enchantments. And since then the Old Wizard has been tutoring him, so it's safe to assume his abilities have grown. He would have recognized any determined effort at overt beguilement. And the use of compulsion or obsession spells is out of the question. Even if he didn't detect it himself, his mortal colleagues would sniff out such interference immediately. No, his attraction to the old man's daughter can't be severed in a single meeting. But I will sever it nonetheless."

Cadilus smiled. "I have the utmost faith in your . . . abilities, Lady Si'entha."

••••

Paul grew impatient with walking and splurged on a cab. He needed to get to McGowan's before Katherine left, and the lie he'd told Coleen about being in the east bay meant that as soon as Katherine was ready to leave, Colleen wouldn't attempt to stall her.

A bank of clouds had rolled in over the city. The cabbie had the radio going and the weathergirl predicted a fifty percent chance of rain. Paul had the cabbie stop about a block from McGowan's, paid the man and climbed out of the cab, then walked cautiously up the street. He stopped about fifty yards from the old man's place and leaned into a shadow. For all he knew Katherine had already left and he'd be standing there waiting all night long.

••••

Karpov got the call just before dinner. "Mikhail here, Mr. Karpov."

"Yes, Mikhail, what is it?"

"You wanted me to call you if the Conklin fellow went out at night. He hailed a cab, went to the Old Wizard's house, but stopped a few doors down and is hiding in the shadows. I'm not sure what he's doing."

"You have eyes on him."

"I do, Mr. Karpov."

"We're on our way. If he moves, stay with him and call me."

Karpov switched off his phone, summoned Vladimir, Alexei and three others. Ag had told him they could summon the Caorthannach only at night. Consulting with the

Winter King, Karpov had prepared a very powerful spell; it had taken three days just to gather the ingredients, and another four to concoct the thing. But he was now ready.

He instructed one of his more powerful practitioners to contact Ag with a scrying bowl and tell them to be ready at that end. He didn't know the preparations they'd made in Faerie, but assumed they'd been as extensive as his own.

On Mikhail's instructions he had his driver drop them off a city block from Conklin's position. They met Mikhail there.

"He's still there, Mr. Karpov. Been waiting for something."

"Or someone," Karpov said.

Karpov turned to Sergei, one of his lieutenants. He'd called the man up from the LA area, his main qualifications being that he was a moderately strong practitioner, and that he'd never had any interaction with young Conklin, or any of the McGowan clan, so was unlikely to be recognized. He did have pronounced Slavic cheek bones, but other than that, his features were rather ordinary, so Conklin would have to be quite astute to make the connection.

"Are you ready, Sergei?"

They'd drilled on the summoning spell for the last three days, and Sergei knew how dangerous it would be. The man simply nodded once. Karpov liked that about Sergei, a man of few words.

6

Fire Returns

AS THE EVENING wore on, the weathergirl's fifty percent probability turned to one hundred, and a light drizzle began to fall. Paul hadn't thought to bring an umbrella but his jacket did shed water, and by staying close to the building behind him, most of the drops missed him. The night wasn't terribly cold for October, but if he did get really wet he'd be pretty miserable within an hour.

About a half hour after the rain started Katherine emerged from her father's house. She'd been smarter than Paul, was wearing a trench coat, and as she walked down the steps to the sidewalk, she popped open an umbrella. The front of the overcoat flared open for a moment, and in the light of a streetlamp he saw she wore one of her dark suits with a blazer and a tight, pencil skirt cut a few inches above her knees. Of course, she had on the mandatory high heels, probably some designer brand he couldn't pronounce.

Paul got lucky; she walked his way so he didn't have to chase after her. He simply waited in the shadows.

When she was about ten feet from him he stepped out into the rain and onto the sidewalk in front of her. She hesitated and stopped walking, but he held up both hands and said, "Don't worry, it's just me, Paul."

The light from a street lamp cast a deep shadow under the umbrella, so he couldn't see her face, but there was no mistaking the wariness in her voice. "You startled me."

He walked forward. "Sorry. Mind if I share some of that umbrella."

She couldn't really refuse that, but as he ducked beneath it he got the impression she wanted to. "Listen, Paul, I've got to run. I've got an important appointment I need to get to."

"What appointment?" he demanded, certain it was a lie.

"I . . . um." She cocked her head and said. "I can't recall exactly, but I know I've got one. I'll just check my calendar on my cell when I get to my car."

"You're avoiding me."

"No, I'm not. I really do have an appointment."

He reached out and gripped the arm holding the umbrella, was careful to do so very lightly and without any aggression. "Yes, you are."

She shook her head, and with her free hand reached up and gripped his wrist. When her hand touched his wrist something strange fluttered through him, and clearly the same happened to her.

"Hmm!" she said. "My aura just got a little shock. But I do . . ."

She hesitated and looked at him oddly. "No . . . I don't."

"Don't what?"

"I don't have an appointment, and for the life of me I can't think of why I thought I did. I must have gotten tonight mixed up with another night. I'll have to check my calendar. Sorry about that."

The raindrops increased in size and came down a little harder. Paul turned to walk beside her and they continued up the street, both huddled under the umbrella, walking past classic, multi-story, Victorian San Francisco Houses. With the exception of one other pedestrian walking their way, the street was empty, not unusual given that they were in a residential area on a dark, dreary, rainy night.

"What did you want to talk to me about?" she asked.

"Nothing really. I just thought you were avoiding me."

As they approached the lone pedestrian coming their way, Paul realized the sidewalk wasn't wide enough for the three of them to pass, so he held back a pace and stepped behind Katherine. When they passed going in opposite directions, the street light momentarily illuminated the fellow's face, and Paul thought he saw eastern European features with high cheek bones. The instant ended and the fellow passed them, but he dropped something.

Paul turned and said, "Excuse me. You dropped something."

The fellow turned, froze and looked at Paul for a moment. Then he spun on his heels and ran like the devil was on his tail, and as he disappeared down the street into the rainy mist, Katherine said, "Now that was odd."

Only then did Paul feel it, a strange, twisted distortion in reality. The sidewalk in front of him appeared to lose its solidity, bubbled and flowed as if it were molten. He backed up a step and bumped into Katherine. "I really don't like this," she said.

Paul continued to back away from it, with Katherine back-stepping behind him. He sensed a spell trigger at his back. "That you?" he asked.

"Yes," she said, "a little protection."

"You know what we're facing?"

"No."

"Something from the Netherworld maybe?"

"No, worse."

He turned to face her. "Why worse? How worse?"

"I don't know," she said, "but it feels really bad. Let's get the hell out of—."

The sidewalk exploded, slamming Paul against Katherine and they both went down with him on top. Fearing she'd bashed her head into the concrete, he put his hands on the sidewalk on either side of her and pushed up off of her. "Are you all right? Are you okay?"

"Ya," she said, blinking rapidly.

He glanced to one side, saw that the explosion had badly damaged the front of the house next to them, noticed a sign above the door that said something about *Law Offices*. The blast had blown the door partially open, and it hung precariously from a single hinge. If Katherine hadn't had the presence of mind to bring some sort of protection spell, they'd both be dead.

"Let's get out of here," he said.

"Ya, let's," she said, but her eyes focused on something behind them and she added, "Oh shit!"

Something screamed out a high pitched wail that sounded like tearing steel. As Katherine's eyes filled with terror, Paul wrapped his arms around her and rolled to one side. A blast of searing hot flame flooded the concrete where they'd been laying a moment before. Paul jumped to his feet and turned to face whatever had come into this world.

Before him stood a ten-foot tall woman with hair that writhed and curled about her head. Two massive ram's horns curled back from her forehead and two six-inch fangs sprouted from her mouth. She wore a dress that appeared to be a mix of peacock feathers and some sort of scaled, green leather. It was cut like an evening gown, floor length with long sleeves, but there was no front to it and it fully exposed her breasts. Her mouth dripped molten flame instead of saliva, and her nipples dripped molten fire in place of milk. Rain now poured down in torrents, but where it touched her it sizzled and crackled, and boiled away in wisps of steam.

She threw her head back, screamed that ungodly cry that sounded like tearing metal, then spit at Paul. A glob of molten flame shot straight toward him and he dove to one side, plowed into Katherine and they both landed in front of the broken door of the house.

"Who the hell is she?" Paul shouted as they both struggled to their feet.

He came up facing Katherine, with the monster behind her. It reared again, and now knowing what to expect, Paul screamed, "Look out."

He grabbed Katherine by the front of her coat, and threw himself backward through the doorway of the house, bringing her with him. She landed on top of him just as a glob of flame splattered off the door above them, showering them with bits and pieces of fire.

••••

Seated in McGowan's study, waiting for him to pour a couple glasses of cognac, Colleen had decided it was time for a serious talk, and she was going to make the old man listen to her. He handed her a snifter with amber liquid in it, then crossed the room to the fireplace and stood in front of it staring at the flames with his back to her. "Paul was way off his game today, preoccupied with something."

"Preoccupied with your daughter," she said.

He nodded and took a sip of his cognac. "They are attracted to one another. I assumed they're dating, or something. Don't tell me he's all gaga in love."

The old man could be such a *man*. "I wouldn't be surprised if their relationship became serious, if they ever saw one another. But they're not dating, not seeing each other at all. In fact, she's avoiding him."

He turned and looked her way with a frown on his face. "Now why would she do that? He's a nice guy, be good for her."

She raised a questioning eyebrow at him and he said, "Ya, I know, I'm a typical father, and I act like I think she's still a virgin and I expect her to remain so until she's eighty or ninety years old, but I'm just giving the boy a hard time."

Colleen decided to voice her suspicions. "I think her avoidance is unnatural."

"What do you mean by that?"

"I think someone's interfering with them."

The old man looked at her angrily. "Why would anyone do that?"

"I think they're stronger together," she said. "I've only seen little hints of it, but I think both of them exhibit enhanced arcane abilities in the other's presence."

He sat down in the chair next to her, his brow creased in thought. "Now that I think about it, Katherine was a middling witch before Paul came along, and now I'd classify her as quite powerful."

The old man had begun following her line of thinking. She prodded him further. "And when we first met him, Paul was quite limited, but after several misadventures with Katherine, now he's anything but. And the growth seems to be permanent, not something that dissipates when they separate."

She let him ponder that for a moment, then she added, "I want to push them to work together more, and I'll need your help to overcome any resistance Katherine exhibits."

"All right," he said, "I'm in. The question is: who's interfering with them?"

She kept her mouth shut and let him think on that, wanted to see if he'd come up with the same conclusion she had. He sat there for a long moment, swirling the cognac in his glass and staring at it. Then he looked at her and said, "That would be so like the fey."

She gave him a big smile. "My thoughts exactly."

"But who?" he asked. "Seelie, Unseelie, or non-aligned?"

"I don't—" She hesitated as she felt something dangerous and powerful manifest on the Mortal Plane.

McGowan started as well, had clearly felt it too. "What the hell was that?"

She stood. "Something fey, and extremely old. Something that doesn't belong here, and it's close."

She looked at her watch. Katherine had only been gone for a few minutes. They both had the same thought and spoke in unison, "Katherine."

••••

The house Paul and Katherine had stumbled into was a classic nineteenth-century, wood-frame with three or four stories of bay windows. Just inside the front door, stairs led up to the next floor, and beside them a hallway led to the back of the house.

Paul had landed on his back with Katherine in top of him just as the gob of fire hit the front doorway. She rolled off him and he scrambled to his feet. The arm of his coat was on fire, so he pulled it off and threw it aside. But Katherine had been on top of him and gotten the worst of it. She was on her hands and knees, using one hand to swat at flames consuming the back of her trench coat. He grabbed the coat's collar, paying no heed to the flames licking at his hands and arms, pulled and tugged until he got it off of her. He threw it aside as she got to her feet and faced him.

A ball of flaming spit shot through the door, passed right between them down the hall and splattered all over the floor there. With flames blocking the back of the hall, they had no place else to go but up the stairs.

"Go, go, go," he shouted.

Katherine turned and raced up the stairs, her high-heels clacking on each step. Paul followed behind her, though she wasn't moving fast because of the heels. When they reached the second floor he grabbed her arm and spun her to face him. "Ditch the damn heels," he said.

She opened her mouth to argue, but flame-bitch let out one of her wailing screams. Katherine hesitated for a second, then said, "That fucking bitch," and she kicked the heels off.

As she did so Paul saw tendrils of smoke rising from the back of her shoulders, realized the flames had burned through the trench coat to the blazer. He reached out, grabbed the blazer's lapels and tore them open.

"What are you doing?" she shouted. "Now's not the time to cop a feel, Conklin."

"You're still on fire," he shouted back.

He spun her around, ripped the blazer off her and threw it down the stairs, leaving her in nothing but a white, long-sleeve blouse and the pencil skirt.

She turned around and shouted at him, "You're never going to get lucky, Conklin, if this is how you undress a girl."

Down below, the ten-foot-tall woman let out an ear-splitting cry, and they heard the snap and pop of tearing lumber. Paul looked down the stairway, saw that she'd shredded the front of the house and ripped a hole in it large enough for him to walk through without bending over; there was no longer any sign of the front door. Flame-bitch stuck her head through the hole, looked up, hocked a loogie and spit a gob of flame at him. He ducked back as the ball of fire shot past him and splattered on the wall. Alarms shrieked as sprinklers in the ceiling unloaded, soaking them even further.

Katherine said, "Thank god they installed a sprinkler system. These places are tinder boxes."

Paul shook his head. "I don't think it's going to matter too much, not the way that bitch is spitting fire."

He glanced again down the stairway; flame-bitch had opened the hole even further and now stood in the hallway below. She saw him and started up the stairs, moving slowly and spitting lungers of fire as she came.

He ducked back out of the way. "We're in deep shit. She's in the house and coming up after us."

They ran down the hall to the stairs that led to the next floor, but Katherine pulled them to a stop there. "We can't just keep going up. This place is a fire trap, and we're going to run out of floors."

"What the hell else are we going to do, sit here and wait for flame-bitch to barbecue us alive?"

Katherine frowned and said, "Maybe that's exactly what you need to do."

"What do you mean?"

Flame-bitch screamed out another cry of tearing steel.

"You have power over the dead," Katherine said. "And that bitch is as dead they come. And she's fey, not nether. And you can transfer between here and Faerie with just a thought, right? Or whatever it is you do."

"Sort of," he said. "Kind of." He thought of his experimental failures in the living room of his apartment.

"Well then you can take her with you, get her off the Mortal Plane. You hide in one of these rooms, I'll draw her attention up the stairs, then as soon as she's past you, you hit her from behind and get her out of here."

"Are you crazy?"

"No, I'm desperate. You got a better plan?"

Flame-bitch screamed again, as if to punctuate the fact that, *No, he did not have a better plan.*

They quickly checked the rooms on the second floor. A door near the bottom of the stairs opened into a room that appeared to be furnished as an office. Paul stepped into it, closed the door and waited.

He heard Katherine thud up the stairs, then heard her shout, "Come on, you bitch. Let's see what you got, honey."

Through the door he heard flame-bitch's shriek, still not close enough, heard Katherine shouting at her, unloading a string of epithets that would have made a dock-worker blush.

Flame-bitch shrieked again, and he realized she'd reached the second floor and stood just on the other side of the door. He waited, heard Katherine screaming more epithets, then flame-bitch screamed again, and it sounded like she'd started up the stairs after Katherine.

He hadn't thought to listen to the door when they'd opened it, to recall if it squeaked or made any noise. He wanted to open it a crack, peek out, confirm the situation and know what he was stepping into. But if the door did make any noise, it would warn flame-bitch, she'd turn him into overcooked barbecue, and then Katherine would die too. So he had no choice; assume he was right, move fast and get it over with. Though if it didn't work and he failed to take flame-bitch back to Faerie, he'd run like hell back down the stairs and try to draw her away from Katherine.

He threw the door open and stepped out into the hall. Flame-bitch stood with her back to him a few steps above him on the stairway leading to the third floor, leading to Katherine. He reached out and gripped her wrist. It surprised him that it was ice cold, painfully so.

At the touch on her wrist she halted and turned slowly toward him. On instinct and a bit of whim, he thought of the courtyard outside the Unseelie Palace. If he was going to give anyone the problem of dealing with this nasty bitch, he preferred it be the Winter King. He recalled that spiral shift in reality between their two worlds, and mentally stepped into it.

7

Fire Exiled

WHEN COLLEEN AND McGowan hit the street, there was no question where they needed to go. They ran towards the flames and stopped in front of the house that had been converted to lawyer's offices. The front door and part of the wall supporting it had been ripped away, leaving a gaping hole fully engulfed in flames. Colleen released a veil to hide them from prying eyes.

"Katherine's in there," McGowan said, his eyes locked on the roaring flames, "with something really bad. I can sense it."

Colleen asked, "Can you handle the flames?"

"Sure," he said. "But I have to pull a lot of power."

At that moment Colleen felt the *something-really-bad* go away. She grabbed the old man's arm, but he looked her way and said, "I felt it too. It's gone. But Katherine's still in there, and I don't know if she's still okay."

He ran up the steps and walked into the wall of fire.

••••

Paul and flame-bitch materialized in the middle of the courtyard outside the Unseelie Palace. He hadn't been sure the place would be there, so he'd chosen that destination with a bit of trepidation, and he thanked whatever gods watched over him he'd found it.

Flame-bitch turned on him, hocked another lunger and spit fire at him. He jumped to the side in a shoulder-roll as a spit-gob of flame splashed on the ground where he'd been standing a moment before. He ended his roll on his hands and knees, and when she spun toward him again he knew he couldn't move fast enough to avoid the next flaming loogie. But before she turned him into an overdone slab of baby-back ribs, an Unseelie warrior in full Sidhe armor stepped in her way and swung his sword. The fire she spit at him splashed off his armor and scattered in little mini-gobs all around them.

Paul should have realized the Unseelie Palace Guard would be sensitive to any-thing like her showing up. Dozens of them flooded into the courtyard, shouting and crying out. Paul knew damn well the instant they realized who he was, he wouldn't live long in the Winter Court; he needed to get the hell out of there now. He hoped flame-bitch would keep them too busy to realize who he was as he recalled the sec-ond floor landing in the flaming house. He was still on his hands and knees as anoth-er warrior stood over him and raised his sword with the clear intent of making Paul's day go from bad to worse. Paul thought of the spiral twist in reality, and mentally stepped into it.

Paul had chosen the second floor landing because Katherine had climbed up to the third and he didn't want to land on top of her and hurt her. But apparently, during the few moments he'd been gone, she'd run back down to the second floor. As usual he didn't return simply standing up, but instead materialized right above her shoulders.

She shrieked as he landed on top of her, a real girly scream very unlike her. They ended up tangled in a heap on the floor of the landing, surrounded by flames, the house filling with smoke, Katherine gripping the high-heel shoes.

He shouted, "You came back for the fucking shoes?"

She gave him an indignant look, sputtered and tried to say something, but clearly couldn't come up with a clever reply.

They untangled their arms and legs, but stayed low, trying to find some breathable air.

"Can you take us to Faerie?" she asked.

He gripped her hand, thought of the leprechaun's huts, tried to step into that spiral twist in reality, but nothing happened. He tried the Seelie Court, and again nothing. He even tried to go back to the courtyard outside the Unseelie Palace—better to be Ag's prisoner than burn to death here—but he failed there too.

"It's not working," he said. "We're so fucked."

There was a bit of panic in her voice as she said, "You know, Conklin, I kind of figured that out."

"Stay low," he said, "see if we can stay under the smoke and flames and crawl down the stairs."

They crawled to the top of the stairway leading down to the first floor, but the stairwell had become a chimney and a roaring torrent of flame ran up the ceiling above them, the heat so intense it forced them away from the top step. He looked in her eyes and knew he didn't have to tell her they'd run out of options. And then a shadowy specter appeared standing above them and said in old man McGowan's voice, "Let's get you two out of here."

••••

Paul had no idea how McGowan managed to get them out of that inferno alive. Out on the street the torrent of rain pouring down on them felt wonderfully cool. Paul helped Katherine down the steps of the burning building into Colleen's arms. Without coats, Paul and Katherine were soaked to the skin.

They heard sirens in the distance as McGowan said to Paul, "Get Katherine back to my place. Colleen and I'll clean this mess up."

"My purse," Katherine said. "It's got my ID and it's here somewhere."

"Don't worry," McGowan said. "I'll take care of it."

It occurred to Paul there must be people looking down from nearby houses, and there'd be hell to pay if they were identified to the police. "What about witnesses?" he asked.

"I'm running a veil," Colleen said. "All anyone will see of us is four shadows. You two get out of this rain and let Walter and I take care of this."

Paul noticed Katherine clutching the high-heels to her chest. She saw him staring at the shoes and threw a defiant look his way. She leaned down and put the shoes on, then strode out ahead of him toward the old man's house. Even in the pouring rain he heard the heels clacking on the concrete of the sidewalk.

McGowan had left the front door unlocked, so they walked right in, staggered down the hall and into the kitchen, both soaked to the skin and dripping rainwater all over the tile floor. Paul leaned on the table in the center of the room, while Katherine walked past him to the counter and gripped the edge of the sink as if she needed it to hold herself up. They were both breathing heavily.

"What just happened?" Katherine asked.

Paul looked up as she turned around, but at that moment couldn't think of a thing to say. They were both drenched, but Katherine wore a white blouse, with a white, lacy see-through bra beneath it. Her breasts were small enough she didn't need a bra made of heavy cloth, and could probably go braless if she wanted to. And Paul saw that the lacy bra was see-through, because soaking wet he saw pretty much everything there was to see through the white blouse. She looked ready to compete in a wet t-shirt contest in some crummy sports bar.

She frowned at the look on his face, obviously noticed the direction of his gaze, then slowly looked down at her chest. She stared at it for a moment, her eyes turning hard and angry, and when she finally looked at Paul, he knew he was in deep trouble.

"Did you get a good eyeful, Conklin?" she asked.

She marched around the table and stopped in front of him. "Here," she said, and shook her chest at him, wiggling her breasts, the dark nipples visible through the wet fabric bouncing from side-to-side. "Take a good look, go ahead and ogle, stare openly if you want. You can even have a conversation with them, and leave me completely out of it. I can simply be Katherine, the thing that's attached to my boobs and just happens to come along with them for the ride."

She was being unfair, though he couldn't really blame her for being a little hysterical after what they'd just been through, but now was not the time to call her on it. He didn't try to hide his frustration as he said, "Cut me a little slack, would you McGowan? You're half naked, I'm a healthy guy, and you're an incredibly attractive woman."

"You can just . . .", she shouted, but then hesitated, and the fire in her eyes dimmed a little. "You . . . What . . . What did you just say?"

"You heard what I said."

She grinned evilly and wiggled her breasts at him again. "I know. I just wanted to hear you say it again. And I'm not half naked."

He made a point of looking at the dark areolas showing through the wet, white blouse and see-through lacy bra. "You might as well be."

She took an aggressive step forward. He stepped back, but ran into the wall behind him. She got that glint in her eye. "You guys are so easily turned on." She stepped forward again, and since he couldn't step back further she ran into him and pressed her breasts against his chest. "Give you a peek at a little dark nipple, and you all turn into a bunch of horny school boys."

"There's more to it than that."

"Like what?"

"The *incredibly attractive woman* part has a bit to do with it."

She stretched upward, stopped with her lips just an inch from his, and pressed her entire body against him. "So, you like me just for my mind, huh?"

He swallowed hard. "Well," he said, having a little trouble speaking, his voice coming out in a husky growl. "I confess I'm not doing much thinking about your mind right now."

"Fess up, Conklin."

"The nippular content . . . does have a bit to do with it."

She brushed her lips against his. "Anything else?"

"Well . . . I do . . . like to look at your—"

"I know," she said and stepped back a pace. She shook her chest at him one more time, saying, "Enjoy it while you can."

He tried not to watch, but then decided, *Aw, fuck it*, and enjoyed the show as her breasts bounced side-to-side.

She said, "I'm going to get a hot shower."

She turned away from him, and as she walked out of the kitchen she called over her shoulder, "You probably need to take a cold one?"

••••

When McGowan and Colleen returned from cleaning up flame-bitch's mess, Paul was seated at the kitchen table, still soaking wet, and Katherine was in the shower. Paul had made a pot of coffee to warm up a bit, and used a towel from the guest bathroom to dry his hair and mop up the puddles of water on the floor. As the old man walked into the kitchen with Colleen behind him, he tossed Katherine's purse onto the table, then demanded, "What the hell happened out there, kid?"

Paul wrapped his hands around his coffee cup, enjoying the warmth. "Katherine and I were walking down the street together, and this flame-bitch from hell appeared out of nowhere."

"No, Paul," Colleen said as she poured a cup of coffee. She did not look pleased with him. "Start from the beginning. Katherine left here alone, and you told me you were in the east bay. How did you get here?"

"Sorry, Colleen," Paul said. "I lied about the east bay thing. I wanted to get Katherine alone, because she's avoiding me." Paul explained his reasoning for the lie, and how he'd waited for Katherine down the street when she came out of the old man's house.

McGowan raised an eyebrow and said, "Stalking my daughter, huh?"

"Oh shut up, old man," Colleen said as she sat down at the table. She held out her coffee cup, and her Irish accent thickened. "And I need something to fortify this coffee, old man."

McGowan said to Paul, "Don't say anything more until I'm back."

He turned and marched out of the kitchen, returned a few seconds later with a bottle of Irish whiskey. He splashed some in Colleen's cup, poured a healthy dose in Paul's, poured a cup of coffee, added some whiskey to it and sat down at the table. He put the bottle in the middle of the table. "Okay, you can continue."

Paul raised his hands in a gesture of helplessness. "Katherine and I were walking down the street, we felt something fey happening, and then flame-bitch showed up just like that."

Katherine walked into the room during his last few words. She wore slippers, a blue terry-cloth robe a few sizes too large, and was drying her hair with a towel. "Don't forget that guy that passed us," she said, "just before flame-bitch came along. And remember how he took to his heels like he was really scared of something."

She poured a cup of coffee and sat down with the rest of them, then reached for the bottle in the middle of the table. She pulled the cork and took a swig straight from it, then added some to her coffee.

Colleen said, "Before we go any further, describe this *flame-bitch*."

Paul and Katherine both supplied bits and pieces to the description. When they finished Colleen and McGowan shared a look. The old man asked her, "The Caorthannach?"

Colleen said, "I believe so."

To Katherine she said, "Some legends have it that she's the mother of Satan, but all agree she spits fire, though they don't agree on much else, and none of them mention dripping molten flame from her nipples."

Katherine shook her hair out, leaned forward, scrunched her nose up, and Paul knew she had something sarcastic to say. "I think she did that just for Paul. She can probably read his mind, and he's got a horny, schoolboy thing for nipples."

Paul wasn't going to let that stand without a rebuttal. "Only for fiery hot ones."

Colleen and McGowan looked at each other, clearly realizing there was some sub-plot here to which they were not privy, but they said nothing. They made Paul and Katherine describe the entire incident in detail, and carefully quizzed them on certain aspects. When they got to the point where Paul removed flame-bitch from the Mortal Plane, Katherine asked, "Where did you take her? You never said."

When he told them, Colleen chuckled and McGowan laughed until he had tears in his eyes. "You dumped her on Ag. Serves that shit right."

Paul said, "That's kind of the way I felt."

McGowan and Colleen were in agreement that the fellow who'd passed them on the sidewalk had probably triggered some sort of spell. McGowan said, "It took a very powerful spell to bring a legend over. And besides me and Colleen,"—he looked at Paul—"and maybe you, there's only one other practitioner in the bay area powerful enough: that ass-hole Russian."

Collen said, "And even he must have had help from Faerie."

The meeting of the four of them broke up. McGowan invited Paul to take a warm shower before going home, but he declined, figured he'd just go back to his apartment, dry off and hit the sack. The old man did lend him a coat since his had gone up in flames.

Katherine said, "Father, if you don't mind, I'm going to spend the night."

He said, "I always keep your old room available."

Katherine and Paul both had to walk down the hall since the stairs to the second floor were just within the front entrance. They walked in silence down to the end of the hall, but as she turned toward the stairs, he paused at the front door before opening it.

"That was unfair," he said. "I don't have a thing for nipples."

She glanced back his way, rolled her eyes and said, "I'm a woman, so I'm never fair." She turned and started up the stairs.

Paul opened the front door but paused there and called back to her. "McGowan."

She stopped half way up the stairs, turned and looked back at him. He added, "Unless they're attached to the right, fiery hot girl."

She frowned thoughtfully and closed her eyes, clearly had to take a moment to string his words together and understand what he meant. Then she smiled, but when

 J. L. Doty

she opened her eyes and saw him still standing there, she killed the smile, reached up and touched her neck where the front of the terry cloth robe was open.

He left her standing on the stairs.

8

A True Alice

HE FIRST NOTICED her on the edge of Union Square, holding the hand of her mother as they walked down the sidewalk. She was a lovely little girl, wearing a pink dress with a white pinafore, white knee-high stockings and little Mary Jane shoes. And her mother hadn't put her in pigtails, had instead let her beautiful blond hair cascade past her shoulders in curls and ringlets. That was so much more truly Alice than the pigtails.

Nooo, the voice said. *A young girl will draw unwanted attention.*

"I have to," he said, keeping his voice low. "I need a true Alice. Not these prostitutes. Even the blond ones don't look like Alice, not a true Alice."

A nearby pedestrian glanced his way and gave him a look of distaste. But the streets of a large city like San Francisco were filled with plenty of odd-balls mumbling to themselves, though most of them looked like street-people, whereas he had nurtured a very ordinary appearance.

Nooo!

He ignored the voice, and followed the mother and daughter. They went into a large, expensive department store just off Union Square, though they were already burdened with a number of packages. He noted several video cameras near the ceiling in the store, knew he was taking a chance, but trailing them proved to be easy. It never occurred to the mother that someone like him might stalk them.

They strolled casually, stopping at one display for several seconds, pausing at another and speaking with a saleswoman. Their leisurely pace allowed him to stay back quite a distance, so he'd not appear in the same frame with them on any of the store's video footage. And in any case, he wouldn't take her today, and when he did the girl would not die of any suspicious cause. She'd just be one of those mysterious cases of a young child whose life came to an end, and there'd be no reason for the authorities to examine video footage of their shopping trip.

He followed them back out onto the street, then down to the Powell Street BART Station. They stopped at a kiosk to buy tickets. He had a monthly pass so he didn't need a ticket, but he couldn't just stop and loiter about, so he chose another kiosk and pretended to buy a ticket. He waited for them to finish, then followed at a distance as they went through the turnstiles.

They boarded a train to the east bay. He wasn't stupid enough to get into the same car, but chose the next one behind it. He found a spot where he could keep an eye on them through the windows of the doors that separated the cars.

They got out at the Walnut Creek Station. They were close to the afternoon rush hour, so he had the luxury of staying within a crowd as he followed them out to the parking lot, and he wasn't the only person following them down the row of cars where the mother had parked her expensive SUV. When she pressed the button on her key fob and the car's lights flashed, he noted the license number and continued walking. He couldn't follow them because he'd left his car in the parking structure in the city. He spotted a couple of cabs near the curb, briefly considered hailing one, but giving the cabbie instructions to follow the woman and her daughter would be the stupidest move he'd ever made. For the time being he'd have to settle for the prostitutes while he figured out a way to convert the plate number to an address. And once he accomplished that, he'd begin the process of making this new Alice his.

His master would gain more strength from her pure and vibrant soul than It did from the degraded prostitutes. They could go after the young McGowan witch even sooner.

••••

Magreth's audience chamber was warm and inviting, though Cadilus suspected that might change shortly. He dropped to one knee before her and bowed.

"Rise, Lord Cadilus," she said as she extended her hand.

He stood, bent deeply at the waist, took her hand in his and kissed the large ruby ring on her maiden finger, a powerful symbol of the sovereignty of the Seelie Court.

When he straightened, she said, "You're here to tell me about the recent unpleasantness on the Mortal Plane, aren't you?"

"Yes, Your Majesty."

"I felt it too, something to do with the Young Mage, I assume."

"Yes, Your Majesty." He glanced around the room at the courtiers and attendants present.

She followed his gaze, nodded, and with nothing more than a whim from the queen of the Summer Court, they disappeared. "You may speak freely now," she said.

He chose his words carefully as he reported the incident, and when he finished the queen merely paused as if lost in thought for a long moment. "The Caorthannach," she said. "That seems rather extreme, don't you think?"

He was relieved to see that her eyes did not fill with flame, and the primordial Sidhe spirits remained quiescent. "There was quite a bit of damage, Your Majesty. The flames completely gutted one building, and caused considerable damage to the two on either side of it. The authorities of the old man's city are conducting an arson investigation, but I have no doubt the Old Wizard cleaned up nicely. I'm sure there'll be no hints of arcane activity."

She brushed that thought aside with a casual wave of her hand. "That's the old man's problem. But the Young Mage has twice now demonstrated the ability to walk the halls of Sidhe."

Cadilus said, "And let us not forget he broke a circle from within, a circle powered by thirteen Unseelie mages, and in breaking it he killed four of them."

"And he murdered Simuth," she said.

Cadilus flinched at her choice of words, though any Sidhe mage would consider the taking of an immortal's life murder. "Our mortal colleagues would not call it murder."

She turned, strode across the room and stopped at a window. He crossed the room to join her, though without a specific invitation, he did not stop beside her, but remained two paces behind her. He saw that the window looked out onto a courtyard below.

"He frightens me," she said.

"Any mage who demonstrates such abilities frightens us all."

"Do you know who summoned the Caorthannach to the Mortal Plane?"

"No, Your Majesty, but we suspect Ag may have been involved."

She sighed. "Oddly enough, the interests of Winter and Summer coincide in this."

Cadilus needed to steer the subject to another issue. "One of my assistants reports that just before the excitement began, there was a minor incident that might have been eclipsed by the more dramatic events that followed. It involved the Young Mage and the Old Wizard's daughter."

She turned to face him and lifted a questioning eyebrow, so he continued. "My agent told me that the mere touch of her hand on his wrist unraveled all their efforts at keeping them apart."

She frowned and said, "That confirms everything we've suspected about their connection."

"It also means that Si'entha's efforts are even more important."

She smiled wistfully. "Yes, simple seduction frequently succeeds where magic fails, though as a precautionary measure, don't abandon your efforts to keep the two young people apart. But I suspect you may not be as effective as we had hoped."

"But Lady Si'entha has made no progress."

Her smile changed from wistful to calculating. "You must have patience, Lord Cadilus. A slow, careful seduction will bind the young man's heart even more tightly to her, and make it easier for her to destroy him when she's ready."

••••

With Ag walking beside him, Vasily Karpov surveyed the damage in the courtyard outside the Unseelie palace. Blackened scorch marks discolored the stone of the palace and the ground about them. Large blocks of stone had been broken and dislodged from the palace walls, and the earth was pitted and scarred.

Ag said, "I wanted you to see this, Vasily."

"Could he have suspected?" Karpov asked. "Is that why he brought her here?"

Ag shook his head as they strolled. "No, I think not. The magics we used to send her your way were consumed in the sending. Anyone who came sniffing about afterward could never trace the spells back to this Court. No, I believe the young man did it out of pure vindictiveness, a simple act of spite."

"Where is she now?"

"It took thirteen mages and an entire platoon of warriors to herd her back to her lair."

Karpov waved a hand. "What will it take to repair all of this?"

Ag halted and Karpov stopped beside him. The Winter King slowly turned around and examined the damage. When he'd completed a full circle, he looked at Karpov and said, "Only a whim and a thought."

He closed his eyes, stood quite still for a moment. In an instant the carnage disappeared, no blackened scorch marks, no broken and displaced stones, no pitted and scarred ground. Karpov found such enormous power frightening, and took comfort in the fact that Ag's abilities were considerably limited when on the Mortal Plane. He suspected that's why the Ag and Magreth never ventured there.

Ag opened his eyes. "What next, my friend? Shall we send demons after him?"

As they turned and began strolling through the restored courtyard, Karpov said, "Not yet. Tell me, how is it the young man brought the Caorthannach back here with such little effort?"

"Perhaps because he is a necromancer." Ag looked at Karpov pointedly, and the Russian saw anger and jealousy in the king's eyes. "We know so little of his abilities."

"Exactly," Karpov said. "Am I correct in assuming no mortal practitioner should be able to do that?"

Karpov watched Ag's anger turn to curiosity. The king nodded. "You are, my friend. What do you have in mind?"

Karpov answered his question with one of his own. "And might that lead you to believe the young man could just as easily bring the Caorthannach from here to the Mortal Plane?"

Ag smiled as they walked into the palace. They entered a waiting room where Vladimir and Alexei awaited them, both looking hungry and anxious. The two were such fools.

Karpov turned to Ag and said, "My young men are hoping your young lady will grace them with her favors again."

Ag grimaced and said, "I'm sorry, friend. The Lady Maor'mith might be willing, but only if you bring at least a half dozen of your young men next time. The two of them alone were barely up to the task of pleasing her."

••••

Paul felt like an old man when he climbed out of bed. He hadn't sustained any serious injuries from his encounter with flame-bitch two nights ago, but he'd been slammed to the pavement, fallen to the floor with Katherine on top of him, fallen back out of Faerie on top of her, and every muscle complained a little.

The hair had been burned away from his hands and forearms, and the skin felt a little raw. He probably had minor burns from tearing Katherine's flaming trench coat off her, though there were only a few blisters so most of the burns were not even first degree.

He showered, shaved, dressed, then made a bowl of cereal and sat down at the small table in his kitchen to gulp it down. He spread the morning's newspaper out beside the bowl of cereal and read as he ate. Flame-bitch's fire had been a front-page article the day before, but the follow-up had now been relegated to page four. Luckily, no one had been killed, though a few people in the buildings on either side had been hospitalized with smoke inhalation and minor burns. The fire department believed arson was involved, but would not comment further on an ongoing investigation. He glanced briefly at a number of other articles, including one about prostitutes dying from a deadly new designer drug that had recently hit the streets.

Madge jumped onto the seat beside him, then up onto the table. She sidled up to him, clearly wanting attention, so he scratched her behind the ears and under the chin. She purred, and a little satisfied grumble escaped her throat.

She sat back on her hind quarters and regarded him with a look a cat shouldn't be able to give. His new neighbor Eileen had seen Madge sitting in the hallway outside her apartment, so she wasn't a hallucination, but there was no doubt the *speaking-like-a-human* bit was. He still hadn't figured out how she managed to get in and out of the apartment without his help.

"You really blew it with that pretty McGowan girl," she said.

He swallowed a mouth full of cereal and said, "What do you mean? What did I do wrong?"

She shook her head sadly. "Staring at her breasts like that."

"I didn't stare," he said. "They were just . . . there. I barely even looked."

She closed her eyes and continued to shake her head.

"Okay," he said. "Maybe I did look a little."

She continued to shake her head. "You looked quite a lot, and you know it."

"She caught me by surprise. I didn't realize I was doing it."

If a cat had eyebrows to raise, she raised one. "That's a pathetic excuse."

"It was an accident."

She licked her paw and refused to say anything more while Paul finished his breakfast. She was still sitting there with a snarky look on her face when Paul walked out of his apartment.

••••

From the window of her apartment Si'entha watched Paul Conklin walk out the front of their building and up the street. She waited until he walked out of sight in the distance, then stood, walked out of her apartment and up the one flight of stairs to his door. She needed to get inside when he wasn't there, knew she could spell his lock, but had to move cautiously with something like that when dealing with a powerful wizard.

She pressed her hand against the door, closed her eyes and sensed the threshold wards he'd placed. From such a cursory examination she couldn't discern their strength.

She reached into the pocket of her jeans and retrieved the charm she'd prepared. She dare not touch the iron of the lock, but draping the silver chain of the charm over the door handle would help considerably.

To make the charm she'd chosen a decorative piece of silver with a sharp point, because she needed blood to activate it. A quick jab into the tip of her finger produced a round drop of blood that she smeared into the rune on the face of the small amulet; she sensed it go active. Carefully, without touching the door handle, she wrapped the chain around it.

Now, when she pressed her hand against the door, closed her eyes and concentrated, she sensed not only the presence of the wards but also their strength, and they were quite impressive. The threshold and perimeter wards of a wizard's home were always strong. She might possibly defeat them, but not in a way that she could reconstruct them, so if she proceeded now he'd know his apartment had been invaded. At this stage, such a complication might arouse his suspicions and make him wary regarding her.

Again, moving carefully so she didn't harm herself by accidentally touching the iron of the door handle, she retrieved the charm and returned to her apartment. She'd have to find another way.

9

A Dangerous Pattern

HE'D LEARNED LONG ago that, with rare exception, people were fundamentally wired to be creatures of habit. They developed a routine that they followed mindlessly, like commuting to work on autopilot, whether driving down the freeway, walking along a sidewalk, or sitting on a bus. Those thoughtless habits made his life much easier, and were almost a necessary prerequisite for abduction. He'd made some progress learning the McGowan witch's routine, but the necromancer's daily habits were a different matter.

He'd hoped to stake out the fellow's apartment and follow him as he went about his daily business, but that proved to be problematic. Like the old wizard's house up on Nob Hill, it was located in a relatively quiet residential neighborhood. He drove by several times and saw a reasonable amount of foot traffic, but it was always residents coming or going, not loitering about. He'd stand out if he tried waiting nearby for the young man to come out of the building.

He drove up and down the street several times, and decided his best bet was a bus stop two blocks from the apartments. From it, he could easily see anyone entering or leaving the building, though, because of the distance, he'd not know for certain if they were the necromancer until he got closer.

His own apartment in The Castro was a little over a mile away, and that made for an invigorating morning walk. That first morning he sat down at the bus stop just before the rush hour, opened a newspaper, and read it while keeping an eye on the entrance to the apartment building. He glanced up every time someone exited the building, ignored women, and men who were clearly too short or tall. But eventually, a man of about the right height and build stepped out of the front door.

He folded the newspaper, stood and tucked it under his arm. Luckily, the fellow walked his way, but he was not the necromancer. He returned to the bus stop and sat down again. After several false starts like that, he decided that staying more than an hour would be dangerous. He left and returned the next morning, but an hour later than the previous day. In that way he bracketed the morning, and on the third day he saw another young man leave the building, and this time it was his target. He followed the fellow to the old wizard's house. He returned the next day at the same hour, but the young man never appeared.

By slow experimentation he learned that the necromancer didn't adhere to a set schedule. He walked to the old wizard's house quite regularly, but not every day, and at differing times, sometimes in the morning, sometimes in the afternoon, and he might remain there for only an hour, or all day.

Frustrated that he couldn't establish a pattern in the young man's daily life, he drove by the apartment building during twilight one evening, and saw the fellow walking down the street away from his apartment. He pulled the car up to the curb and parked in a no-parking zone. He watched the fellow walk into a place named *Jessie's Bar & Grill.*

He found a parking place on the street and shoved several coins into the meter, then returned to the apartment building. At night the street was a series of bright oases illuminated by overhead lamps, but between them were many shadows in which to find anonymity. He chose one across the street from Jessie's and waited. An hour later the young man emerged, picking his teeth with a toothpick.

Over the next week he learned the fellow frequently dined at the pub, not every night, but often enough to establish a pattern. What better time to take someone than after dinner, with the satisfied feeling of a full stomach, and maybe a little buzz from a beer or two?

••••

McGowan had cut Paul's tutelage short that day, claiming he had some important errands to attend to. Paul left the old man's place for his apartment shortly after lunch, and with nothing really demanding his time he thought he might get in a few hours of work. For the last year his life had been so upside down and inside out he couldn't commit to a full time job, had instead made ends meet by contracting out on a job-by-job basis. It paid the bills, met his rather modest needs, and he could work at home any time of the day or night.

He opened the door to his apartment, stepped in, and the instant he closed it someone knocked on it from the outside. He turned around, looked through the peephole and saw only an empty hallway. He slipped his hand into his coat, rested it on the butt of the nine-millimeter, then carefully opened the door just a crack. He relaxed when he saw Anogh standing there looking very much like a normal, mortal resident of the city. The Sidhe mage was clearly wearing a glamour to hide the shoulder length hair, though Paul seemed to have the ability to pierce the illusion enough to see the pointed ears sticking out through the hair. He took his hand off the gun and lowered it to his side.

Anogh smiled and said, "It's time for your first lesson."

With all the excitement surrounding their little adventure with flame-bitch, Paul had forgotten about his request to learn how to fight with a sword. He did find it uncanny the way Anogh knew he had no responsibilities for the afternoon.

"Okay," Paul said. "How do we do this?"

Anogh reached out, but paused with his hand inches from Paul's face. "With your permission I'll take us to Faerie."

Paul nodded. "You have it."

Anogh touched his cheek, and Paul felt that spiral slippage in reality he'd come to associate with transferring to and from Faerie, or *walking the halls of Sidhe*, as Anogh and his Seelie Court colleagues called it. The walls of Paul's apartment dissolved slowly and were replaced by the familiar yellow stone of Magreth's castle. Standing before him Anogh now wore a suit of fantastic Faerie armor, draped in lapis lazuli, silver and mother-of-pearl, with a masked helm that hid his eyes and nose, exposing only the lower half of his face. He had a silver rapier strapped to his side.

Paul had not considered what he should be wearing, and remained dressed in his rather plain, mortal attire. Anogh took one look at him and said, "No, this won't do."

He waved a hand with almost casual indifference, and Paul felt everything about his clothing shift and change. He looked down at himself and found that he too was now dressed in Sidhe armor, including a silver rapier strapped to his side, though he was thankful the Summer Knight hadn't included the masked helm.

Anogh's sword hissed with a scrape of metal as he drew it from the sheath. "Draw your blade," he said.

Paul's rapier made a similar sound as he slid it from the sheath, and it occurred to him this seemed rather dangerous. "Shouldn't we like . . . start with something like wooden blades . . . or staves? You know, for safety's sake."

"Wooden blades?" Anogh asked, clearly incredulous Paul would make such a suggestion. "We are in Faerie, and I am the Summer Knight. You have not the skill to harm me, and I do have the skill to not harm you."

Anogh started with instruction on how to properly hold the rapier. He showed Paul a few stances and techniques for swinging it. Then, over the next two hours, Paul learned that Anogh's definition of *harm* did not coincide at all with his. Neither of them drew blood, but when the Summer Knight returned Paul to his apartment, he had bruises everywhere, and every muscle ached.

Standing in the middle of Paul's living room, Anogh said, "Until the next time, Young Mage," then disappeared in a cloud of smoke.

Paul wondered if he would survive the next lesson.

••••

As the cab pulled into the driveway of Katherine's house Colleen recalled her conversation with the old man's daughter the day before. Colleen and McGowan had agreed to push Katherine and Paul to work together as much as possible. They wanted to see how well their arcane abilities developed when they worked in unison. But when Colleen had called Katherine yesterday and invited her to the old man's house today, the young woman had seemed almost desperate to avoid them—to avoid Paul, Colleen reminded herself.

"Keep the meter running," Colleen told the cabbie. "I'll be back out in just a few minutes." She gave the fellow a twenty to ensure he didn't get impatient.

Colleen climbed out of the cab, walked up the steps to the front door and rang the doorbell. When Katherine opened the door she frowned and said, "Colleen, I wasn't expecting you."

"Just thought I'd drop by, dear."

Katherine stepped aside and said, "Come on in. Would you like some coffee? I've got a full pot."

"Yes, I'd love some," Colleen said as she stepped into the house. She noticed Katherine was dressed casually in a pale-blue, long sleeve blouse, cream colored slacks, and comfortable flats. Colleen guessed the shoes, though casual in appearance, would still be an expensive brand name.

In the kitchen, Colleen plopped her purse on the counter and threw her coat over the back of a chair. As Katherine poured a mug of coffee, Colleen opened her sight and examined the young woman's aura; nothing unusual there. Colleen closed off the sight and said, "I hope I didn't interrupt anything."

Katherine handed her the mug. "No, nothing at all. Just working at home today, a lot of paperwork to do."

Colleen had expected as much. "What happened to that important appointment you have?"

Katherine frowned. "Appointment?"

"Yes, yesterday, on the phone, you said you couldn't come to Walter's house today because of an important appointment."

Katherine shook her head. "I don't recall saying that."

"So there is no appointment?"

"No. Never was."

Time to spring the trap. "Good. Then you can come with me now to your father's house. Paul and he will be glad to see you."

Katherine looked at her watch. "But, I have all this paperwork. I really can't come right now. You'll just have to go on without me."

Colleen opened her sight again and there it was, a faint, dark gray tendril of compulsion tangled within the young woman's aura. It had been subtly done by a powerful mage, a spell that went quiescent when not needed, but triggered at the application of some stimulus, probably the mention of Paul's name, perhaps coupled with the thought of any action that might bring her into his presence.

Keeping her sight active, Colleen said, "My dear, you're acting under a compulsion spell."

"Nonsense," Katherine said, giving her an angry, impatient look. "I told you I have an appointment."

"No," Colleen said. "You just told me you don't have an appointment."

Katherine closed her eyes and shook her head. When she opened them she seemed dazed and confused, which was so unlike her. "I can't be under compulsion. I'm warded."

With a small charm concealed in the palm of her hand, Colleen reached out and gripped Katherine's wrist as an excuse to press the amulet against the young woman's skin. The charm triggered, and Katherine shivered.

The spell Colleen had concocted was the blackest of black, an obedience spell. It usually took one dark spell to combat another. Walter had helped her prepare it; otherwise she might not have gotten past Katherine's protections, and with his help she was confident her spell would not harm the young woman.

"Let's get you a coat," Colleen said.

Katherine spoke dreamily, as if she was only half conscious. "Okay. Where are we going?"

"To your father's place, dear."

Katherine looked down at her feet. "Have to change my shoes, can't go out in these flats."

"Okay, dear. We'll take care of that first."

Such spells didn't change one's fundamental nature. Colleen led Katherine into her bedroom, and the young woman carefully picked out a pair of terribly uncomfortable looking, but probably quite fashionable, high-heel shoes. She also selected a navy-blue blazer that went nicely with the cream colored slacks. The spell did produce some confusion, so Colleen helped her change her shoes and pull on the blazer, then they walked out to the cab waiting in the driveway. They headed for McGowan's place.

••••

When Paul knocked on the door to McGowan's house, the old man answered it personally. "Paul, glad you could make it. Come on in."

Paul hung his coat on the rack near the front door and followed McGowan down the hall to the kitchen. He was disappointed he didn't see Katherine there. He didn't want to be obvious so he asked, "Are Colleen and Katherine going to join us?"

"Most definitely," McGowan said as he handed Paul a cup of coffee. "Colleen went to fetch Katherine, just called a moment ago to tell me they're on their way."

Paul wondered why Colleen needed to *fetch* Katherine.

Perhaps the look on his face made the question in his thoughts obvious, because the old man said, "Someone's been messing with my daughter's head, and she's been avoiding you." The look on McGowan's face hardened into anger. "And we're going to fix that today."

McGowan pointed at the kitchen table and said, "Sit down, kid." The old man walked out of the kitchen.

Paul pulled out a chair, sat down and tested the coffee, but it was too hot to drink. He blew on it to cool it a bit, and was still blowing on it a couple minutes later when he heard the front door open. Colleen called out, "Walter, we're here."

Paul stood, and was surprised to see Colleen walking down the hall behind Katherine, guiding her with her hands on her shoulders as if she was blind. Katherine's eyes were open, but she appeared dazed and confused. McGowan stepped out of his study into the hallway behind them.

When they got into the kitchen, Colleen stopped Katherine about a pace away from Paul, facing him squarely. To Katherine she said, "Just stay where you are, dear."

Paul started to turn away, but Colleen raised her hand. "No, Paul, I want you to stay where you are as well."

McGowan asked, "I take it the black was necessary, as we suspected?"

"Yes, it was," Colleen said.

Paul asked, "What's wrong?"

McGowan said, "Opposing black spells."

Paul didn't try to hide his confusion. "Whose?"

"One is mine," Colleen said. "The other we're not sure of yet, but I have my suspicions."

"I thought black spells were always harmful."

"They usually are," McGowan said. "But frequently the only way to fight one black spell is with another. Don't worry, we were careful with the one we prepared. It's actually protecting her right now."

Colleen added, "And we want to try a little experiment with you two. Don't do anything yet, but in a moment, when I tell you to, I want you to reach out and touch her. It's got to be skin-to-skin, but it can be something simple like merely touching her cheek. If it works, I'll remove my spell a moment later. If not, we'll have to unravel the two spells more slowly."

While Colleen fished in her purse for something, Paul stood there facing Katherine, the look on her face vacant and unfocused. He thought she still looked pretty, but without the spark in her eyes it didn't have the same effect on him. That little glint, and the threat of mischief it brought with it, was the thing that took her from pretty to drop-dead gorgeous in his eyes, and to see it gone made him angry at whoever had done this.

"Here it is," Colleen said, holding up a small, silver charm. She looked at Paul. "Are you ready?"

He nodded once.

"If it works," Colleen said, "she'll react like someone coming out of a deep and very realistic dream. She may be disoriented for a moment, and since you're the focus of the compulsion they've placed on her, she'll probably react very strongly to your presence, possibly act on pure instinct. I warn you, she might even be quite angry with you, but it'll pass. You can help her by doing whatever she needs."

A pissed-off Katherine was the last thing he needed. "Yes, ma'am."

Colleen smiled at his remark. "Then go ahead."

Paul reached up, but hesitated with his hand an inch from Katherine's cheek, then he touched her and traced his finger along her jaw line.

She gasped, shivered and blinked her eyes rapidly.

Behind her, Colleen stepped forward and pressed the charm to her neck.

The shivering stopped, the blinking slowed, her eyes focused on Paul and she smiled dreamily. Then her eyes stopped blinking and she stepped forward aggressively. As she reached up, he wasn't sure if he should duck or cringe, but she put her arms around his neck and kissed him. Her tongue explored his mouth as she backed him across the room until he ran into the wall and could go no further. Without interrupting the kiss she pressed her body tightly against him.

"That's okay, Paul," Colleen said. "Just go with it. She'll come out of it in a moment."

Next to Colleen, McGowan hissed, "She's practically shoving her tongue all the way down his throat."

"Oh, old man," Colleen said. "I don't think there's any *practically* about it. I'm surprised the poor young man can breathe."

"Oh, they're breathing all right," McGowan said. "The hot and heavy kind. Tell him he's not supposed to enjoy this."

Paul was trying hard not to enjoy having Katherine in his arms and rubbing against him, but failed miserably.

Colleen said, "She's clearly enjoying herself, isn't she?"

Colleen waved a finger at Paul. "Try not to enjoy yourself, Paul, but don't interrupt her, let her come out of it on her own. Remember, you're doing this for Katherine, purely for medicinal purposes, of course."

There was nothing medicinal about the way Katherine kissed him. But then she froze, and her eyes widened as she looked into Paul's face. She pulled her tongue out of his mouth, stepped back and screamed in his face, "Mother-fuckers!"

Paul asked, "Me?"

"No, *those* mother-fuckers!"

"What mother-fuckers?"

"*Those* mother-fuckers."

"I don't know what mother-fuckers you're talking about."

"I don't either, but they're mother-fuckers anyway."

She spun around and looked at Colleen and McGowan. "What mother-fuckers am I talking about?"

Colleen looked aside at McGowan, who was still seething. "Certainly fey," she said. "I'm guessing Seelie. What do you think, old man?"

McGowan made a visible effort to calm down. He looked at Colleen and said, "Ya, Cadilus and Magreth. It would have to be someone that strong to penetrate Katherine's wards. I helped her create them myself."

Colleen said, "Perhaps we should have a little chat with the Summer Queen and her High Chancellor."

The old man shook his head. "No, I'll warn them off, but talking doesn't do any good."

He stood there for a moment looking into the distance with a thousand-yard stare, then said, "Tomorrow, National Cemetery, we're going to see how well the two of you can do with a boundary when working together."

Katherine turned back to Paul, started to say something but glanced downward and froze. She stepped forward, but didn't press against him as she'd done before. She leaned toward him and whispered in his ear. "I was in the way so I don't think they saw it."

Paul didn't need her to tell him he had a visible bulge in his pants.

"Sorry," she said. "Didn't mean to be a tease."

He whispered, "Is this payback for the nippular thing?"

She grinned. "No, Conklin, I haven't yet figured out how you're going to pay for that one."

She started to turn away but paused and turned back. She brushed her lips against his earlobe. "Though a girl can't help but be flattered."

10

An Imposter

HE DID A little homework on the internet to determine the worst time to go to a DMV office. The longest wait times were on the first and last day of the week, and noon to 2:00 PM because of the lunch hour. But the worst time for everyone else would be the best time for him. A stressed-out, overworked public employee trying to satisfy long lines of impatiently waiting people would be much less likely to recall any single person. Perhaps he was being overcautious, but such attention to detail had kept the local practitioners off his trail for years.

He walked into the DMV office at a quarter past noon and took one of those little pieces of paper with a number on it. He looked around for a place to sit and wait, but the office was so crowded there were no seats available. He was forced to stand along with quite a number of other people. Good!

A large screen on the wall showed a list of numbers with a letter of the alphabet next to each. He milled about for more than an hour waiting for his number to appear, and when it did he noted the letter G next to it. He pulled out his driver's license and triggered the spell he'd woven into it, then walked over to counter G and smiled his most ordinary smile at the overweight Asian woman behind it. She didn't smile back, just waited for him to state his business.

"I need a print-out of the vehicle registration record for my car," he said. He'd learned on the internet that they had a standard procedure for providing exactly the information he needed.

"License number," she said.

He gave her the license number of Alice's mother's SUV. She typed it into the computer keyboard in front of her, looked at her screen for a moment, then said, "ID, preferably California Driver's License."

He laid his driver's license down on the counter and slid it across to her. When she picked it up and the spell flooded through her, he realized she too was a practitioner, and he almost panicked. Her eyes blinked rapidly for a moment, but she didn't cry out, which meant he was probably stronger than her. She fought the spell for a few seconds, but was unable to defeat it, and when it finally took control her eyes stopped blinking. Only then did he realize he was much stronger than her. Occasionally, a relatively weak practitioner demonstrated unusual skill at a single talent. This woman could apparently hide her arcane abilities from someone even as powerful as him.

She looked at his driver's license and compared it to the information on the screen, then said, "Yes, Mr. Sellers, this appears to be in order."

She used the computer's mouse to click on something on the screen, then reached below the counter and produced a piece of paper. She put it and his license on the counter and slid them across to him.

If she hadn't been a practitioner he could have just walked away. She'd feel slightly disoriented for a few seconds, then resume her normal daily activities. But a witch would know something was wrong, and anyone who delved in the arcane arts could detect the traces of his black spell, a loose end he couldn't allow to survive. So as she slid the paper and license toward him, he reached out and touched her hand before she pulled it back. Skin-to-skin contact allowed him to reinforce the spell, and add another directive to it.

"When do you get off work?" he asked.

"My shift ends at five."

"I'm an old friend," he said. "You'll be glad to see me."

"Yes . . . old friend."

He released her hand, turned and walked out of the building.

The wait was intolerable, three hours during which almost anything might go wrong. Hunger gnawed at him, but he dare not leave to get lunch and come back at the end of her shift. She might feel ill because of the extra control he'd asserted and clock out early to go home sick. Or a hastily done spell like that could unravel, quite possibly leaving her aware of what he'd done to her. She struck him as exactly the kind of woman in whom such treatment would spark anger, not fear, and she could identify him. She might even summon up her memory of looking at his driver's license, and then she'd know his full name and address.

He had one stroke of luck: a weather front came in off the ocean as the afternoon progressed, blanketing the bay area in low lying clouds. As the five o'clock hour approached, mist rolled in and a light drizzle began to fall. She came out of the building at a quarter after five. Since it was October, the sun was low on the horizon, and the drizzle encouraged her fellow employees to get to their cars without lingering.

He followed her as she walked out into the parking lot, held back as she opened the door of an old Toyota and climbed in. He looked around, saw no one nearby, no one looking his way, so he approached her from the driver's side. He tapped lightly on the window.

She looked at him, and the suggestion he'd implanted that he was an old friend kicked in. She smiled as she rolled down the window. "Hello . . ." she said. "You're—"

He leaned down to get his face close to hers, opened his mouth, and the oily, black stain flowed out of him and into her. She shook violently, trembled and gurgled, white foam appearing on her lips. She seized up into a rigid, catatonic state, remained that way for several seconds, then went limp.

He waited, and nothing happened, so he said, "You mustn't stay."

But I'm stronger if I leave a hint of my power with her.

"She's a practitioner. She'll have friends who are practitioners, and they'll discover you, and they'll come after us. Leave her, and I'll get you another whore—tonight."

The dark stain erupted from her mouth, and he inhaled, taking it in. He tasted her death in it and got an immediate erection. He'd learned to enjoy taking it back and loved the intimate contact with violent death.

He straightened and looked around; still no one paying attention to him.

As he walked back to his car he looked at the registration report she'd given him. The SUV was registered to Richard and Janice Sellers, and he now knew their Walnut Creek address. The report didn't list the name of their daughter, but no other name mattered because she could only be Alice.

••••

Si'entha knocked on Paul Conklin's apartment door. After a few seconds the peep hole darkened as the young man looked to see who stood in the hall. When he opened the door, she was a bit disappointed he didn't show more interest.

"Hi, Eileen," he said. "What's up?"

She frowned and said, "Do you have a screw driver I could borrow? I've got one, but I haven't completely unpacked and it's still hidden in a box somewhere. And maybe a hammer too?"

"Sure," he said. "Come on in and I'll get them. I'm pretty certain I left them in one of the kitchen drawers."

He turned away, leaving the door open. She stepped into the living room of the small apartment and watched him disappear into the tiny kitchen. She glanced around the room and saw what she was looking for: a framed mirror on the wall. While she heard the clatter and clank as he rummaged through a drawer, she crossed the room to the mirror. She touched the tip of her index finger to her tongue, activating the blocking spell there with a bit of saliva. Then she reached out, confident now that it would not trigger any wards, and touched it to the mirror's frame.

Yes, he had warded it. She sensed strong wards that would block any nether life. They'd been in place for some time and he'd obviously reinforced them on a regular basis. She also sensed the recently added wards against fey intrusion, but they were weaker, and a little amateurish. She had heard he was powerful, but uneducated in the arcane arts. Confident now that she could circumvent the fey wards, she quickly returned to where she'd been standing when he'd left the room.

A few seconds later he stepped out of the kitchen carrying some tools. "I found a pair of plyers too, thought that might be helpful as well."

"Oh, thank you so much, Paul. I really appreciate it."

When she took the tools, she made sure the skin of their hands touched for just a second, though no magic or spells. Little bits of contact like that would help her build the attraction, even without spells or beguilement.

Back in her own apartment she dropped the tools on her kitchen table. She'd been careful to rent an apartment identical to his, which would help her now. In her bedroom she opened a dresser drawer and paused for a moment to regard her mundane, mortal clothing. She missed the elegant gowns of the Seelie Court, and absolutely abhorred jeans and sneakers.

From beneath the clothing she retrieved a small, hand-made, wooden box, carried it to her bed and sat down there. She opened the box and took from it a leather-wrapped bundle, then peeled back the layers of soft kidskin to reveal an ornate hand mirror, an ancient device of polished silver. She'd used it for centuries and brought it from Faerie. She looked at her image in the mirror and focused her thoughts.

When she'd touched the frame of the mirror in Paul's apartment with her finger, she'd left a bit of saliva behind, and that would make this a lot easier. She lifted the finger to her mouth and again placed a little saliva on the tip of it, then touched it to the edge of the mirror in her hand. She concentrated on her image, and said, "Saliva to saliva, frame to frame, mirror to mirror."

Her image swirled and distorted, but the fey wards on his mirror blocked her. She carefully neutralized them into a quiescent state in such a way that she could reactivate them when finished. Then her image disappeared, revealing a view of the interior of his apartment as seen through his mirror. As she looked on he walked in front of the mirror, then out of sight, completely unaware he was being observed.

She waited and watched, and he passed before the mirror several times, but finally stepped in front of it carrying a coat. He threw on the coat, then stepped out of sight, and she heard the door to his apartment open, then close.

She focused, sent a piece of her consciousness into the mirror and closed her eyes. And though she was not physically there, it felt as if she stood in the middle of his living room; if she was wrong about him leaving, he'd see nothing visibly present. She quickly glanced into the bedroom, the bathroom and the kitchen, and when satisfied that he had truly left, she completed the transference and now stood physically in his living room.

She walked slowly around the apartment, carefully examining everything. Nothing in the living room, kitchen or bathroom would be of use, but she found what she was looking for in the bedroom. A half-dozen pictures had been carefully arranged on top of the dresser, images of a pretty young woman and a small girl child. She knew of the young man's dead wife and daughter, but hadn't known the details of Suzanna's appearance. His wife had worn her brownish-blond hair cut chin length, and Si'entha noted that the color was not much different from her own, though the young woman had worn hers much shorter. From a picture in which Paul and his wife stood side-by-side, it was clear Si'entha and her were of similar height and build. And apparently she'd liked light summer dresses in pastel colors.

Si'entha retrieved a small charm from the pocket of her jeans. She'd prepared it for just this purpose. She pulled out her cell phone, and took a quick picture of the photos on top of the dresser, though not to record the images they contained; the phone's camera wasn't that good. Then she triggered the charm, lifted each photo one at a time and carefully touched the charm to the image. When she was done she deactivated the charm and returned it to her pocket. Then she examined the photograph she'd taken with her cell phone, and carefully adjusted the position of each picture to ensure she hadn't displaced it in any way. She could have done the same without the cell phone by using a rather complex spell, but this was so much easier. Mortal technology helped in so many ways.

This was going to be rather easy.

••••

As Paul approached McGowan's front door, the piercing cry of a hunting hawk startled him and he flinched. He quickly scanned the rooftops around him, not really sure what he'd do if that seven-foot-tall crazy woman decided to take off his head with that sword of hers. He knew he was getting paranoid, but he recalled the motto he'd adopted when all the weirdness had started: *better paranoid than dead*, though recent experience had taught him there were worse things than death.

McGowan's assistant, Sarah, answered the door. A witch of medium strength, strange and unusual events did not surprise her. As Paul stepped into the house, she leaned close to him and said, "Those unpleasant Russian fellows are here. Mr. McGowan apologizes for not warning you, but he didn't know they were going to show up unexpected."

"Thanks for the warning," Paul said. He'd come prepared to accompany the old man to the cemetery to work on boundaries, and wondered now what that Russian bastard was after.

Sarah smiled and took his coat. "Mr. McGowan wants you to join them in his study."

Paul stepped through the door into the large office Walter McGowan called his study. The old man and Karpov were both seated, McGowan behind his desk, Karpov in one of the wingback chairs in front of it. Both held snifters of an amber liquid. Boris and Joe Stalin stood to one side, dressed in their cheap, horse-blanket suits. They eyed him warily as he came into the room. Their real names were Vladimir and Alexei, but at the looks they gave him, he decided to stick with Boris and Joe.

McGowan said, "Come in, Paul. Have a seat."

He lifted his glass. "Care for a finger of whiskey?"

"No, thanks," Paul said, shaking his head.

He sat down in the other wingback chair opposite Karpov.

"Mr. Conklin," Karpov said. As always, he pronounced it meester, instead of mis-ter. "You look well."

There was no doubt in Paul's mind that the Russian ass-hole and his colleagues would like to change that. "And you too look well, Mr. Karpov."

McGowan looked at his watch. "Sorry to be abrupt, Vasily, but Paul and I have an appointment with a couple of ladies, so we don't have a lot of time. You wanted to meet with Paul and me, we're here, so what's on your mind?"

Karpov looked down at his glass and swirled the whiskey there, then looked at Paul. "Mr. Conklin, what were you thinking, summoning a fey monster of enormous power to the Mortal Plane?"

Paul hadn't expected that, and from the look on his face, nether had McGowan. Paul said, "I didn't summon it. Someone else did."

Karpov gave Paul a smarmy smile. "And who would this someone else be?"

"I don't know," Paul said, anger rising up in his gut. "A stranger. He passed us on the sidewalk going the other way, triggered a spell and dropped it at our feet."

"He's speaking the truth," McGowan said.

Karpov shook his head sadly. "The only practitioners in this city capable of such a summons are me, Valter, and Colleen. And even we would have to join forces to do so."

Paul leaned forward and didn't try to hide his anger. "Then what makes you think I can do it?" As soon as he asked the question, he realized his mistake.

"You are a necromancer," Karpov said. "You have extraordinary power over the dead, and we know the fey do not have souls, so your power extends to them. You demonstrated the ability to take the Caorthannach back to Faerie without assistance, so you are the only one who could single-handedly summon her."

McGowan said, "You're assuming quite a bit, Vasily. We both know that returning her was probably easier done than summoning her."

Karpov shrugged. "Paul, I think you were experimenting with your unusual powers, and made a mistake. We all make mistakes, but you can't be allowed to make such disastrous errors."

"You're flat wrong," Paul said.

"And I think I'm right," Karpov replied. "Nevertheless, I intend to consult with several of my colleagues on the matter."

He stood and placed the snifter on the old man's desk. "It has been a pleasure, Valter. Thank you for your time."

Paul and McGowan stood, and the old man said, "I'll see you to the door."

As they left the room, Karpov paused in the doorway and looked at Paul. "There are others who will think like me, Mr. Conklin."

By the time McGowan returned, Paul was absolutely livid. "That fucking ass-hole."

"Calm down," McGowan said. "Karpov is just being the shit-head Russian we all know he is. Unlike him, my colleagues will look at the evidence before drawing such a conclusion, though it occurs to me I should do a little preemptive lobbying on your behalf."

McGowan slapped him on the back. "Come on, kid. Let's grab our coats, hail a cab and head to the cemetery."

"Where are the ladies?"

"They went out early to do a little shopping. They'll meet us there."

11

The Boundary Between Where and When

KATHERINE HAD LEARNED her lesson, and was not about to find herself once again tromping through some dirt field in Faerie wearing a tight skirt and spike heels. For the little misadventure her father had planned that day she'd opted for a black, wool, pleated skirt that ended just above her knees, a really cute, gray sweater tight enough to drive Paul bonkers, and a gorgeous little Kate Spade jacket. She finished the outfit with some ankle-high Prada boots with a zipper up the side, a wedge sole and great looking clunky heels. The heels were only three inches high, and thick enough that they wouldn't sink into the ground if they ended up in some field in Faerie. Very practical indeed!

After some serious therapeutic shopping, she and Colleen met the two men in the National Cemetery, and the four of them headed for the back boundary. As they walked, Katherine glanced back over her shoulder, and noticed Paul behind her looking suspiciously at her Pradas.

When they stopped at the edge of the cemetery, she turned to him and said, "Like the shoes, huh? I saw you checking them out. I decided to go practical this time, no pencil skirts or spike heels."

Her father said, "He didn't notice your shoes; he was too busy looking at your ass."

She couldn't hide a grin. "Was he now?" She wiggled her butt a little bit.

Her father's eyes narrowed with disapproval. "I thought I told you not to act slutty."

"I wasn't acting slutty. Paul was being slutty by checking out my ass."

She heard the frustration in Paul's words as he said, "I wasn't checking out your ass."

He sounded like he was telling the truth, which disappointed her a bit, though she was careful not to let it show.

Colleen waved a hand, indicating the cemetery's boundary, and made an obvious effort to change the subject. "Is this where you tried before?"

"And failed completely," Paul said.

"That's why Walter and I want you to try again, but with the two of you working together."

McGowan added, "And without me or Colleen. Just you two."

Colleen asked, "Where in Faerie do you want to go?"

Paul looked at Katherine with a question on his face, and said, "I was thinking the leprechauns."

Katherine recalled the quaint little huts, and the pink sun burning off a low morning mist. "Works for me."

"Good choice," Colleen said. "You've both been there, and they seem to favor the two of you. And you'd be wise to stay away from either of the Courts without some guarantees."

Katherine felt a bit nervous about all this. "I don't know any more about this boundary stuff than Paul."

McGowan said, "Colleen and I think you'll find it rather easy with the two of you working together. But remember, it has to be a slow and continuous shift in the possibilities of your existence in the two realms, and both of you need to picture the destination in your minds."

He spoke to Katherine, "But let Paul manipulate the probabilities. On the first try you're just along for the ride. If he succeeds, we'll try again with you twisting the possibilities while he goes along for the ride. Ready?"

Paul held his hands up in a gesture of resignation.

Katherine said, "As ready as I'll ever be."

••••

Colleen told Katherine to hold Paul's hand as he tried the boundary. She said she felt they'd have a better chance if they were in physical contact. Paul looked down the length of the boundary and concentrated hard, started with a hundred percent probability that they were on the Mortal Plane, and zero for Faerie.

Before they took the first step, Katherine said, "Thanks for coming back for me."

Paul wasn't sure what she meant. "Coming back where?"

"Flame-bitch's burning house."

Paul looked at her, surprised she needed to thank him. "Did you ever doubt I would?"

She cocked her head and thought about it for a moment, then smiled and said, "No, I guess I didn't. But thanks anyway."

"My pleasure, McGowan."

"Of course it was your pleasure, Conklin, especially since you got the full-on, wet-blouse boob show."

He looked at her, leered at her chest and said, "Guess I should thank you for that."

"My pleasure, Conklin."

"Does that make us even?"

"Not by a long shot."

They walked parallel to the boundary of the cemetery down the gravel strewn path, taking each step in a slow, steady rhythm. Paul tried to avoid counting the possibilities down like a NASA engineer at a Cape Canaveral launch, instead decided to believe there was a slight possibility they existed in Faerie near the leprechaun's huts. After a dozen paces Katherine said, "Look," and pointed at the horizon.

It had brightened a bit, as if the sun was about to rise, when in fact they were approaching the noon hour in San Francisco. The sky had also taken on a purplish hue, with a slight pinkish tint to it. As they walked further the row of trees thinned out, became little more than a line of low-lying shrubs with a rather odd look to them, though Paul had seen them before. Their green leaves had a violet cast that made them appear to shimmer, with flowers so deeply purple they were nearly black. Paul felt reality slipping from his grasp along that strange spiral track, a sensation he'd experienced more than once. And when the slippage ended they stood among the leprechauns' huts in a green and verdant countryside of low rolling hills, the pink sun shining down upon them.

"You did it," Katherine said.

A trilling female voice said, "Dannie boy, it appears we have some visitors."

Paul and Katherine both started and looked toward the voice. A pretty little female leprechaun stood on one side of the trail, with a male seated above her on a large rock. Both were younger versions of the little people Paul had met before, with similar features, but lacking the craggy lines of age in their faces. The girl wore a bright yellow dress, with a gray apron, her hair a wild mass of red curls. The boy wore green breeches tucked into black boots, a red doublet, with a blue felt hat on his head. He jumped down off the rock, bowed deeply and said, "Dan'Dandio is the name, and beside me stands the most beautiful lass in all of Faerie, my betrothed, Sally'm'sweet."

"I'm Paul Conklin," Paul said, turning to introduce Katherine, "and this is—"

"We know," Dan'Dandio said. "Do you think we're unaware when the Young Mage and the Old Wizard's daughter come to Faerie? The fates twist around the two of you like thread on a bobbin."

Paul asked, "Does that mean Winter and Summer know we're here?"

"Aye," Dan'Dandio said. "The Courts'll be watching. But don't pay them no nevermind. You'll not come to harm here."

Jim'Jiminie emerged from one of the huts, and Boo'Diddle from another.

"Paul, me boy," Jim'Jiminie said. "'Tis good to see you, and glad we are you brought the pretty lass as well. To what do we owe the pleasure of your company?"

Katherine said, "We're learning how to do boundaries."

"A valuable skill, that," Boo'Diddle said. "But be careful. If you twist the fates at the wrong moment, the consequences can be dire."

Jim'Jiminie doffed his felt hat and bowed deeply to Katherine, his bald head sporting only a few wisps of red hair. "And you, sweet darlin', twist them more than most."

He straightened, donned his hat and turned to Boo'Diddle. "But isn't that always the way of a woman."

"Aye," Boo'Diddle said. "You've got the right of that, Jimmie-me-boy."

McGowan and Colleen expected them to return almost immediately, and Paul didn't want to worry them. "The Old Wizard is expecting us, so we should be getting back."

"Of course," Jim'Jiminie said. "Wouldn't want him and Lady Armaugh to worry."

Paul wondered how they knew Colleen waited with McGowan. It wasn't the first time the fey exhibited unusually informed knowledge of the Mortal Plane.

Paul and Katherine turned to walk back the way they'd come, but the sharp cry of a hunting hawk startled him and he froze. He looked up, spotted it circling high overhead and descending rapidly toward them.

"What is it?" Katherine asked.

"It's that crazy nut-case," Paul said. "The one that wants to kill me with the heart arrow."

He gripped Katherine's hand tightly. "Get ready," he said, preparing to pull them back to the Mortal Plane in an instant along that spiral track, but fearing he'd fail the way he had in the burning house with flame-bitch. "If I have to I'm getting us out of here the hard way."

"Hold on there, boy-oh," Jim'Jiminie called. "She'll not be a-harming you here."

Paul recalled the way she *hadn't* tried to kill him in his apartment when she'd swooped out of the mirror on his wall, had merely wanted to see *les flèche du coeur*, and to kiss it. He held his ground reluctantly, and continued to hold onto Katherine's hand so he could move quickly if necessary.

The hawk rocketed toward them in a dive, its wings pulled into its sides. He cringed, felt Katherine do the same, but at the last instant it flared its wings, pulled up a few feet off the ground, killed its speed, and transformed into the tall humanoid shape. Obscured by shadows that fluttered about her maddeningly, Sabreatha faced Paul and Katherine squarely from about ten paces with a strung bow in her left hand and a shadowy broadsword in her right. Then slowly the darkness that enveloped her dissipated, and one-by-one her features cleared.

Katherine asked, "Who the hell is that?"

Paul recalled that she had never seen the black fey warrior up close. The woman stood seven feet tall, with pale golden hair twisted into dreadlocks that fluttered slightly as if touched by a light breeze, though the air remained still. She walked toward them, one cautious, careful step at a time, though her attention appeared focused on Katherine. The color of her eyes shifted continuously. "That's Sabreatha," he said.

She stopped at arm's length, and with one fluid motion sheathed the sword. Then she slowly raised her hand, reached up and lightly touched Katherine's cheek. Katherine's eyes widened with fear, and still holding her hand, Paul felt her flinch.

Sabreatha lightly brushed a lock of Katherine's hair back, then opened her mouth, and when her lips moved, her voice sounded like the haunted whisper of a chill wind on a bleak winter day. "So pretty," she said.

Katherine's voice trembled as she spoke. "Why do I feel as if there are several souls standing before me?"

Sabreatha smiled and said, "And worthy."

She lowered her hand, turned away from them, took two steps, broke into a run, leapt into the air and spread her arms, transformed into the hawk, and rose into the sky on the beat of powerful wings.

Katherine turned to Paul. "What the hell was that about?"

"I have no idea," he said. "But she's a nut-case, so it doesn't have to be about anything, does it?"

Katherine opened her mouth to say something but hesitated. Then she said, "Can you please get me out of here?"

They held hands and walked back the way they'd come. Paul found it rather easy the second time around, and they emerged back in the National Cemetery about a hundred yards from McGowan and Colleen. Katherine breathed a long sigh of relief.

"You okay?" he asked.

"Ya," she said, "I guess so, though that was just plain weird."

She visibly relaxed, and as they walked toward her father and Colleen, she said, "This morning, when we first came into the cemetery, you *were* checking out my ass, weren't you?"

He looked at her. She had a little smirk on her face, but refused to meet his eyes and continued to look straight ahead. "No," he said, "I was checking out your legs. I was going to check out your ass next, but your father interrupted me."

She was clearly trying to suppress a smile, so he leaned toward her and whispered in her ear, "By the way, they're really nice legs."

The smirk turned into a cheesy, self-satisfied grin, so he added, "And I did finally get a chance to check out your ass, enjoyed that quite a bit too."

"Gee, Conklin, you're such a silver-tongued devil. You sure know how to sweet-talk a girl."

She looked so smug he decided to pull her chain a little, though he'd have to lie to do so. "You know, they stick out."

"What are you talking about?"

He hadn't really seen her breasts all that well that night in McGowan's kitchen, with her white blouse soaking wet, but he so rarely got the chance to gain the upper hand with her, he couldn't resist the lie. "When they're cold and wet, your nipples stick out quite prominently. Guys love that kind of thing."

She blushed and turned absolutely scarlet.

····

"You're blushing," Colleen said. "What happened?"

"Nothing," Katherine said. She wasn't about to tell them what Paul had just told her, so she decided to change the subject. "That black-fey warrior woman paid us a quick visit while we were in Faerie."

Her father's eyebrows shot up. "She did, did she? What did she want?"

Katherine described the incident with Sabreatha.

When she finished, Paul said, "That crazy woman is a nut-case."

Colleen shook her head. "We don't understand the black fey, so it might be a terrible mistake to assume their actions are without logical motive."

"Let's try the boundary again," her father said. "This time Katherine twists the possibilities while Paul's just along for the ride."

Katherine took Paul's hand and they walked side-by-side back the way they'd just come, moving at a slow, steady pace. She looked straight ahead as she hissed, "You saw that much through my blouse, huh?"

"And more."

Her face grew hot, and she knew she was blushing again. She found it difficult to focus on the changing possibilities, had to concentrate hard to do so. The sky had shifted a bit toward that pink-tinged purple, the tree line had thinned out and those strange plants appeared. She still felt the heat of her blush and knew she needed to concentrate on the bucolic scene with the leprechaun huts. It occurred to her that she mustn't think about either of the Courts, or Magreth or Cadilus or any of the other fey.

"Actually," Paul said. "I lied. I was just pulling your chain. To be honest I really didn't see all that much."

She stopped and turned to face him. His self-satisfied smirk softened into an apologetic shrug, and she realized that lately she'd teased him rather unmercifully. "Truce," she said.

"Truce," he agreed.

She kissed him on the cheek, a chaste little peck.

He said, "I prefer the full-on lip-locks."

"I'll bet you do."

"Nicely done, High Chancellor."

Katherine recognized Magreth's voice at the same instant Paul's eyes widened. She looked past him and saw only the yellow stone walls she recalled from her last visit to the Seelie Court, not the quaint little leprechaun huts. They both looked toward the sound of the voice and saw Cadilus standing beside Magreth.

"It wasn't all that difficult," Cadilus said. "She's inexperienced at manipulating the probabilities, and she was distracted for some reason. Getting her to think of us was easily done."

Paul hissed, "I'm getting us out of here the hard way."

He reached for her, but strong hands grabbed her elbows from behind and dragged her away from him just as a Seelie warrior stepped between them, raised a silver rapier and leveled it at Paul's chest. Katherine struggled, but her captor had her arms pinned behind her back, and clearly had her out-classed in the strength department.

"Not so fast, Young Mage" Magreth said. "We're not going to allow you the physical contact you need to take her with you. We may not be able to stop you from walking the halls of Sidhe on your own, but you'll have to leave her behind."

Paul turned away from the warrior with the sword and faced Magreth and Cadilus. "You have no right to hold her."

Cadilus shook his head sadly. "But we do. You come into our Court uninvited and unannounced, with no guarantees. You're no better than intruders. Perhaps you intend to spy upon us, or cause us harm."

Katherine said, "You tricked me."

Magreth's eyebrows lifted as if to say, *So what?*

"What do you want?" Paul asked.

"A little agreement," Magreth said. "You, Young Mage, agree not to walk the halls of Sidhe until we release you. We, in turn, agree to treat you as guests and to release you in a matter of minutes, unharmed and unmolested."

"Why?" Paul asked.

"We wish to test the two of you."

Katherine saw it in Paul's face as he considered the offer. "Don't," she said.

Cadilus said, "If you don't, we are free to treat her as an intruder."

"I'll agree," Paul said, "as long as you agree no rape, no beguilement, no compulsion or obsession."

Magreth seemed almost offended. "Here in the Summer Court we treat our guests far more kindly than Winter."

Paul had told Katherine of his first visit to the Seelie Court, and the way the Summer Princess Nae'eth had beguiled him in front of them all. He'd reluctantly admitted that he'd had an overwhelming urge to throw her to the floor and fuck her right in front of everyone. He'd managed to resist the compulsion and passed the test, but had later confessed that it had been a close call. If that was Magreth's idea of treating her guests *far more kindly*, then she had a twisted idea of hospitality.

Paul demanded, "Do you agree to my terms? Say it plainly."

Magreth smiled, and Katherine knew they were in trouble.

"I agree," the queen said.

Paul said, "Then I too agree."

Katherine asked, "What kind of tests are you going to perform?"

Magreth's smiled broadened as she turned her head to look at Cadilus. "What say you, High Chancellor?"

Cadilus stared at Paul as he raised an eyebrow in thought. "I was thinking perhaps . . . Tolstoy."

Paul asked, "You mean . . . the Russian author?"

Cadilus grinned and Katherine felt reality shift. The yellow stone walls of the palace grew translucent, blurred by an overlaid image of horse drawn carriages rattling down a busy street in a city from a long ago past. Standing only a few paces away, Paul now wore the uniform of a nineteenth century military officer. Katherine noticed that her shoulders were cold. She looked down at her outfit and saw that the pleated skirt and sweater were gone; she now wore a floor length gown with an empire waist. Cut low in the front and back, it exposed her neck and shoulders.

"Katerina."

Reality completed the shift and Katerina Magovana turned toward the voice.

12

A Night in Petersburg

"LIEUTENANT KONKLINOV."

At the sound of Major Sukharov's voice, Pavel Andreyevich Konklinov put down the boots he'd been polishing, stood, turned, snapped to attention and saluted. "Sir," he said.

Sukharov stood in the doorway of the room, a short man about Pavel's age, but with a gut that protruded over the top of his belt. He glanced around the small barracks at the four bunks, a look of distaste on his face. Unlike most officers in the Imperial Russian Army, Pavel had neither the money nor connections to garner a private room, and was forced to bunk with the non-commissioned officers. The small inheritance he'd received from his father had been just enough to buy a low-level commission and equip him as an officer. Two years ago that had seemed like a good idea.

Sukharov crossed the distance between them, sloppily returning the salute and saying, "Stand at ease."

He held out an envelope with a wax seal on it. "The regimental commander wants you to take this message to the Winter Palace immediately. I've ordered the stables to have your horse saddled and ready for you."

Pavel took the envelope from the major's fingers. "Yes, sir."

Sukharov looked Pavel up and down disapprovingly. "And look sharp. You're going to the palace." The major spun on his heels and marched out of the room.

Pavel was an experienced officer, had fought in Persia, but to men like Sukharov he was no more than a messenger boy. He pulled on his boots, threw on his coat, doffed his hat and stuffed the envelope into a pocket sewn into the coat's lining. He hurried out of the Horse Guard's barracks and found a stable hand waiting in the courtyard with his horse saddled and ready. It was early evening with the sun low on the horizon, but in July in Petersburg it wouldn't completely set until quite late.

The streets were packed so Pavel had to guide his horse carefully, and more than once he thought he might have gotten there faster had he gone on foot. In the palace he was told to wait in case there was a reply, so he paced back and forth in a small sitting room for hours. Sometime after midnight he learned there would be no reply and he was free to go.

Pavel had missed dinner and his stomach growled as he rode back to the Horse Guard's barracks. In the wee hours of the morning the streets of Petersburg were all but deserted, so he was surprised to hear a commotion up ahead. As he rounded the corner at the intersection of two streets, he saw a young soldier sitting on the sill of a third-floor window, his legs dangling out over the street. The light from the room behind him cast his features in shadow.

Pavel pulled his horse to a stop, not sure what to expect. The fellow had his head thrown back, with one hand holding the mouth of a bottle to his lips as he guzzled its contents, the other clutching at the edge of the sill to keep from falling to his death. He finished the bottle, jumped to his feet, and standing on the window sill he turned and shouted back into the room, "It's empty. I win." Then he jumped into the room and disappeared from sight. Pavel couldn't see the fellow's friends, but he heard them cheering and shouting, and he concluded it was just a bunch of drunken soldiers gambling on a daredevil stunt.

Pavel nudged his horse forward into a walk, but just as he approached the building, the drunks spilled out of it into the street in front of him, one of them leading a young bear on a chain. Only then did Pavel realize he knew the drunk who'd just guzzled an entire bottle of liquor while sitting on the window sill: Dolokhov, a handsome, rakish soldier with curly hair and blue eyes. Swaying unsteadily on his feet, Dolokhov looked up at him and frowned, looked again, and slurring his words badly he shouted, "Konklinov? Pavel Andreyevich, is that you, old friend?"

Fyodor Ivanovich Dolokhov was one of the last persons Pavel wanted to see in Petersburg. The man found trouble where none existed, though he usually managed to come out of it unscathed while others paid the price for his folly. He staggered up to Pavel's horse, grabbed at the sleeve of his arm, and it was either dismount, or be pulled from the saddle. Pavel quickly swung a leg over the rump of his horse and stepped onto the cobbles of the street.

Dolokhov gripped his shoulders and held him at arm's length. "How long have you been in Petersburg?"

"Just transferred in last week."

Dolokhov wrapped his arms around Pavel, and though the drunken soldier was the shorter of the two men by a couple of inches, he lifted Pavel off his feet in a crushing bear hug. "Old friend, my brother in arms, it's good to see you."

As Dolokhov put him down Pavel lied. "Fyodor Ivanovich, it's good to see you too."

Dolokhov turned and shouted, "Anatole, Pierre, come here."

As two young men approached, both wearing fashionably expensive clothing, Dolokhov shouted, "This man saved my life in Persia."

Dolokhov introduced one of the two fellows as Prince Anatole Vasilyevich Kuragin, a handsome young man of average height in whom Pavel sensed the weakest of arcane abilities, though the young man was probably not even aware of it. The other, a large, gangly fellow with awkward movements, was simply, "Monsieur Pierre." At thirty years of age, Pavel guessed he was older than all of them by six or seven years.

"He saved your life?" Pierre asked.

"Aye," Dolokhov said, leaning drunkenly on Pavel. "Sword thrust to my thigh, festered, would have died slowly if he hadn't treated it. He's a sorcerer, you know, can heal with magic."

Pavel stiffened as Pierre's eyes widened, while Prince Anatole raised an eyebrow and looked him over in a calculating way. In some parts of the world people viewed practitioners with fear, and Pavel had learned to keep his abilities a secret.

"Fyodor here is a superstitious peasant," Pavel said. "All I did was make a poultice the way my father taught me. When I was a young boy we used them on pigs to keep minor scrapes from festering, and I thought it might work on a man as well." That was mostly the truth; he'd used only a little magic to enhance the effect of the poultice.

"Well there you have it," Dolokhov said, slapping Pavel on the back. "I'm no better than a pig."

"You should join us," Prince Anatole said, still looking at Pavel in that calculating way.

"Yes," Pierre said meekly.

"By all means," Dolokhov bellowed.

"I can't," Pavel said, trying to think of any excuse to avoid spending more time with Dolokhov. "I'm on duty. Perhaps another time."

Dolokhov slapped him on the back so hard he staggered. "Well I owe you a drink or two, and that's a debt I intend to pay, even if not tonight."

The drunken soldier turned and staggered away, shouting something about the young bear. Pierre followed him, but Anatole remained. "You may be able to help me with something," he said, "and in return I will be most grateful. Come see me tomorrow."

If Anatole liked spending his time with a psychopath like Dolokhov, Pavel wanted nothing to do with him either, but it might be dangerous to refuse a wealthy aristocrat. "I'm not sure I can get away. My company commander keeps me quite busy."

"What's his name?"

"Major Sukharov."

Anatole's eyes narrowed, still with that calculating look. "Fear not. I'll have a word with him."

The next morning Major Sukharov made it clear Pavel was not merely free to leave the barracks, but was, in fact, required to visit Prince Anatole as requested. He handed him a note in which Anatole had specified a time later that afternoon, and said, "Wear your best uniform, and be prompt."

Pavel had one uniform that he reserved for special occasions. He'd worn it very little so it remained relatively new. He hurriedly put it on and left the barracks.

Anatole's residence was not far from the Horse Guard's barracks, so Pavel walked there. The servant who admitted him to the house escorted him to a spacious sitting room. Pavel had heard rumors of some sort of incident the night before shortly after he'd left the drunken young men. It apparently involved Anatole, Pierre, Dolokhov, a policeman and the bear, though he had yet to hear of any ramifications developing.

Some minutes after the servant left Pavel waiting in the sitting room, Anatole showed up, looked at him with distaste and said, "Is that your best uniform?"

Pavel thought his uniform was perfectly good, but apparently not up to Anatole's standards. "Yes, it is, Prince Anatole. I apologize if it's not adequate."

"Well," Anatole said, "it'll do for today, but we'll have to do something about that in the future."

Pavel wondered what Anatole had in mind for the *future*.

Anatole called for a carriage, they climbed into it, and as it rattled along the cobblestoned streets, he said, "There is a particular woman I want your help with. She is closer to your age, but I find her the most beautiful woman in Petersburg, and she ignores me completely."

"How can I help?" Pavel asked.

"Dolokhov said you're a sorcerer. Can you not do something magical?"

Pavel now understood Anatole's sudden interest in a simple, common officer of the hussars[1]. "But I meant it last night when I said Dolokhov is merely superstitious. I have no special talents."

Anatole leaned back in his seat and eyed Pavel carefully. "Well, we shall see."

The carriage stopped at a stylish address not far from the Winter Palace. The footman held the carriage door for the two men, and Pavel followed Anatole into the building. A servant escorted them to a large sitting room filled with people of many different ages and types, though Pavel guessed they were all part of the fashionable elite of Petersburg.

•••

A feeling of unease crawled up Katerina Valtrovna Magovana's spine as her arcane senses alerted her to something she couldn't define. She smiled at Prince Andrew Bolkonski and Monsieur Pierre, pretended to listen to their discussion of the upcoming

---

[1] A type of light cavalry used by most European armies during the 18th and 19th centuries.

war while she looked past them and scanned the crowd of aristocrats and soldiers in the room. She wondered what had alerted her.

She spotted the beautiful Princess Helene Kuragina, a young witch of limited ability. The girl wasn't strong enough to mask her powers, certainly not strong enough to detect even a hint of Katerina's capabilities. But even though wholly untrained, she'd managed through pure instinct to use her arcane talents to seduce several of the wealthiest men in the room. No doubt she would eventually take one as a husband. Pity the poor fellow.

No, the Princess Kuragina was not the cause of Katerina's sudden unease. So what, or who, had alerted her arcane senses? If the cause was a practitioner, then he or she was extremely powerful to remain undetected by Katerina.

Helene's brother, Prince Anatole, had just entered the room. Katerina wouldn't really call him a practitioner, since he didn't practice at anything other than seeking amoral pleasure. But he did have some minor arcane ability, though she'd long ago determined it was so faint he remained completely unaware of it. He was accompanied by a handsome young army officer, a hussar who appeared ill-at-ease. Katerina guessed the fellow to be several years older than Anatole, probably closer to her own thirty years of age.

Anatole paused just within the room and scanned the crowd. He spotted Katerina, smiled and nodded his head, then leaned toward the army officer and spoke to him in a confidential way.

Katerina knew immediately that she was not going to like the young army officer, even if for no other reason than that he had such poor taste in friends.

••••

When Pavel followed Anatole into the room full of people he immediately noticed the beautiful young woman speaking with Monsieur Pierre and another man. She had auburn hair and dark-brown eyes, and he thought her the most attractive woman there. She wore a low-cut, pale-blue gown with an empire waist, the style most fashionable throughout Europe. He also sensed that she was a very strong witch.

Anatole hesitated, scanned the crowd and leaned close to Pavel. "See that woman speaking with Pierre," he said, pointing out the young woman Pavel had just noticed. "She's the one I told you about: Katerina Valtrovna Magovana. She's a witch, or at least all the women believe so. I think they go to her for potions and such, and probably to have their fortunes told. Her father is quite wealthy, but not titled, and reputedly somewhat eccentric. He's a bit of a recluse, though apparently Emperor Alexander values his counsel and consults him regularly."

"I know Monsieur Pierre," Pavel said, "but who is the other man?"

"That, my friend, is Prince Andrew Nikolayevich Bolkonski. His father is extremely rich, a famous man, you may have heard of Prince Nicholas Andreyevich Bolkonski. He found it expeditious to retire from the army when the late Emperor Paul exiled him to his country estate, and he's lived there since. Come, I'll introduce you."

Pavel followed Anatole as he crossed the room in a carefully orchestrated dance. The prince paused briefly to speak to a young woman, introduced Pavel, then moved on to another acquaintance, as if just casually wandering from one to another without any specific destination in mind. Pavel lost count, but crossing the room resulted in at least half a dozen such pauses and introductions. As they slowly approached the group around Katerina Valtrovna, he knew this could not end well. He wasn't about to pull out a compulsion spell and force the poor woman into Anatole's arms, and short of that, there was nothing he could really do to help the prince. That would probably anger the fellow. No, this would not end at all well.

Anatole deftly inserted them into the small group around Katerina, greeting them by saying, "Prince Bolkonski, Monsieur Pierre, Mademoiselle Magovana."

They politely returned the greeting, though Pavel noticed Katerina remained a bit cold and aloof. Anatole said, "Let me introduce Lieutenant Pavel Andreyevich Konklinov."

Pierre said, "Dolokhov told us he fought bravely in Persia, even saved Dolokhov's life."

"An experienced fighting man?" Bolkonski said. "What brought you back to Petersburg?"

Pavel shrugged, "Orders. They didn't tell me why, but I assume the emperor and his staff want to move more troops to the western front to face Bonaparte."

Anatole said something about stopping Bonaparte and the glory of war, but Pavel couldn't look away from Katerina. As Anatole spoke she had a pleasant smile on her face, but it extended only to her lips, while her eyes smoldered angrily. Clearly, she harbored a considerable dislike for the young man. As Pavel looked at her she slowly shifted her gaze from Anatole to him, and the burning disapproval remained. Apparently her dislike for Anatole had rubbed off on Pavel.

"Ah, the glory of war," she said, addressing Pavel directly. "Do you hunger for the glory of war, Lieutenant?"

For some reason she had chosen to bait him. "I think many young men hunger for the glory of war . . . until they actually get their first taste of it, and learn what a bitter fruit it can be."

Her eyes narrowed, and now he wasn't sure if she was angry with him, or just distrustful.

"And a philosopher, too," Pierre said.

"So you fought alongside Dolokhov?" Bolkonski asked. "I'm told he's a bit of a scoundrel."

No matter how much he disliked Dolokhov, Pavel wasn't about to be lured into a condemnation of a fellow soldier. "He is a man of many talents, though sometimes not terribly civil."

"Tell me, Anatole," Katerina said, "is it true that you, Pierre and Dolokhov tied a young bear to the back of a policeman and threw them in the Moyka Canal to swim about?"

Pavel had only heard a rumor or two and no details, but Pierre confirmed the story when he lowered his eyes shamefully. Anatole merely shrugged indifferently and said, "There may be some truth to that, though it was really Dolokhov's idea?"

Pavel thought it telling that Anatole attempted to shift the blame for their mutual foolishness to someone not present.

Bolkonski said, "The man sounds like a complete brigand. Why do they keep him around?"

"Among Dolokhov's many talents," Pavel said, "he's good at killing enemy soldiers."

Bolkonski nodded and gave him an appraising look.

Pierre said, "Dolokhov thinks Lieutenant Konklinov is a sorcerer, and believes he used magic to save his life in Persia."

Pavel quickly said, "As I told you last night, Dolokhov is as superstitious as any peasant."

Katerina gave him an appraising look, and he saw deep suspicion in her eyes.

••••

A sorcerer! Katerina thought. It could be, though this Pavel Andreyevich would have to possess quite a bit of innate talent to completely mask his abilities from her. She detected nothing, just that uneasy feeling that had come over her. And now that she thought about it, the sensation had come upon her just as he'd entered the room with Anatole.

To test the man's reaction, she said, "So you're a practitioner of magics?"

At her words, she saw his discomfort grow. "No," he said. "In fact, I firmly believe magic is nothing but superstitious mumbo-jumbo."

"Is it?" she said.

"Lieutenant," Anatole said angrily. "I believe you've upset Mademoiselle Magovana. She is reputed to possess hidden talents of her own, or at least all the ladies believe so."

Clearly, this Pavel Andreyevich had not had as much practice as Katerina at diverting such talk. She said, "I know a few herbal remedies, Prince Anatole, but nothing more. They're popular among the ladies only because they lessen certain discomforts only we women suffer. I quite agree with Lieutenant Konklinov; there is no such thing as . . . *magic*."

Anatole leaned toward her with a smarmy smile on his face. "But a woman like you who possesses such beauty . . . why, it could only be magic."

It was such a trite compliment, but it gave her an opening she needed. "So, Prince Anatole, you believe any attraction I might possess is merely some sort of glamour or illusion. I suppose you think that beneath the deception I'm actually a wrinkled old woman with warts."

His eyes widened. "Oh no, Mademoiselle, I didn't mean it that way."

Prince Bolkonski's lips twitched as he suppressed a smile, while Pierre frowned and looked from Anatole to her, clearly not understanding the byplay between them. Lieutenant Konklinov turned his face away from Anatole to hide a grin he couldn't suppress. Perhaps the fellow wasn't such a bad sort after all.

13

Encounter in Moscow

"I THOUGHT SHE was supposed to be in Moscow," Magreth said as she stepped back from the image in the scrying bowl.

"She was," Cadilus said. He dismissed the image, and now the bowl contained nothing more than simple water.

Cadilus sensed the queen's anger rising as she paced back and forth across her private audience chamber. "Then what happened? How did she end up in Petersburg? Not only that, within a single day they find themselves face-to-face."

"I know not the answer to that, Your Majesty. I can only surmise that with the two of them here in Faerie, the fates twist around them like smoke in a whirlwind."

"Get her out of Petersburg. Get her to Moscow. Now. With him in Petersburg and her there, the fates should calm down nicely."

"Yes, Your Majesty. I'll make the arrangements immediately."

••••

When Mikhail answered the knock on the door, he knew immediately that the young man who stood before him was an Unseelie mage. It wasn't the fellow's outward beauty, which certainly was considerable, or for that matter anything about his appearance, but rather the sense one mage has for another, especially when that other makes no attempt to mask his abilities. "I wish to speak with Mr. Karpov," the young man said. "I have a message from my king. May I enter?"

Mikhail knew he should not be surprised that the fellow attempted to trick him; the Sidhe always sought advantage. Had he been stupid enough to simply say, "Yes," this mage would have been granted free access to the building with only a few restrictions on his actions. Mikhail shook his head and said, "I could ask him to come here to speak with you, but he might not bother. If you want to enter, then I must have your parole. You know the formula."

The mage smiled unpleasantly. "While I am your guest, I'll take no action against you, your family, friends, guests, acquaintances, colleagues or enemies. I'll leave nothing behind, not a hair, a fiber, a whim or a wish, nothing magical, nether, or mundane. I ask of you only audience with your superior. You have my parole, and that of my king. But only while I am your guest."

Mikhail stepped aside and held the door open. "You may enter."

Mikhail led the fellow to the back of the warehouse to Mr. Karpov's office. He knocked on the office door, opened it a crack and stuck his head in. Karpov looked up from the lunch spread before him on his desk.

"Mr. Karpov," Mikhail said. "There is an Unseelie mage here who wishes to speak with you. He says he has a message from his king. I've properly taken his parole."

Karpov tilted his head slightly and raised an eyebrow. He waved a fork impatiently and said, "Bring him in. And you come in too."

Mikhail opened the door wider and held it for the mage, who walked past him into the office. Mikhail followed him in and closed the door.

The mage stopped in front of Karpov's desk and reached into his coat. Even though the fellow had given his parole Mikhail tensed instinctively, and his hand reached for the knife he always carried. If the Unseelie mage had some sort of betrayal in mind, cold iron would do considerable damage to that pretty face. But the mage only retrieved some sort of square picture and held it out toward Karpov.

Karpov raised the fork again and said, "Wait." He waved at Mikhail. "Come here. I want you to see this too."

Mikhail crossed the room quickly and stepped around behind the desk. Standing beside Karpov, he now saw that the picture was actually a small mirror.

"Proceed," Karpov said.

The mage didn't move in the least, but the shiny surface of the mirror clouded over for a moment, then slowly cleared, revealing the image of King Ag. "Vasily, my friend," Ag said. "Forgive me for being abrupt, but we have an opportunity. We might facilitate the death of the Young Mage, and in the process blame it on Magreth."

"Really," Karpov said.

"Yes, but we have to move quickly. I need the young McGowan girl's ex-husband, here, now, without delay. If we use him, we can keep our hands clean."

Karpov looked up at Mikhail and didn't need to ask.

Mikhail said, "Reichart's here in the warehouse."

Karpov smiled, looked back into the mirror and said, "You'll have him immediately."

••••

Katerina's host in Petersburg was Anna Pavlovna Scherer, maid of honor and favorite of the Empress Marya Fedorovna. When the afternoon soiree broke up, Katerina joined Anna in her carriage for the ride back to the Scherer residence. "Please, my dear," Anna said as the carriage rocked and swayed down the streets of Petersburg. "Won't you stay a bit longer? Just another day or two."

"I can't," Katerina said. She'd already delayed her return to Moscow by three days, had done so on a whim, and now wasn't even sure why. "Marya Dmitrievna is expecting me and I'm long overdue."

"Ah, yes," Anna said. "You mustn't keep the terrible dragon waiting."

Tall, stout and of middle age, Marya Dmitrievna Akhrosimova spoke her mind with a frank and sometimes biting tongue. Both Moscow and Petersburg laughed privately at her rudeness, though somehow she never garnered the wrath of the more powerful aristocrats, perhaps because everyone respected and feared her a bit. What they didn't know was that she was a strong witch, though by no means as strong as Katerina, which meant the younger woman more often than not escaped the lash of the older woman's tongue, and was frequently treated as a favored daughter.

When they reached the Scherer residence Katerina learned a letter had arrived from Marya just that afternoon. In polite, but direct language Marya encouraged Katerina to return to Moscow as soon as possible. It confirmed her sense that she had delayed overlong.

She gave the servants instructions to pack her belongings. She'd leave in the morning, though she wondered if she'd ever see that handsome young officer again. She struggled for a moment to remember his name: Konklin—no, Konklinov. In any case, she'd decided she didn't like the fellow, so what did it matter?

••••

When they left the soiree near the Winter Palace, Anatole Kuragin expressed his extreme displeasure with Pavel's performance regarding Katerina Valtrovna. Apparently, the young man expected him to cast some sort of spell that would compel her to come to his father's residence, lift her skirts and willingly spread her legs for him. Pavel didn't want to anger an aristocrat, so he lied and told the prince he would gladly help him if he could, but since his sorcerous abilities were limited strictly to those in Dolokhov's imagination, doing so was completely beyond his power. Such compulsion spells were possible, but he didn't admit that to the young nobleman. They were the blackest of magic, and might be permanently harmful to the victim, so Pavel had avoided them throughout his life, and didn't intend to start crafting them now.

The next morning Pavel joined the other young officers in the Horse Guard's barracks for breakfast. During the meal he learned that, after a brief investigation the previous day, the authorities had decided to punish the perpetrators of the incident with the bear and the policeman. Dolokhov had lost his commission and been demoted to the rank of a common soldier, Pierre had been exiled to Moscow, and while Anatole Kuragin's father had managed to hush up his contribution to the incident, the young man had been ordered out of Petersburg and would probably go to Moscow as well. Pavel breathed a sigh of relief that he'd no longer have to put up with the amoral, young prince, though throughout the meal he couldn't put Katerina Valtrovna out of his thoughts. He wondered if he'd ever have an opportunity to meet her again; most likely not, which was probably best since she had clearly taken a dislike to him.

While Pavel's comrades laughed at the details of the bear and the policeman's swim in the canal, a corporal walked through the door at the far end of the room. The man paused, looked around for a moment, then marched their way. He stopped next to Pavel and said, "Lieutenant Konklinov, you're to report to Major Sukharov's office immediately."

In the week since Pavel had come to Petersburg, Sukharov had often demonstrated that he was prone to impatience, so Pavel left his meal unfinished and hurried to the major's office. After stopping in front of the man's desk, saluting and announcing himself, and receiving the usual sloppy salute in return, Sukharov leaned back in his chair and regarded Pavel, saying nothing for several seconds. Then he said, "Tell me what happened yesterday."

"As you instructed, sir," Pavel said, "I went to Prince Anatole's residence at the appointed hour, and at his request accompanied him to a gathering."

Sukharov put his elbows on his desk, steepled his fingers in front of him and his eyes narrowed. "Tell me about this gathering."

Pavel gave the major a carefully edited summary of the events of the previous day, eliminating any references to arcane abilities, or to Anatole's desire to bed Katerina Valtrovna by any means possible. When he finished, Sukharov again stared at him silently for a long moment. "Well, Lieutenant, it appears you're doing a good job of climbing the social and aristocratic hierarchy of Petersburg."

"I don't know what you mean, sir."

"Oh come now, Konklinov, I'm not stupid. First Kuragin, and now Bolkonski. Just a coincidence, eh?"

Pavel had no idea what had upset Sukharov so. "I really don't understand, sir."

"Prince Bolkonski is leaving for Moscow tomorrow. He's been appointed aide-decamp to General Mikhail Illarionovich Kutuzov, commander-in-chief of the Imperial Russian Army, and he wants you to join his personal retinue. And of course I dare not deny him. If such a man chooses to be your patron, you have an enormous opportunity here. I'm assigning you to him. Do what he says and try not to bungle this."

Moscow! It would be just Pavel's luck that he'd run into Anatole there. And it occurred to him that with Katerina here in Petersburg, he probably would never see her again.

••••

Monsieur Pierre joined Prince Andrew's retinue for the trip to Moscow and the journey proved uneventful. The prince did not maintain a large retinue, but since his wife Lise was with child, they brought along several attendants to see to her needs. Pavel noticed Andrew spent very little time with her. Small of stature, though quite pretty, everyone called her *the little princess*. But in her presence, Andrew always appeared distant and cold, as if she displeased him in some way.

Prince Andrew monopolized Pavel's time, quizzing him incessantly about the realities of battle. He and Pierre listened intently to Pavel's every word, though Pavel had a difficult time making war sound glorious, and he suspected that disappointed them a bit. At the soiree where he'd met Bolkonski he'd spoken from personal experience when he'd talked of the bitter taste of the glory of war. His most vivid memories were of gut-wrenching fear during a charge as musket balls, grapeshot and canister shot shredded the bodies and lives of the men and horses around him.

One day, after they'd questioned him at length about the slaughter at Ganja in Persia, Pavel said, "I fear I sound like a coward."

Pierre asked, "Did you ever turn and run from the enemy?"

Pavel shook his head and felt a bit indignant that Pierre would even ask. He couldn't hide the anger in his voice when he said, "No, of course not."

"Well there you have it," Pierre said. "The mark of a coward is not the presence of fear in his heart, but letting that fear rule him so he acts in a cowardly way."

Andrew seemed to consider Pierre's words for a long moment, then said, "When I think about it carefully, I suppose a man who is fearless at a time like that—truly without fear—is not necessarily brave, but simply a foolish psychopath. But the man who feels fear, and still performs his duty—he is the bravest among us."

"You see," Pierre said, giving Pavel a friendly pat on the back. "You are a man of honor and bravery."

Pavel shrugged and said, "Well, if you measure bravery by the amount of fear in a man's gut, then I must be the bravest man in the world."

They got a good laugh out of that.

Andrew had a residence in Moscow where he insisted Pavel stay, saying, "The food and accommodations at the barracks are barely tolerable." However, on reaching Moscow, Andrew stayed only long enough to introduce Pavel to the staff, then left to escort Lise to his father's estate located about a hundred miles outside of Moscow. She would remain there while Andrew rode off to war.

Before they parted, Andrew said to Pierre, "Take care of our friend Pavel Andreyevich here. Make sure he meets the right people."

"Gladly," Pierre said.

The next morning Pierre showed up with a tailor in tow. Pavel learned that Prince Andrew had asked Pierre to supervise, and left instructions with his staff to ". . . make sure Pavel Andreyevich's wardrobe is up to the standards required of a gentleman on my staff." Apparently that meant several new uniforms, all with extra bits of piping, embroidery and embellishments, outfits Pavel would never have been able to afford without the prince's patronage.

When the tailor finished the first uniform and Pavel tried it on, Pierre clapped his hands and said, "You look splendid, quite the dashing army officer. And I have just the occasion where you can wear that. Count Rostov has invited me to dinner this evening. And when I mentioned that Prince Andrew had asked me to introduce you around, he extended the invitation to you."

••••

Pierre and Pavel arrived at Count Rostov's only a little before dinner. Pierre formally introduced him to the Rostov family, then sat down in a chair in the middle of the drawing room. To Pavel's surprise, Pierre turned stiff and awkward, and as the Countess Rostova tried to engage him in conversation he responded in monosyllables, glancing about the room nervously, and adjusting the spectacles on the tip of his nose. It occurred to Pavel that Pierre might be most comfortable in a small group, not large gatherings like this. He'd been quite animated on the trip from Petersburg when the conversations were limited to just him, Pavel and Prince Andrew.

When Count Rostov heard that Pavel had fought in Persia, he introduced him to a young Russian lieutenant named Berg, and a German captain named Eric Reichart. Pavel immediately sensed that Reichart was a practitioner, though it was clear the fellow had attempted to mask his arcane abilities. Pavel was confident the fellow could not detect his own capabilities.

"Persia, eh?" Reichart said, speaking French with an atrocious accent. If Catherine the Great hadn't made French the official language of the Imperial Russian Court more than thirty years before, Reichart would probably speak Russian with an atrocious accent. "I heard Ganja was a slaughter. Were you at Ganja?"

"Yes, I was," Pavel said, "and there was a great deal of unnecessary killing." He got the impression that Reichart had taken an immediate dislike to him, and didn't understand what he'd done to offend the fellow.

Everyone seemed ready for dinner, and only when Count Rostov asked his wife, "Hasn't she come yet?" did Pavel realize they were waiting for someone.

A few minutes later Pavel heard a commotion at the entrance to the residence, then a tall, stout, middle-aged woman entered the room, and he immediately sensed that she possessed arcane abilities and was a strong witch. Everyone but the oldest of women rose, a clear sign of respect, but Pavel also sensed a bit of fear in them. The stout woman stood there for a moment, surveying the guests and arranging the folds of her dress. As she did so, to Pavel's surprise, Katerina Valtrovna stepped out from behind her to stand beside her. Of the two, the younger woman was by far the more powerful witch.

Standing next to Pavel, Pierre leaned close to him and whispered, "That is Marya Dmitrievna Akhrosimova, called the terrible dragon by many in both Moscow and Petersburg because she speaks her mind, frequently with a sharp tongue. And you know Katerina Valtrovna, her protégé."

The older woman spoke in a commanding voice, complementing the count and countess, though she called the count, ". . . you old sinner," and she called his pretty, young daughter, Natasha, a Cossack. While she spoke, Katerina glanced around the room, and as her eyes brushed past Pavel she smiled pleasantly at him, then seemed to think better of it and gave him a stern and disapproving look.

Pavel whispered to Pierre, "Don't her barbs get her in trouble?"

"Somehow she escapes the wrath of the most powerful," Pierre said, "perhaps because she always speaks the truth, though it certainly doesn't hurt that she is favored by the imperial family."

Marya Dmitrievna turned her attention on Pierre and crossed the room toward him, saying, "Come here, my friend. Come closer."

Pierre immediately stepped forward, and they met in the middle of the room. She chided him in a friendly way about the incident with the bear and the policeman, then she noticed Pavel and said, "And who is this young man. I don't believe I've met him before."

Pavel crossed the room to stand beside Pierre, who introduced him.

"Konklinov?" Marya said. "I know that name."

With a mischievous glint in her eye, she looked at Katerina. "This is the young officer you told me about, isn't he?" She leaned close to Katerina as if to whisper in her ear, but her words were clearly spoken. "And he is every bit as handsome as you said he is."

Katerina's eyes widened and she blushed, turned absolutely scarlet. For some reason that made Paul—Pavel—think he'd seen her blush that way before. But when he thought about it he knew for a certainty he hadn't.

They proceeded to the dining hall, and Pavel thought he might try to sit near Katerina. Reichart beat him to it, though Katerina looked none too happy that the German had taken a place next to her. Pavel ended up at the far end of the table where he would be seated next to the commanding presence of Marya Dmitrievna. But as he held the older woman's chair for her, she looked up and down the table and said, "No, no, this won't do."

Everyone froze as she turned to Pavel and said, "Forgive me, Lieutenant Konklinov, but I do so wish to speak with Captain Reichart during dinner."

She marched around the table, took Katerina by the arm, escorted her back around the table to Pavel. "You sit here, my dear," she said. "I want to sit by the good Captain."

Katerina again blushed, while Reichart gave Pavel a nasty look.

••••

Katerina was at a complete loss for words. She certainly had told Marya that Lieutenant Konklinov was quite handsome, but Marya had made it sound as if she'd gushed like a school girl, and then this pretense to have her sit next to him. It was all so embarrassing, she could only sit and stare at her food as a servant placed the first course before her.

"I wasn't expecting to see you here in Moscow," Pavel said.

Katerina didn't want to be openly rude, so she pulled her eyes away from the food and looked at him. Besides being handsome, he appeared kind and thoughtful, and she couldn't help but smile, though she tried to keep the look on her face a bit aloof. "I consider Moscow my home, though I travel regularly to Petersburg."

He smiled pleasantly. "When I came to Moscow I thought I might never see you again, and I'm glad I got to."

She couldn't help but be flattered, though at that moment she glanced past Pavel and noticed Eric Reichart and Marya Dmitrievna. Marya was speaking to the captain and probably dominating the conversation, but while Eric had leaned slightly toward her as if to listen carefully to her words, his eyes remained locked on Katerina in a disapproving stare.

She was curious how far Pavel's relationship with Anatole went. "Prince Anatole Vasilyevich is here in Moscow, you know. Have you seen him?"

"No," he said, and the look on his face darkened.

"I thought you were friends."

"No, not friends exactly," he said. "He wanted something from me, and insisted that I accompany him to the soiree where we first met."

"Did you give him what he wanted?"

"No, but because of his stature it was difficult to extricate myself from his company. There was one consolation."

"What was that?"

"I got to meet you."

If he disapproved of Anatole Kuragin that way, her opinion of Lieutenant Konklinov ratcheted up a notch, and the evening passed rather nicely. She watched him relax in her presence, and near the end of the dinner she thought she might catch him off-guard and learn something. "Pierre thinks you're a sorcerer."

"No," he said. "Pierre said Dolokhov thinks I'm a sorcerer. I'm not sure what Pierre thinks, and we all know Dolokhov is just superstitious."

She gave him a penetrating look as she said, "Is he?"

He shrugged knowingly, as one conspirator in a cabal might to another, implying that they both shared some secret. "He certainly is superstitious, but I think you really mean to ask: Is he correct in this instance?"

"Well, is he?"

"I would think you'd know, being a witch. Pierre did tell me you're a witch, or rather all the women believe you're one. Can't you just tell, in some way?"

"Yes, I can," she said, giving him a smile that implied she knew exactly what his capabilities were, when in fact she did not.

"As can I," he said, returning the smile. "May I call on you tomorrow?"

She wanted to say yes, but still wasn't certain of him. His words implied he was a practitioner, but that could be no more than polite banter. "No, I think not."

She saw the disappointment in his face, but at that moment she noticed Reichart giving her a nasty, jealous look, so without thinking she said, "But later this evening I'm sure there'll be dancing. And if you were to ask me to dance, I might agree to do so."

14

A Pleasant Outing

AFTER DINNER THE guests dispersed throughout the Rostov residence into two drawing rooms, a sitting room and the library. One of the young girls demonstrated her ability on the harp, playing a pleasant little ayr. "Come," Pierre said, taking Pavel by the arm. "I believe the count is going to play cards in one of the sitting rooms, but let's go to the drawing room for drinks."

As they walked toward the drawing room, Pierre glanced about surreptitiously, then paused and leaned close to Pavel's ear. "But first I must warn you. Be careful of Reichart, my friend. He and Katerina Valtrovna were betrothed several years ago, and it is rumored they had a tumultuous affair. But apparently he was overly possessive and it didn't last long. It angered him greatly when she broke it off, and he has since been quite persistent."

"Did she ever marry?"

"No, he took his revenge on her by quietly letting it be known she was no longer . . . *marriageable material*, one might say."

Pavel said, "That seems a rather cowardly thing to do."

"Exactly. It amazes me he thinks she'll treat him with anything but absolute contempt. But do be careful, my friend. While we might agree he is a reprehensible coward, that does not make him less dangerous."

The young girls played more tunes on the clavichord and harp, Natasha demonstrated that she had a lovely voice, then one of the young boys sang as well. Pavel found a chair from which he could see into the next room where Katerina sat discussing something with the other ladies. He sat quietly and listened to Pierre and an older gentleman argue politics, and occasionally Katerina glanced his way and caught him looking at her. Then Count Rostov's young daughter came in and insisted Pierre dance with her. He took the little girl by the hand and walked with her into the other room.

Professional musicians took up their instruments and the young people danced in the contredanse style. Then the count and Marya Dmitrievna emerged from the sitting room where they'd been playing cards with most of the older people. The count demanded the musicians play his favorite dance, he took Marya as his partner, and all of the visitors gathered from the various rooms to watch them. Pavel stood at the back of the crowd and leaned against a wall casually.

"I thought you were going to ask me to dance?"

Pavel started, recognizing Katerina's voice, and turned to face her.

"I would," he said. "But I don't know this dance."

At that moment the dance ended, and the musicians struck up another tune.

"Ah," she said. "It's that new dance they call the waltz. A man and woman dance together face-to-face and turn as one while they maintain a close embrace."

"I don't know that dance either," Pavel said. "But I would definitely enjoy a waltz with you. Perhaps you could teach me."

She smiled shyly but did not blush.

Reichart appeared beside her, took her arm and said, "Come, my dear. Let's dance."

He didn't wait for a reply and took a step, but she held her ground and didn't move. To continue he would have to actually drag her out onto the dance floor, making a horrible scene. Several people had already turned to look their way, so he stopped and released her arm. "I want to dance with you," he said.

"I'm sorry, Eric," she said. "But I've promised this dance to Lieutenant Konklinov."

He glared at her. "Then I'll take the next."

"No," she said, her voice an icy, soft whisper. "I'm afraid my dance card is quite full. Perhaps another time."

Reichart looked at Pavel, his eyes hardened and his upper lip puckered up. Then he spun about and walked away.

Katerina spoke as if nothing had just happened. "I've only just learned the rudiments of this new dance myself, so we'll both be stumbling about a bit, and I think you'll have to hold me in that close embrace rather tightly."

Pavel held out his arm, she took it, and as he escorted her out onto the dance floor, he said, "I think I'm going to enjoy dancing with you, Katerina Valtrovna."

She turned to face him. "And I you. Now let me show you how to hold me very tightly."

Pavel noticed several couples moving about the floor in halting steps, and realized he was not the only one learning this new dance step. When the music ended everyone insisted the musicians play another waltz. The old count asked Katerina to be his partner, and Pavel stood on the sidelines as he swirled her about the floor. That evening the count took a turn with almost every lady present, but after that one dance Katerina returned to Pavel, saying, "I'm afraid one dance is not enough of a lesson for you, so further instruction is required."

Pavel bowed and said, "I am humbly grateful, my lady."

She smiled, and he saw a playful glint in her eyes. "You should be."

After that she danced only with Pavel. At the end of the last dance, as the evening was coming to an end, she looked into his eyes and said, "I've changed my mind. You may call on me tomorrow. Come mid-morning, and bring your horse; we'll take the air in Sokolniki Park."

Pavel and Pierre left the Rostov residence in a hired carriage, and as it rattled down the cobblestone streets, Pierre said, "Captain Reichart was clearly displeased with you. Heed my warning, friend, for he is also known to be a skillful and experienced duelist."

••••

As a child Katerina had been raised on her father's estate outside Moscow and considered that *home*. Her father and Marya Dmitrievna had been her principal tutors in the arcane arts and she enjoyed the older woman's company, so when in Moscow she always stayed at Marya's residence. She also enjoyed the life of the city and spent a considerable amount of time there.

She and Marya were seated in the drawing room when a servant escorted Lieutenant Konklinov into their presence. He crossed the room, and as Marya extended her hand he bowed and kissed it. He repeated that with Katerina, and as he kissed her hand she wondered what it would be like for him to truly kiss her. But recalling her disastrous affair with Captain Reichart, she quickly put that thought out of her mind.

Marya stood, clapped her hands and said, "Come. The carriage and the footmen are waiting."

Though autumn was near, the day was warm and clear. Marya and Katerina rode in an open carriage, while the lieutenant, mounted on his horse, trotted beside them. The ride to the park was only a few miles, and when they reached it the coachman slowed their pace to little more than an easy walk.

"So," Marya said to Lieutenant Konklinov as he rode beside them, "you fought in Persia beside that scoundrel Dolokhov. And you saved his life with sorcery, I hear."

Katerina had carefully briefed Marya on her previous interactions with Konklinov and everything she'd learned about the man. She also told her of the unusual sensation she got whenever he came near. She was certain he was a true wizard, and she had enlisted the older woman's aid in an effort to prove that one way or another.

Konklinov casually shrugged off Marya's remark. "I merely made a poultice from some fungus the way my father taught me. It worked, and Dolokhov, being a superstitious man, attributed his recovery to magic, or something of that nature."

That had not been the reaction Katerina had hoped for. In fact he hadn't reacted in any way, hadn't so much as blinked, merely denied the accusation with a calm and composed demeanor. But Marya could be quite tenacious, and Katerina had every confidence the older woman would learn his secrets. That was the only reason Katerina had allowed him to call on her today, and the fact that she was attracted to him had nothing to do with it.

She was attracted to him! Until that moment she hadn't realized that. But she could easily put that aside, wouldn't let that get in the way of unraveling the mystery of Pavel Andreyevich Konklinov.

"Just a poultice, eh?" Marya asked. "And you know nothing of magic?"

He frowned as if the question perplexed him. "There was a hedge witch in our village. But from what I saw she mixed potions that didn't work, and told fortunes that never came true."

Katerina asked, "You don't believe in magic at all?"

He smiled knowingly. "Do you?"

They rode that way for some time, Marya and Katerina probing, and the lieutenant deftly parrying each stroke like a skilled swordsman. Finally, Marya said, "I tire of this conversation. A fat, old woman like me can ride in a carriage all day, but you young people need to get some exercise."

She called to the coachman. "Stop the carriage."

Katerina was careful not to react. This was not in the script she and Marya had discussed. The older woman instructed Lieutenant Konklinov to dismount and tie the reins of his horse to the back of the carriage. "Now," she said to him, "help Katerina out of the carriage, and you two walk ahead while I rest and enjoy the ride and the warm sun. I may even nap a little, as we old people do."

Katerina gave her a nasty look as she stood, but the older woman ignored her, so she leaned close to Marya and said, "Don't you dare start matchmaking again."

Marya merely smiled like a cat who'd just swallowed a mouse.

••••

Pavel took Katerina's hand and helped her down from the carriage. She gave him a strained smile as she straightened the folds of her dress, and all he could think was that he wanted to take her in his arms and kiss her.

"Oh, Lieutenant," Marya said, and both Pavel and Katerina looked her way.

Marya wagged a finger at him like an adult scolding a recalcitrant child. "You'll be walking alone with her so don't you dare attempt to kiss her. As your chaperone I mustn't allow it, though, if I'm napping, and she wants you to kiss her, how will I stop you?"

Pavel felt heat rushing to his face.

"And he blushes too," Marya said. "Both handsome and modest."

Katerina put a hand to her mouth and uttered a quiet little laugh. Pavel held out his arm, she took it, and they walked ahead of the carriage. He kept his eyes locked straight ahead and didn't know what to say.

"She is hopeless," Katerina said. "She's well known for embarrassing people that way."

Pavel asked, "Does she read minds too?"

Katerina stopped, forcing him to stop as well, and she turned to look up at him. The carriage behind them stopped as he looked down at her. She had a glint in her eye as she smiled and said, "That seems to imply that when she told you not to kiss me, you were thinking you'd like to do exactly that."

He felt heat rushing to his face again.

Her smile broadened. "And you just confirmed it with that blush."

He was rescued by the sound of hooves pounding on the dirt. They both looked toward the sound; Pavel saw Eric Reichart astride a horse galloping their way and bearing down on them as if he would trample them. Pavel reached out and wrapped his arms around Katerina to protect her, and prepared to pull her to one side or the other at the last instant. But Reichart reined his horse to a stop just short of them, and a small cloud of dust wafted past them.

Seated above them on his horse, Reichart demanded of Katerina, "What are you doing here with him?"

Only then did Pavel realize he was holding Katerina in a tight embrace, much tighter than the waltzes of the previous night. She looked into his eyes and said, "Thank you, Pavel Andreyevich. But I'll handle this."

Pavel released her and stepped back, but stood ready to intervene if Reichart proved to be as unstable as he appeared.

"Answer me?" Reichart demanded.

Ignoring him, she carefully straightened the folds of her dress, and brushed away imaginary dust.

Reichart almost shouted, "I asked you a question."

She looked up at him and gave him a cold, unyielding smile. "A question you have no right to ask."

His eyes flared, and Pavel stiffened, fearing the fool might actually do something violent.

Katerina added. "And a question I choose not to answer."

She turned her back on Reichart and said to Pavel, "Come, my dear friend, let us return to the carriage." She took Pavel's arm. "I tire of this park"—she glanced over her shoulder at Reichart—"and the company we're forced to endure here."

Reichart spun his horse about and put his spurs to its flanks, galloping away in a cloud of dust.

Pavel returned Katerina to the carriage, mounted his horse and they rode back to Marya's residence. Pavel helped Katerina out of the carriage, then he helped Marya, but as the older woman's feet touched the ground she stumbled. He caught her by the elbow and she didn't fall, but leaning close to him she whispered, "She does want you to kiss her, you know. She just doesn't know she wants you to kiss her. And as a gentleman, Pavel Andreyevich, it is your solemn duty to give a lady what she wants."

••••

After the ride in the park Marya invited Lieutenant Konklinov to join them for tea, which did not displease Katerina. He had proven to be quite the gentleman, and she'd rather enjoyed the way he'd wrapped her in his arms to protect her from Reichart. It also pleased her that, when she told him to let her handle Eric, he hadn't become over protective, hadn't turned all *man* on her and tried to shield her from the unpleasantness. He'd clearly been ready to defend her if necessary, but hadn't treated her as a frail and stupid girl, had perhaps understood that she'd long ago learned to be her own woman. Eric Reichart had forced that lesson upon her when she was much younger, though she almost wished that pig of a German would do something else to make the lieutenant embrace her again, and so tightly she'd been pressed against him, almost like a lover.

With Marya and Katerina seated in the drawing room, the lieutenant standing near the hearth, he seemed a little ill-at-ease. Katerina had seen Marya stumble as he helped her from the carriage, wasn't sure if the older woman had said something to him at that moment, and now suspected she had. Was that the cause of his discomfort?

A servant brought in a tea service and placed it before Marya. As hostess, she carefully served each of them.

Katerina sipped her tea and said, "Thank you, Lieutenant, for letting me handle Eric."

At the mention of Reichart, his face hardened, and perhaps she caught a glimpse of the experienced soldier there. He said, "I learned long ago that when I don't know the situation, or the players, it's best to let someone who does handle it."

Marya remained strangely silent.

The hard look he'd had a moment ago softened. "Especially when that someone is strong and can handle herself quite nicely."

Katerina tried not to grin like a flattered schoolgirl, but failed miserably. Then she recalled her own tarnished reputation. "Surely you've heard the rumors about me."

Marya raised her teacup to her mouth and sipped, but gave her a disapproving look over the cup's rim.

He said, "I've heard many rumors about many people. But I find that when I get to know the individuals themselves, the rumors are frequently irrelevant, so it doesn't matter if they're true or not."

"Is that always the case?"

"No," the lieutenant said. "Take Reichart, for example. I've heard he's committed some rather cowardly acts, and I'm learning that those rumors are quite relevant."

Katerina couldn't rid herself of the grin so she sipped at her tea to hide her mouth behind her teacup.

Addressing the lieutenant, Marya finally spoke. "You're going to have trouble with him, you know."

••••

"I don't like the direction this is going," Magreth said.

Peering at the image in the scrying bowl, Cadilus agreed with her. "Neither do I. We send her to Moscow to separate them, and the story sends him there as well. And they're reunited almost immediately."

"Exactly," Magreth whispered.

The Young Mage and the Old Wizard's daughter grew more powerful with each scene in the story, and it had taken on a life of its own. Cadilus said, "Their natural personalities are resurfacing, and little by little I'm finding it more difficult to guide the story in the direction we desire."

"Should we end it?" she asked.

"That might be the wisest course of action, Your Majesty."

A crow cawed, a sharp cry that startled them both and they turned away from the scrying bowl. Cadilus glimpsed the bird in flight in the middle of the room for only an instant, then it transformed into an old crone wearing a long, hooded cloak and hunched over a walking cane. She had a twisted nose with warts and moles all over her face, and what few teeth remained in her mouth were crooked and brown. Cataracts clouded her left eye, and her right drooped with some sort of palsy.

She cackled and laughed maniacally. "Your magics cannot defy the fates."

She walked toward them slowly, leaning heavily on the cane, but between one step and the next she became a beautiful young maiden with long tresses of golden blond hair that hung well past her shoulders. One eye sparkled a pale blue, while the other flashed an emerald green, and she wore a shimmering, translucent gown draped over the curves of a tall goddess. The fabric of her dress left little to Cadilus's imagination. She smiled at them and spoke in a lovely voice, "Their story will play out as it is meant to."

In the next step she turned into a naked, skeletal corpse, ribs protruding visibly, dried up old breasts withered to nothing, gobbets of rotted flesh hanging from her face, maggots filling her eyes and mouth. Her skin appeared to have the texture of old leather, with a sickly, yellowish cast that hinted at disease and pestilence. "Beware," the corpse croaked, "lest you twist the fates to your own detriment."

In the wink of an eye the triple goddess disappeared.

"I . . ." Magreth said. "I . . . ah . . ."

In all the centuries Cadilus had served the queen of the Seelie Court, never before had he seen her left speechless.

15

A Challenge

THAT REICHART HAD shown up in the park bothered Katerina. He couldn't have known they were going there, but he was a reasonably skilled wizard, so perhaps he had used some sort of spell to track her. And how had he known Lieutenant Konklinov would be there as well? She didn't believe in simple coincidence, not when it came to practitioners.

She was finding it hard not to like the lieutenant, especially since he knew of her tarnished reputation, and he'd made it clear he didn't care. She considered the possibility that he was attentive to her only because of the rumors, and hoped to use her for a casual fling and a few nights of pleasure, then discard her. She'd met other men like that—Anatole Kuragin, for one—and had not fallen for their deceits. But for some reason she felt confident Lieutenant Konklinov was not the type of man to be so casually cruel, almost as if she had already known him for some time, and knew he was kinder than that.

She had to be careful with the lieutenant. They'd had no success determining if he was a practitioner, and if he had no arcane abilities . . . well, relationships between a practitioner and a mundane lover rarely lasted long.

Marya's blatant matchmaking didn't help any, and frustrated Katerina to no end. In the drawing room that day after the ride in the park, Marya had stood without warning and said, "We should have something to eat along with the tea." Then she'd left the room to give instructions to the kitchen. She could have rung for a servant to come to her, but leaving the room left Pavel and Katerina alone together, which she didn't mind so much. And then he'd become unsure of himself, which she did mind. Katerina was now almost certain Marya had said something to him when she'd stumbled while he helped her out of the carriage that day. And knowing Marya's tricks well, the stumble had likely been no accident.

The next morning Katerina had an appointment with a dressmaker across town. She could have had the dressmaker come to her, but she enjoyed getting out of the house, and this allowed her to see all of the fabrics at the woman's disposal, not just those the seamstress chose to show her.

As Katerina prepared to leave, Marya said, "My dear, you'll be going rather close to the Rostov's on the way back, won't you?"

"Why, yes," Katerina said. "I will."

Marya handed her an old book. "Be a dear and stop there will you? At that little gathering the other night, when you danced all night with Lieutenant Konklinov, I promised Countess Rostova I'd lend her this book. Could you give it to her for me?"

"Of course, I'll be happy to."

"I hope it's not too far out of your way."

"Not in the least."

Katerina needed a new ball gown for a large event a few nights hence. She'd already been through two fittings, and when she tried it on at the dressmaker's shop the woman tugged a little here, and a litter there, then said, "The only changes required are quite minor. If you'd care to have a cup of tea, I can have them completed for you by the time you're finished, and you can take the gown with you now."

Katerina was not in the mood for tea, so she chose to bide her time by examining the new fabrics in the shop. She selected a few, told the woman to keep them in mind for her, tried the gown on one more time, then left with the dress in hand.

The sky had clouded over, and a light drizzle fell as the coachmen pulled the carriage into the courtyard of the Rostov residence. A servant rushed out with an umbrella and held it for her as she crossed the short distance to the entrance. She asked them to tell the countess that she was merely there to deliver a book from Marya Dmitrievna, and wouldn't stay long. But the countess showed up a few moments later.

"Katerina," she said. "What's this about a book?"

"Marya told me she promised to lend it to you the other night."

The countess looked at the book and frowned. "I honestly don't recall asking for this. Oh well, we old women do get forgetful. We're about to dine. Do join us."

Katerina started to decline, but the countess said, "No, no, no, I insist."

"Very well," Katerina said.

The countess's eyes narrowed in a conspiratorial look. "That handsome young cavalry officer you sat next to at dinner the other night, then danced with throughout the evening . . ."

"Yes, Lieutenant Konklinov, what about him?"

The countess glanced over her shoulder, then said, "He's here. I'll see to it you're seated next to him."

As they dined, just out of curiosity, she asked Pavel, "Yesterday, when you helped Marya Dmitrievna from the carriage, and she stumbled, what did she say to you?"

"Oh," he said. "It was nothing, nothing at all. I don't even recall it."

It pleased Katerina that he was such a terrible liar, and his words confirmed her suspicions. Marya had said something to him, and it was something he didn't want to repeat.

She learned that shortly after dinner the other night, the count had invited him to come today and speak with his son Nicholas, who would be leaving soon for the regiment, and had no experience of war. Pavel said, "He wanted me to give the young man an idea of what life for a lower-ranking officer will be like. Though, with his money and connections, I think young Nicholas will live far better than I ever did."

"And when the count extended his invitation," she asked, "was Marya Dmitrievna present?"

"Why yes," he said, "she was. In fact, she suggested it. How did you know?"

"Just an educated guess."

She decided it would be unfair to take her ire out on poor Lieutenant Konklinov, just because two conspiratorial, old matchmakers had set their sights on steering him her way. And in any case, she thoroughly enjoyed herself that afternoon, though she was not about to admit that to either Marya or the countess.

••••

Between the countess and Marya, the two old women somehow managed to make sure Katerina and Lieutenant Konklinov ran into each other daily, for the next three days. They were quite deft at making their encounters appear to have occurred purely by coincidence, even though Katerina did everything in her power to thwart them, though perhaps she didn't try as hard as she might have. It turned into a bit of a game in which each day she wondered how Marya would again trick her into being at a certain place just as Pavel arrived.

She had to admit that she was a bit torn. She did like the lieutenant, and found herself thinking about him quite a lot, even looked forward to their next *accidental* encounter. But no matter how hard she tried to anticipate Marya's next move in the game, she'd walk into a room and find herself face-to-face with him without any warning. So by the fourth day she capitulated, and gave up entirely on any attempt to resist. And yet, as the afternoon dwindled toward evening, and she prepared for the Razumovski's ball, there'd been no sign of Lieutenant Konklinov.

She stood before a mirror and looked at herself in the new ball gown she'd purchased. In the fashion of the day it was cut low in the front and back, exposing her neck and shoulders and the swell of her breasts. Perhaps she'd see Pavel at the ball. She thought he'd like the way she looked in the dress.

August had been comfortably pleasant, and the Razumovski's were throwing a gala to take advantage of the last warm evenings of summer. Prince Andrew Nikolayevich

Bolkonski had returned from his father's estate and would undoubtedly attend. Certainly, he'd be accompanied by the lieutenant. She realized that the prince's return meant they would soon depart for the war, and Pavel might be injured or killed.

When Katerina and Marya arrived at the Razumovski's the event was in the early stages. The musicians played softly while everyone mingled. She scanned the crowd, but didn't see the lieutenant anywhere, though she spotted Prince Andrew. She wanted to march up to the prince and ask him if Pavel would be attending, but she dare not be so brazen.

She decided to stay close to Marya, though that meant she ended up chatting with Prince Anatole, and he never took his eyes off her breasts. Prince Andrew joined them, and greeted them kindly.

"When will you be leaving for the war?" Katerina asked him.

"Two days hence," he said.

She wanted to ask him about Lieutenant Konklinov, but couldn't think of how to do so without seeming obvious.

Marya gave Katerina a knowing look as she asked Andrew, "Will Lieutenant Konklinov be joining us this evening?"

"Yes," Andrew said, "I believe he will."

Katerina tried not to beam with obvious pleasure.

Prince Andrew looked at his watch and said, "I'm surprised he's not here yet. Something must have delayed him."

When the dancing started Anatole asked her to dance, and she couldn't refuse him without being rude. She noticed Eric Reichart hovering close to a pretty, young girl. She pitied the poor child but was glad he'd focused on someone else for a change. She danced with Monsieur Pierre who had just inherited his father's vast wealth, and was now Count Bezukhov. Later she saw Princess Helene Kuragina hovering about the young man. The girl had never paid him the least bit of attention before, but now that he'd gained such wealth, she'd probably seduce him, perhaps even marry him. Poor fellow!

An hour after the festivities had started she tired of dancing, so she quietly slipped out of the ballroom into one of the gardens. The air was warm and didn't chill her in the least, so she wandered deeper into the garden and stopped in a brightly lit gazebo. The pleasant scent of flowers drifted on the night air.

"Katerina."

She stiffened at the sound of Eric's voice, and turned slowly to face him. He stepped into the gazebo and stopped about two paces from her. He must have used a minor spell to approach her without being heard. By any standard he was so incredibly handsome, but knowing him as she did, nothing about him attracted her.

"You've been avoiding me."

She took a deep breath and sighed. "Captain Reichart, I don't avoid you, and I don't seek you out. In any case, earlier it appeared you'd found a new conquest."

"She's a child," he said, and took one aggressive step forward.

He now stood uncomfortably close, but she refused to be intimidated and held her ground. Looking past him toward the light spilling out of the doors to the ballroom, she realized she'd wandered quite deep into the garden and was now alone with him.

"I wasn't much more than a child myself."

"You were a woman in every way that counted."

"Yes, I suppose I was, but children are your forte."

He stepped forward, and this time she did step back, though she bumped against the wall of the gazebo. He closed the distance between them, grabbed her arm and pulled her against him, wrapping his arm around her waist.

She spoke softly. "Please take your hands off me."

He pulled her even more tightly against him, and she felt his erection pressed against her hip. He tried to kiss her, but she turned her face away. He groped at her breast, and only then did she understand he might be insane enough to rape her then and there.

••••

Pavel had spent the afternoon at the Horse Guard's barracks discussing with other officers their coming deployment to the western front. He wasn't able to get away until early evening, and then half way back to Prince Andrew's residence his horse began limping so he walked the animal the rest of the way. By the time he'd changed his uniform and taken a hired carriage to the Razumovski's, he was considerably late.

Prince Andrew and Pierre, the new Count Bezukhov, greeted him warmly. He saw Marya Dmitrievna, but no sign of Katerina. Marya saw him looking her way and imperiously marched across the room like a general leading troops.

"Lieutenant Konklinov," she said as she joined them, "how good to see you."

She made an obvious point of scanning the crowd and grinned. "I don't see her either."

"Who are you looking for?" Pierre asked.

She said, "I was wondering where Katerina had gotten to."

The new count frowned thoughtfully. "I think I saw her step out into the gardens a short while ago."

"Be a dear," she said, "and show the good lieutenant where she is."

Pierre led Pavel around the periphery of the dance floor to a set of open double doors. They both stepped out into the warm night air, but Pavel saw no sign of

Katerina. He noticed another couple wandering among roses off to one side, and in the distance a copse of trees was illuminated by the glare of light from a gazebo.

Katerina's voice suddenly broke the silence of the night. "I told you to take your hands off me."

Pierre's eyes widened, he looked at Pavel and hissed, "The gazebo!"

Pavel ran toward the gazebo with the sound of Pierre's boots crunching on the gravel pathway behind him. As he approached the lighted structure, he saw a man in a cavalry officer's uniform struggling with someone pressed against the wall of the gazebo. Katerina shouted again, "Unhand me, you pig."

Pavel recognized Reichart just as the man raised his hand to strike her. He wanted to hit the fellow and knock him to the ground, but he knew he should avoid escalating the situation to outright violence. So he reached out and grabbed the German's raised wrist, halting it above his head. Reichart struggled against Pavel's grip for a moment, then Pierre shouted, "Release that woman immediately."

Reichart glanced over his shoulder, and apparently realizing he now had witnesses, one an incredibly wealthy, titled aristocrat, he hesitated.

Still holding Reichart's wrist, Pavel said, "Katerina asked you to release her. Do so, now."

Reichart grinned. "Or you'll do what?"

Pavel was surprised at how deadly his voice sounded. "Something you'll find quite unpleasant."

Reichart must have seen something dangerous in Pavel's face because he frowned.

Pavel said, "Take your hands off the lady."

Reichart released Katerina and stepped back. Pavel released his wrist.

"Lady!" Reichart said. "She's no lady."

Pavel stepped toward Reichart, anger rising up in his gut. "You say that only because you're no gentleman."

Prince Andrew stepped out of the darkness to stand beside Pierre. "Captain Reichart," he said, "I think you should leave."

Reichart lifted an arrogant eyebrow, then stepped past Pavel, nudging him with his shoulder. He walked out of the gazebo and strode confidently toward the ballroom.

"Katerina Valtrovna," Pierre said. "Did he harm you?"

"No," she said. "Thanks to you gentlemen, I'm quite all right."

"Actually," Pierre said, "thanks more to Pavel Andreyevich."

She looked at Pavel and smiled like a cat about to devour a meal. "Yes, you're quite right. Do you mind if I have a word alone with the good lieutenant?"

The two men turned and quietly walked away. When they were out of sight Katerina stepped toward Pavel, and the look on her face made him back up a step.

"Thank you, Lieutenant."

"I would not let him harm you, ever."

"I know," she said, slowly walking forward while he stepped back. "You want to kiss me, don't you?"

He backed into the wall of the gazebo and stopped. She didn't stop advancing until she stood with her face only inches from his. "You wanted to kiss me that day in the park when Marya made you blush, didn't you?"

"I . . ." he said. "I must admit that kissing you has certainly . . . crossed my mind."

"You want to kiss me," she said, "and Marya has made it rather obvious she wants you to kiss me, so why don't you?"

For Pavel there was one question she hadn't answered. "She is rather obvious about it. And I do want to kiss you. But do *you* want me to kiss you?"

She gave him that cat-anticipating-a-meal smile. "You'll know the answer to that only when you try."

He put his arm around her waist, but he didn't have to pull her against him because she leaned forward and took care of that herself. He lowered his face toward her, and as he brushed his lips across hers, her tongue dragged lightly along his lower lip.

"Shall I take that as a *yes*?" he asked, his lips brushing against hers as he spoke.

"I'm sorry, lieutenant, but you won't know until you truly try."

He pressed his lips against hers and her tongue explored his mouth. With her body pressed tightly against him, he learned her answer.

••••

When their lips parted, she said, "I suppose we should return to the ball or my reputation will be ruined. Though I guess I really don't have much of a reputation to preserve."

The young man in Pavel would have preferred to stay in the gazebo all night and explore more ways to kiss Katerina Valtrovna, but that would be utterly scandalous. They kissed again and she remained pressed against him.

He said, "I'm finding it difficult to let you go."

"Good," she said, and stepped out of his arms.

With Katerina on his arm, the two of them walked back to the ballroom. Marya Dmitrievna stood in the garden just outside the doors, apparently waiting for them. As they stepped into the light that spilled out from the ballroom, she reached out and pressed a hand against Pavel's chest, halting him. She retrieved a small, white handkerchief from the folds of her dress, reached up and smudged at his lips, saying, "You don't strike me as the type to wear a woman's lip paint, Lieutenant."

Pavel stiffened.

Looking at Katerina, Marya added, "Though I have no doubt she put it there herself."

Katerina blushed, and at the heat he felt in his own face Pavel guessed he was doing the same.

Marya finished wiping his lips and said, "And I'll bet you thoroughly enjoyed the way she did so, didn't you?"

Thankfully, the older woman didn't press the issue, though as they stepped into the ballroom, she all but clucked like a thoroughly pleased hen. She leaned toward them and whispered, "The whole place is abuzz with that German's despicable behavior."

Katerina said, "No doubt, some of them believe I lured him out there."

"My dear," Marya said, "there are always fools present."

There wasn't much left of the evening. Pavel and Katerina danced a few times, then people began to depart. Pavel, Pierre and Prince Andrew accompanied Marya and Katerina to their carriage. They were waiting in the courtyard when Eric Reichart approached, and all conversation ceased. He stopped a few paces from Pavel, took the gloves from his belt, and threw one at Pavel's feet.

"No," Katerina said.

Reichart said, "I want satisfaction."

Pavel had no choice. He reached down, picked up the glove and handed it to Reichart. "I accept."

"Dawn," Reichart said. "Tomorrow. To first blood. My second will contact yours with the location."

"I'll second him," Prince Andrew said.

Reichart nodded, turned around and strode away.

"To first blood," Katerina said. "That means even a minor injury ends the duel, does it not?"

Prince Andrew looked quite unhappy. "Reichart likes dueling, and has fought many, always to first blood. But he is an expert marksman, and it is uncanny how frequently his bullet finds his opponent's heart."

He looked pointedly at Katerina. "With that man, first blood usually means death."

••••

The scrying mirror clouded over for a moment, and when it cleared Vasily Karpov saw his own reflection, with Ag standing beside him and the walls of the Unseelie King's drawing room behind them both. Karpov didn't turn to Ag, but instead looked at the king's image in the mirror when he spoke. "But isn't this all just illusion? Regardless of the outcome of the duel, won't he simply wake with nothing more than memories?"

"Ah, my friend," Ag said, throwing an arm around Karpov's shoulders. "Here in Faerie, an illusion is so much more, and so much less, than merely an illusion."

At the moment, Karpov's support among the other senior wizards was questionable, and he could no longer afford to be associated with something like this. "Are you sure they can't detect your tampering?"

"Trust me," Ag said. "Mr. Reichart has been so much a part of recent events in the lives of both the young woman and young man, as well as an intimate part of her past, it's only natural he would appear in this. Have no fear. The blame will be laid at Magreth's feet. As long as Mr. Reichart performs his part well, we'll soon be rid of the Young Mage—permanently."

••••

"Can you stop this?" Magreth demanded. "If he is harmed in any way, we will incur obligations that will complicate matters no end."

"I'm sorry, Your Majesty," Cadilus said. "The triple goddess has taken the story to her bosom, and we are now no more than spectators."

16

Satisfaction

FOR THE DUEL, Reichart had chosen a secluded clearing in the forest just outside of Moscow. Since dueling was officially illegal, though unofficially tolerated, the clearing offered the privacy necessary for murder.

Prince Andrew brought along his personal physician, and Reichart had chosen another German officer as a second. The sun had just broken over the horizon as Pavel, Andrew, Reichart, his second, and the physician assembled in the clearing. Not far away Pavel sensed a ley line deep in the forest.

They gathered around Prince Andrew. "You have met here on the field of honor," he said, looking from Pavel to Reichart. "If you both agree, you can depart now without bloodshed, and your honors will be preserved."

Pavel said, "I'm willing to end it at this."

Reichart clearly took that as a sign of weakness. He gave Pavel a scornful look and shook his head. "We agreed to first blood, and so to first blood it will be. Otherwise, you are without honor."

Andrew said to Pavel, "You may decline because of the rank difference and still retain your honor."

They'd discussed this beforehand. The unwritten code of dueling forbade duels between men of different ranks. That a captain had challenged a lieutenant had badly damaged Reichart's reputation, which, after the rumors of his conduct toward Katerina, wasn't much to begin with. Pavel could refuse to fight Reichart and walk away with his honor intact. But for Pavel, this wasn't about honor. Reichart needed to know that he would not be allowed to molest Katerina without consequences. Pavel shook his head.

To mark the positions where Pavel and Reichart would stand, Prince Andrew and Reichart's second walked the field of honor, then plunged two sabers in the ground separated by thirty paces. Andrew had provided an expensive dueling pistol for Pavel, and Reichart had brought his own.

As Pavel examined the pistol, Andrew said, "The barrel is very accurate, and I personally charged and loaded it. You need not fear a misfire."

Reichart and Pavel exchanged pistols, each examining the other's to ensure nothing untoward. Among practitioners it had long ago been agreed no arcane forces would be used in a duel. It would create difficulties for all of them if two practitioners threw around a lot of magics in front of mundane witnesses. Pavel would play by the unwritten rules, even though he'd masked his own abilities and was confident Reichart knew nothing of his power. But he knew the German all too well, so he examined the fellow's pistol carefully for any spells that might give the bullet more force or greater accuracy. It would be so like the man to spell the weapon so the bullet sought his heart. He detected nothing.

Once both of them were satisfied, the two men returned the pistol's to each other, removed their coats and handed them to Andrew's physician.

"We will separate you by fifty paces, with the sabers between you," Andrew told them. "You will each stand facing your opponent, though your pistols must remain aimed at the sky until I drop this." He flourished a white, silk handkerchief. "When I do, you may aim at your opponent and fire immediately, or, if you choose, you may walk forward before firing, and fire at any time, but you may not walk any closer than the two sabers. If the first to fire his weapon draws blood, that is first blood and his opponent may not fire his weapon. If both weapons are discharged and no blood is drawn, if either of you wishes, you may end this at that time with your honor preserved. Otherwise, the weapons will be reloaded and we'll repeat. Understood?"

Pavel nodded.

Reichart said, "Yes."

With his heart pounding, Pavel cocked the ornate hammer on his pistol, raised the gun so its muzzle pointed at the sky, turned and walked slowly toward his designated spot. But half way there he sensed something strange, a gathering of arcane forces, and he realized Reichart was drawing power. Pavel glanced over his shoulder and saw the German walking confidently to his position.

Reichart must have prepared some sort of spell and was clearly applying it now to his own pistol, probably to make its bullet seek Pavel's heart. Pavel would bet good money Reichart had never challenged another practitioner, only men without arcane abilities who could not sense his treachery. He now had no choice and drew his own power in self-defense. He'd always had the ability to use his power to throw a knife with uncanny accuracy, but he'd never tried it with a musket ball. He didn't know if it would work, but it was his only hope.

He walked past the sabre with its point plunged in the ground, walked another ten paces and turned to face Reichart. At that moment he sensed a spell in his own pistol activate. The bastard had placed something arcane on his pistol while examining it, and at the time Pavel had been too focused on inspecting his opponent's weapon to notice. He felt the pistol twist slightly in his hand, probably an incantation that would deflect the barrel just enough to ensure Reichart's safety.

Andrew extended his arm, the handkerchief dangling from his fingers. With no carefully crafted spells, Pavel could only hope he might overcome Reichart's deceit with raw arcane force, so he pulled on the nearby ley line and drew every bit of power he could from it.

Andrew dropped the handkerchief and it fluttered to the ground.

Pavel aimed his pistol at Reichart's chest but the spell pulled it to one side so the muzzle pointed a few feet off target. The German bastard simply walked forward at a slow and measured pace, his pistol still aimed at the sky. With his spells in place to control the two weapons, and believing he faced a mundane human with no arcane defenses, he had nothing to fear.

Pavel couldn't force the barrel of the gun back on target, so he drew all the power he could handle, fed it into the ball of lead in the pistol, and pulled the trigger. The gun roared and kicked in his hand, emitting a cloud of grayish white smoke that momentarily hid his opponent from view. He didn't think of Reichart's chest or arms or legs or any specific target. He simply willed the bullet to strike him anywhere and fed it power.

He tensed, waiting for Reichart's bullet to fly through the cloud of smoke and pierce his heart. But a light breeze slowly dissipated the gray haze to reveal the German bastard standing arrogantly about forty paces distant, an egotistical grin on his face. His confidence was so great he still hadn't aimed his weapon at Pavel and it remained pointed toward the sky. But then the grin disappeared, he blinked uncertainly, frowned and looked down.

Reichart wore a white blouse, and in the middle of his stomach a bright red stain slowly blossomed.

"First blood," Andrew called. "This duel is over."

Reichart grimaced, shook his head and aimed his pistol at Pavel. Looking down the gun's barrel, Pavel pulled on the ley line and summoned more power just as the bullet exploded from the muzzle with a flash of gun powder. Pavel released the power, willing the musket ball to divert to one side. When it tore into his arm it felt as if he'd been hit by a hammer wielded by a brawny peasant worker. He spun and staggered, but managed to remain standing.

Andrew and the physician rushed to him. "How bad is it?" Andrew demanded.

As the physician examined the wound, Pavel didn't feel like a dying man, and he wasn't surprised when the doctor said, "Just grazed him. I'll bandage it, though it'll be quite sore for several days, but he'll be fine."

Forty paces away Reichart lay on the ground, groaning piteously, his second kneeling over him. Pavel said, "Then why don't you see to him. His wound appears to be much worse."

The physician looked Reichart's way and his face clouded with anger. "He fired after first blood. That shot was not part of the duel, so it was an attempt at murder. I'm not inclined to treat such a man."

Pavel said to Andrew, "But I wish it."

Andrew grinned slyly and said, "After such cowardliness, what little honor he has will be completely erased if he is magnanimously treated at Lieutenant Konklinov's request."

The physician nodded and matched Andrew's grin. The three of them walked over the wounded man. The physician knelt and examined him, then declared, "A gut wound. Very nasty!"

••••

"He failed," Ag shouted, sitting up in bed next to the beautiful Unseelie witch he'd fondled during the duel. "He was completely unaware he was dueling against another practitioner. Is he that stupid?"

Karpov had been witness to Ag's famous temper a number of times, and knew he could not reason with the king until he'd fully vented his anger. "Reichart is not stupid, but is frequently blinded by overconfidence."

The witch growled angrily as the king climbed out of bed, leaving her languishing naked on the sheets. She made no attempt to cover herself, nor did Ag, for that matter, his erect penis slowly drooping.

When the king had invited Karpov to join him to witness the duel, he'd had no idea Ag would provide a sideshow to entertain Vladimir and Alexei. The king had laid back in bed, watching the event play out in the scrying mirror, while the witch performed various acts of pleasure on him. The Slav and the big, dumb bear hadn't paid the least bit of attention to the duel, and were now having trouble hiding the bulges in their pants.

Karpov said, "Couldn't you have helped Reichart, even if only to make him aware of his opponent's capabilities?"

"Absolutely not," Ag said, pacing back and forth across the bedchamber. "If I'd done anything more than simply insert him into the story, Magreth would have suspected something, and we'd not walk away from this with our hands clean. We had to count on his animosity toward the Young Mage to drive him to some sort of violence."

He stopped beside the bed. The witch rolled over onto her hands and knees and crawled across the bed to him. "Darling," she said, as she reached out and stroked his limp penis.

"Not now," he shouted, and hit her with a resounding slap that knocked her onto her back.

She lay there with her legs spread, a trickle of blood running down her cheek. And she smiled, her eyes looking hungrily at the king's penis, which was now rising to a state of excitement. She and Ag were both so . . . Unseelie. *Yes*, Karpov thought. The only way to truly describe them and their proclivities was *Unseelie*. By itself that one single word carried so much meaning.

••••

In the drawing room of Prince Andrew's residence, Katerina paced back and forth in front of Marya, who sat on a comfortable couch. She suddenly realized that she was wringing her hands like a fearful maiden, so she forced them down to her sides. But as she imagined Pavel lying wounded and dying, without conscious thought her hands crept back together.

"Sit down, child," Marya said. "Your pacing is upsetting to an old woman."

Katerina turned on her and stood over her. "I can't. What if he's horribly wounded, or even killed?"

"The fates will do as the fates will do."

Katerina threw her hands up. "I know, I know."

She began pacing again.

That morning she'd insisted on attending the duel, had thrown a bit of a tantrum when everyone else, men and women included, had refused her. At least Prince Andrew had allowed the two of them to wait in his drawing room so she'd know the outcome immediately upon their return. She absolutely loathed the idea that she would appear to be the fearful woman waiting to learn the fate of a man, but she could no longer hide her feelings.

Katerina heard the clop of the horse's hooves and the rattle of a carriage's wheels on the cobblestones in the residence's courtyard. She turned toward the front of the building, but Marya called after her, "Child, help a fat, old woman up."

Katerina turned back and helped Marya stand, then spun about and rushed to the front of the house. She met Andrew, his physician and Pavel entering. Pavel wore his coat merely thrown over his shoulders, and her heart skipped a beat when she saw the bloody bandage wrapped around his left arm just above the elbow. The look on her face must have prompted the physician to speak. "It's nothing, a minor wound."

Andrew smiled mischievously. "And Pavel Andreyevich took first blood from Captain Reichart."

Katerina whooped, wrapped her arms around Pavel's neck and kissed him, but when his eyes widened she came to her senses and remembered they weren't alone. She released him, and stepped away from him, blushing like a schoolgirl.

The physician raised an eyebrow and grinned. "That German behaved in a most reprehensible fashion."

"I need a brandy," Andrew said.

They retired to the drawing room, where Andrew served drinks and related the events of the duel.

"Firing his weapon after first-blood," Marya asked. "That's not allowed, is it?"

The physician's face took on a hard and angry look. "No. And doing so is a cowardly act, tantamount to an attempt at murder."

The physician had another appointment awaiting him, so Andrew escorted him to the courtyard. As the door to the drawing room closed, Pavel turned to Katerina and Marya. He held out the arm with the bloody bandage, "I'd like a practitioner to look at this, make sure it doesn't fester. And I'm not very good at healing."

Katerina guessed the wide-eyed look on Marya's face reflected her own. "Practitioner?" the older woman said, enunciating each syllable of the word carefully. "Then you are . . ."

"Yes," Pavel said. "I am, just as you two are. You should also spread the word among practitioners that Reichart spelled both pistols, his to achieve greater accuracy, and mine to divert the musket ball from him."

Katerina said, "But that's forbidden."

"Yes," he said. "I would wager good money he's never challenged a practitioner before, and probably wouldn't have challenged me had he known I could detect his treachery."

Andrew returned. "Come, Pavel Andreyevich. We have much to attend to if we're to leave tomorrow morning."

••••

Pavel dearly wanted to spend his remaining hours in Moscow with Katerina, but with so little time before he and the prince rode to the western front, and with so much to do to get ready, that proved impossible. He and Katerina managed only a few minutes alone that evening. He stole a few kisses, though he didn't have to try terribly hard to steal them.

"Wear this," she said, handing him a small, silver charm attached to a leather thong.

He sensed the magic she'd woven into it. "What is it?"

"I'll know if you're hurt, and I'll know where you are."

He tied the thong around his neck, then hid the charm beneath his blouse so it rested against his chest.

"You must come back to me, Pasha," she said.

The next morning Pavel and Andrew rode out of Moscow, not sure where they'd catch up with General Kutuzov.

"As an aide-de-camp to the general," Andrew said, "I'll no longer have a retinue, so I petitioned Kutuzov on your behalf, informed him of your experience in Persia.

You've been promoted to captain, and you'll be in command of a squadron of hussars."

Pavel said, "My thanks, Your Excellency."

"It's the least I can do. Because of you, I'll be that much more prepared for my first experience in battle."

Pavel didn't think anyone could be prepared for that. He recalled his first experience in battle and the gut wrenching fear that had almost overwhelmed him; fear that he'd be killed, and also fear that he'd lose his nerve and run like a coward. He reached up and touched the charm Katerina had given him, and wondered if he would ever see her again.

••••

Five days after Pavel left for the western front, Katerina stood at the window watching heavy rain pelt down and soak the Moscow streets. Behind her she heard the rustle of Marya's skirts as she walked into the room. The older woman stopped beside Katerina and said, "You've done nothing but brood since that young lieutenant of yours left the city, and I tire of your mood."

She'd tried to put Pavel out of her mind, but he filled her thoughts during every waking moment of the day.

"I'm sorry," Katerina said. "I'll try to be more pleasant."

"That rain will soon turn to snow."

"Yes, winter is not far off."

"I've been thinking," Marya said. "I have a dacha on the outskirts of Lviv in the western Ukraine. It'll be a bit warmer there than here in Moscow, and Lviv is a charming city, so I've decided to spend the winter there. I would like you to accompany me. It would comfort me."

"I don't know," Katerina said, unable to tear her thoughts away from Pavel, and her fear that he might be hurt or killed.

"It would also be that much closer to the war."

Katerina looked her way, wondering what Marya had in mind. "Isn't that a bit dangerous?"

Marya shook her head. "It's still a few hundred miles east of the armies, so there's nothing to fear. But we'll hear of any developments much sooner than here in Moscow."

Katerina had no doubt there was more, so she waited for her to say it.

"And should your young lieutenant be hurt, you'll be able to get to him in about a week's time, much faster than a month-long journey from here."

Katerina smiled.

17

War and Defeat

ANDREW AND PAVEL caught up with General Kutuzov in Poland in mid-September. The commander-in-chief was a bit portly, with silver-gray hair, but he had a commanding presence. Andrew introduced Pavel to the great man.

"So you fought in Persia?" Kutuzov asked.

"Yes, Your Excellency."

"Prince Andrew tells me your superiors spoke well of you. It's good to have you with us. I need experienced officers in this war."

They immediately assigned Pavel to a squadron of hussars. He considered himself lucky when he learned half his men were experienced veterans.

News came that Napoleon had chosen not to invade England, had instead marched south from Boulogne with close to 200,000 troops. Kutuzov's army spent the rest of September travelling southwest through Poland and Bohemia. During that time their Austrian allies met the French in a number of battles west of them. Pavel's squadron was given the duty of scouting the countryside in that direction, which entailed carrying dispatches between the Austrian and Russian armies. They heard news of disastrous losses and one defeat after another. Then in mid-November, as they retreated east, Kutuzov trapped one of the French divisions in a valley between two Russian columns, and even though Pavel was not privy to the discussions of the general staff, he knew they would now fight a pitched battle.

His squadron assembled with the rest of their regiment on a ridge overlooking the trapped French about five hundred paces below them. The hussars had skirmished throughout the day. As light cavalry, it was their job to patrol the flanks and ensure no surprises came their way. The constant pop of musket fire filled the late-afternoon air, along with the whistle of cannon balls streaking by overhead. Great clouds of grayish-white gunpowder smoke wafted across the battlefield, frequently as dense a heavy morning mist. Pavel knew he wasn't alone in hoping it would prevent the French marksmen from seeing them well enough to aim their muskets accurately.

The Russian infantry had the French badly outnumbered, and assaulted them on three sides. Pavel's regiment had been tasked with crushing their flank with a massed charge, not a tactic normally employed by hussars and other light cavalry. But it was their regiment ready and present just where the assault was needed.

The terrain separating them from the French was ideal for cavalry: open, unfarmed grazing land with a thin carpet of grass and only the occasional rock or tree. Unfortunately, it also gave the French a clear line of fire when aiming their weapons. Pavel checked the two flintlock pistols holstered to his saddle, an action he'd already performed a half-dozen times.

The colonel commanding Pavel's regiment drew his sabre and spurred his horse forward a few paces so that all could see him. Pavel and the other squadron commanders responded by doing the same. At that range they had little to fear from musket fire, and the French artillery officers held back, knowing their grapeshot and canister shot would be much more devastating at closer range.

The colonel raised his sabre high and spurred his horse into a trot. Pavel and the other squadron captains mimicked him and the men behind them followed suit. Pavel fought to restrain his own mount as it pulled at its reins, eager to break into a premature charge. They'd covered fifty yards when the colonel increased his horse's stride to a canter. Pavel and his men did likewise, and his horse no longer fought his control. When they reached a range of four hundred paces the colonel shouted, "Charge," and spurred his horse into a gallop.

That was always the moment that sent a shiver up Pavel's spine, the sound of hundreds of horses' hooves thundering on the ground, the animals struggling and grunting with the effort, the men shouting. Three hundred paces from the enemy, the French line fired its first volley and musket balls hissed past Pavel's head. A rider on his left grunted and fell out of his saddle, a horse on his right collapsed with its rider. At two hundred yards the French cannons belched massive clouds of smoke, and canister shot hissed through the ranks of cavalrymen.

Pavel's horse stumbled and slowed, but didn't fall. He spurred it hard, but no matter how much he tried it slowed further and fell behind the main line of the charge. The animal had dropped back to an uneven limp and Pavel guessed it had taken a musket ball somewhere. Then grapeshot from a French cannon took off its head and it collapsed, falling to one side. Pavel managed to jump clear just as it hit the ground, landed on his feet and converted his forward momentum into a shoulder roll. As he came up a musket ball slammed into his chest, high and to one side near his left shoulder, dropping him to the ground.

His head swam as intense pain washed through him, and he struggled to hold onto consciousness. A musket ball zinged off a nearby rock. He needed to find cover from the French fire or die, so he took a chance, raised his head just enough to look about, and spotted the carcass of a recently killed horse. He crawled toward it on his stomach, his left arm a useless weight dragging at his side. When he reached the dead animal and took cover behind it, he tried to burrow into the mud of the battlefield. The repeated thump of musket balls slamming into the animal's body warned him the French were blanketing the field with withering fire. He could do nothing but lay there and hope he survived the night.

A hunting hawk screeched somewhere high above him, and for some reason that drew his attention away from the battle. He rolled over onto his back and looked up into the slowly darkening late-afternoon sky. Through drifting clouds of gunpowder smoke he spotted the hawk easily, circling above him and gradually descending. It cried out again, an eerie sound, then pulled in its wings and plummeted toward him in a dive. At the last instant the hawk flared its wings, pulled up a few feet off the ground, killed its speed, and transformed into a tall humanoid shape obscured by shadows that fluttered about it maddeningly. The shadows dissipated, and an enormous woman stood over him easily seven feet in height. She had pale, golden hair twisted into strange, roped tendrils that hung past her shoulders, wore a tight, gray leather outfit with leggings and no skirt. She held a shadowy broadsword in her right hand with an unstrung bow strapped to her back. He marveled that no musket ball touched her as she stood over him in the midst of the battle raging about them.

He felt consciousness slipping from him, knew he must be hallucinating. "Sabreatha," he said, though he had no idea how that name had come to him.

She sheathed the broadsword in one quick motion, then reached down, gripped him beneath his armpits, and lifted him as if he weighed no more than a child. She threw him over her shoulder like a bag of potatoes, and with his chin bouncing against her back she walked off the battlefield. Pavel found it an exceedingly uncomfortable way to travel.

••••

In the drawing room of Marya's dacha in the Ukraine, Katerina sat at a small writing table composing a letter to Pavel. Nearby, the older woman sat reading a book and softly humming a little peasant tune.

When Katerina finished the letter, she stood and crossed the room to a window. Outside wet snow fell from a gray sky as sunset approached. It was too warm for the flakes to last long, though they did dust the ground briefly before melting, but that would change once night fell and the temperature dropped. Her hand tightened about the charm mated to the one she'd given Pavel, and only then did she realize she'd clutched it desperately.

They'd heard rumors of the Austrian defeat at Ulm, and finally had it confirmed only a few days ago. As Bonaparte's victorious army advanced eastward, they'd considered returning to Moscow, but had decided against that for now. With Kutuzov's army present to oppose the French advance, they'd have plenty of opportunity to leave should further disaster strike.

Without warning the charm came to life. Katerina gasped and stepped back from the window.

"What's wrong, dear?" Marya asked.

Through the charm Katerina sensed pain and fear washing through Pavel. She also sensed a confused scene of strange images consistent with a semiconscious mind. She turned to Marya and said, "It's Pavel. He's been hurt . . . badly."

With an effort, the stout woman rose from the couch. "Can you tell if he's still alive?"

"Yes, he is?"

"And you can locate him?"

"Yes."

Marya nodded thoughtfully. "I'll instruct the coachman to prepare to depart tomorrow. We'll find your lieutenant and make sure he's cared for properly."

••••

Pavel drifted back to consciousness lying on his back on a cot. He heard men groaning piteously all around him, a few crying out in agony. He raised his head, though that was about all he had the strength to do. Someone had carried him off the battlefield; he had a vague memory of a strange, giant woman, but he dismissed that as the ravings of his fevered mind. He recalled regaining consciousness lying on the ground back on the ridge from which his regiment had begun their charge. Then some soldiers picked him up and piled him into a wagon with other wounded. As he scanned his surroundings he realized someone had deposited him in a field hospital located in a large barn somewhere. It was filled with wounded soldiers, some lying on cots and some on the dirt floor.

He lay back and drifted in and out of consciousness for some unknown time. Then several pairs of hands lifted him off the cot, and the pain in his shoulder returned with renewed intensity.

They placed him gently on a wooden table. Two officers loomed over him, one on each side, a major and a young lieutenant, both wearing bloody aprons over their uniforms. Four orderlies stood behind them looking on. The older of the two officers with gray at his temples said, "Ah, you're awake. That's a pity. We're going to have to dig that musket ball out of your chest."

He stuck a plug of leather in Pavel's mouth and said, "Bite down on that. It'll help . . . a little."

He looked at the orderlies. "Hold him down."

Pavel had never been under the surgeon's knife for anything as serious as this, but knew on an intellectual level what was coming. The orderlies grabbed his arms and legs and clamped them to the table by leaning heavily on them. The surgeon produced a long, thin metal instrument encrusted with both fresh and dried blood. When he inserted it into the wound, a sharp jab of pain shot through Pavel's chest, he bit down on the leather and groaned. As the surgeon probed about for the musket ball, jolts of agony washed up and down Pavel's left side; he spit the plug of leather out and screamed. At some point he mercifully lost consciousness.

••••

As the coach rode toward a large, old barn, Katerina nodded to Marya and the older woman called out to the coachman, "Please stop at that barn."

The coachman pulled the carriage up to the front of the barn and reined the horses to a stop. Almost immediately a footman opened the carriage door, then assisted both women down out of the carriage. An open wagon filled with wounded and dying soldiers had been parked at the entrance to the barn. A group of burley men lifted a soldier out of the wagon and carried him inside. Another wagon carrying wounded pulled up as they stood there, while an empty one drew away. There were also men carrying draped bodies on stretchers out of the barn and placing them on the ground to one side. Somewhere far in the distance they heard the faint pop of musket and cannon fire. The smell of burnt gunpowder permeated the air about them.

Katerina clutched at the charm hanging from her neck, and from it she sensed that Pavel lay somewhere within, gravely ill. To Marya she said, "He's inside."

With soldiers moving about everywhere, the two well-dressed women stood out. A young Austrian officer approached them. He bowed and spoke to Marya. "May I be of assistance, madam,"

"Yes," Marya said. "We're looking for a Russian hussar officer named Pavel Andreyevich Konklinov. We received word that he was gravely wounded and taken here."

"If you please," he said, "follow me."

He led them into the barn to a young officer seated at a table, gave the fellow Pavel's name and asked about his condition. The fellow consulted some papers, then said, "I have no record of a Konklinov, though there are many here who remain unidentified. Are you a relation?"

Katerina said, "I'm his wife." It was a lie she and Marya had agreed upon.

The young officer waved a hand toward rows of wounded men lying on cots and the dirt floor. "You're free to look around, see if you can find him."

Katerina didn't need to *look around*. She turned slowly, her hand clutching the charm, and when she faced Pavel's direction it pulsed steadily. In that way they quickly found him lying on a cot, a bandage on his left shoulder, his pale and drawn face covered with streaks of mud and a sickly sheen of oily sweat.

Katerina knelt on the dirt floor, caring nothing for her dress. With Marya standing over her, she carefully peeled back the dressing on his wound to reveal a nasty hole in his chest near his shoulder. The skin around it had an inflamed reddish hue, with yellowish puss oozing from the hole.

"The puss is a good sign."

An older officer with gray at his temples and wearing a bloody apron stood beside Marya. He added, "That means the bad humors are being expelled from his body."

Practitioners understood far more about infection than the mundane medical profession, and Katerina wanted to scream at the man.

"You're his wife, I hear."

"Yes. May we take him with us?"

He hesitated. "I'm not sure—"

"Come now, major," Marya said forcefully, taking him by the arm and leading him a short distance away.

Marya was more than capable of handling the man. In a matter of minutes the major had a couple of the burly orderlies carry Pavel out to their carriage, and with the assistance of Marya's footmen, they bundled him inside.

••••

While Katerina may have been the stronger witch, Marya was by far the better healer. As the carriage bumped along the road headed east, the older woman immediately began cleaning the wound and expunging the infection with a series of spells and charms she'd prepared in advance. The first night they stopped at an inn frequented by well-to-do travelers.

Marya ordered hot water brought up to their room in buckets. They stripped Pavel down, cutting away most of his uniform, then bathed him carefully with sponges, hot water and soap. As they washed him he showed not the least sign of life other than a constant and shallow intake of breath.

"Will he live?" Katerina asked, fearing the answer.

"I don't know," Marya said. "The infection is bad, and it's had almost a week to fester. He certainly might have died under the care of that surgeon. We'll just have to be diligent and hope for the best."

They forced the coachman to push the horses, and late in the afternoon on the fourth day of travel they reached Marya's dacha. Pavel still burned with fever, and when not comatose, he mumbled weak, incoherent words about strange visions. Sometimes his words were so faint his voice was barely audible. At one point she thought he said, "Katerina," so hoping he had regained consciousness she put her ear close to his lips.

"Katerina," he said, his voice barely a whisper. "Katerina," he repeated, and she realized he was still not lucid.

"What about Katerina?" Marya asked.

"Should have . . ." he mumbled, ". . . told her . . . stole my . . . heart."

As Katerina blushed, Marya smiled knowingly and said, "I'm going to make sure this young man lives so he can tell you that to your face."

Marya showed Katerina how to use her raw, arcane power to burn the infection out of him. They took turns caring for him through the day and night, and each time Marya relieved her, Katerina fell into an exhausted sleep. On the third night back at the dacha Pavel took a turn for the worse. Katerina tried to sleep when it was her turn, but she lay awake, restlessly rolling back and forth beneath her covers. She finally gave up on getting any rest, lit a candle, threw a robe over her nightgown, and wandered down to Pavel's room. She found Marya seated in a chair beside his bed. The older woman looked exhausted.

"Get some sleep," Katerina said. "I'll watch him."

"Thank you, dear," she said. "He's alternating between fever and chills. When the chills come, pile blankets on and do whatever you can to keep him warm."

Sitting in the chair beside his bed, Katerina found it difficult to keep her eyes open. She drifted off, then snapped awake, and repeated that several times. She was close to losing the battle against sleep when the sound of Pavel's teeth chattering brought her fully awake.

She stood, grabbed a spare blanket and draped it over him. The shivering continued, so she added another blanket, and another. The room seemed stiflingly hot, but that was just her fear and sense of helplessness, overheating her with anxiety. ". . . do whatever you can to keep him warm," Marya had said.

Katerina untied her robe and let it drop to the floor. She was warm and he was not, and skin-to-skin she could transfer warmth to him more readily, so she untied her nightgown and let it drop to the floor as well. She lifted the blankets and slipped into bed beside Pavel, wrapped her arms around him, and fed him power.

She awoke at Marya's touch on her shoulder, her body still wrapped around Pavel, the rays of the morning sun splashing through the window.

"My dear," Marya said. "I think you and he are connected in some way. I should have let you help more with his healing. The fever has broken."

18

A Stolen Heart

WHEN PAVEL AWOKE he lay on his back in a comfortably warm bed in a nicely appointed room, his head and shoulders propped up on a wealth of pillows. Rays of sun splashing through a window lit the room, and through the blurry panes of glass he saw snowflakes falling outside. He didn't know if it was morning or afternoon.

He lay there for a while without moving, simply glad to be alive and not dreaming the unreal hallucinations of a feverishly delirious mind. He recalled that strange giantess he'd called Sabreatha carrying him off the battlefield and laying him down gently out of harm's way. That had certainly been a hallucination. And Marya and Katerina, he hoped his dim memories of them were real, though he did have one recollection of a beautiful, young Katerina lying naked next to him in bed, her body wrapped protectively around him. That was certainly another delusional memory, though one he wished had actually been real.

With his right hand he carefully touched the bandage near his left shoulder. The wound was quite tender, and any pressure sent an agonizing shock through his left side. But the hole in his chest no longer throbbed with the burning pain of infection, and he breathed easily.

"Ah, I see our patient has returned to the living."

He recognized Marya Dmitrievna's voice, tried to turn his head, but pain in his shoulder prevented him from turning far enough to see her. The stout woman stepped up beside his bed with a towel draped over her arm and a maidservant standing beside her. The maid held a pail from which steam rose in faint wisps.

"We were about to bathe you," Marya said, "and change your dressing."

Pavel was completely naked under the blankets and the maid blushed at the implication in Marya's words, while the older woman didn't show the slightest bit of color.

"But that can wait," she said. "Since you're conscious and lucid, let's get some food into you."

She turned to the maid. "Leave the pail of water and go to the kitchen. I believe we still have some roast pork from yesterday's supper. Tell the cook we'll have some of that, and some hot tea. And tell Katerina Valtrovna that our young man is awake and would probably like to see her. That should do for now."

••••

Though Pavel started out weak as a kitten, under the care of Marya and Katerina he healed quickly. Marya pushed him to get on his feet as soon as possible, saying, "The sooner you're up and about, the quicker you'll heal and grow strong."

At first Pavel couldn't stand without aid. "Katerina will help you," Marya said. "I would, but I'm much too old and fat to support a strong, young man like you leaning on me. Why, I'd probably topple over."

Pavel had no objections to that. It meant he and Katerina spent hours together with her on his arm holding him tightly, sometimes just taking laps about the drawing room, sometimes bundled up and walking through the snow-covered gardens of the dacha. In a matter of days he progressed to the point where he could walk without assistance, so to his disappointment Katerina stopped gripping his arm tightly.

"No, no, no, no, no," Marya said. "In the early stages of healing, weakness can come and go, so hold him tightly, my dear, lest he fall."

Katerina rolled her eyes, but complied. Pavel didn't mind.

After a few more days of Marya's and Katerina's spells, and regular walks with Katerina on his arm, Pavel stopped wearing a sling. At that point there was no doubt in his mind he'd not weaken again, but Katerina continued to hold his arm as they walked, so either she hadn't realized yet that she was no longer needed, or she liked it as much as him. He hoped it was the latter.

One afternoon Marya went into the city to visit some friends and do a little shopping. "I'll be staying the night with my friends, and won't return until tomorrow sometime."

Standing at a window in the drawing room, Pavel watched Katerina and Marya walk to the waiting sled arm in arm, a light snowfall dusting everything. A footman helped Marya into the sled and the two women exchanged a few final words. The coachman snapped the horse's reins and the sled pulled away from the property. Katerina waved until it was out of sight, then turned and walked back into the dacha.

Pavel would soon be well enough to return to his regiment, and that depressed him. He heard the rustle of skirts behind him as Katerina crossed the room. She stopped beside him at the window, both of them looking out at the falling snow. "What are you thinking?" she asked.

"That soon I must return to my regiment."

"Oh dear, I don't want to think about that at all."

He turned to face her. "Then you don't want me to go?"

She hesitated for a moment, then turned to him with a thoughtful look on her face. "Tell me, why did you befriend Anatole in Petersburg? You two are so different."

"I didn't befriend him," Pavel said. "He befriended me when Dolokhov told him I was a sorcerer."

"Why?"

"He wanted me to use arcane power to help him with something."

"Help him with what?"

Pavel hesitated, but Anatole's proclivities were well known, so he decided the truth was in order. "He desperately wanted to seduce you, and was willing to use any means possible to do so."

She smiled and emitted a soft chuckle. "Yes, he was so obvious. So what did he want from you?"

"Since you had spurned his advances, he thought I might compel you with sorcery."

Her eyes flashed with anger. "You agreed to help him seduce me?"

"No," Pavel said. "I didn't agree."

"But you befriended him, or at least you accompanied him to that soiree to help him."

"No. He spoke to my superior officers, and he's a nobleman, so I couldn't refuse him."

"So then you did agree to help him, eh?"

Pavel realized he was digging himself into a deeper and deeper hole. "I lied. I told him I'd gladly help him if I could, but I couldn't because the only arcane powers I had were in Dolokhov's imagination."

"So you would have helped him then?"

"No."

"Then why aren't you trying to seduce me yourself?"

Pavel had been ready to throw out some sort of defense to the next accusatory question, but to that, all he could say was, "I . . . I . . ."

She smiled and raised an eyebrow. "Stammering like that makes me think you wish you could."

He decided to try something different, hopefully to change the subject. He reached out, put his arm around her waist and pulled her against him. She didn't resist, so he said, "Perhaps all I was hoping for was another kiss."

"But I'm a tainted woman. That's why Anatole thought he could have me so easily. Is that your intent, Pavel Andreyevich?"

He purposefully ignored her question and said, "Let me ask you a question."

She waited for him to speak, looking at him curiously.

He recalled the naked body lying next to him during his delirium. "I have a faint and indistinct memory of you lying beside me, giving me warmth with your body while I was most ill. Was that just a dream?"

Her eyes widened, and he had his answer.

"Well I thank you for that. And I also recall that you were completely naked at the time. Was that just a dream?"

Her eyes widened further, and she blushed.

He lowered his head and put his lips against hers, and the kiss she gave him was passionate and hungry. He sensed something between them, that they were connected in some way. When their lips parted she smiled at him, all the shyness and blushing gone.

"Did I really steal your heart?" she asked, her lips brushing faintly across his.

"Like a thief in the night," he said. "But I have one more question."

She looked at him suspiciously.

"Perhaps I want to seduce you," he said, "but do *you* want me to seduce you?"

She gave him that same cat-anticipating-a-meal smile she'd given him in the garden that night at the ball. "You'll know the answer to that only when you try."

In the fashion of the day she wore a gown cut low in the front and back. It exposed her neck and shoulders and a hint of her breasts. He kissed her again, and as their tongues fought a pleasant little war she pulled her body tightly against his. When their lips parted he lowered his head further, planting kisses down the side of her neck and along her shoulder. When he brushed his lips across the swell of her breasts above the gown she gasped.

He had the strangest feeling. "Why do I feel as if we're nothing more than characters in a historical novel?"

She grinned and said, "I've had the same feeling, but if that's all we are, then I'm rather enjoying the story."

That afternoon Paul learned that undressing a woman in an early nineteenth century dress with an empire waist took quite a bit of time, which he didn't mind. It involved a great deal of pins and straps and ties. He thoroughly enjoyed the lesson, and Katherine clearly enjoyed teaching him.

••••

"You have to stop this, now," Magreth shouted, pacing back and forth across the audience chamber.

Cadilus cringed as the queen's eyes filled with flame, and primordial Sidhe spirits fluttered about the room like startled sparrows.

"We can't have them as lovers," she said. "They'll become too strong."

"I'll try," Cadilus said. "But I can't succeed if the triple goddess resists me."

"I don't care," she shouted. He had never before seen her so agitated. "Just do whatever you can."

A rather creative thought occurred to him. "I have an idea, Your Majesty."

She stopped pacing, looked at him pointedly and said, "What?"

"I may not be able to stop them from becoming lovers in this dream, but they still must return here."

She calmed down and gave him a curious look. "And?"

"And we'll have ready access to them, so they'll be subject to our power. I can counter the triple goddess by instilling doubt in both of them. And I'll tell Si'entha to move more quickly. She needs to control the young man through his heart."

The flames disappeared from the queen's eyes and she smiled like a hungry predator.

••••

Katerina---Katherine—Katerina— *No*, she thought, *I'm Katherine*.

Katherine had expected to wake up in bed lying beside Pavel—Paul—Pavel. Instead she found herself standing in Magreth's audience chamber with Pavel—Paul— beside her, both of them facing Magreth and Cadilus. The two fey looked at them smugly, as if enjoying some joke at their expense. The queen's eyes were not filled with flames, which was some comfort.

Katherine looked down at her clothing. Gone was the early nineteenth century dress, cut low in the front and back, exposing her neck and shoulders. Once again she wore the black, wool, pleated skirt, gray sweater, Kate Spade jacket, and the ankle-high Prada boots. They had returned to where they'd started as if only a few seconds had passed, when in fact they'd been in Russia for months. From the look on Paul's face, the transition had stunned and disoriented him as much as her.

She recalled their afternoon and night together and the way he'd kissed her, kissed her in a lot of places she quite liked. She'd enjoyed the feel of him in her arms and his touch, enjoyed him so much she wanted to remember every second of it. But she forced her thoughts back to the moment, realizing their love making had all been an illusion, nothing but a dream. She looked at Pavel—Paul, and wondered if he'd shared the same dream, or experienced something completely different.

"You lied," Paul said, taking a step forward aggressively. "You said we'd be here for only a matter of minutes, but we've been gone for months."

The two fey looked at each other and smiled knowingly, then looked again at Paul. Magreth said, "Dear Mr. Conklin, we have kept the terms of our bargain, for only a few seconds have elapsed since we put you in Tolstoy's story."

Paul staggered back a step and shook his head as if dazed. Both of them had so little real experience with the fey, it was quite possible Magreth had spoken the truth. Katherine realized she needed to snap out of the stunned, prissy woman act and join him on the offensive.

"No," she said, and was pleased that her voice came out hard and angry.

At her irate tone the two fey frowned.

Think, she told herself. It had been months—no seconds—since Paul had struck the bargain with the two fey. But it felt like months, and somehow she needed to recall the terms.

"As I recall," she said, her voice still strong and hard. She paused, as if doing so for dramatic intent, when in fact she was stalling for time to gather her thoughts.

"As I recall, the terms of our bargain included *unharmed and unmolested.*"

She pointed at Paul. "He suffered a musket ball buried in his chest, then the agony of having it dug out of him using barbaric surgical procedures and without anesthesia."

Both of the fey frowned uncertainly, and the queen lifted her chin haughtily, as if doing so could deny Katherine's accusations.

Katherine continued. "Then he suffered weeks of fever and delirium, and came very close to dying. And I know that illusions in Faerie carry with them so much more than illusion."

With her chin still held high, Magreth said, "And your point is?"

Katherine put her hands on her hips and gave the queen a nasty grin. "You broke the terms of our bargain, so you are now further indebted to him."

Magreth stepped forward angrily and slashed a hand through the air like a sword. "Absolutely not."

Katherine wasn't sure her next gambit would work, but it was worth a try. "We should ask the little people. Don't they arbitrate such disputes?"

Magreth's eyes filled with fire, and little shadows darted about her like a flock of starlings. "They are not neutral in this."

Clearly, the queen did not want the leprechauns involved. And since she and Paul had been there for just a few seconds, it was only the previous day that they had uncovered the spells Cadilus and Magreth had used to keep the two of them apart. Katherine lifted a hand and examined her fingernails as if bored. "I'd also like to see what they think about the spells you used to make me avoid Paul." She looked up from her fingers and into the queen's eyes. "My father is even more unhappy with you than I am."

Cadilus stepped forward, leaned close to Magreth and whispered something in her ear. As he spoke her lips tightened into a pucker and her nose wrinkled with fury. When he finished, the queen simply vanished.

Cadilus said, "We'll consider your petition."

"It's not a petition," Katherine said. "It's a demand."

She looked at Paul, noted he still appeared stunned and disoriented. Having a little cat-fight with Magreth had cleared her head nicely. She turned her back on Cadilus, held out her hand to Paul and said, "We're leaving."

Paul took her hand, and Katherine found it quite easy to return them to the boundary in the National Cemetery.

Her father and Colleen were waiting for them, and her father said, "Well that was quick. How'd it go?"

19

A New Alice

PAUL LET KATHERINE lead him like a blind man. He couldn't wrap his head around the fact that it had all been illusion, an enormous hallucination that had lasted for months—seconds, he reminded himself. A part of him wanted to return to it, because there he'd tasted the scent of Katerina's skin, or had it been Katherine's? But had she experienced the same illusion, and he wondered now if they really had made love, or he'd just imagined it.

When they approached McGowan and Colleen, the old man said, "Well that was quick. How'd it go?"

That confirmed it. They hadn't really experienced anything more than a few seconds of a dream. "We were in Faerie for months," Paul said.

Colleen and McGowan both frowned.

"Faerie?" Colleen asked.

"Months?" McGowan asked.

Katherine had clearly recovered from the disorientation of the illusion much better than Paul. She explained how she'd mistakenly taken them to Faerie, told them of Paul's bargain with Magreth and Cadilus, and that they'd both experienced a months-long hallucination, though she didn't elaborate.

The old man said, "I think Colleen and I need to hear this story in detail. Let's go back to my place."

McGowan hailed a cab and they rode back to his house in silence. That gave Paul an opportunity to recover from his confusion, and by the time they assembled in the old man's study, he could finally put two thoughts together with some sort of clarity.

Colleen and Katherine sat down in the two wingback chairs in front of McGowan's desk. McGowan offered Colleen a shot of whiskey, but she declined. Paul stood by the hearth, while McGowan poured two glasses, then handed one to Katherine and the other to Paul. "You two look like you really need this," he said.

They sat in silence for a few moments. Paul sipped at his drink, while Katherine upended hers and tossed it down in a single gulp. She held out the glass to her father. "I could use another."

He retrieved the bottle, crossed the room and splashed more whiskey into her glass, then she started talking. She told her story, her eyes gazing absently at the whiskey in her glass as she swirled it around. The parts that involved Paul—Pavel—were pretty much as he remembered, though in her version there was no mention of a love affair between Pavel and Katerina. They were merely acquaintances, not even a kiss. He learned a little about Katerina's life as she talked of times when he wasn't present. She finished by telling them of her argument with Magreth about breaking their bargain. Then all three of them gave Paul a questioning look.

"That's pretty much how I remember it," he said. He wasn't about to tell them he'd dreamed he and Katherine—Katerina—had become lovers, not if Katherine hadn't shared that same dream. He told them of how he'd come across Pierre, Anatole and Dolokhov the night of the incident with the bear and the policeman, and of other times when Katerina wasn't present, no mention of kisses or love making. Since Katherine hadn't experienced that part of the illusion, he wasn't about to tell them he had.

"Straight out of *War and Peace*," Colleen said. "Amazing!"

One thing still troubled Paul. "Magreth said they wanted to test us. What were they testing?"

"I can only guess," Colleen said. "Perhaps they wanted to see your normal response to unusual circumstances. They like to manipulate mortals—you two in particular—and to do that they need to know and understand you as individuals."

McGowan said, "I think they also suspect you two are stronger together, and wanted to confirm that."

Colleen stood and crossed the room to Paul. "May I examine your wound?"

Paul shrugged and unbuttoned his shirt. She slid the collar aside, then delicately touched the skin around the healed wound. It was still a little tender.

"There's a nasty, puckered scar here," she said, "exactly the kind a musket ball would make. Did you have that before?"

Paul couldn't understand how illusion could be so real, and yet not. "No, never been shot by a musket before."

"There might be some residual scar tissue," Colleen said, still probing the wound. "I'll look at it later today and clean up anything I find. But that proves you were injured, that you did not come out of this unharmed, and as Katherine pointed out, Magreth violated the terms of your agreement and is further indebted to you."

McGowan said, "I'll see to it word gets around, make sure the little people hear of this. She's going to owe you big time, kid."

As Paul buttoned his shirt he heard the muffled sound of a cell phone. Katherine retrieved hers from her purse and looked at the display. "It's the hospital. I have to answer it."

She put the cell phone to her ear and said, "Dr. McGowan here."

She listened for several seconds and her eyes widened. "Thank you," she said. "I appreciate the call."

She put the cell phone back in her purse and smiled rather unpleasantly. "Eric was brought into the ER this morning with a gunshot wound. Most of the staff there is aware he's my ex-husband, and a few thought I'd want to know. His story is that he now collects antique firearms, was restoring an old flintlock pistol, and accidentally shot himself in the abdomen. He's out of surgery now, but he's got a nasty case of peritonitis."

Her smile broadened into a satisfied grin.

••••

It took Paul a couple of days to get to the point where the Tolstoy hallucination didn't dominate his thoughts, and to come to terms with the fact that he and Katherine, or Pavel and Katerina, weren't lovers. He was now quite certain Pavel and Katerina's lovemaking had been strictly his illusion, one Katherine hadn't shared. Because of that, since returning from nineteenth century Russia, he'd thrown himself into his work and avoided the McGowan clan. He took a break one afternoon and walked down to Jessie's for a sandwich.

On the way back to his apartment building he ran into Eileen Cleary on the sidewalk and noticed there was something different about her. Her hair, it had been fairly long before, but she'd had it cut chin length. "You cut your hair," he said.

"Yes," she said, brushing a few strands out of her eyes. "I like it shorter. It's so much easier to take care of this way."

The new style she'd adopted seemed familiar in some way, but he couldn't quite place it, and he thought she looked much more attractive with it cut that way.

"How about that beer I owe you?" she said.

His first thought was of Katherine and he was about to decline, but when he opened his mouth he surprised himself by saying, "That sounds good."

He followed Eileen up the stairs to her apartment. She wore an overcoat which she pulled off and dropped on her couch. She had on a light summer dress in pastel blue that ended just below the knees, and he liked the way she looked in it. Her apartment was laid out exactly like his, a small one-bedroom with a bathroom, living room and tiny kitchen.

"Grab a seat and I'll get those beers."

He pulled off his jacket and tossed it over a chair, then dropped down onto the couch next to her overcoat. He heard a refrigerator door open, the clink of a couple bottles, the door closing, then the pop and hiss as she opened the beers.

She walked out of the kitchen carrying a beer in each hand, and as she leaned over to hand one to him, the top of the pastel dress billowed out, and there was no doubt she was not wearing a bra. He lowered his eyes to the beer and kept them there.

"So what do you do?" she asked as she sat down on the other end of the couch, the overcoat between them.

"I'm self-employed, an architect, do contract work for some of the firms in the city."

The pastel dress was a little sheer, and he realized he could see dark areolas through it. He looked into her face, decided to keep his eyes locked there, and noticed there was something familiar about her that he found attractive—not just the hair. It was a face he enjoyed looking at.

They sipped their beers and chatted. She'd recently moved to San Francisco and was looking for work. He tried not to stare at her.

When he finished his beer he stood and said, "I've got to run."

He tossed his jacket over his shoulder and turned toward the front door. He noticed a mirror hung on the wall, and in it saw his own reflection and that of Eileen. For just an instant he thought he saw the reflections of Cadilus and Magreth standing in the room with them. But it was just a momentary flash of his imagination, and he realized the two fey were too much on his mind.

He crossed the room and opened the door, then turned back to say good-bye. He hadn't realized Eileen had followed him to the door, had done so without making a sound, and he ran right into her. She stumbled and he grabbed her shoulders to keep her from falling. She smiled at him invitingly, and he had the strongest urge to kiss her.

"Thanks for the beer," he said, his voice a little unsteady.

"No, thank you," she said softly, reaching up and putting her hands on his upper arms, "for helping me with the TV that day. Any time you want . . . another beer . . . or anything, for that matter, just stop by. You don't have to call first."

Paul felt a little pinch on his arm where her hand rested, but thought nothing of it. He wasn't sure how he got out of there without kissing her, but somehow he managed it, though he questioned his own sanity for not making the attempt. He found her attractive in a way he couldn't define, and couldn't put her out of his mind until he opened the door to his apartment and stepped inside.

Madge the cat was curled up on his couch. She stood and arched her back, stretched, then sat back on her haunches. "So," she said, "you scored with Katerina. Who's next, the pretty girl downstairs? Is she your consolation prize since you can't nail Katherine?"

"Score, nail" he said, unable to keep the frustration out of his voice. "I told you I'm not trying to score with anyone. You sound like a pubescent high school boy telling stories in the locker room."

She licked a paw, shook her head and rolled her eyes as no cat should. "You need to listen to old Madge here. Do what I say and you'll get your rocks off with the right girl."

"Get my rocks off!"

••••

When the door to her apartment closed, Si'entha crossed the room and stopped in front of the mirror hung on the wall. Magreth and Cadilus stood within it.

The High Chancellor made no effort to hide his displeasure. "I asked you to accelerate your efforts. If you'd tried just a little harder you would have had him in your bed this day."

Cadilus's ire did not frighten Si'entha. "Yes, I would have. But I'd merely have had the pleasure of his body. I'd not now have his heart, and I need his heart in chains to bind him to me. That's the only way I can truly sever his attraction to the young woman."

Magreth nodded and said, "She's right, High Chancellor. If she can bind the strings of his heart, she can destroy him thoroughly. And simply luring him to her bed will not accomplish that."

Magreth and Cadilus had thoroughly briefed her on Paul and Katherine's little sojourn in Tolstoy's Russia. "You said they became lovers in the *War and Peace* illusion?"

"Yes," Magreth said. "That was unfortunate."

"I don't think that will hinder you," Cadilus said. "We've clouded their memories so each thinks the other did not share that illusion. It may even make the young man more amenable to an alternative relationship."

"You know," Si'entha said, "he caught a glimpse of you in the mirror, but I clouded his thinking with a bit of beguilement."

"We'll have to be more careful," Magreth said.

"Using beguilement," Cadilus asked, "was that wise?"

"I had no choice," Si'entha said, "and I only used the slightest bit, just enough to turn his thoughts away from what he saw. His own household wards will have easily washed it away as soon as he stepped into his apartment."

Magreth said, "I must compliment you, my dear. Adopting the appearance of his dead wife is a stroke of genius, especially since most of it is merely mechanical."

"Yes," Si'entha said. "Simply wearing her preferences in clothing, and cutting and styling my hair as she did, leaves no arcane scent. We're of a similar height and body type, and my facial features are not far from hers. But as his attraction to me grows, I'll have to use some arcane forces, which means I can't see him in his apartment, within his wards."

Magreth asked, "What magics did you have in mind?"

"I'll have to use a tiny bit of glamour to complete the appearance of his wife's facial features. And if he were to realize on a conscious level that I'm her doppelganger, he might begin to wonder about my appearance. I'll also have to cloud his thinking a bit, and that does carry some risk of discovery, especially since you clouded their memories of the illusion in Russia."

"It's worth the risk," Magreth said. "But while you should move cautiously, do take the High Chancellor's words to heart, and also move expeditiously."

She bowed her head respectfully. "As you wish, Your Majesty."

When the conversation ended, and the scrying mirror became just a mirror, Si'entha sat down and examined the short, blond hair she'd pulled from Paul's arm as he left her apartment. "Perfect," she said.

Using it, she carefully constructed a spell keyed to signal her when he came near. Then she walked out of her apartment and up one flight of stairs. With a bit of saliva she pasted the hair to the stair post at the top of the stairs just outside his apartment. She applied a little arcane power and the hair disappeared, but the spell remained.

She returned to her apartment, confident that every time he came down the stairs, the spell would let her know he'd stepped outside his household wards.

••••

Nooo, the voice said. *The little girl is too dangerous.*

Seated in his car, he watched her walk off the soccer field to her waiting mother. "But she's a real Alice," he said, "a true Alice."

If this alerts the necromancer, we could be destroyed.

"But I have to," he said. "I need her, I want her so badly. She has to be mine."

We can find others less dangerous.

"No more prostitutes," he said. "They're not true Alices. They don't look at all like Alice."

The voice continued to haunt his thoughts, but he ignored it.

The girl's mother was one of those helicopter moms, constantly hovering about the child, which presented a serious problem. She filled the girl's every waking moment with some sort of activity. When she wasn't in school, she had soccer practice, an art class and additional tutoring. He couldn't just casually walk by and spell the girl. He'd have to spell the mother as well, and trying to get them both at the same time would be just too dangerous. And even if he succeeded, the authorities would find it odd that both mother and daughter had died on the same day of no apparent cause. He'd have to think carefully about his approach this time.

He started the car and drove away, but an accident on the freeway turned it into a parking lot, and it was well after dark before he got clear of it. The Saturday traffic on the Bay Bridge was light, but the accident had delayed him enough that it was well into the evening by the time he parked his car in the monthly permit garage he used in the city. He locked the car and walked out onto the street.

A group of young people in wild costumes passed him on the sidewalk. They'd clearly been drinking and partying, though not excessively. But when he spotted another group of young people in unusual outfits it gave him pause. And then he recalled that it was Saturday night on the weekend before Halloween. With the holiday next Tuesday, tonight would be costume-party night for all the young professionals who worked during the week. He wasn't a party person.

He walked on toward his apartment, but about half way there he saw another Alice, a real Alice, and his heart leapt. She was a lot taller than the other Alices, and her dress appeared to be too small.

He stopped and waited while she and her friends walked toward him, laughing and enjoying themselves. As she got closer he realized she was older than his previous true Alices, probably in her twenties, and wearing a very sexy version of Disney's classic Alice outfit. The plunging neckline exposed considerable cleavage, he thought the little skirt might be called a minnie, and she wore white stockings up past her knees supported by black ribbon garters. And while the shoes were Alice shoes, they included platform soles and extremely high, spiked heels. So it wasn't exactly a true Alice costume, but she was beautiful beyond imagining. Could she be a true Alice?

Yes, the voice said. *She is a true Alice, and she won't be as dangerous as one of the younger ones.*

"And she won't have a mother hovering over her," he said.

He hadn't realized he'd spoken out loud until a middle-aged woman passing by gave him a wary look, then veered away from him to the edge of the sidewalk before walking past him. He ignored her and watched the young woman and her friends walk away. She could be a true Alice, or at least very close, certainly so much better than the prostitutes.

He had no trouble following her. She and her friends were loud and boisterous, and in their outlandish costumes he easily tracked them from a distance. They led him to an apartment building, but they pressed a button at the front of the building and waited to be admitted; probably a party, and certainly not her building.

He glanced up and down the street, spotted a cheap restaurant about a hundred feet away. Just outside he bought a newspaper from a machine. The rush-hour for dinner had ended some time ago, and it wasn't the kind of place frequented by tourists or young professionals, so he had no trouble getting a table near the window where he kept an eye on the building she'd entered.

He ordered a cup of coffee and sipped at it while pretending to read the paper. After an hour, the waitress hovered near his table more frequently, so he ordered a sandwich and some fries, and that seemed to satisfy her. He hadn't had dinner so he ate the sandwich quickly, but he nibbled slowly at the fries to make them last. He continued the pretense of reading the paper while he watched small groups of costumed young people enter and leave the building at regular intervals. A little over two hours after he'd sat down she emerged with a young man. There was no mistaking his Alice.

He called the waitress, got his check and paid quickly, left her a nice tip, but nothing too extravagant; the little things could make one stand out, and she might remember him.

It was easy to follow Alice and her companion since they frequently stopped and shared a passionate kiss. They led him to an apartment building some blocks away. He watched her fumble in her purse for her keys, then open the front door. Satisfied he now knew her address, he turned and walked away, happy that after some preparation, Alice would soon be his.

Only then did he realize he had come to think of her as a *true* Alice.

••••

Breathing heavily, Paul back stepped and barely managed to avoid the tip of Anogh's sword as it hissed past his nose. They disengaged and circled one another.

It sure didn't feel like they were just practicing. He'd tested his Sidhe sword, and he could have shaved with it quite comfortably, though that would be a bit awkward since it was longer than his arm. And when Anogh swung his blade or thrust it at Paul, he did so with no restraint and lightning speed. But every time Paul expected to find himself spitted on the Summer Knight's sword, the Sidhe miraculously stopped his own momentum in a heartbeat. They'd freeze, and Anogh would point out something Paul had done wrong.

"Enough," Anogh said. He lowered his sword and backed away from Paul. "You're doing well."

The Sidhe didn't say it, but in the tone of his voice Paul heard the implied finish to the sentence, "—for a mortal."

Paul didn't feel like he was doing well. He'd now been through several lessons with the Summer Knight, and he'd learned that real sword fighting was nothing like in the movies, two skilled opponents trading blow after blow: strike, parry, thrust, strike, parry, thrust. Instead, two swordsmen faced one another, circling, judging, looking for an opening. When one finally did strike, their blades met no more than two or three times, and it was over in a flash. If neither won, they circled to try again.

Paul raised his rapier and looked at it. His gut told him they were doing something wrong. Not that Anogh was anything less than an incredibly skilled swordsman and instructor, but they'd missed something. It occurred to him that maybe it was the rapier that was wrong.

"You seem troubled, Young Mage," Anogh said as he sheathed his sword and approached Paul. He followed Paul's gaze and looked at the upraised rapier. "You never did tell me the true reason you want to learn the sword."

Paul looked into Anogh's eyes. They were vertically slit like a cat, and amber in color. "To be honest, I really don't know why I want to learn the sword. It's just that some instinct tells me I should."

Anogh's eyes narrowed in thought. "I see nothing about you that hints at compulsion."

Vertically slit eyes, Paul thought. He was almost certain that somewhere he'd encountered another being with vertically slit eyes, but definitely not one of the denizens of Faerie. And there was the memory of a sword, a vague and indistinct recollection like that from a dream. "I seem to recall a sword," he said, looking once again at the rapier in his hand. "But it was nothing like this." He fought to recover that memory, and an image came to him. "The hilt was long enough for a two-handed grip, with a simple cross brace, and a straight, wide, double-edged blade covered in runes."

Anogh's eyes widened, and Paul realized that never before had he seen the Seelie mage show consternation or surprise. "You're describing a broadsword, a weapon for cutting, not thrusting. Can you recall the runes?"

Paul shook his head. "No, they're just a blur."

"Where did you see this blade?"

"I'm not sure," Paul said. "But I think . . . maybe in a dream."

Anogh flinched and frowned. "The triple goddess frequently compels us through dreams."

Paul recalled the Faerie nut-case who shifted between an old crone, a beautiful young maiden, and a naked, skeletal corpse, all three of them just plain batty.

Anogh's eyes grew distant as he considered Paul's words. He said, "It is always dangerous to ignore hints from the Morrigan. We'll practice with broadswords from now on. Apparently, that's what she wants."

••••

Paul was still having trouble getting the whole *War and Peace* thing out of his system. It felt as if months had elapsed since he and Katherine had accidentally stumbled into

Faerie, when in fact it had been less than a week ago. He spent the morning working on a contract-job for old man Strath, his former employer from before all the crazy stuff had started. But his thoughts kept returning to Katerina and the taste of her skin.

No, he thought. *That had been Pavel Andreyevich, a character no more real than their love-making.*

About noon he decided to break for lunch, but there was nothing at all appetizing in his refrigerator. He didn't want to go to the trouble of preparing something, so he decided to go down to Jessie's and get a burger. He grabbed his coat, walked out of his apartment and locked the door. But one floor down he ran into Eileen Cleary on the stairs. Again, he was struck by the thought that he'd met her before and knew her from his past.

"Paul," she said, giving him a big smile.

He tried to return her smile, tried not to appear dazed by the disorientation he still felt from the Tolstoy adventure. "Hi, Eileen. How's it going?"

"Great," she said, pulling on her coat. But then she hesitated and frowned at him in a thoughtful way. "Can you spare five minutes?"

He wasn't in any great hurry, so he said, "Sure, what do you need?"

"I'm trying to mount that TV on my wall, but I can't lift it and handle a wrench at the same time. I've got everything ready, so it'll just take a couple minutes."

"Let's do it," he said.

She'd purchased one of those telescoping TV mounts that allowed her to pivot the screen so she could see it from the kitchen or the living room. She'd already screwed the thing to the wall, with the flat-screen TV resting on the floor beneath it. Paul made a quick double-check to be sure the thing was solidly attached to the wall. Then he lifted the TV and held it in place while she used a wrench to bolt it to the mount. They tested it by pulling the set away from the wall and pivoting it from side to side.

When they were done, a thought occurred to Paul. "Say, I was just going down to Jessie's for a burger. Want to join me?"

"Jessie's?" she asked.

"Jessie's Bar and Grill, just down the street; good food, and not expensive."

"Oh ya," she said. "I'd love to join you. I've noticed that place, was curious about it. But we're going Dutch, all right?"

Eileen demonstrated a healthy appetite. Paul learned a bit more about her job search; she was hoping for a position as a receptionist in a large law firm downtown. After they finished lunch they continued talking for another hour, then she went on her way to take care of some errands, and Paul returned to his apartment to finish old man Strath's job.

He felt good, felt refreshed, and realized it had been the first time he'd put aside his disappointment that his affair with Katerina had been nothing but an illusion. When he was with Eileen he thought only of her, and their past together.

No, that was wrong. They didn't have a past together, he reminded himself. So why did he keep thinking they did?

20

Compulsion and Desire

THE LUNCH WITH Eileen helped Paul get the whole Tolstoy thing out of his system. He felt some sort of attraction to her he couldn't explain, as if he'd known her for a long time.

The day after he had lunch with her the phone rang, and it was McGowan. "Colleen and I have been talking about your training. One thing we've avoided so far is compulsion spells, and the spells to defend against them."

"You mean, like black magic?"

"Yes, binding, compulsion and obsession spells, they're a subset of the black stuff. But they can be especially dangerous and damaging if you can't defend yourself against them, so Colleen and I think it's time you learned."

Paul recalled the way the witch Belinda had bound him to her with such spells. He might as well have been trussed up like a pig for the roasting pit. Once she'd wrapped him up that way, she'd delivered him to her demon master with ease, and he'd barely escaped with his life, thanks to Katherine.

Paul asked, "Why have we waited until now to do something about it?"

"Because these type of spells are extremely difficult, and dangerous. That's why they're pretty much reserved for advanced training, sorcerer grad-school kind of thing. But you're much stronger now, especially when you work together with Katherine. So we've asked her to train you. Can you go by her house this afternoon, say two o'clock?"

"Sure," Paul said, glad for the excuse to see her again.

Paul had spent the morning working at home trying to finish up the job for Strath, and hadn't bothered to clean up. So he ate a light lunch, showered, shaved, brushed his teeth, threw on his clothes and headed out the door with more than enough time to get to Katherine's. One floor down he ran into Eileen again just coming out of her apartment.

"Paul," she said. "Nice coincidence running into you this way. I really enjoyed lunch the other day. We should do that again. In fact, why not today?"

Paul almost said, "Great, let's go," but caught himself, remembering that he had an appointment with—

Looking into Eileen's face, into her eyes, he was so drawn to her he had to think for a moment to recall the appointment was with Katherine. He wanted to take Eileen into her bedroom and make love to her the way they'd made love so many times before. Even after Cloe had been born, he and she had found little ways of steeling an intimate—

He stumbled as he realized where his thoughts had gone. "Sorry," he said, stammering a bit. "I have an appointment."

He turned, and walked in a daze down the stairs, trying desperately to clear his thoughts.

••••

Paul managed to regain his composure by the time he reached Katherine's house, and had stopped thinking like a horny high school kid. Though when he thought about it, he hadn't been thinking like a pubescent boy trying to get laid for the first time, he'd been thinking how much he loved her, and that was way out of line. He was so not in love with Eileen Cleary. He barely knew her.

Katherine owned one of those two-story fifties houses in the Sunset district, with half the bottom floor taken up by the luxury of an enclosed garage, and a stone stairway that climbed up through the front yard to the entrance. Paul had been there once before, the night the Tertius caste demon had trashed the place. Then Karpov and his thugs had showed up and abducted him and Katherine.

He rang the doorbell, and when Katherine answered, she seemed a little uncomfortable. She probably hadn't yet gotten over the months they'd spent in Tolstoy's Russia. Paul sympathized with her on that.

"Come in," she said, her eyes meeting his for only the briefest of moments, then darting away to look elsewhere.

She had on a pale-blue blouse made of some shimmery fabric—probably silk or satin—and a tight pencil skirt cut just above the knees, though she stood there in her stocking feet, no high-heel shoes clacking on the travertine tile floor. She turned around and he followed her into the living room, thinking how much he wished she'd shared the illusion of Pavel and Katerina's love-making. It might have led to something more between them.

She paused in the middle of the room, looked over her shoulder without turning around, and the Katherine he knew returned. "And no checking out my ass."

"Why not?" he said. "What if I like checking out your ass?"

She grinned, but didn't turn around to hide her butt from him. "Well that would be just plain rude."

"Not if I do it when you're not looking."

She laughed. "Come with me," she said as she continued on through the living room and into a hallway on the far side.

At the far end of the hall he followed her into what he now recognized as a practitioner's workshop. It had a utilitarian workbench with a couple of stools, and several tall, enclosed cupboards. He glanced through another door and noticed it led directly into her bedroom. Apparently, as particular as she was about her own appearance, she was not one to make her bed.

The bedroom had two entrances: the one he stood in now that connected it to the workshop, and one directly off the living room. He was about to turn away and join Katherine when a small black-and-white cat sauntered into her bedroom from the living room. The little cat had a black splotch on her upper lip that looked like a half-Hitler mustache. He recalled that Eileen had seen Madge in the hallway outside her apartment when he'd helped her with the TV, so he had some hope the little feline wasn't a hallucination. She jumped up onto the unmade bed, sat on her haunches, licked a paw and winked at Paul.

Paul turned around and saw Katherine rummaging in one of the tall cupboards. "You got a cat?" he asked.

"Sort of," she said without turning around to face him, "though it's more like she got me."

"How do you mean?"

Katherine closed the door of the cupboard, then turned and walked to the workbench carrying several items. "Couple of days ago she streaked right between my legs when I opened the front door, and I haven't been able to get rid of her—kind of like she adopted me."

"Anything unusual about this cat?"

"Only that she seems a bit too healthy for a stray. Why do you ask?"

Paul crossed the room to the workbench. "Couple of weeks ago she adopted me the same way."

Katherine had placed a couple of little trinkets along with several other items on the workbench. The trinkets appeared to be made of silver. She looked at Paul curiously and said, "Really! How did she get all the way from your apartment to here?"

"She gets around."

"Are you sure it's the same cat?"

"I'm sure."

"Well, we'll have to pick a name for her."

"Her name's Madge."

Katherine shook her head. "Madge! That's a horrible name for a cat. It's so uncool. What made you pick that?"

"I didn't pick it. That's just her name. She told me so herself."

Katherine froze and her eyes narrowed. She spoke carefully. "She told you so herself?" She said it the way one might talk to a nut-case.

"Yes, in English, speaks it rather well for a cat. I think she can speak any language she wants to, but I wouldn't understand her if she spoke in Chinese. Told me that too."

From the look on Katherine's face she clearly wasn't sure if he was joking or serious, or just plain nuts. He added, "She said she's my familiar."

Katherine grinned and rolled her eyes. She'd clearly concluded he was teasing her. "We don't have familiars. That's just a thing fantasy writers put in stories."

She turned her attention to the two trinkets on the workbench. "We frequently use silver in charms and spells because it's a conductor of energies. But before we do anything else I'll make a little something we can use to kill the spells when we're done with them."

Among the items on the workbench were a plastic water pitcher, a large spoon, and a cylindrical container of salt. She picked up the pitcher, walked out of the room and a moment later Paul heard running water in the kitchen. A few seconds after that she returned carrying the full pitcher, placed it on the workbench, then poured a few teaspoons of salt into the water and stirred it with the spoon until the salt dissolved. Paul recalled that salt muted the power of arcane forces, and could be used to cancel or mitigate spells.

She opened a small jar with a commercial label that read *Bay Leaves*. "Bay is frequently used as a protection against black magic, but we can reverse that by adding blood to it."

She placed two dried bay leaves on the surface of the workbench.

"I need a few hairs," she said. From a drawer in the workbench she retrieved a pair of scissors, reached up to her own hair, carefully isolated a couple of strands and cut them. She laid them on the workbench, then cut a couple of Paul's hairs and placed them beside hers.

Explaining as she worked, she knotted together one of her hairs with one of Paul's. "In some spells the type of knot you use can have quite a bit of significance, but for these it doesn't matter. Just make sure they're tightly bound together."

She placed the knotted hairs on one of the bay leaves.

She swabbed her finger with rubbing alcohol, then produced a small, plastic device of some sort. "This is a disposable safety lancet used by diabetics to draw a few drops of blood."

She placed the tip of the lancet against a finger, Paul heard a snap and she tossed the lancet into a waste basket. She dripped a single drop of blood onto the knotted hairs on the bay leaf. "I used my index finger because we're going to try a repulsion spell first. After that we'll try an attraction spell, and for that we'll use the ring finger."

"It matters?" he asked.

"Oh, yes," she said. "The part of your body from which you take blood for a spell has enormous significance. The blackest of spells are sometimes created using . . . various body parts I won't mention."

"You mean naughty bits?" he asked.

She wrinkled her nose and nodded. "The naughtiest."

She swabbed the finger again with alcohol, placed one of the silver trinkets on the blood, hair, bay leaf combination, and lifted a candle. "Between the moment I light this candle, and the moment I blow it out, I'll be feeding power into the trinket, and everything I think or say will become part of the spell. So you have to be careful while the candle burns."

Paul sensed the flow of power as she lit the candle with a minor spell. Then, with her eyes locked on the trinket, she said, "I call upon the circle of friendship and alliance. May it spiral in reverse and repel the joy of common bond. I command thee, I bid thee, I pray thee, to make it so."

She blew out the candle, took the trinket off the top of the knotted hairs and set it aside, then lifted the hairs. "Now, to activate the spell."

He watched her touch a finger to her tongue and transfer a bit of saliva to the hairs. They flared brilliantly for an instant, and when the light died the hairs had disappeared. She looked at him and smiled like a school teacher. "So what do you feel?"

He didn't feel anything, and he said so. "Nothing." In fact, he was irritated with her that she'd use him as a guinea pig that way. "Nothing at all." His words came out a little harsher than he'd intended.

She lifted pitcher and poured a little salt water onto the bay leaf where the hairs had been. The feeling of irritation disappeared in an instant, and his eyes widened.

"It's quite subtle, isn't it?" she said. "What did you feel?"

He told her how he'd become irritated with her, as if it had been a natural development of her actions and his own thoughts.

"Now you try it. But this will be an attraction spell, nothing strong or powerful, just a little pleasant attraction. If it works I'll feel nothing more than a vague sense of happiness that you're here today, much like you felt a mild sense of irritation."

With the items they hadn't yet used, they repeated the combination of bay leaf, knotted hairs, blood and trinket. But this time it was Paul's blood, and she told him to use his ring finger to draw it. Katherine wrote something on a piece of paper and said, "Say exactly these words and feed power into the trinket while the candle burns, then blow it out."

Paul used a simple fire spell to light the candle, noticed Madge wandering into the workshop with a satisfied look on her face. He tried not to think about her crudely stated goal of *getting him laid*, nor how desirable he found Katherine. He looked at the paper Katherine had handed him and read the words carefully. "I call upon the circle of friendship and alliance. May it turn as it was meant to and yield the joy of common bond. I command thee, I bid thee, I pray thee, to make it so."

He blew out the candle.

"Now this time you're going to activate it by weaving it into my hair, which is a good way to hide it and make it stay with me wherever I go. It can also amplify the effect a little." She leaned forward. "Just tie the knotted hairs to one of mine and touch them with a little saliva."

Paul took the knotted hairs, isolated one of Katherine's hairs, and tied them together, then placed a little saliva on them. Like her spell, the hairs flared brilliantly, and when the light died, they were gone.

Katherine leaned away from him, cocked her head to one side and gave him a questioning look. "You did activate it, didn't you?"

"Yes," he said. "Is it working?"

She shook her head. "No. Nothing."

She frowned and shrugged. "It should have worked."

She paused, clearly waiting for something to happen, then she shrugged again and said, "Sometimes these things take practice. Father'll be disappointed, but we'll try again another time. How about tomorrow? And we can try a couple of tricks to counter compulsion spells. But I have an appointment so I have to get to the office now."

Paul agreed to come by the next day, and Katherine escorted him to the front door. He paused there, turned to her and said, "Anyway, thanks for trying."

"I'm sure it'll work next time," she said. She leaned close and gave him a friendly kiss on the cheek, a peck little more than the air-kisses he'd seen celebrities share on the red carpet at Hollywood events.

She started to pull away from him, but hesitated, then gently brushed her lips lightly down the side of his neck. He wasn't sure what to make of that.

She did pull away then, but paused with her face only a few inches from his and looked into his eyes. He'd never before noticed that her brown eyes had a hint of amber to them, which gave them a kind of sparkle. This time he came to her, leaned in and touched his lips to her neck, and she responded with a deep breath and a little shudder.

He whispered, "What about your appointment?"

She stepped back and away from him, her eyes wide. "Yes, my appointment, I don't know what came over me."

It irritated him that she'd start something like that with no intention of finishing it. So he stepped forward, closed the distance between them and put an arm around her waist.

"No," she said. "I'm sorry. I don't mean to be a tease, but I really do have an appointment, no Seelie interference this time."

He released her. "I won't say I'm not disappointed."

She smiled, a mischievous look in her eyes. "But I do have time for a real kiss."

She put her arms around his neck. He responded by wrapping his arms around her and pulling her close. She gave him a real curl-your-toes kiss, and he had trouble controlling his reaction.

Their lips parted and she said, "I've wanted to do that ever since we left Russia."

She leaned forward and nibbled on his earlobe.

He said, "But . . . you're . . . appointment."

"Yes," she whispered breathlessly, "my appointment. What about it?"

She planted a line of light kisses up the side of his neck, her lips barely brushing against his skin. She slid her lips across his chin and stopped at his mouth. The kiss she planted there was anything but delicate, and he sensed in her a hunger and need he wanted to fulfill.

"I think my appointment can wait," she said.

She thrust her hips against his and there was no way he could hide his own reaction.

"Gee, Conklin," she said, "I guess I'm rather flattered."

"I don't know if *flattered* is the right word," he said, having a little trouble speaking. "My thoughts are leaning toward something a lot more visceral right now."

With her pelvis pressed against him, she said, "That's rather obvious."

They kissed again, staggering in an odd little dance toward her bedroom, neither of them wanting to release the other, both moving in little, stuttering steps. About halfway there she grabbed his wrist and pressed his hand against her breast outside of her blouse, a very aggressive move that surprised him. They paused in the middle of the living room, and while kissing he unfastened the top button of her blouse. She growled like a hungry animal, and ground her hips against him.

In that way they progressed slowly across the living room: step, pause, kiss, undo a button, grope at each other for a moment or two, then repeat. By the time they reached the door to her bedroom he'd completely unbuttoned her blouse, and it hung open, revealing a lacy, pale-blue bra of a color that matched the blouse. She pushed him against the doorjamb, and while kissing him reached around behind herself. He heard the short wiz of a zipper, and the pencil skirt dropped to the floor. The lacy slip she wore beneath it followed a second later. His pants felt rather loose, and he realized that at some point she'd unbuckled his belt and unbuttoned his trousers.

She grabbed his wrist again, but this time slid his hand up underneath her bra. "I need you," she said, her breath coming out in gasps as she shoved her hand down his pants and grabbed him. "I want you so badly I need to have you. I must."

Must, need! he thought, trying to tell himself to forget it and just enjoy what was about to happen. *Why* that *choice of words?*

Must, need! The words had come out filled with desperation and longing, the way he'd felt about the witch Belinda, when she'd wrapped him in one compulsion spell after another so she could present him to her demon master Cassius. There'd been no joy in their lovemaking, just release at the fulfillment of a desperate need.

He and Katherine had worked their way to her bed, and over her shoulder he saw Madge the cat sitting there with a satisfied look on her face. She winked at him.

The spell! Katherine had said everything he thought or said while the candle was lit would become part of the spell. And Madge had wandered into the room just after he'd lit the candle, prompting him to think briefly of the little cat's efforts to *get him laid*, and how much he desired Katherine and would enjoy exactly that.

"Conklin," Katherine growled, breathing like a sprinter who'd just finished a race.

But what if he was wrong? What if he refused Katherine, and she was so insulted he never got another chance. Behind her Madge smiled the way no cat should smile.

Standing in her panty hose, bikinis and bra, Katherine tried to shove Paul's hand down her panties. "I am so ready," she said.

There was only one way he could be certain. He gave Katherine a shove, the back of her knees hit the edge of the bed, and she fell backward onto it, bouncing once.

"Ooh, Conklin," she said, pumping her hips at him, "are we going to do the big he-man thing?"

He lied, "I gotta pee first."

She widened her eyes and said, "Don't take too long, Mr. Macho."

He spun about, crossed the room and stepped into her workshop.

"That's not the bathroom," she said.

At the workbench he grabbed the canister of salt and upended it over the pitcher of water, pouring a steady stream of the stuff into it. If he was right, he needed it to be as salty as possible.

"What are you doing?" she asked. He didn't look over his shoulder, but from the nearness of her voice he knew she'd followed him into the workshop.

He lifted the large spoon, plunged it into the water and stirred desperately as he heard her cross the room.

She grabbed him by the arm and spun him about, then pressed her body against him. The panty hose were gone, and she'd unfastened the back of her bra, but hadn't removed it so it hung there loosely.

"No true gentleman just walks away from a girl in need."

He reached to the side, grasped the handle of the pitcher, lifted it, and dumped the contents over her head.

"Ahhh!" she shouted and stepped back from him. She looked at him, her eyebrows arched, her nose scrunched up in absolute fury, her dripping wet hair hanging lankly about her shoulders. "What the hell did you do that for?"

"I . . . uh . . ." he said, demonstrating his magnificent command of the king's English, and now realizing maybe he'd been wrong about the spell.

"What got into you?"

He decided to try a new tack. "I . . . uh . . ."

Somehow she managed about ninety Decibels. "Pouring water all over me."

"I . . . uh . . ." That didn't seem to be working any better.

She dabbed at the water on her face, then touched her fingers to her lips. "Saltwater?"

"I . . . uh . . . the spell."

She stepped forward and put her nose only inches from his. "Spell. What spell?"

"The . . . uh . . . um . . . attraction spell."

"Spell. There was no spell."

"Uh . . . well . . . uh . . . actually, there was."

Madge, sitting off to one side and licking a paw, gave him a pathetic look and said, "Mr. Articulate, wowing us with his lightning repartee."

"Spell," Katherine shouted, spitting drops of saltwater in his face. But then she flinched and looked at him oddly. Her voice dropped several octaves and she said, "Spell?"

Her eyes shifted from a hard, angry stare to an uncertain frown. Without moving her head she looked from one side to the other, as if only now understanding where she stood. Then she slowly lowered her head and looked down at herself, standing there in nothing but a pair of bikini panties and an unhooked bra that threatened to fall to the floor at any moment.

She spoke in an uncertain whisper. "Spell? You spelled me?"

Only then did he truly realize that he'd been right. He had triggered the blackest of spells.

She hugged herself, wrapped her arms tightly around her chest in a childlike attempt to hide her nakedness. "You . . . tricked me."

He saw the betrayal in the look she gave him. "No. I didn't mean to. The cat made me do it."

She looked at him the way he looked at the Faerie nut-cases he found so exasperating. "The cat?"

"Yes," he said. "You know, the talking cat."

The look on her face shifted to pure disgust. "Don't blame it on the cat, you fucking ass hole."

With her arms still clutched desperately—protectively—about her breasts, she turned and walked across the room. "I'd prefer you just . . . leave."

She walked out of sight into her bedroom. A moment later he heard a door slam, then the sound of a shower spraying water.

"Meow," Madge said.

Paul spun toward the cat, and while tucking his shirt in and buttoning his pants he made no attempt to hide his fury. "You did that, didn't you?"

She licked a paw and said, "Meow."

Paul knew he'd lost any semblance of control. "Don't *meow* at me. You made me think of just the wrong thing at just at the wrong moment."

"Meow."

"You did that. You made that happen."

"Meow."

"So now you only speak cat, huh?"

"Meow."

Paul tried to calm down. "I'm talking to a fucking cat," he said, and headed for the door.

"Meow."

21

Careful Preparation

KATHERINE LET THE warm water cascade over her head and down her shoulders. Everything had gone so terribly wrong. Paul's compulsion spell had been subtle, but quite powerful, more so than anything the witch Belinda had used on him. Such spells were exceedingly dangerous, and she couldn't understand what had prompted him to do that. It occurred to her that she should have Colleen check out her aura, make sure he hadn't harmed her.

As she stood there relaxing under the torrent of warm water, she fantasized about being in bed with Paul. But she crushed that thought; it was probably a little residual from the spell. It would have been better if the spell hadn't worked and they'd simply made love to satisfy their natural desires. That, she would have enjoyed thoroughly, though she crushed that thought as well. When she considered the way she'd acted—throwing herself at him that way, shoving her hand down his pants, forcing his hand up under her bra, and trying to cram his hand down into her panties—she wasn't sure she could ever face him again.

She toweled off, pulled on a bra and panties, then called her office. While the phone rang at the other end, the little black-and-white cat jumped up on the bed, sat on her haunches and began licking a paw.

Her receptionist answered, "Dr. McGowan's office."

After licking her paw, the little cat rubbed it behind her ear, grooming herself.

"Judy, it's Katherine. Something's come up and I'm going to miss my next appointment, and probably the one after that."

"Meow," the little cat said.

"I'll make your apologies for you," Judy said, "and reschedule."

Katherine switched off the phone and laid it on the night stand next to her bed. She stood there for a moment, took a deep breath, looked at the little cat and said, "Why does everything have to go so wrong?"

"Well, dear," the cat said. "That's quite your own fault, isn't it?"

"My fault?" Katherine said, the fury she'd directed at Paul now aimed at the cat. She curled her hands into fists, planted them on her hips, then leaned over the little animal and shouted. "I didn't do anything wrong."

The cat rolled her eyes. "Sweetheart, you want that man so bad it's pitiful. And here you were, all set to get your horns clipped, and you blew it."

"Horns clipped! Blew it. I didn't blow it. He's the one who killed the spell, not me. If he hadn't poured saltwater all over me, we could have gone right ahead—"

Katherine couldn't believe what she was saying. "Wait a minute. You've . . . you've got this all twisted around. And I don't need my horns clipped."

"Oh, honey," the cat said. "You so do. You need a little assault with a friendly weapon, a bit of bam-bam in the ham, some banana in the fruit salad." She shifted into a western accent. "You need to let that cowboy in your saddle so he can ride you like a stud-bronc on a mare."

"Friendly weapon," Katherine said. "Bam-bam . . . fruit salad . . . saddle . . . stud-bronc . . . you're . . . you're a complete potty-mouth. I'm not going to stand here and talk to a foul-mouthed cat."

She turned around and marched into her walk-in closet. Putting on some nice clothes would calm her, and a little shopping might help as well. A new pair of shoes would do wonders for her soul after the conversation she'd just had with that cat.

. . . conversation she'd just had with that cat!

"Meow."

Katherine spun around, found the cat seated on the floor in the closet doorway licking a paw.

"You . . . you . . . you talked."

The cat let out a dramatic, drawn-out sigh. "Do I have to go through the same conversation with you that I had with your young man?"

Katherine tried hard not to stammer, but couldn't seem to quite manage it. "But you . . . you talked."

The cat rolled its eyes. "Of course, I did."

"You didn't . . . just meow . . . you talked in English."

The cat spoke in a bored monotone, "And my next line is, 'Of course I spoke English. You wouldn't understand me if I spoke Chinese.' Then you say, 'But— But— You're a cat.'"

The cat grinned. "Am I right?"

Katherine knew that hysteria had gripped her, but she didn't care. "Exactly."

"I just have one question," the cat said. "I want to know why you think the name Madge is so uncool. You'd probably give me a stupid, cute name like Mittens. That would be so much more uncool than Madge."

••••

It was so much easier stalking a person in a large city like San Francisco, and as he mapped out the daily routine of his twenty-something Alice, he longed to see her in that lovely costume again. Of course, she'd only worn it for the Halloween parties she'd attended that night, and probably wouldn't wear it again for another year. But he wasn't about to wait that long to see his desire fulfilled, so he resolved to do something about it.

He decided he rather liked the *sexy* version of the costume she'd worn, rather than the conservative, Disney, young-girl look. On the younger girls the sexy outfit would not be at all appropriate and would destroy the appearance of innocence he so loved. But he'd come to realize that on this more mature Alice, this beautiful young career woman, the sexually appealing outfit only enhanced her attraction.

It wasn't difficult to find sexy Alice-in-Wonderland costumes. He simply did a search on the internet for exactly that and came up with hundreds of styles available for sale at prices he could easily afford. Some looked more like something a prostitute would wear, and he'd had his fill of hookers, so he studied the selections carefully; his Alice would not look like some cheap street-walker.

He chose an outfit that looked much like the costume she'd worn the night he'd first seen her. It was pale blue, with little touches of white satin that gave the impression of a pinafore, though that was purely an illusion. It had a short, little skirt that flared out from the waist with a frill of white lace, and a plunging neckline that exposed considerable cleavage on the model in the picture on his computer screen. From behind, the skirt was short enough to expose a hint of the integral panties sewn into it. He saw the crease where the model's thighs met her bottom, and an inch or two of her butt as well. He searched the internet to learn that he was looking at what was referred to as a bit of exposed *butt-cheek*, the kind of thing visible when young girls wore very short shorts.

He especially liked the little white collar connected to the back of the dress. It was much like the collar on a man's dress shirt, though it didn't connect in any way to the front of the outfit, but buttoned around her neck from behind without covering any of her chest or cleavage. He also selected a pair of white stockings that went up to mid-thigh, and a pair of black, ribbon, bow-tie garters to hold them up. He added a push-up bra to really emphasize the cleavage, and as an afterthought, he threw in a thong. Thongs were very attractive.

He had a little trouble finding the right shoes. That night on the street in San Francisco his Alice had worn high stiletto heels with platform soles beneath the toes. He wanted something similar, but they had to be shiny black with rounded toes like the Mary Janes a true Alice would wear. He eventually found a pair with two-inch soles and six-inch heels. And since he didn't know anything about women's sizing for clothing or shoes, he ordered three of everything in a range of sizes.

He found a small warehouse for rent in South San Francisco not far from the airport. Before signing the lease he spent several nights wandering the streets nearby to be certain there was little or no foot traffic after dark. The warehouse consisted of a single, large, open space, with steel beams and girders supporting the roof about twenty feet overhead. It had a one-room enclosed office at the back that included a small water-closet with a sink and a toilet, though it was otherwise unfurnished. He didn't want to give his Alice a place to hide from him so he brought in a contractor to remove the walls that enclosed the water closet, which turned the office into a single, square room with a sink and toilet against one wall. He added a bed and mounted a full-length mirror on the wall. It was a dark mirror, basically a pane of glass painted on the back side with flat-black paint. He mounted an identical full-length, dark mirror on the outside wall of the office.

One criteria for choosing this particular warehouse was that the office was not connected to any exterior walls, but was contained completely within the space of the warehouse near the back. That way he could enclose it in a nice, tidy circle, and no one would hear her screams.

••••

When Paul walked into McGowan's kitchen he found Colleen seated at the table, nursing a cup of coffee. Katherine stood near the sink leaning against the counter. The look she gave him should have dropped the temperature in the room about ten degrees.

Paul asked, "Where's your father?"

"In his office," she said.

Her tone should have dropped the temperature in the room another ten degrees, something that Colleen clearly noticed. The older woman's eyes narrowed as she looked at Katherine, though she didn't ask why Katherine was so obviously angry with him.

"He's on a call from New York," Colleen said. "I think with Charlie Stowicz."

Paul recalled the McGowan-class wizard from New York. Stowicz looked like a dockworker, short, stocky, a little overweight, heavily muscled, and he had a permanent five-o'clock shadow. Paul had met Stowicz in Dallas at the mansion of a woman named Salisteen, a witch in the same class as Colleen. Salisteen was a tall, elegant black woman, African-American, looked like a retired model a bit past her prime, but still drop-dead gorgeous. She staffed her mansion with low-level practitioners, all male, young, muscular, and runway model handsome, made them wear little white coats and tight black pants.

Paul walked around the table to the coffee pot on the counter, which took him close to Katherine. As he came near she walked away from him, walked around the table as if to put it between them for protection. Somehow he had to get her alone and apologize for the attraction-spell snafu.

Paul turned away from her to the coffee pot, poured a cup, and as he turned back old man McGowan walked into the kitchen, a look of distaste on his face. Not fear or anger, Paul thought, but clearly distaste.

Colleen asked, "What's wrong, Walter?"

All he said was, "Amen's coming."

Colleen disappeared into one of her shadows.

"Exactly," McGowan said, and Paul guessed Colleen's reaction had been instinctive.

McGowan poured a cup of coffee and sat down at the table opposite Colleen. "Karpov's made a lot of accusations," he said, "about Paul summoning the Caorthannach."

Colleen's shadow dissipated and she looked perplexed. "Paul didn't summon the Caorthannach."

McGowan drummed his fingers on the table and Paul saw his anger building. "That hasn't stopped that Russian ass-hole from making the accusations, and at this point, the best we can hope for from the others is that they'll withhold judgement until they have the facts."

Paul couldn't put Colleen's reaction out of his thoughts. "Who's Amen?"

McGowan's eyes lost their focus, and he appeared to think for a moment before answering. "Very powerful wizard from Egypt. Charlie said he'll be in New York next week, and the two of them will be here a day or two after that. They've also called in Salisteen. She'll be arriving about the same time."

"Amen?" Paul asked, thinking that for some reason he was supposed to be wary of Egyptians. "Like you say at the end of a prayer?"

"No," McGowan said. "Amen, like the Egyptian god. There were a number of ancient pharaohs named Amenhotep, which means something like 'Amen is satisfied.' Just like him to choose the name of a god."

When Katherine spoke, Paul realized she was thinking along the same lines as him. "The two of you seem upset that this Amen fellow is coming. Why?"

Colleen said, "Because he's . . ."

When she hesitated, McGowan finished for her. "Because he's just plain scary. He's very powerful."

"Like you two?" Paul asked.

Both of the older practitioners shook their heads. McGowan said, "No, Amen is in a league all his own. I wouldn't take him on even if I had Colleen, Charlie and Salisteen to back me. The four of us might lose."

Katherine whistled and said, "Holy shit!"

"Exactly," McGowan said. "Last time I saw him was in Omaha. A practitioner named Dwayne Eagers, one of our contemporaries"—he looked at Colleen—"had been experimenting with demons, brought a nasty one over and was feeding it human lives. Charlie, Salisteen and I went there to put him down, and Amen came to help. Not sure if we could have done it without him."

"That's what bothers me about Amen," Colleen said. "When he shows up, someone always dies."

Colleen, McGowan and Katherine turned their heads and looked at Paul.

••••

When Katherine opened the front door of her house, she was relieved to see that Colleen had come alone as she had requested. As the older woman tossed her purse and coat on the couch, she said, "I'm curious why you want to see me without your father, and why he can't even know I'm here."

Katherine ignored the implied question. "I've made some tea. Would you care for some?"

Colleen raised an eyebrow and gave her a curious look. "Yes," she said.

Katherine poured them both tea, and they sat down at the small table in her breakfast nook.

"So," Colleen said. "We have tea, we're seated, and I'm here. Forgive me for being blunt, but let's not waste time with small-talk. Something's wrong, and I think you should tell me what."

Katherine didn't know where to start. "I had some difficulty with Paul, and if father heard about it he might become . . . very angry."

Colleen leaned back in her chair, steepled her fingers in front of her, and gave Katherine a penetrating look. "I'm listening."

"He spelled me," Katherine said, "a compulsion spell, and I'd like you to check me to be sure he didn't do any harm." After she'd said it, she realized it sounded more like an accusation than a simple statement of the facts.

Colleen leaned forward, reached out and took Katherine's hand. "If you're concerned he harmed you, then it must have been a very powerful compulsion spell."

Katherine simply said, "It was," though when anger clouded Colleen's features she knew she wouldn't be allowed to leave it at that.

"Okay," Colleen said. "Sit still and I'll check."

Colleen's eyes focused at a far distant point, and they both sat there without moving for several seconds. Then the older woman's eyes refocused and she said, "I see no damage, no harm done. What kind of a compulsion spell was it?"

"Sexual compulsion. I tried to teach him a simple attraction spell, and he turned it into strong sexual need."

Colleen shook her head vehemently. "That would be a truly despicable act, and that doesn't sound like Paul. Everything I've seen of him tells me he's a nice guy."

"Maybe he didn't mean to," Katherine said, feeling a little guilty she'd implied otherwise.

Colleen stared at her for several seconds, then said, "Tell me about it—everything."

Katherine purposefully skipped a few small pieces of the story, wasn't about to admit she'd shoved her hand down Paul's pants. When she finished, Colleen said, "You've left a few little bits out, haven't you, dear?"

Katherine felt her face growing hot.

Colleen continued. "I'll bet you were quite aggressive, which is a common symptom of such a spell. In fact, you were probably just plain slutty."

Katherine shook her head. "I just don't understand why he did it."

"Is it possible it was an accident?"

"Yes, I suppose."

Colleen's brow wrinkled thoughtfully as she sipped her tea. "Don't forget this is all new to him. It's been a little over a year since we first met him. Did you carefully explain that he had to control even his thoughts while the candle was lit?"

Katherine couldn't hide a grimace. "I said it, but I didn't make a point of it."

Colleen gave her a motherly smile. "It's quite clear you're attracted to each other, not just emotionally, but sexually as well. He probably had a thought or two along those lines while the candle was lit, not realizing how it would influence the spell. And you didn't react immediately, so he thought your natural attraction to each other drove your actions. When he realized otherwise, don't forget that it was he who broke the spell. He did the gentlemanly thing, so no other explanation fits with what I know of him."

Guilt washed through Katherine's thoughts.

"And I'll bet you're feeling rather embarrassed at the aggressive way you behaved. Threw yourself at him, didn't you?"

Katherine couldn't hide a grimace as she said, "Yes."

"But you shouldn't feel embarrassed. It was the spell, not you. Though if the two of you are attracted to each other the way I think, that would magnify the effects of the spell."

Katherine grimaced. "I kind of ended it badly. I think I owe him an apology."

"I'll bet he feels he owes you one as well."

Katherine prepared a light lunch and they talked about her adventures in Tolstoy's *War and Peace*. It was clear Colleen suspected she'd left out a few parts of that story as well, but the older woman didn't press her on the matter.

They called a cab. A few minutes later, as Katherine stood on her front porch watching the taxi pull away from the curb, Madge rubbed up against her ankles, and Katherine realized she'd forgotten to tell Colleen about the talking cat.

"No," Madge said. "I really don't think you and your young man should tell anyone about me. In fact, I'm rather confident you won't."

22

A Lesson From the Black

THE SHARP CRY of the hunting hawk startled Paul. He grabbed a towel and turned away from the sink full of dishes in his kitchenette, drying his hands as he walked into the living room. He stopped by the end table next to the couch where he kept one of the Sig Sauers, and slid the drawer open enough to grab it if he needed it. With his eyes locked on the mirror hung on the wall of his living room, he thought he knew what to expect, and Sabreatha didn't disappoint him.

The hawk shot out of the surface of the mirror, spread wings that almost filled his entire living room, and shifted into the shape of the seven-foot-tall crazy woman. Standing in the middle of his living room, she turned her head slowly and looked at him, her eyes constantly shifting color. Her pale, golden-haired dreadlocks fluttered in a light breeze, even though no wind disturbed the still air of his apartment. As always, she wore tight gray leathers, had that enormous broadsword strapped to her side, and held a longbow in her left hand.

He recalled that she hadn't tried to kill him in their last few encounters so he didn't reach for the gun, but he stayed close to the open drawer of the little end table. In fact, she'd saved his life by carrying a wounded Pavel off the battlefield in 1805 Austria. She opened her mouth, and as always seemed to have trouble speaking. When her lips moved her voice was just a whisper of thought. "Summer wishes me to aid you."

Paul had to think about that for a moment. "Summer? Do you mean Anogh?"

She slowly nodded her head once. "I know the broadsword better than he."

Again, Paul had to think carefully to get the meaning of her words. "You mean . . . it's time for a lesson?"

She looked over her shoulder at the mirror on the wall. "The Summer Knight awaits."

Paul had a couple of hours before he needed to be at McGowan's place, and he wondered again how Anogh knew the time was *convenient*. "Okay," he said, not sure what to expect. "I guess it's sword practice time."

He shut the drawer on the end table and tossed the towel across the kitchenette into the sink.

Apparently, that was all the permission she needed. She did that thing where she crossed the room in an inhumanly freakish instant. She wrapped her arms around him, reality shifted and he fell toward the mirror on his wall, then through it. Below him he saw nothing but air and a drop of several hundred feet. He gasped, but he didn't fall because of the massive talons supporting him, wrapped around him and pinning his arms to his chest. Above him he heard the whoosh of air displaced by the beat of giant wings, while the countryside of Faerie slid by below. Beneath him he saw a castle built of yellow stone.

Sabreatha circled above its battlements and descended slowly. As they got lower Paul saw a lone figure standing in the castle's empty courtyard, and he recognized the armor of the Summer Knight.

Sabreatha swooped over the wall of the castle and down into the courtyard. As the ground rushed toward him Paul gasped again. But the hawk pulled up at the last instant and deposited him on his feet wearing Sidhe armor with a broadsword strapped to his side and facing Anogh. The seven-foot-tall crazy women materialized beside the Summer Knight.

Anogh had a self-satisfied look on his face as he said, "Sabreatha wants to help. Draw your sword, Young Mage."

Paul drew his sword. The thing was just plain heavy. He'd already had two lessons with Anogh in broadsword fighting, and had learned that it felt only a little heavy at first, but after an hour of swinging it his forearms ached, and he struggled to hold the damn thing up.

Anogh stepped back as Sabreatha drew her sword and gripped it with both hands; there was no sign of the longbow. Paul and crazy-woman circled slowly, then she attacked, and he was thankful she didn't use that *move-in-a-blink* speed against him. She came in with an overhand strike, and he deflected it, their swords ringing loudly as they made contact. They separated and circled again.

Feeling clumsy and unskilled, Paul tried to go on the offensive and swung his sword in a flat arc. Sabreatha back-stepped just out of range, then in one motion she took her left hand off the hilt, wrapped it around the tip of the blade, and holding the sword at both ends she stepped in and slammed the hilt into Paul's jaw.

He must have gone down like a sack of potatoes, though he didn't recall how he got from standing up to lying on his back in the dirt, his head spinning, the side of his face throbbing painfully. He tried to open his mouth to groan, but a lightning-hot lance of pain shot up the side of his face and he realized she'd broken his jaw.

Standing over him, Sabreatha reached down with one hand, grabbed the front of his armor and lifted him to his feet. She held him there, and as the ground tilted crazily beneath him, he realized he couldn't have stood on his own. "You have much to learn," she said.

Without moving anything but his lips and speaking through his teeth, Paul hissed, "You broke my fucking jaw."

She smiled, reached up and brushed her fingers along the side of his face in an almost loving caress. The pain went away. It didn't recede slowly, it simply vanished in an instant. Paul's head cleared and he no longer had trouble standing. He experimented with his jaw, moving it up and down and side-to-side. Nothing! No pain or sign it had ever been broken.

Standing to one side, Anogh said, "Sabreatha can wound and heal with a gesture. And lucky for you, mortal, she doesn't want to kill you today."

Sabreatha said, "The lesson has only begun."

Paul backed away from her as she lowered herself into a crouch, her right foot back, her left foot forward, the hilt of her sword gripped in both hands. He tried to mimic her and did the same.

Once again they circled, Paul watching for an opening, but at the same time bracing for an attack. She lunged at him, spearing the point of her sword at his gut. He deflected it downward, enjoying a moment of satisfaction that he'd finally done something right. But she spun around in a flash, and the edge of her blade sliced through his Sidhe armor and cut a searing line across his stomach. He dropped his sword, hugged his abdomen with both arms and fell to his knees as blood poured out of the wound. His hand felt a slimy lump of flesh protruding from the muscle wall of his belly, and then a length of intestine spilled out. He desperately tried to keep the wound closed, but ended up on his knees with a true understanding of what it meant to literally spill his guts. He knelt there staring at his own insides hanging out of his abdomen and piled on the ground in front of him, then he vomited on them.

Sabreatha stood over him shaking her head sadly, then she leaned down and touched his stomach. The intestines in front of him squirmed and writhed as if they had a life of their own. Then they wriggled, and foot by foot slithered back up into his stomach like snakes crawling into a pit. The wound in his abdomen closed, the blood disappeared, and only the rent in his Sidhe armor remained as evidence of the ordeal.

Sabreatha stepped back two paces, gripped her sword in both hands, dropped into a crouch and said, "Get up, pick up your sword, and fight."

"You gotta be kidding," Paul said.

Her face remained expressionless. "Get up and fight, mortal."

Paul staggered to his feet, picked up his sword, and like the broken jaw he felt no aftereffects of his wound, of being gutted. He dropped into a crouch and again they circled.

She came in with an overhead strike. Paul stepped back and swung his sword up, the ring of the heavy blades sending a jolt up his arms and into his shoulders. His parry had deflected her sword to one side, forcing her to release one of her hands from the hilt. He lunged in, tried her little trick of gripping the tip of the sword with his left hand while holding the hilt with his right. The heavy gauntlets of his Sidhe armor protected his left hand from the sharp edges of the blade as he used it like a fighting staff. He swung the hilt upward and slammed it into her gut, landing a solid blow that forced her to grunt and stagger back.

Paul returned his left hand back to the hilt and pressed his advantage, lunging at her, aiming the point of his sword at her chest. But she side-stepped, blocked the tip of his sword downward with the palm of one gauntleted hand, and swung her sword with the other.

As the blade cut through his right wrist, it sounded like a butcher's cleaver chopping into a large hunk of meat. His hand popped off the end of his arm, and it and his sword dropped to the ground. He staggered backward and gripped the stump of his wrist as blood sprayed out of it in long, arcing spurts.

He could still feel the fingers that were no longer there, and a schizophrenic part of him realized he was experiencing phantom nerve sensations, while the rest of his mind silently screamed out his terror. The pain was so intense all he could say was, "Fuck, fuck, fuck!"

Crazy woman leaned down, casually picked up his severed hand and removed it from the remains of the gauntlet. It was caked in blood and dirt, and she didn't bother to wipe any of it off as she grabbed his arm and planted the hand on the end of his stump. All the pain and blood disappeared.

"You're learning," she said in that whisper-soft voice. "You did well that time."

"I did well," Paul hissed, feeling hysteria taking control. "You break my fucking jaw, spill my guts all over the ground, cut off my hand—and you say I did well."

The color of her eyes shifted randomly. "Yes, and you may yet master that blade."

Paul reached down, picked up his sword and held it out in front of him. "Why do I feel a need to take sword lessons? Why do I need to master this blade?"

She shook her head slowly, as if instructing a dim-witted child. "You know as well as I the blade you hold now is not the blade you must master."

He did recall the rune inscribed blade of his dreams, but riddles and conundrums only fueled his anger. "You sound like Dayandalous."

One of her eyebrows lifted sharply at that reference. She smiled unpleasantly, and that infuriated him even more. He dropped the sword to the ground, stepped toward her and made no attempt to hide his anger. And oddly enough, even though she towered over him, he saw fear in her eyes, and he sensed it in all the souls hidden within her.

Off to one side, Anogh said, "Necromancer, please do not draw power against her."

Paul turned on Anogh and marched toward him. He wasn't sure what he intended, only that someone was going to get hurt. But he was just a few paces from the Summer Knight when Jim'Jiminie and Boo'Diddle materialized on either side of the Sidhe mage.

Both leprechauns extended their hands in a warning for Paul to stop. Jim'Jiminie said, "Hold, Young Mage."

Boo'Diddle said, "Anogh and black Sabreatha are not your enemies. Do not use the power you've drawn against them."

Paul hesitated and stopped in his tracks. He looked into Anogh's eyes, and saw the same fear he'd seen in Sabreatha's. Only then did he understand he'd pulled a mountain of raw power without realizing it. It shimmered in the air around him, little motes of it dancing up and down his Sidhe armor, tickling his eyebrows and the hairs in his nose. The leprechauns were right.

He closed his eyes and concentrated, allowing the power to dissipate slowly.

Sabreatha returned him to his apartment the same way she'd taken him from it, wrapped in the massive claws of the giant hunting hawk. Standing in his living room and facing each other, she said, "Do not fear me, mortal. And please do not hate me."

She shifted into the shape of a hawk and disappeared into the mirror on his wall.

He carefully examined himself. All his limbs were there, all the pieces still intact, a few bruises, but no serious injuries, not even a scar.

He sat down on his couch, buried his face in his hands, and said, "Shit, shit, shit!"

••••

He'd purchased a cheap table and set it in a corner of the warehouse where he used it as a workbench. Without a hair, or at least a sliver of fingernail, or some physical piece of her to work with, the spell would require his master's help and every ounce of skill at his command. He assembled a carefully selected set of ingredients on the table: charcoal from a fire thirteen nights cold, a fresh bay leaf, a silver charm from a cheap bracelet, and a small piece of square parchment paper.

He used a pair of scissors to cut the parchment into a carefully-formed, round disk, then placed it squarely on the table in front of him. He'd made the charcoal himself, had extinguished the fire in which it was created at solar midnight exactly thirteen nights ago, and he used it now to draw a circle just inside the edge of the parchment. He then drew a pentagram inside that, with its five points just touching the charcoal circle. In the center of the pentagram he drew the *Crux Satana*, the Devil's Cross, a double cross above an infinity sign, a figure eight lying on its side, the symbol for eternal damnation.

He stood and unzipped his pants, reached in and pulled out his penis. Taking up a single-edged razor-blade, he carefully pricked the flesh on the most sensitive area of skin where there were many small scars from previous incantations. It had to be a small cut, for it was imperative he carefully control the flow of blood. He leaned over the table and cautiously dripped thirteen drops of blood onto the bay leaf, then shoved his penis back into his pants and zipped them shut.

Using the scissors, he cut the bay leaf into thirteen pieces of near equal size and placed them on top of the *Crux Satana* in the center of the pentagram. He retrieved a dark mirror and a bag of salt from a cupboard, and walked out of the office into the warehouse proper

Two days earlier he'd carefully laid out and painted a small pentagram enclosed within a circle on the concrete floor in a far corner of the warehouse. He'd painted a similar, larger circle and pentagram that completely enclosed the office at the back of the warehouse, but he wouldn't use that tonight; the smaller one in the corner would do nicely for a straight-forward summons. The dark mirror was a smaller version of those he'd mounted on the walls of the office, a pane of glass with black paint on the back side, though he'd secured it in a cheap frame with an attached stand to hold it upright. He placed the dark mirror at the center of the painted diagram, and positioned it so he could see into it from outside the circle.

He used the painted lines as a template to put down a circle and pentagram of salt, then returned to the table and retrieved the silver charm and the parchment containing the charcoal diagram, bay leaf fragments, and blood. Careful not to disturb any of the lines of salt, he placed the parchment in the center of the pentagram just in front of the dark mirror, and laid the silver charm on top of it. He walked out of the circle stepping carefully to avoid the lines of salt.

He checked his watch; he'd set it to solar time, and he still had a few minutes before true midnight on the thirteenth night after creating the charcoal. He spent the time standing outside the circle in meditation, calming his nerves, for he always grew excited at the prospect of being in the presence his master.

A few minutes before the appointed hour, he placed a candle at four of the five points of the pentagram, and lit each with magical fire. He stood at the fifth point, and summoned a flame to flicker in the palms of his hands, then fed power into the circle of salt.

He chanted, "Dark master of mine, I humbly summon thee into my presence. I implore thee to grace me with thy power and malevolence, and to allow me to bask in thine own glory and hatred. I bid thee, I pray thee, I beg thee to come forth, my Lord and Master Abrasax."

He repeated that twelve more times, keeping a close eye on his watch, and with each repetition the mirror appeared to become more of a mirror. He timed the thirteenth repetition so the second hand on his watch touched midnight just as he spoke the last word, and something in his soul rang out like a massive bell in the tower of a corrupt and debased church.

He saw his own face now reflected in the dark mirror, with blood-red, goat-slitted eyes. He bowed his head to the image and said, "Master of my soul."

They did not trade words or speak in any way, and his master's thoughts did not come into his head, but the darkness in the mirror knew his desires. If he was going to circumvent the powerful young witch's wards and control her, then do the same with the necromancer, he needed a charm imbued with his master's power. His twenty-something Alice wouldn't be protected by such wards, but she'd still make a nice test case to ensure the spell worked properly. Her death, and the consumption of her soul, would also bring him far more joy—and his master far more strength—than the damaged and degraded souls of the prostitutes.

The parchment flared and burst into flame. He watched it slowly burn down and die out until nothing remained but the charm.

He bowed his head again. "I thank you, my Master."

It always saddened him when his master departed. If only he had the power to bring It truly over to the Mortal Plane, then he could bathe in Its malice and evil. But while he was far more powerful than most mortal wizards, he did not have the power of a necromancer, and must content himself with his little joys and pleasures.

He broke the circle and retrieved the charm. Tomorrow night he would have his Alice.

23

Apology Aborted

SI'ENTHA SAT AT the window of her apartment, watching the street below. A short while ago she'd received a message from one of the Seelie mages following Paul Conklin, and knew he was headed her way.

She'd completed the glamour that gave her the appearance of his dead wife, though she'd been careful to do it in small steps, and at each stage had made sure that Paul had seen her, even if only briefly. Several times they'd stopped and chatted for a few minutes while passing on the stairs. Then she'd had lunch with him that day, and another time she'd asked him to help her hang a heavy painting on the wall of her living room. Each time her appearance had been just that much more like the young woman in those pictures on his dresser, but never enough of a change that it disturbed him. What disturbed him was that he grew more and more attracted to her each time they met. And Si'entha threw in a little beguilement here and there to cloud his thinking, just to ensure he didn't connect the dots. Now the time had come to wrap the strings of his heart in chains.

The sidewalks weren't terribly busy with pedestrian traffic, so she easily spotted him when he rounded a corner. As he walked up the street, she grabbed her coat and rushed out of her apartment.

••••

Just as Paul approached the front steps of his building, the front door opened and Eileen Cleary stepped out. "Paul," she said, her face lighting up with pleasure as she walked down the steps. "How have you been?"

"Busy," he said, noting that she wore an overcoat open at the front, and beneath that a pastel summer dress. He thought that might be a bit chilly for a November evening in San Francisco, but she did look awfully good in it, and it sparked a fond memory from somewhere, though he couldn't quite place it.

"Lots of work?" she asked.

"Yes," he said. It was only half a lie.

"You know," she said. "I really had a great time at lunch the other day."

"So did I." That was the truth. "Maybe we should do dinner some time."

"That sounds great." She paused thoughtfully. "In fact, I was just going out. Why don't you join me, unless of course you've got other plans."

"No, no plans." He considered it for a moment, decided he didn't want to spend another evening alone. "Okay, that's a great idea. Let's go have dinner."

She gave him a big smile that reminded him of someone else, but he couldn't quite place the memory. "There's a new place," she said, taking his arm and leading him up the street. "Couple blocks away. Thai food, I think. You like Thai food?"

"Thai works for me." Walking with Suzanna—Eileen—on his arm, Paul felt at peace for the first time in a long time.

The new restaurant was a little family-run affair. Paul and Eileen sat across from one another at a small table. The restaurant staff were still working out a few kinks in the table service. The couple that owned the place were training their daughter to wait tables, and she made a few mistakes, but the food was great.

Throughout the meal Paul couldn't take his eyes off Eileen, though she caught him staring at her a few times and blushed a bit, but didn't seem to mind. There was something about her that stirred a warmth and joy in his soul he hadn't felt in a long time. He tried to think it through and couldn't quite put his finger on exactly what it was about her that drew him so. He wasn't in love with her, nothing like that, but the line of her jaw, the color of her eyes, everything about her struck him as perfect. He recalled the last time they'd gone to Golden Gate Park on a lazy Saturday afternoon with Cloe. It had been a wonderful day.

Paul shook himself, realized he'd mixed up different memories.

"What's wrong?" Eileen asked.

He shook himself again and said, "Nothing. Just a little preoccupied."

••••

Katherine turned the Jaguar onto Paul's street three blocks up from his apartment building. Colleen's comments had forced her to think long and hard about Paul, and the apology she owed him. It had been about a year since she'd first met him, and in that short time he'd progressed from a rather ordinary, mundane person to a strong practitioner. When it came to wielding raw power he was almost on a level with her father, something she hadn't realized until forced to think about it. His training in the craft of magic had gone well, and he was a quick study when it came to spell crafting. But when she considered the situation carefully, while his progress had been quite admirable, he was still working at a rather elementary level. The strength of an unusually powerful wizard, combined with the struggles of a beginner, must keep him in a state of constant imbalance.

It occurred to her that she had progressed as well. When she'd first met Paul, she had been a middling witch, quite skilled at the craft of magic, but not strong in handling the forces needed for the most difficult spells. She'd been stronger than a run-of-the-mill practitioner like Sarah, her father's assistant, but now she could wield forces she would have never considered a year ago. That left her as much off balance as Paul.

No, he clearly hadn't meant to spell her, and he had killed the spell when he realized what was happening. She'd simply overreacted because of her embarrassment at the way she'd thrown herself at him—not his fault, not her fault.

She recalled kissing him, recalled kissing Pavel and their night of love-making in Marya Dmitrievna's dacha, and a little piece of her wished Paul hadn't killed that spell. So having thought about it carefully, she'd decided to drive to Paul's apartment and give him that apology in person. And who knew what might happen after that.

As she approached his building she slowed the Jaguar, looking for a parking place. There weren't any other cars on the street so she didn't have to worry about some irate driver tailgating her while she drove at a snail's pace. She still hadn't found an open slot as she passed Paul's building.

She slowed further and noticed a couple walking toward her on the sidewalk. The young woman was quite pretty: chin-length, brownish-blond hair. Cleary attracted to the young man, she held his arm tightly and laughed openly at something he said. And the young man, he was . . . he was . . . he was Paul—smiling, happy, beaming like a schoolboy—Paul.

Katherine passed them and almost ran into a parked car, but she hit the brakes in time and came to a stop. With the engine idling, she looked over her shoulder and watched their backs as they walked down the street. She watched them walk up the steps of Paul's apartment building, watched Paul fumble for his keys and watched him open the front door. Only then did the pretty, young woman release his arm and step through the door. Paul followed her and closed it.

Katherine decided if Paul was going to pick up some girl and take her back to his apartment—well, the apology could wait.

••••

Dinner had been great, Paul thought as he followed Eileen up the stairs. The food had been okay, but they'd chatted and talked about all sorts of things, just like old times.

No, he thought, a flood of confusion washing through his thoughts. There were no *old times* with Eileen.

On the third floor landing she stopped, turned to face him and he almost ran into her.

"Why so preoccupied?" she asked.

He couldn't tell her the truth so he made up a lie. "Oh, you know . . . work, stuff like that. Got a big contract I've got to jump on tomorrow."

She smiled, almost as if she understood he'd lied. "Well that's tomorrow. Right now I don't want the evening to end, so why don't you join me in my apartment for a glass of wine?"

He started to make up some sort of excuse, but she shut him up by kissing him. No, maybe he kissed her; it was all so confusing. It had been so long since he'd held his Suzanna in his arms, he couldn't resist. But she didn't taste like Suzanna, and in his arms she didn't feel like Suzanna, not his Suzanna. He ended the kiss, stepped back from her, looked into her eyes, the eyes of his Suzanna, but not his Suzanna. It was quite clear that if he followed her back to her apartment, he'd get a lot more than a glass of wine.

He panicked. "I have to go," he said, then turned abruptly and marched up the stairs, taking them two at a time, fearing to look back because he might stop and return to her, his Suzanna, but not his Suzanna.

••••

For more than a week he sat at the bus stop across the street from the parking garage near Katherine McGowan's office, and developed a thorough understanding of her routine. He also followed her in the morning as she walked from the garage to her office, and in the afternoon back to the parking structure. When maintaining office hours, she returned to her parked car almost like clockwork at a quarter after six. Like most mortals, she was a creature of habit, and he needed to know the patterns of her behavior intimately.

A few days ago, satisfied that he now knew the schedule she followed, he drove his car to the entrance of the garage, and used his master to follow her arcane scent to the house in the Sunset District. It was a lovely little home, probably built in the fifties, situated on a raised lot above the street. It had a single-car garage, level with the street and beneath the rest of the house.

He wanted to know every aspect of her routine, which would allow him to make a nice, intimate connection to her, the same way he connected with his Alices. To do that he needed to actually follow her, not just the trail of her arcane scent, so a little after five o'clock he found a metered parking spot on the street about a block from the garage in the city. He shoved coins into the meter to max it out at its two-hour limit, then walked to the bus stop across from the garage and sat down. Right on schedule, at a quarter after six, he spotted her walking up the street. He knew her routine enough to wait until she entered the garage before standing and walking to his car. He had no need to hurry.

He started his car, pulled out into the street, and he understood her timing so well that just before he drove past the exit from the garage, she pulled out onto the street in front of him. He followed her south on Van Ness, then west on Geary across the city to Park Presidio Boulevard. It was such a predictable route to the Sunset District, but then all his Alices had been predictable, so why should the young witch be any different?

He watched her park her car in the small garage at street level. She walked out of it, the automatic opener closing the door behind her, then walked up the steps in the front yard to the front door. Apparently, the old fifties house didn't have an internal passage from the garage to the interior, or perhaps the garage had been added in a later remodeling of the place.

He pulled the car up to the curb a few houses down from hers, put it in park and stopped, thinking he must be quick and not linger. He retrieved a camera from the glove compartment and took several photos of the place and the surrounding neighborhood. It was late afternoon, just after rush hour, and it occurred to him that he should come by again at night, because that's when he would take her. But he needed another mundane Alice or two before his master would be strong enough to go after the witch.

He returned the camera to the glove compartment, put the car in gear and drove away. It was time to forget about the old wizard's daughter, time to satisfy his master's need, time for his true Alice.

Like the McGowan witch, he'd watched his Alice closely since the night of the Halloween parties in the city, and knew her schedule rather well. She had a job at one of the department stores near Union Square. Her hours varied with the day of the week, but tonight she'd get off at 8:00 and walk back to her apartment south of Market. She too was a creature of habit and always followed the same route home.

He parked his car in the structure on O'Farrell Street, then walked to Powell, bought a newspaper, and entered the diner he'd checked out several days ago. He took a seat at a small table near the window with a good view up the street, ordered a cup of coffee, paid his bill immediately, opened the newspaper and pretended to read it. At a little after 8:00 she came walking down Powell, right on schedule. He left a small tip, stood, stepped out onto the sidewalk and walked up Powell toward her. As she passed him going the other way he bent down and, holding his master's spelled charm hidden in his hand, pretended to pick something up off the sidewalk.

"Miss," he called after her, extending his hand toward her. "Miss, you dropped something."

She stopped, turned, frowned and hesitated.

"You dropped this," he said.

With a few steps she crossed the distance between them and held out her hand, still frowning and appropriately wary of a stranger on the street. He dropped the charm onto her palm, and the instant it touched her skin she shivered and her eyes fluttered.

She looked at the charm and said in a dreamy voice, "No, this isn't mine."

"Oh," he said, holding his hand out palm up. "I'm sorry."

"That's all right," she said, dropping the charm into his hand.

"Take BART to the South San Francisco Station," he said. He'd left a small attraction charm just inside the back door of the warehouse. Under the influence of his master's charm, once she got within range it would pull her in. "From there, you'll know the way. There's a back entrance off the alley to one side. Just let yourself in, and if I'm not there yet, wait for me."

"BART," she said dreamily. "Back entrance. Wait."

He turned and walked away from her, walked back to his car. As he had anticipated, traffic was heavy and BART got her to the warehouse before him. She was waiting for him, standing complacently just within the back entrance. He led her to the one-room office that contained nothing but the bed, full-length mirror, toilet and sink. Earlier, he'd laid out the sexy Alice-in-Wonderland costume on the bed. He pointed to it and said, "Change into that. Then sleep."

"Change," she said. "Sleep."

24

The Egyptian

MCGOWAN WAS SEATED behind the desk in his study, with Colleen seated in one of the two wingback chairs in front of him, and Katherine and Vasily Karpov standing to one side. Standing near the fireplace, Paul was happy that, for once, the Russian hadn't brought Boris and Joe Stalin, though they were probably waiting on the sidewalk outside. The older practitioners were visibly nervous; that this Amen fellow from Egypt made all three of them uncomfortable scared Paul no end. And for some reason he felt he should be suspicious of anyone from Egypt, though he couldn't recall what made him feel that way.

The door opened and Salisteen stepped into the room. The tall, elegant black woman had cut her hair into a short afro, then bleached it to a slightly off-color blond. "Darling," she said, leaning down and giving Colleen a Hollywood-style air kiss. She did the same with Katherine, then crossed the room to Paul. He really wasn't practiced in air-kisses, but it turned out he didn't need to be because she planted a smacker right on his lips, though since he'd had to endure forced celibacy now for quite some time, he kind of didn't mind it. Katherine glared daggers at both of them, though she'd treated Paul like a bad smell all morning, so her feelings on the matter had him a bit perplexed.

Salisteen let him up for air, looked him in the eyes and said, "You taste delicious, darling."

She wrapped her arms around him and hugged him tightly. He tried to ignore the way she pressed her breasts against his chest. She released him, gripped his shoulders with her hands and held him at arm's length. "Shoulders," she said as if eyeing a particularly delectable desert. She squeezed Paul's upper arms. "I like a man with shoulders." Somehow Salisteen always made Paul feel like he was about to be served up for dinner, though, in another time and place, and under different circumstances . . .

He decided not to run with that thought, especially since *daggers* no longer properly described the look Katherine was now giving him. Daggers were much too small. The look in her eyes needed to be described with much bigger knives. He decided she was staring swords at him, really big ones like broadswords with incredibly sharp edges.

He wondered if Katherine was clairvoyant, and had somehow intuited the rather unchaste thoughts he'd had regarding Salisteen while she was kissing him. He'd have to ask Colleen if there was some sort of spell for reading minds, though she'd probably say something like, "No, that's not necessary, dear, because we can see your disgusting, lurid thoughts written plainly on your face."

As Salisteen sat down in the other wingback chair Paul heard the front doorbell. Then he heard Sarah's voice greeting someone, though he couldn't make out any words, and a few seconds later the door to the study opened again. Charlie Stowicz stepped into the room. Built like a fireplug, with a permanent five-o'clock shadow, he always reminded Paul of the kind of actor Hollywood studios cast as a dock worker in a movie. Behind him, a short, little fellow with deep olive skin stepped into the room wearing an ill-fitting, but expensive looking suit. He couldn't be more than five feet tall, had a decided paunch, a head completely devoid of hair, and a hook nose that made Jim'Jiminie's beak appear quite unremarkable.

"Walter," he said in a soft, meek voice.

McGowan stood as the little man crossed the room and they shook hands. McGowan said, "Amen, it's good to see you," though he didn't sound like he really meant it.

Amen looked at Katherine, smiled and crossed the room to her. "You must be Walter's daughter—Katherine, is it not?" He spoke with no discernable accent.

She smiled and shook hands with him, though Paul saw the strain overlaying the pleasant look she gave him.

"You are quite lovely," he said, "and I sense that you're a strong witch. I can see why your father is so proud of you."

He turned away from her, slowly scanned the room, and for some reason Paul thought of a snake turning its head toward its prey just before striking. The little man's gaze took in each of them and finally settled on Paul. The smile he'd bestowed on Katherine disappeared. He stood on the other side of the room, but then in no more than a heartbeat he stood before Paul. Paul flinched, but apparently no one else had noticed the way he'd covered the distance in an instant, or perhaps he hadn't and Paul had just zoned out for a few seconds with fear.

Amen looked into Paul's eyes and smiled, though Paul saw no warmth in his face. "You must be the young man I've heard so much about, the necromancer."

Paul extended his hand, saying, "Paul Conklin."

Amen reached out with both hands and wrapped Paul's hand in an almost intimate embrace. "It is a pleasure to meet you, Mr. Conklin."

Paul caught a whiff of a slightly unpleasant odor, nothing terribly offensive, but the kind of disagreeable scent some people are forever stuck with because of hormones, or something like that. Paul had known a fellow in high school who had practiced impeccable hygiene, but could never get rid of the last trace of that smell.

Amen continued to hold Paul's hand as he said, "I hear you were attacked by the Caorthannach. That must have been a most unpleasant experience."

Karpov said, "An unpleasant experience brought on by his own foolishness."

Facing Paul at one end of the room, the little Egyptian had his back to everyone else present. Continuing to hold Paul's hand and still looking into his eyes, he didn't turn to face Karpov when he asked, "And why do you say that, Vasily?"

"He's a necromancer. Such a powerful fey monster could not have come to the Mortal Plane without his summons."

Amen finally released his hand, and Paul had a sudden urge to go to a bathroom and wash it. The little man turned to face Karpov. "But we don't know that's true, Vasily. And we do know there are several of us in this room who could have accomplished it . . . with the help of one of the fey courts."

McGowan stood and leaned on his desk. "And Paul is not on trial here."

Stowicz took a step forward. "And he's demonstrated to my satisfaction that he's a responsible practitioner, definitely not the loose cannon you imply, Vasily. I'll vouch for him."

"And I," Colleen said.

Salisteen gave Paul one of those I'm-ready-to-eat-you-for-dinner looks and said, "And I," though the way she said it, he wasn't sure if she vouched for his reliability as a practitioner, or for some hoped-for sexual liaison. Katherine gave her the daggers look again, then she gave Paul the swords look.

They argued for the rest of the afternoon. At one point Amen's opinion shifted and he appeared to align with Karpov. Then later he shifted back to Paul, then back to Karpov. Shortly before they broke up, he said to Paul, "It is believed a necromancer comes along only when truly needed by the Mortal Plane. Let us hope matters don't become so dire we need you to be our salvation. But let us also hope you are not our bane."

••••

It was time to use the large circle and pentagram that completely enclosed the office at the center of the warehouse. He'd purchased a fifty-pound bag of salt, and as he'd done with the smaller diagram in the corner when making the charm, he carefully used the painted lines as a template to lay out the circle and pentagram of salt. It was large enough that little salt remained in the bag when completed. The arcane circle he would create this night must be a more complex structure than the simple circles employed by practitioners in the normal exercise of their abilities. It would have to contain his Alice and the demon, prevent them from escaping, but allow him to freely enter or leave while it was active. Few practitioners were skilled enough to accomplish such a complex weave of arcane forces.

He placed a candle at all five points of the pentagram, then lit each with a fire spell. He had access to a nearby ley line, but ley power was anathema to a demon summons, so standing outside the circle, he cleared his thoughts and called forth his own personal power. Using it would weaken him considerably, but once his master fed, his reward would more than make up for that.

From outside the circle, he carefully placed one foot inside it, and also inside one of the points of the pentagram that touched it. Now straddling the circle, one leg in, one leg out, he raised his arms to either side, closed his eyes, tilted his head back and fed the power he'd summoned into the lines of salt on the floor. The circle coalesced before him, and as it took solid form he chanted, "Circle of my making, vessel of the forces I call forth, contain not me but encompass all else that lives, and all that doesn't. Prove thyself impenetrable to all but mine own mortal flesh. I command it be so."

He closed the circle with a thought, and felt a painful tightening in his crotch and chest where it touched him. It hurt terribly, as if someone had kicked him in the groin and stabbed him in the heart with a white-hot blade, but he dare not demonstrate weakness by crying out. He clamped his mouth shut, the muscles of his jaw bunching with the effort. For several seconds nothing changed, then the pain receded, slowly at first, then more quickly as he proved his personal strength was up to the task. Arcane forces were almost like conscious beings, like dogs constantly pulling at their leash, and it was frequently necessary to demonstrate who was master.

When the pain had finally withdrawn completely, to calm down he took a deep breath and let it out slowly. He opened his eyes, and since the circle exactly bisected his body, he had the strange sensation of seeing it from inside with one eye, and from outside with the other.

He stepped out of the circle and examined his handiwork. Careful not to disturb any of the lines of salt, he lifted a foot and placed it in the circle, pleased that he encountered no resistance. Confident now that he had succeeded, he stepped wholly into the circle, then into the center of the pentagram. He stopped in front of the full-length, dark mirror he'd mounted on the outside wall of the office. It was identical to the one he'd mounted on the inside wall in the room where his Alice now lay sleeping on the bed. He'd carefully prepared both mirrors by infusing them with identical conduction spells.

"Dark master of mine," he said, "I humbly summon thee into my presence. I implore thee to grace me with thy power and malevolence, and to allow me to bask in thine own glory and hatred. I bid thee, I pray thee, I beg thee to come forth, my Lord and Master Abrasax."

With the charm he'd prepared earlier gripped tightly in one hand, he didn't need to repeat the chant, or use charcoal from a fire thirteen nights old, or time it for exactly solar midnight. His master was ready for him, and the corrupt bell in his soul rang out immediately, washing him in his master's power and malice. Again, he saw his own face reflected in the dark mirror, with blood-red, goat-slitted eyes.

He sensed his demon master testing the boundaries of the circle containing them. It had not truly manifested on the Mortal Plane—he was not a necromancer and didn't have that kind of power—but It could reach out from within the mirror, and torment or give pleasure with ease. If It sensed that Its reach extended beyond the circle, that he had failed to construct it properly, the temptation to feed on all the mortal souls within reach might be too much for It, and he might easily suffer the same fate as his Alice.

His master finished probing the circle and apparently found no weakness in it. *Is she ready?*

When the thought brushed across his soul, he felt true joy. "She is, Master of my soul."

The surface of the mirror cleared, and through it and its twin, he now saw into the room where she lay. To one side, the edge of the toilet was just visible, while he saw nothing of the sink. But directly in front of him his Alice lay on her back on the bed, spelled into sleep by the magic of the charm he and his master had created. Dressed in the sexy costume, the swell of her breasts emphasized by the push-up bra, he watched her chest rise up and down in a slow, even intake and exhale of breath.

With the charm still clutched in his hand, he lifted it to his mouth and blew on it lightly. Several seconds passed, then her eyes fluttered for a few heartbeats and finally opened. At first she didn't move, but then she slowly raised her head and looked around the room, frowning as she did so. She would have no memory of passing him on the street and being spelled, nor of the instructions he'd given her. To her it would seem as if she had walked down the street on her way home from work, and in the blink of an eye, she had awakened here.

She rose up on her elbows, looked down at the outfit she wore and her frown deepened. She sat up, swung her legs off the bed, and apparently, only when she put her feet on the floor, did she realize she wore the platform, high-heeled Mary Janes. She stood and wobbled a little awkwardly—perhaps the shoes didn't fit her well enough—crossed the room to the mirror and looked into it. To her it would appear to be an ordinary mirror in which she saw her own image.

Examining her reflection carefully, she spun around slowly and turned full-circle, the frown deepening even further. As she leaned forward to peer into the mirror, his master said, *It's time.*

He raised the charm to his lips a second time and blew on it again. From his vantage looking through the mirror in the office, he couldn't see what she saw in its twin, but he knew she caught a glimpse of his master's blood-red, goat-slitted eyes overlaid on her own reflection. Her eyes widened, she gasped, straightened and back-stepped desperately across the room.

"What's going on?" she pleaded. "Who are you? What are you?"

His master waited patiently, for It would gain much more from the feeding if It allowed her terror to peak.

She glanced around the room. He'd positioned the mirror so he had a clear view of the bed and the door to the warehouse where he now waited. She saw the door, and without taking her eyes off the mirror edged her way to it, then turned, grasped the handle and tried to open it. But of course he'd locked it with a dead-bolt that would thwart even a skilled burglar.

She pulled on the handle desperately, the little skirt of the sexy Alice outfit bobbing up and down as she tugged on it. She glanced over her shoulder at the demon eyes in the mirror and pounded on the door with her fist. "Let me out. Please. Please, let me out."

With each word her tone rose higher in pitch, and the last came out with a decided tremble in her voice.

Instinctively, he knew the time was right, and he watched an oily, black cloud emerge from her mirror and drift toward her. She looked over her shoulder, saw it, turned and huddled with her back against the door. "No," she said, tears streaming down her cheeks. "No, no, no."

She slid along the wall away from the cloud and into a corner, but it followed her, and as it enveloped her, she clutched at her throat and screamed. It was so much better this way, without any beguilement or enchantment to cloud her perception of the pain and terror. His master took her slowly as she screamed again, and again, and again.

She dropped to her knees, still clutching at her throat, then dropped to the floor and lay on her side, screaming out her horror and dread. It took more than an hour for the screams to slowly dwindle to quiet whimpers, and then she died. Such a long, drawn-out process meant his master had gained considerable strength from her death, from her terror.

He stood there for a while just staring through the mirror at her lifeless body. It had been so easy to use the charm to compel her to change from her street clothes into the sexy outfit. But when the authorities examined the body, the Alice costume might raise some concerns, so now he'd have to personally reverse the process. Before dumping her back in the city, he'd have to remove every bit of the outfit and put her back in the clothing she'd originally worn, and he hated touching female flesh.

You have done well, his master said. *I am strong now, strong enough to go after the young witch. And once she's neutralized, we'll take the necromancer.*

25

Deception Unmasked

KATHERINE AWOKE FEELING anything but rested. She'd slept sporadically all night long, alternating between dozing off briefly, and laying there wide awake thinking of Paul and that pretty young woman she'd seen him with. Last night she'd started out angry with him for betraying her that way, but she couldn't deny that she had no claim on him. If he wanted to take that little slut up to his apartment and . . . well, that was his business, not hers.

Later, she thought about the times she'd kissed him, and chided herself for being such a tease. A tease wasn't a tease as long as she delivered, but it was too late to change that now. Paul had seemed quite taken with that young woman. Katherine could have probably shrugged it off if he'd only been interested in some meaningless sex, but he'd beamed at her like a schoolboy in love, and that had hurt more than anything else.

It was Saturday, and she had the day off, so she crawled out of bed and walked into her closet. The cedar box on the shelf above caught her eye. She reached up and retrieved it, carried it into the bedroom and placed it on her bed. She opened it, carefully unfolded the navy-blue, cashmere, Donna Karan, couture dress, then carried it back into the closet where she had a full-length mirror on the back of the door. She held it up against her, and thought again that she would have liked to wear it for Paul.

She decided to do a little medicinal shopping to get her out of her melancholy mood. Time to buy some new shoes.

She put away the Donna Karan dress, wolfed down a bowl of cereal, then showered, dried her hair, and applied her makeup. She put on a black, silk camisole, and over that a blood-red blouse, then a dynamite DKNY suit. She was damn well going to look good when buying clothes to look good in. She pulled on a pair of Louis Vuittons, grabbed the matching purse, then walked into her closet to take one last look in the full-length mirror, just to be sure.

She started when she saw Madge the cat in the mirror. She looked down at the floor next to her, and there was no little black-and-white cat beside her. She looked again into the mirror, and only then realized she didn't see her own reflection there, just the cat, seated on a table up against the mirror in a strange room, a room that was not her closet reflected in the mirror.

The little cat jumped out of the mirror and landed on the floor beside her. "Oh shit," Katherine said. "This isn't going to be an Alice-Through-the-Looking-Glass thing is it?"

"Come on," Madge said. "It'll be fun."

Katherine put her fists on her hips and said, "Not on your life."

"Oh lighten up," the cat said. She rolled her eyes the way no cat should. "Jeez, you really do need to get those horns clipped."

Katherine wasn't about to listen to any of this. "Would you kindly cut the potty-mouth talk?"

Madge gave her a conspiratorial look. "Don't you want to see the inside of Paul's apartment? He's not there." She winked. "You can snoop around all you want."

"No, I don't want to go snooping around in Paul's apartment."

Madge sat back on her haunches. "But there's something important there you need to see."

"What do you mean?" Katherine asked, thinking she was a damn fool for falling for this malarkey.

"It'll answer all the questions you have about him and that young woman."

"I don't care in the least about that woman."

Madge rolled her eyes again and jumped into the mirror. She landed on top of the table in Paul's apartment and turned back to Katherine. "You'll truly regret it if you don't come."

Katherine shook her head and said, "I can't believe I'm buying into this."

She put her hands against the frame of the mirror, lifted her right foot and extended it carefully. She expected it to bump up against the glass of the mirror, but instead it sank into it with no resistance whatsoever. The table-top in Paul's apartment was several inches below the bottom of the mirror and she had to step down carefully to place her foot on it. Then she was forced to turn sideways to squeeze her butt and her boobs through the mirror. Last came her head and shoulders, then her left foot.

The mirror in Paul's apartment was much smaller than the full-length one in her closet, and her new stature now reflected that. Up on that table beside the cat, she didn't stand much taller than one of the leprechauns, and the drop to the floor was well over her newly diminished height.

"Oh," Madge said. "Don't you worry your pretty little head about that. I'm here to take care of such things."

There came a moment of vertigo, then Katherine found herself standing in the middle of Paul's small living room, once again her full height. She stood there for a moment trying to calm down while looking around.

She'd never been in Paul's apartment before, but saw immediately that it was quite small and Spartan. She glanced briefly in the little kitchenette, saw nothing of importance there and turned to Madge. "So where is this really important thing I need to see?"

Madge grinned and said, "Just look around. You'll know it when you see it."

Katherine had had enough. "You're grinning just like a fucking Cheshire Cat."

Madge shook her head sadly. "Now look who's the potty-mouth."

Katherine demanded, "Do we really have to play guessing games?"

Madge ignored her and licked a paw.

Katherine threw her hands up and walked through the living room looking for anything that might be important. She stopped briefly in the small bathroom and saw nothing there. She finished in the bedroom: still nothing.

She sat down on the bed and scanned the room slowly, hoping some inspiration would strike her. She saw absolutely nothing out of the ordinary, just the bed, a night stand with a lamp on it, a dresser with some pictures on top of it, and a small desk and chair. A very modest place, a lot like Paul Conklin.

Out of curiosity she stood and crossed the room to the dresser, picked up one of the pictures and looked at it. Her heart lurched, and she felt as if she'd been punched in the gut. Paul and that woman had become so close he had pictures of her in his apartment. How long had their relationship been going on? Had he hid it all this time, from her, from her father, from Colleen?

She picked up another picture. In it, Paul and that woman were seated on a blanket with a young girl about eight or nine years old. They were having a picnic in a park. Paul's eyes were focused on the child, and the look on his face made it quite clear he loved her deeply. Katherine's chest tightened painfully as she realized Paul's girlfriend must have a child from a previous marriage or something, and somehow Paul had fallen in love with her and her child.

She recognized the location: Golden Gate Park. Paul had once told her he, Suzanna and Cloe had loved to picnic on a Saturday afternoon in . . .

"Yes," Madge said, hoping up onto the bed beside her. "I told you it would be important."

Katherine's thoughts raced through her mind in a jumble of rapid-fire confusion. She'd never seen Suzanna or Cloe, didn't know what they looked like. And the Paul in the picture looked to be a few years younger than the Paul she knew, didn't have those little lines of aging that came with the kind of pain and grief he'd been through after losing them. "But who?" she asked.

"Just think it through," Madge said, licking a paw.

"Someone's playing with Paul's mind."

"Much more than that," Madge said. "Someone's trying to take him away from you."

Katherine couldn't believe it. Losing a wife and daughter like that was a wound that never truly healed. But to reopen it that way! "That could destroy him, imitating Suzanna like that. Who would do that? Who *could* do that?"

Madge didn't say anything, and in that moment of silence Katherine found her answer. Absolute fury welled up in her heart. "The Sidhe, of course, one of the Courts."

She thought of the woman she'd seen hanging on Paul's arm and said, "That bitch, I'd like to wring her fucking neck."

Madge licked a paw. "I think a little potty-mouth can be excused at a time like this. And there's one other thing you should know: he didn't sleep with her. He's strong enough to recognize, at least on a subconscious level, that something didn't ring true with her. So no parking the beef bus in Tuna Town for them."

Katherine spun on the little cat. "But he brought her into this building. Why would he do that if he didn't take her up to his apartment?"

Madge leaned back on her haunches. "Now let's think this through. Why would he let her into the building if he had no intention of batter-dipping the corn dog?"

Katherine screamed, "Give me a god damn hint, would you?"

"You're potty-mouthing again."

Katherine wanted to strangle the little cat, but she wanted to strangle the Sidhe bitch more. And then it hit her. "She lives in the building too, doesn't she?"

"Finally!" Madge said, rolling her eyes. "You're not very quick on the uptake, are you, dear? But you can get away with that because you're so pretty."

"Don't patronize me," Katherine said. "Where . . . where's her apartment. You know exactly, don't you?"

Madge grinned. "Just follow me, dear."

••••

Katherine stuffed one of the pictures of Paul and Suzanna into her purse, and as she followed Madge out of his apartment and down the stairs, she asked, "So he didn't screw that Sidhe slut?"

"No," Madge said. "No creaming the Twinkie. No gland-to-gland combat. No launching the meat missile. No—"

"Would you kindly stop that? Just shut up."

"You want me to clam up completely?"

"Yes."

"Okay, but I've got a great one about clams. You want to hear—"

"No."

Madge stopped on the third floor. "You're kind of snotty, for one who's not too quick on the uptake."

Katherine stopped, clenched her fists, held her hands at her sides and bit back every retort that came to mind. "Please just lead me to her apartment."

Madge smiled. "Gladly, dear."

Madge led her down the hall on the third floor and stopped in front of the door to apartment three-ten. "This is going to be interesting," she said.

Standing just outside the apartment door, Katherine closed her eyes and allowed her arcane senses to expand outward. She couldn't discern much, but there was no question the witch she was about to confront bore allegiance to the Seelie Court.

It occurred to her that before confronting the Sidhe witch, she should contact her father. She stepped to one side of the door and retrieved her cell phone from her purse, then dialed her father's number. After a couple of rings he answered. "Hi, Katherine, what's up?"

"Is Paul with you?" she asked.

"Yes, he is. Colleen and I've been keeping the boy rather busy."

"This is important, father, so listen carefully."

"That sounds ominous."

"It's not good," she said. "I've just discovered there's a Seelie witch living in Paul's building who looks exactly like his dead wife Suzanna. Not just a *lot* like her, but *exactly* like her, a complete, absolute doppelganger, and she tried to seduce Paul." The *seduce* part was a guess, but certainly a good one.

The phone was silent for several seconds, then McGowan said, "Those assholes."

He'd reacted as she'd expected. "I think you, Colleen and Paul should come here right away. But don't say anything to Paul until he gets here."

Her experience as a shrink had kicked in. "If she's done what I think she has, he's going to need to see this for himself, kind of like an intervention. She's in apartment three-ten. I'm there now, and I'm going to confront her."

"I think you should wait until we get there."

She didn't want to wait one second. She wanted to knock on the door, then kick the bitch's ass. But she forced herself to cool down. Her father's home was just up at the top of Nob Hill, so it shouldn't take him long. "I'll give it ten minutes, but if you're not here by then, I'm really pissed off, so she and I are going to have a little chat."

"We're coming right away."

Katherine ended the call and put her cell phone back in her purse. She paced up and down the hall for a few minutes, but her impatience got the best of her.

She always carried a couple of defensive, protection charms—just in case. She retrieved one now, hid it in the palm of her left hand, then licked the tip of her left index finger. Triggering it now might alert the Seelie witch in the apartment; this way, if she needed it, all she had to do was touch the saliva on her finger to the charm to activate it. She slung her purse over her left arm and retrieved the picture from the purse, holding it in her right hand.

She rang the doorbell. Nothing happened for several seconds, then the peephole darkened, and at the same time she felt faint tendrils of magic probing at her. She suppressed all traces of her own arcane abilities, and with the growth she'd experienced in the last year, she thought she could conceal her talents from even a powerful Seelie witch, especially on the Mortal Plane where she had the advantage.

The door opened, and Katherine faced the young woman she'd seen walking down the street with Paul, the young woman in the picture.

"What can I do for you?" she asked, appearing every bit the mundane mortal.

Katherine raised the picture to hold it just in front of the witch's face. "You're pretending to be Paul Conklin's dead wife, Suzanna."

The witch raised an eyebrow, looked at the picture carefully, but didn't appear in the least perturbed by the accusation. "Is that what she looked like?" she asked. "I didn't know. And I'm not pretending anything. If he's attracted to me because I look a little like his dead wife, well that's . . . not surprising . . . though a bit creepy, don't you think?" She gave Katherine a nasty grin.

Katherine lowered the picture. "You're right. What you've done is very creepy."

"Me?" the witch asked. "I think you're just jealous. I'm just a simple working girl. It's not my fault—"

"No," Katherine said. "You're a Seelie witch, and you're wearing a glamour and beguiling him."

The witch hesitated for a moment, her eyes narrowing. She looked Katherine up and down carefully, and made it clear by the look on her face she didn't like what she saw. "Oh yes, you're the McGowan girl, aren't you?"

"Katherine!" At the sound of her father's voice, they both looked down the hall and saw him, Colleen and Paul coming their way.

Katherine said, "That was fast."

Her father said, "Paid a cabbie a big tip to get us here quick."

Paul frowned and looked quite confused. "Katherine, what are you doing here?"

He looked at the Seelie witch standing in the doorway. "Eileen," he said, and his eyes narrowed with doubt.

That was the clue Katherine needed. The witch had used a little beguilement when near Paul so he wouldn't realize how strange it was to encounter someone who looked *exactly* like Suzanna. But she couldn't do that undetected with two mortal witches and a powerful wizard present. Katherine handed the picture to Paul. "Look at that. She's a Seelie witch, and she's beguiled you so you won't realize she looks exactly like Suzanna."

Paul looked at the picture, then at Eileen, then at the picture again. Then he closed his eyes, lowered his head, and whispered, "My god!"

Her father stepped forward and faced the Seelie witch. "Tell Magreth I'm very upset she's chosen to mess with my apprentice this way."

The witch shrugged and gave them an unconcerned look. "We've done nothing wrong. I'm free to live on the Mortal Plane for a while and wear any guise I choose. The young man was merely attracted to me, so you have no recourse."

Katherine stuffed the picture and the unactivated defensive charm into her purse. She wanted her hands free.

McGowan looked at Katherine and said, "She's right."

Katherine had considered this carefully. The Seelie witch had most likely set up powerful house wards, but they'd only be effective against someone inside the walls of the apartment. And they'd only trigger automatically against offensive or defensive arcane forces. Against anything else, the witch would have to trigger them overtly, and by then it would be too late. Katherine smiled and said, "But I do have a recourse."

The witch rolled her eyes. "And what might that be?"

Katherine thought of the witch Belinda the night they'd faced each other in the Secundus caste demon's mansion. She made sure she didn't completely mask her abilities and drew power in preparation for an arcane attack. The Seelie witch sensed the gathering of arcane forces and raised a sardonic eyebrow as if to say, *Really, you think you can best me in my own abode?* But drawing power was just a fake, the kind of feint a boxer might make with one hand while delivering the knockout punch with the other. Without making any obvious movements, Katherine curled her right hand into a fist and said, "This," and punched the bitch in the nose.

She let the arcane power dissipate without using it.

••••

Watching Katherine stand in the middle of the hallway shaking her hand and shouting, "Owe, owe, owe," Paul wasn't sure if he should thank her or not.

The Seelie witch staggered back a few steps into the middle of her living room, her hands cupped over the lower half of her face, blood streaming between her fingers, tears pouring out her eyes. Paul said to Katherine, "Thank you."

She ignored him and said, "Owe, owe, owe."

"Nice right jab," McGowan said. He reached out and took hold of her injured hand. "Here, let me see that." He examined it carefully. "Nothing broken. We'll just put a little ice on it. And I could use a drink."

As they walked down the third floor hall away from the Seelie witch's apartment, Paul was still trying to absorb what he'd just learned. Walking beside him, Colleen took his arm and said, "Are you okay?"

He had to think about that. He'd been happy and excited in Eileen's presence, and yet there'd been something about her that bothered him, though he couldn't say exactly what. Whenever she'd turned on the sexually inviting charm, the *I'm reading, willing and able* allure, some sort of alarm in his gut had driven him away from her. And when he wasn't in her presence, there hadn't been the kind of attraction that made him long to see her again. Thinking of that he glanced at Katherine walking beside her father in front of them.

Colleen noticed his look and said, "Exactly! I think you're going to be just fine."

Paul carefully recalled the whole sequence of encounters with Eileen Cleary, and the way he just happened to run into her by chance time and again. Looking back, he now understood how easily they'd set him up. "No," he said. "I'm not going to be all right. I'm pissed off, angry at Magreth, and I'm only going to get angrier."

McGowan glanced over his shoulder. "Glad to hear it. Let's go to your place, get some ice for Katherine's hand."

The cheap refrigerator in Paul's small apartment didn't have an automatic ice maker. Colleen and Katherine sat on the couch in the living room and McGowan dropped into a seat in the breakfast nook. It occurred to Paul he should probably augment the rather Spartan furnishings that came with the apartment, perhaps put a chair or two in the living room, something to sit on besides the couch.

Paul had one question for Katherine that kept surfacing in his thoughts. "Where'd you get that picture of me and Suzanna?" he asked as he broke several cubes out of a plastic ice tray, sealed them in a zip-lock plastic bag, and wrapped that in a terry cloth towel.

Katherine had stopped saying, "Owe, owe, owe," and as he crossed the living room and handed her the ice pack, she gave him a confused look. "I . . ." she said, hesitating, "I . . . don't recall."

Colleen helped her wrap the ice pack around her hand. "Let's get the swelling down, then I'll take a look at it later. It's probably just bruised."

"And I need a drink," McGowan said.

Paul didn't have anything like the expensive whiskies the old man served. "I've got some white wine and a couple bottles of beer in the fridge."

Colleen stood and walked into the kitchen. "I'll take a little white wine."

McGowan stood and said, "Think I'll take one of those beers. Hope it's descent stuff."

With the two of them in the kitchen, Katherine whispered. "Madge the cat. That's how I got the picture. But with them here, I couldn't say the words. Just couldn't say them."

As if on cue, Madge walked out of the bedroom then sat back on her haunches. "Meow," she said.

Colleen returned from the kitchen carrying two glasses of white wine. She handed one to Katherine, saying, "Thought you might want one as well."

She noticed Madge and said, "Oh, you got a little kitty. And what a cutie she is."

Madge licked a paw and said, "Meow."

26

Set the Trap

AMEN SHOWED UP at McGowan's house quite frequently when Paul was present. Besides McGowan and Colleen, one or more of the other senior practitioners—Stowicz, Salisteen or Karpov—were often present as well, which made Paul feel more like a specimen under a microscope, and sometimes turned his apprenticeship lessons into a rather crowded affair. Paul noticed that Amen's presence muted even Salisteen's playful flirtatiousness, though nothing and no one could completely extinguish it.

There was no getting around the fact that Amen gave Paul the creeps, though Paul wouldn't have admitted that to anyone. The fellow seemed nice enough, was rather meek and unassuming for such an enormously powerful wizard, and actually gave Paul no reason to dislike him so. McGowan had used the word *scary* with regard to the Egyptian, and the way the old man and Colleen had described his arcane strength meant he could certainly be something to fear. But brute strength in arcane forces didn't bother Paul so much; he simply found the little man disturbing, creepy, weird, words with an altogether different dimension from just *scary*.

That morning Paul didn't know what to expect as he walked up the steps to McGowan's front door. He'd been working with McGowan and Colleen on methods of defense against compulsion spells—the disastrous attraction spell screw-up at Katherine's house had ended any possibility of further training by her—and was scheduled for more of the same. When he rang the doorbell he certainly hadn't anticipated Salisteen answering the door.

"Paul," she said, licking her lips as if she was about to devour a delicious meal. She had on a tan dress that ended well above the knees, exposing long and shapely legs; nice legs. The dress included a high collar, though she'd left several buttons undone, displaying quite a bit of cleavage. He couldn't tell if she wore a bra, but if so it certainly didn't do anything to hide the points of her nipples protruding quite visibly through the fabric of the dress. "We've been expecting you," she said.

She took his arm and held it tightly against her as they walked side-by-side down the narrow hall to the kitchen at the back of the house. He was conscious that she had his forearm jammed right up against one of her breasts.

In the kitchen, McGowan, Colleen and Amen sat at the table, while Katherine stood leaning against the counter. When Paul and Salisteen stepped into the room Katherine's eyes narrowed and she crossed her arms like an angry schoolmarm. She clearly thought he was coping a feel—which he sort of was, but not by choice.

As Salisteen released Paul from boob-feel captivity, Amen stood and faced him. He took Paul's right hand and did that thing where he wrapped it completely in both of his. "Paul," he said, his voice barely above a whisper, a pleasant smile on his face. "It's good to see you again."

Every time they met he greeted Paul the same way, and it really creeped him out. Feeling rather awkward, Paul said, "Nice to see you too."

McGowan said, "Amen would like to do some tests, Paul."

Standing there with the creepy Egyptian still shaking his hand and growing more uncomfortable with each second, Paul asked, "What kind of tests?"

Amen finally released his hand, then turned away from him and sat down at the table with McGowan and Colleen. Still smiling, he pointed to the empty chair directly opposite him and said, "Please sit there, Paul, and I'll explain."

As Paul pulled out the chair and sat down he noticed that everyone else in the room seemed a bit uncomfortable. Previously, Amen had stood in the background, observed Paul's training, and only occasionally made a comment or offered some advice. This was the first time Paul had sat opposite him face-to-face, their eyes on almost the same level. For just a heartbeat the room lights caught Amen's eyes at an odd angle, and Paul saw a brief flash of red, when in fact the fellow's eyes were dark brown and a little bloodshot.

"We know so little about necromancers," Amen said, articulating each syllable. "We have rumors, and myths and supposition, but no facts or experience."

"What do you hope to learn?" Paul asked.

Amen's smile disappeared. "I'm told you fed like a demon on one of Mr. Karpov's subordinates."

"Not like a demon," McGowan said. "Whatever he did, he didn't gain any strength from what he took from Alexei. He simply weakened the fellow, which makes it quite different from a demon feeding."

It was true that Paul had gained nothing by feeding on Joe Stalin when the ass-hole was trying to shove his hand into the whirring blades of a blender. He'd merely weakened Joe enough to save his own hand from serious mutilation. He'd never told anyone that when he'd fed on Cassius, the witch Belinda's demon master, his strength had temporarily grown to superhuman proportions. Cassius had thrown him against a wall and slammed him into an ornate desk, shattering the heavy wooden piece like part of a breakable Hollywood set. It should've killed Paul, should've broken his back and every bone in his body. Instead he just felt the power within him diminish with each blow from the demon, like using up the fuel in a car. Paul decided it would still be best to keep that information to himself.

"And how do you know this, Walter?" Amen asked, never taking his eyes off Paul.

McGowan's face hardened with anger as he said, "I questioned Paul quite thoroughly on the matter."

"So you only have his word. And do you know his word is good?"

McGowan placed a hand flat on the table and leaned forward. "Yes, I do."

Amen smiled unpleasantly and continued to look at Paul. "I'm glad you have such confidence in the young man. Nevertheless, some old texts hint that a necromancer must have some trace of demon blood in his veins."

McGowan countered with, "And some hint that he must have a trace of fey blood as well."

"Yes," Amen said. "Both are possible. In fact, both may be prerequisite, or it might be that the different combinations of lineage produce necromancers with different strengths. A necromancer with traces of fey blood might be quite different from one with demon blood, and those quite different from one with both. We just don't know."

"But we don't know how to test for that," McGowan said.

Amen's smile broadened into a grin. "I think I do."

Throughout the exchange he'd never taken his eyes off Paul. He reached out now with both hands and said, "Give me your hands." It was not a request.

Paul extended his hands across the table and Amen grasped them. "I'm going to examine you carefully," the Egyptian said. "I'm not sure what I can learn, but I must try. Close your eyes, and try to relax."

Paul closed his eyes, but knew there'd be no relaxing involved. He grew conscious of the feel of the skin of Amen's hands. He would have expected them to be soft and smooth, but they were weathered, as if he regularly worked at some difficult, manual labor.

Paul felt the tendrils of some sort of foreign, arcane power brushing at the edges of his thoughts. And then without warning he stood alone in the blasted landscape of the Netherworld. He and Katherine had been transported there once before when he'd punched the Tertius caste in the face outside the hospital. That had been when all this wizard stuff was new to him and he thought it nothing more than suspicious mumbo-jumbo. The two of them had faced a chicken-headed, shake-legged demon back then, and the same demon now stood in front of him.

"I will own you," it said. "I will possess you, and with you I will control all that is mortal." It laughed at him, and the ground shook.

The demon disappeared and next he stood in the halls of the Seelie Court facing the mad queen Magreth. "Kill him," she screamed. A dozen Seelie warriors swinging silver rapiers charged at him from all sides.

Next he stood beneath Ag's throne, and the cruel Unseelie king said, "Do not kill him. I want him alive to feel the pain as we destroy everything he loves."

Now he stood in the countryside of Faerie, watching the seven-foot-tall crazy woman fire the heart arrow at him. But this time it didn't slow down and circle him carefully. It drove straight for his heart, but at the last instant it diverted to one side. He followed its progress as it raced toward Katherine and slammed into her chest.

His last memory was standing over her as she lay there in a pool of blood, the spark of life gone from her eyes.

••••

Paul slowly opened his eyes. It took him a moment to realize he was still seated at the table in McGowan's kitchen, the side of his face resting on its surface. His cheeks were sticky with dried tears.

Colleen stepped into his field of view at the end of the table. "He's awake," she said.

Paul peeled his face off the table and sat up. McGowan, Katherine, Salisteen and Colleen stood around him, all with concerned looks on their faces. There was no sign of Amen.

"What happened?" McGowan asked.

"I don't know." Paul said. "You tell me what happened."

Katherine said, "When you closed your eyes you went rigid, then passed out. It was over in a matter of seconds."

"Where's Amen?"

Colleen said, "He released your hands, said you have no demon or fey blood in you, then left."

Paul felt like he'd just run a marathon. He was tired and exhausted, and needed sleep. "I need to lie down," he said.

McGowan helped him up the stairs to a bedroom, let him lay down on top of the covers in his clothes, then closed the door and left.

Paul couldn't put his finger on exactly what bothered him about Amen, but everything that had happened that day only confirmed the creepy, weird feeling he had about the fellow. He fell asleep trying not to think about it.

••••

At first he was concerned about the necromancer, since the only routine the fellow followed was the occasional dinner at Jessie's Bar & Grill. He could improvise for an Alice with no arcane skills, but with a practitioner, he'd be much happier if he established a predictable pattern. Unfortunately, the young wizard seemed to go to the pub on a whim on random nights of the week. At least, that's the way it appeared—at first—but after several weeks of observation a pattern did emerge, hidden within the fellow's daily activities.

The necromancer did go to Jessie's on the occasional random night, but he always ate there on Saturdays, even if he went there no other night of the week. He probably suffered from the *home alone on Saturday night* syndrome. His master was adamant that he neutralize the witch first, so he'd abduct her on a Friday night, kill her, then take the young wizard on Saturday. How convenient!

The McGowan witch would be a much more difficult challenge than the last Alice, but she'd also make a truly wonderful prize, both for him and his master. However, she'd have personal wards to protect her, so he couldn't approach her on the sidewalk and use the *Miss, you dropped something* ploy. He had no doubt he could overcome her wards with the charm his master had helped him create, but her reaction might be unpredictable, and she might not be as complacently controllable as the last Alice had been. Attempting to take her in broad daylight, with witnesses nearby, was not even a consideration.

Thankfully, daylight savings time had ended earlier that month, which meant that when the young woman adhered to her habitual schedule, twilight ended and true night settled over the city shortly before she got home. He drove by her place several times just after dark. Her quiet, residential neighborhood saw only a little pedestrian traffic during the day, even less after dark, and literally none at the time she got home, probably because that was during the dinner hour.

His master was now strong enough to take her, so early Friday morning he sat down at the bus stop across the street from the parking garage where she left her car during the day. From there, he watched her drive into the garage, then, when she emerged on foot, he followed her to her office. He returned to the garage every hour to be certain her car was still in the reserved stall on the fourth floor. He checked the last time shortly after 5:00, then got into his own car and drove down to the Sunset District, confident she was following her pattern that day. He drove around the area to kill time, staying away from her street until just after dark. By his estimate, he parked his car across the street from her house about ten minutes before she would get there.

That night the conditions were ideal: no moon and a coastal-effect fog settling over the area. Dinner hour in a dark, quiet, residential neighborhood; add to that a moonless night, and a little fog, and with no witnesses to interfere he'd take her easily.

Besides the powerful compulsion charm his master had helped him prepare, he'd created two charms with the Sidhe style glamour that forced one's eyes to look away.

He activated one now and left it on the passenger seat of the car. He'd activate the other later when he had control of the witch, just to ensure none of the neighbors saw him leading her to the car. The fog had thickened enough that he might not need them, but it never hurt to be careful.

He climbed out of the car, crossed the street and walked up the stone stairway to her front door. She had a light on the front porch that turned on automatically with the coming of night. He unscrewed the bulb and tossed it into the bushes, then replaced it with a low wattage lamp. Her suspicions might be aroused if the light was completely out; she might notice the dimmer glow, but it was unlikely to trigger any real concern.

He retrieved the powerful compulsion charm from his pocket. He didn't activate it because she might sense it, would wait until the last instant before triggering it. He stepped into the shadows at the side of the porch, and with his master's help, masked any sense that he or his magic was present.

••••

During the drive home Katherine thought a lot about Paul. She'd been ready to apologize for her overreaction to the compulsion-spell screw-up, but before she could do so she'd seen him with that Seelie witch Eileen—or whatever she called herself. She'd gone all jealous on him, and after she learned what was really going on with that bitch, she hadn't gotten him alone long enough to say she was sorry. She decided to call him tomorrow and invite him over, maybe for dinner, get him alone and apologize. Who knew what that might lead to?

A light fog had settled in over the city, and it appeared to thicken as she approached her house. She noticed a car parked across the street, but she chalked it up to a guest visiting one of her neighbors. As she pulled into her driveway she pressed the button on the remote to open the garage door. The garage had been a retrofit sometime after the house was originally built, but before she bought it. Her Jag barely fit, and she had to ease carefully out through the door. She walked out of the garage and pressed the button on the remote to close it.

As she walked up the stone stairway to her front door the porch light seemed dimmer than usual; probably an effect of the fog. She paused on the porch beneath the lamp and opened her purse to retrieve her keys, and had trouble finding them because of the dim lighting. Perhaps the bulb was close to burning out.

When she found them she had to peer at them carefully to select the right one— again because of the light. She inserted the key into the lock on her front door and the dead-bolt clacked loudly as she turned it. As she reached for the door knob she sensed the flow of arcane power.

She crouched down and spun, triggering her personal wards as she swung her purse like a club. She connected just as a hand slapped the side of her face, triggering a powerful charm. She stood upright and staggered back as her wards and the charm fought for dominance, but her wards ran out of juice first. Her last thought was that the purse was a beautiful Salvatore Ferragamo she'd gotten for a to-die-for price, and she hoped she hadn't damaged it.

••••

The young witch reacted faster than he expected. She spun and swung her purse, slamming it into his shoulder with painful force. He hit her with the charm just as she triggered her wards. Her defenses were strong and sophisticated, and he almost failed as she fought the compulsion for several seconds, but the power his master had instilled in the charm overcame her, and she slumped to the stone of the porch. She lay there with her eyes fluttering, the fingers of her right hand twitching spasmodically. Unfortunately, her wards had neutralized the compulsion, so all he had to show for his efforts was a semi-conscious female. That would have to do.

He reached into his pocket and triggered the other charm with the Sidhe style glamour, hadn't triggered it beforehand because she would have sensed an active spell.

He'd needed to carry a few of his Alices in Dallas, but they'd been eight- or nine-year-old girls. The young witch wasn't a large woman, but she certainly weighed more than those Alices. He checked her to make sure the charm had her locked tightly within its power. He looked at the twitching woman lying at his feet and doubted he could lift her. "Stand up," he said. "Get on your feet."

Her legs jerked and convulsed as she tried to move them, which meant some elements of the compulsion had taken hold. He slipped his arms underneath her armpits from behind. "Stand," he said again, straining to lift her. "Get up, damn it."

He repeated that over and over as he struggled to get her on her feet. With minimal help from the compulsion spell, it took all his strength to get her to a reasonably upright position, leaning heavily against him. While doing so one of his hands accidentally cupped one of her breasts, and he quickly released it. He hated the flesh of women.

"Walk," he said, "and come with me."

She still twitched uncontrollably, and he barely managed to keep her on her feet as they staggered down the stone steps to the street. It helped that the charm had her locked in a somewhat rigid barely-conscious state.

When they reached his car he had to repeat every command a half-dozen times, and he had to push her and force her to bend at the waist, but he managed to get her into the passenger seat. As she sat there twitching, he glanced back and saw one of her high-heel shoes on the lawn near the front porch. He looked at her feet and saw that both her shoes had fallen off. He walked back up to the porch and found them. He also retrieved her purse and several items that had fallen out of it. He tossed everything in the bushes beside the porch and returned to his car. Not until he had the engine running, put the car into gear and pulled away from the curb did he again breathe easily.

The drive back to the warehouse was uneventful. Again, he had to repeat every command and carefully support her to get her out of the car, into the building and onto the bed in the office. Thankfully, when he laid her out on her back on the bed she stopped twitching and fell into a comatose state.

At that point he was faced with the unpleasant fact that without the compulsion, he couldn't simply tell her to change into the Alice outfit. At least he'd had some practice when he'd changed the last Alice out of the sexy outfit and into her street cloths before dumping her body, so he knew how everything fit together. He started undressing her, realizing he'd have to guess at the right sizes. He hated female flesh.

27

Slutty Alice

KATHERINE SLOWLY DRIFTED back to consciousness as the spell that had en-trapped her dissipated. She opened her eyes and realized she was lying on her back on a bed. As she raised her head and looked downward, the first thing she saw was the top of her breasts and a swelling of cleavage, much more than she had a right to. Someone had stuffed her into a push-up bra, and they'd done a rather poor job of it, with half her left areola protruding above the top of it—uncomfortable to say the least.

She sat up and looked around. She was alone in a small room with a concrete floor, a door in one wall, the bed on which she sat, a full-length mirror on the wall opposite the door, a toilet and a sink. But other than that, the room was empty and the walls unadorned.

She looked down at her clothing and said, "Oh shit!"

Someone had dressed her in a pale-blue dress, and white knee-high stockings, end-ing in a pair of Mary Janes on her feet, classic shiny-black round-toed shoes. The dress appeared to be a few sizes too small. She tugged on the top of the bra; it was twisted to one side, and it took a little effort to get it properly into place; still uncomfortable be-cause it was a push-up and at least one size too small.

She swung her legs off the bed, and only when she put her feet on the floor did she realize the Mary Janes were platforms, with two inches of sole beneath the toes and six-inch, stiletto heels. She'd never been a fan of platforms, and the shoes were a size or two too large, so when she stood up, she wobbled unsteadily on them and pin-wheeled her arms for a moment until she got her balance. As she crossed the room she had to walk carefully, like someone navigating an icy sidewalk.

She went straight to the door, gripped the knob and tried to turn it; no luck. Above it, the plate for a dead-bolt only accepted a key with no finger latch. She gripped the knob with both hands and pulled, straining with all her might. The door didn't budge. She pounded on it and shouted, "Let me out of here."

She turned around and scanned the room. Movement to one side caught her attention, but when she looked that way she realized it was nothing more than her own reflection in the mirror. She marched over to it and stopped in front of it. Someone had put her in a blond wig with curls and ringlets cascading past her shoulders, then tied a cute, little, blue ribbon into it, with a bow on the top of her head. She decided then and there that she hated cute, little blue ribbons. As her temper rose she tugged at the wig, but shouted when she almost pulled her own hair out by the roots. She worked at it for a bit to find the bobby pins and clips that held the wig in place. She removed them, then tossed the wig aside, throwing it with considerable force.

That act of defiance made her feel a little better. Her own auburn hair had been pinned up to hide it beneath the wig. She removed those pins, and shook her hair out, letting it fall down to her shoulders. As a last show of disobedience she kicked off the damn shoes and sent them skidding across the floor. One of them slammed against the wall, breaking off the stiletto heel.

She considered removing the entire outfit, but she didn't have anything else to wear, and she wasn't about to prance around naked. It occurred to her that her abductor might be monitoring her, but when she scanned the room she didn't see any obvious cameras mounted on the walls or near the ceiling.

She tried to calm down, took a deep breath and let it out slowly, then looked more closely at her image in the mirror. Now she realized that while the dress was a few sizes too small, it was, in fact, just the right size if she wanted to look like a street-walker.

A little white collar encircled her neck, like the collar of a man's dress shirt. But it was up there all by itself, because beneath it she saw nothing but skin between the collar and the top of her breasts. The dress had no shoulders, with puffed up little sleeves that started a few inches below her collarbone. The top of the dress was cut low, with a plunging neckline that ended at the top of her bra. The push-up bra barely covered her nipples, and bunched up what cleavage she did have. Her breasts weren't large, but large enough to deliver cleavage when she wanted to, so the push-up bra was pure overkill and made her look like a tramp. The dress ended well above mid-thigh, was little more than a micro-minnie that flared out like a cheerleader's skirt, though it was considerably shorter than that. She lifted the hem and was thankful to see that, like a cheerleader's skirt, it incorporated an integral pair of panties.

Then there were the knee-high stockings, which weren't really knee high, but went all the way to mid-thigh, with black ribbon garters holding them up. And she'd been right about the fit of the dress; it was at least one size too small, which made little embarrassing bits of her stick out even more. She turned around and looked at her butt in the mirror, and to her horror confirmed her worst fears. The panties were so tight, and the skirt so short, that it exposed an inch or more of her butt cheeks. Someone had dressed her up like a slutty street-walker, and her temper was rising beyond a boil. But she'd be damned if she was going to give the ass-hole what he wanted.

She pinched the hem of the little skirt between her fingers and tried to tear it. That didn't work. She tried to tear her sleeves, and quickly learned that with just her fingers she wasn't going to be ripping undamaged material the way some super-heroine might in a cheap movie. The white, mid-thigh stockings also proved to be stronger than her, though she did manage one small rip in the right leg.

She looked at herself in the mirror again and paused. There was still something un-comfortable about the skirt and panties that didn't add up.

She lifted the skirt again, slid her fingers under the edge of the panties, and discov-ered the problem. Beneath the panties, whoever had dressed her had put her in a thong.

A thong!

She turned around and shouted to the ceiling, "A thong! You can't be serious. Butt cheeks and a thong! You fucking perv."

••••

As he'd done with the last Alice, when it came time for the kill he set the large circle that surrounded the office, then stood looking into the dark mirror he'd hung on the outer wall of the structure. He summoned his master, and again saw his own face re-flected in the mirror, with blood-red, goat-slitted eyes. The surface of the mirror cleared, and he saw the young witch lying on her back on the bed, dressed in the sexy costume, the swell of her breasts emphasized by the push-up bra, her chest rising up and down in a slow, even intake and exhale of breath.

He lifted the charm to his mouth and blew on it lightly, releasing her from its spell, all as before, all as planned. But when she awoke, her reaction surprised him. She marched to the door and pulled on it, her anger clearly rising with every second. Then she turned, walked to the mirror and stopped in front of it. She ripped off the blond wig and threw it to one side, then kicked off the shoes hard enough to send them skid-ding across the room. She examined herself carefully in the mirror, tugged at her skirt, then at a sleeve. She pulled on the material of the stockings and ripped a small tear in one. She turned around, looked at her butt in the mirror, then called him a *fucking perv*.

He needed fear and terror, not anger and defiance. And he was not a pervert. He was an experienced practitioner wielding powerful arcane forces. At least her defiance wouldn't last long when the moment of truth came, when she faced his master. He took some satisfaction from that thought.

He lifted the charm to his mouth and blew on it again, and again nothing happened as it should. His master didn't appear before her, didn't spill out of her mirror in a cloud of oily smoke, didn't consume her soul, nothing.

No, the voice said. *We need her alive.*

"But why?" he pleaded.

We need her so we can control the necromancer. And we need to control him so he can bring me over to the Mortal Plane.

••••

Katherine forced herself to calm down, though it took some effort. She thought about trying the door again, but that would be a waste of time. She examined the room carefully: door, toilet, sink, bed and mirror. The room had been stripped of everything else. Nothing under the bed, nothing she might use to escape. She wished she still had her purse because she always carried a couple of charms she could use to call forth defensive spells in an instant.

"Focus," she told herself. *And stop the wishful thinking.*

She was a strong witch, had access to arcane forces so she should damn well use them. She sensed the compulsion spell hovering at the edges of her aura, like a caged, live animal waiting to be freed to devour its prey. She tried to summon power, felt it close at hand but just out of reach. She closed her eyes and sensed no spell that might block her power that way. Without a complex spell, the only way to so completely block a practitioner from manipulating arcane forces was by locking them in a powerful circle.

Who would have locked her in a circle? It would have to be someone quite powerful. Could it be that Russian ass-hole Karpov? No. He'd gotten away with abducting her once before only because she was aiding Paul, and at the time even her father thought he was a rogue, summoning demons without the proper protections. Kidnapping her without an extremely good reason would get him in hot water with all the other senior practitioners.

Something bothered her about the slutty outfit she'd been stuffed into. She stepped up to the mirror again and looked at it carefully. It was pale blue, with little touches of white satin shaped something like a bib or an apron . . . or a pinafore.

Oh shit, she thought. *Oh shit, oh shit, oh shit!*

She returned to the bed and sat down on the edge of it.

They'd never hunted down the Alice-in-Wonderland killer back in Dallas, though it appeared they'd neutralized him by freeing the girl's souls from the demon corruption left behind. And this wasn't his MO; he liked young little girls, not grown women, and especially not a powerful witch. In any case, he was in the Dallas area, not San Francisco.

Could he have tracked them all the way to the Bay Area? And if so, why bother? She prayed it wasn't him, because she wasn't terribly confident she could fight him alone, not without Paul.

The compulsion spell flared and tightened around her aura with smothering force . . .

She must have lost consciousness. When she awoke she again lay flat on her back on the bed. She propped herself up on her elbows and the curly locks of the blond wig settled about her shoulders. While she'd been unconscious he'd also put the platform Mary Janes on her feet again, and replaced the torn stocking. She swung her legs off the bed, pulled one shoe off and was about to throw it across the room, when she noticed that the floor was littered with bits and pieces of something that glinted in the light. She leaned down and picked up one of the glittering fragments. He'd scattered broken glass on the floor. She put the shoe back on.

She stood and one of the shoes was even more uncomfortable than before. She recalled that when she'd kicked them off, she'd broken the heel on one. He'd replaced it with another of an even larger size, which made it all the more difficult to walk in them.

Okay, she thought, *I'll wear the fucking shoes, for now.*

She sat down on the bed to consider her situation. Her captor clearly wanted to orchestrate a particular setting and image, to the point of obsession. That kind of manic fixation produced an enormous psychic investment, which could be a very dangerous vulnerability for a wizard and sorcerer. If she disrupted the scene he envisioned, it could weaken whatever spell or arcane force he intended to use on her. Combine that with willful defiance, and she just might have a powerful weapon to use against him, even though he'd cut her off from her own arcane abilities.

She stood up and wobbled a little on the platform shoes. She had to assume he was observing her somehow, so she tried not to be obvious as she walked across the room, her eyes scanning the shards of glass that crunched beneath the soles of her shoes. It didn't take long to find what she needed, a piece of glass about the size of a silver dollar, and triangular in shape.

She pretended to wobble unsteadily on the platform shoes, crouched down and put the palm of her right hand flat on the floor as if to steady herself. She felt the sharp sting of a glass splinter cutting her palm, but she'd put her hand down on the large, triangular piece, and she palmed it as she straightened up. It was a crude deception, but hopefully it worked.

She returned to the bed and sat down. Without being obvious about it, she pressed one edge of the shard against the side of the slutty dress just above her waist line, then sliced back and forth a couple of times. The sharp edge of the glass opened a small cut in the material. She inserted her finger into it, and found that with an already opened cut, she could easily tear the cloth further.

She glanced down and noticed a smear of blood had stained the material from a small cut in the palm of her hand. It hadn't occurred to her to use blood, but that could be a very powerful addition to the disruption she hoped to produce.

••••

Watching the young witch through the mirror, as she raised one shoe over her head, he thought she might toss it across the room before realizing he'd sprinkled shards of broken glass on the floor. But she hesitated, reached down and picked up a piece of glass, examined it, then put the shoe back on. Good. That had worked.

She sat down and looked thoughtful for several seconds, then stood and walked half way across the room, wobbling unsteadily on the platform shoes. She almost fell, and crouched down to put her hand on the floor to keep from doing so. She apparently learned a little caution from that because she returned to the bed and sat down.

He was reluctant to leave the warehouse with her conscious, but the compulsion spell he'd woven into the charm hadn't worked as planned, so he decided to abandon it. With his master's help he spent an hour feeding power into the circle so it could keep her imprisoned for days without him present. The circle would be a good alternative to the charm, and anyway, he wouldn't be gone that long.

He needed another circle. He had the large one laid out around the office, and the small one in the corner, but he needed another small one near that. His master wanted him to contain the witch and the necromancer in separate circles within sight of each other. He retrieved the can of paint he'd used on the other two circles, then carefully laid out and painted another small circle near the one in the corner. He also made another small dark mirror, so he had one in each of the two small circles.

When he finished that he walked across the warehouse to the table he used as a workbench. The charm, even bolstered by his master's power, hadn't worked that well on the woman. Her wards had reacted strongly to the compulsion in the spell. If she'd fallen completely unconscious in front of her house, he doubted he could have lifted her and carried her down to his car. And he wouldn't have been able to simply leave her there. He would have had to kill her right then, which would have been a disaster. The necromancer's personal wards were likely similar, so it was time to reconsider how he'd take the young wizard. Perhaps another charm, but without any compulsion; perhaps something that merely sapped the will and generated confusion, with no coercion or induced need to act against his nature. But he'd have to move quickly to be ready. It was Saturday, and creating such a charm might take most of the day.

28

Abduction

COLLEEN NEEDED A breath of fresh air and it was clear Salisteen felt the same way. McGowan's study was crowded with Amen, Charlie and Vasily questioning the old man incessantly about Paul's development, and what they'd learned about necromancy. Amen was especially interested in the way Katherine's arcane development had accelerated recently, and how she and Paul were stronger when working together. The discussion had gotten rather heated so Colleen had stayed out of it, and she noticed Salisteen had done the same.

Colleen looked at her watch. Noon was approaching, so she leaned close to Salisteen's ear and spoke softly. "I need to get out of here."

Salisteen's eyes brightened. "Me too. What do you have in mind?"

"I'll give Katherine a call. I know a great French restaurant near the China Town gates. We can have lunch, just us girls, then do a little shopping."

"Excellent idea," Salisteen said. "We can leave these old men to their bickering."

Colleen stood and announced, "Salisteen and I are going to lunch."

McGowan said, "I can have lunch brought in."

Salisteen stood as Colleen shook her head. "No, we're going out, just us girls. You men can do what you please."

The two women walked out of the room without waiting for a reply.

Colleen called Katherine, but it went immediately to voice-mail, so she left the name and location of the restaurant, and asked her to join them if she got the message in time. Katherine never did show up, or return the call. Near the end of lunch Salisteen asked, "Do you think something's wrong."

Colleen said, "No. She owes Paul an apology, and I'm pretty sure she went to his apartment today to deliver it in person."

"Why does she owe him an apology?"

Colleen told her of the accident with the compulsion spell, and Salisteen threw her head back and laughed.

"So she goes there to apologize," Salisteen said, an evil grin on her face. "And they both have their cell phones turned off for a couple of hours."

Colleen returned Salisteen's grin. "That's kind of what I'm thinking. But don't say anything to any of the men, especially Walter. I'm the only one Katherine told."

They did some shopping in the department stores around Union Square, then sat down in a little pub to have a glass of wine and chat. Colleen called Katherine again and left another message. But as the afternoon was winding to a close it bothered her that Katherine hadn't checked her messages and at least returned her calls. She was usually quite punctual about that, so Colleen called Paul.

He answered immediately. "Paul Conklin here."

"Hi, Paul, it's Colleen. I was wondering if you've seen Katherine today."

"No. Been working all day by myself. Why?"

"Nothing. Just wanted to chat with her about something."

After she ended the call, Salisteen asked, "She wasn't there?"

"No. And he hasn't seen her all day."

"Are you worried?"

Colleen wasn't sure if she was worried or not. "It's probably nothing."

Salisteen stood. "There's been a lot happening lately, so let's grab a cab and swing by her house."

As the cab pulled up to Katherine's house, nothing about the place appeared out of the ordinary. Colleen had all her arcane senses on full alert as she and Salisteen walked up the steps to Katherine's front door, and because of that she picked up the faint residual of a spell.

Salisteen paused and said, "You sense it too, don't you?"

"Yes. How old do you think?"

"Several hours at least, perhaps even a day or two."

She was about to ring the doorbell when she noticed the front door was ajar. She nudged the door open and called out, "Katherine. It's Colleen. Are you home?"

Nothing but silence.

Colleen retrieved a defensive charm from her purse, and prepared to trigger her personal wards, then pushed the door open completely. She and Salisteen walked into the living room cautiously and didn't see anything to concern them. They checked each room in the house and found no sign of Katherine, and nothing unusual or out of the ordinary.

Colleen said, "I'm going to check out back."

"And while you're doing that," Salisteen said. "I'll take a closer look at the residual of that spell out front."

Colleen stepped out onto the back deck, glanced around quickly, and even looked over the edge to the garden below. Nothing.

She stepped back into the living room and saw Salisteen standing in the open front door holding an expensive looking purse and a pair of high heel shoes. "I found these in the bushes next to the front door. And the residual of that spell reminds me of our creepy friend from Dallas."

••••

He walked past the necromancer's apartment building and down the street to Jessie's Bar & Grill. When he stepped into the dimly lit pub the bartender, who looked like a weight lifter, greeted him with, "Seat yourself anywhere you like. We're pretty casual here."

"Thank you," he said. "Are you Jessie?"

"Yup, that's me. Having dinner?"

"Yes, I am."

He chose a small table near the entrance. A couple of menus were wedged between salt and pepper shakers, so he grabbed one and opened it. Jessie gave him a few minutes then stopped at the table. "Like to start with a drink?"

"A glass of wine will be nice. And water too, if you don't mind." With the arcane forces he intended to manipulate that evening, it would not be wise to cloud his thinking with alcohol, so he'd make the one glass of wine last through the meal.

"Haven't seen you in here before."

"I just moved to the city," he said. Since he was in a residential neighborhood he needed a plausible excuse for his presence. "I'm shopping around for an apartment."

He ordered a sandwich, the bartender returned with a glass of wine and he sipped it while waiting for his dinner. He'd chosen his timing perfectly, because the sandwich and the necromancer arrived at almost the same time. The necromancer took a seat at the bar and ordered a steak and a beer.

As he ate his sandwich he carefully avoided any appearance of interest in the young wizard. He finished his sandwich well before the necromancer finished his steak and he asked for the check. The wine glass still had several sips left in it, so when the check arrived he placed cash on the table and let it sit there while he pretended to finish his wine. Several minutes later the necromancer finished his steak and pushed his plate away, then sat there for a while to finish the beer.

He waited until the young wizard asked for the check, then gulped down the last of his wine, stood and walked out of Jessie's ahead of the fellow. Night had settled over the city during his time in the pub, and that was good.

He'd carefully parked his car about half way between the pub and the young man's apartment. He took a flashlight and a map of San Francisco from the glove compartment, then unfolded the map on the hood of his car and switched on the flashlight. He retrieved the new charm from his pocket. He'd briefly tested it on the witch and it left her complacent, without the visible struggle between her wards and the spell. It would sap the young man's will without coercing him, leaving him open to suggestion. He didn't activate it because the fellow might sense it before he could use it, would instead wait until the last instant before triggering it.

He glanced up and down the street and was happy to see only a few pedestrians on the sidewalks. They didn't really concern him because the new charm produced almost no reaction in its victim. It would leave a strong residual a practitioner could detect for several hours afterward, but he'd be long gone by then and they couldn't track him from that, not without a demon helping them. But could they track the scent of his very powerful master, the way It had tracked the senior wizard and his daughter?

Have no fear, the voice said. *Only another demon can track me that way.*

At that moment the young wizard stepped out of the pub and onto the sidewalk, then walked toward him. So with his master's help he masked any sense he was a practitioner of the arcane.

The necromancer would have to walk right past him.

••••

Another Saturday night alone, so Paul threw on his coat and walked down the street to Jessie's for dinner, though just before he stepped into the place he heard the sharp cry of a hunting hawk. He paused in front of the pub, turned around and looked up into the sky, thinking, *Not now, you crazy bitch.*

He saw a couple of small birds, but no large hawks, and the seven-foot tall mad-woman didn't make an appearance. He shrugged it off. Probably just a normal, ordinary, red-tailed hawk.

Even though he was one of the regulars, he didn't really *hang out* at Jessie's, so there were several people present he didn't recognize. He saw a few familiar faces, and some of them nodded to him or smiled in recognition, but he didn't really know their names. A couple of attractive young women were seated at a table in the corner with glasses of wine in front of them. One gave him an inviting smile as he walked in, but when he considered doing something about it, his thoughts turned to Katherine. He pretended not to notice the smile and took a seat at the bar.

Jessie approached him and placed a dinner menu in front of him. "How's it going, Paul?"

He shrugged. "I'm working too much."

"All work and no play, eh?"

Paul ordered a steak and a beer, and chatted with Jessie a bit as he ate. After he devoured the steak he took his time finishing the beer, then paid his check, and walked out into the night, thinking he might order a movie from pay-per-view. Another Saturday night alone.

As he walked down the sidewalk, up ahead he noticed a fellow leaning on the hood of a car looking at something with a flashlight. He looked to be in his late forties, with light brown hair and fairly nondescript features, and Paul recalled seeing him eating dinner in Jessie's. As Paul got closer he realized the fellow was looking at a map and trying to trace something on it with his finger, shaking his head and frowning. Just as Paul approached him, his frown deepened, and he looked up the street away from Paul, craning his neck.

Paul stopped and asked, "You lost?"

The fellow started in surprise and turned to look at him. "Oh . . . no, not lost." He pressed a fingertip onto the map. "I'm new to the city, trying to find an apartment building on this street here"—he tapped the map with his fingertip—"but I'm not even sure I know how to pronounce the name."

San Francisco had its share of strangely named streets. "I know the area a little," Paul said. "Let me take a look."

The fellow handed Paul the flashlight and stepped to one side, still holding his finger pressed to the map. Paul leaned over the hood of the car, and saw that the finger was pointing to Powell Street. Odd that anyone couldn't figure out how to pronounce *Powell*; the fellow didn't have an accent, but maybe he was from somewhere where English wasn't the native language.

Paul's cell phone rang. He retrieved it from his coat pocket, saw that the call was from Walter McGowan and answered it. "It's Paul, Mr. McGowan."

"Where are you?" McGowan sounded upset.

"Near my building. What's up?"

"Katherine's missing, and we suspect it's that demon thrall from Dallas . . ."

Something touched the back of Paul's neck and he felt confused. McGowan on the phone . . . Katherine missing . . . And why was he standing on the sidewalk at night looking at a map on the hood of a car with his cell phone pressed to his ear?

"Paul," the cell phone said. "Paul, can you hear me?"

Someone took the cell phone out of his hand. Paul turned to find a man standing next to him, and he seemed vaguely familiar. "Is something wrong?" the man asked as he dropped Paul's cell phone to the concrete.

Paul thought that might damage it, was trying to think of how to protest the action, when the fellow stepped on the cell phone with his heel and crushed it. He took the flashlight from Paul's hand and said, "You seem confused. I'll get you home."

Home! Paul had trouble recalling how to get home.

The fellow opened the door to his car. "Get in, and I'll take you there."

Paul looked at his crushed cell phone, then at the passenger seat in the car. A pair of hands gently guided him into the seat, pulled the safety belt across his chest and lap and buckled it into place.

"You look tired. Why don't you rest while I drive?"

Paul leaned his head against the window and closed his eyes.

••••

It took two cabs to get them all down Nob Hill to Paul's apartment building south of Market Street. Colleen rode with McGowan and Salisteen in one, while Karpov, Stowicz and Amen rode in the other.

"I tell you he suddenly went all dreamy on me," McGowan said, "like he was under some sort of influence."

Colleen knew he meant that Paul sounded as if he'd been spelled, but the old man was editing his remarks because of the presence of the cabbie.

He added, "And I heard another voice in the background just before the line went dead."

When the six of them spilled out of the taxis in front of Paul's apartment building, Karpov had his cell phone to his ear. "Get down here right now," he said.

Salisteen spoke softly so only Colleen and McGowan could hear. "I assume he's bringing in those unpleasant young men of his."

Colleen said, "No doubt."

McGowan also spoke softly. "We'll spell the locks on the building and I'll take the others up to his apartment. But it sounded like he was out on the street when it happened, so you two cover the sidewalks outside."

Salisteen hooked a thumb over her shoulder and said to Colleen, "I'll go up the street, and you go down it."

McGowan said, "He said he was near his building, so a couple blocks either way should do it."

Colleen turned and walked up the sidewalk while Salisteen went the other way. There was no need to walk slowly and sniff about as she did so. If someone had recently spelled Paul, the residual would be fresh and strong. She walked two blocks without sensing anything, so she crossed the street and walked back on the other side. In the glow of a street light in the distance she saw Salisteen doing the same. She was about a half block from Paul's building when Salisteen started waving her arms.

As Colleen hurried toward her, Salisteen crouched down and picked something up off the sidewalk. Colleen sensed the strong residual of the spell a good ten feet away from her, but not until she stopped next to her did she catch the demon stink.

"What did you find?" Colleen asked.

Salisteen held out her hand palm up. In it rested a cell phone with a cracked screen.

Colleen pulled out her own cell phone and called McGowan. He answered immediately. "Hi, Colleen. We've got nothing up here."

"Down here," she said, "we've got a broken cell phone, the strong residual from a spell, and demon stink."

In less than a minute McGowan and the other wizards spilled out the front of Paul's building, then rushed down the street to the two women. "Yes," he said, standing next to her and examining the cell phone. "I wouldn't know if it's Paul's, but with the residual of the spell and demon stink, I think it's safe to assume it is."

Colleen asked, "Do you think we can follow the demon stink?"

The old man grimaced uncomfortably. "I don't know. We couldn't have tracked just a wizard, but the demon stink, maybe."

"No maybe about it," Amen said in his characteristically mild tone. They all paused and watched him closely as he walked back and forth through the spot where Salisteen had found the phone. He even sniffed several times as he did so, then he stopped, turned to them and said, "We can definitely track It, because It's a Primus caste."

29

The Sideways Slippage

THE WAREHOUSE HAD its own small parking lot; a nice convenience. He parked his car, turned off the ignition and stepped out of the driver's side. He walked around to the passenger's side and opened the door.

The necromancer looked up at him vacantly, so he reached down and unbuckled the fellow's safety belt. "Come," he said. "Get out of the car."

"Car?" the young man asked.

He reached in, took one of the fellow's hands and pulled on it gently. "Yes, get out of the car."

He had to lift the fellow's feet with his hands and place his shoes on the tarmac outside the door, then pull on him and cajole him into standing. The charm had sapped his will so completely he needed to stand behind him, place both hands on his shoulders, and guide him like a sleep walker. He led him through the door into the warehouse, and as he was about to close it he heard the cry of a hawk, which he'd learned was not uncommon in California.

Once he released the witch from the large circle that encompassed the office structure, he'd have no more need for it. Tonight, he'd use the two smaller circles he'd painted on the floor of the warehouse in the far corner. He'd prepared them in advance by placing a dark mirror in each and salting the painted lines.

He removed the necromancer's coat, beneath which he wore nothing but a T-shirt. He tossed the coat aside, led the young man to one of circles and got him to sit down on the floor in the middle of it. The fellow had disturbed some of the salt, so he repaired the lines. He placed five candles at the five points of the pentagram, lit them with magical fire, straddled the boundary of the circle with both feet, and activated it so it would hold his master and the necromancer, but allow him to freely enter and leave. He tested it carefully by walking into and out of it, then walked across the warehouse to the office.

When he looked in the mirror he saw his new Alice seated on the bed, but to his horror, her lovely Alice dress was stained and torn in a dozen places. The stockings were torn as well, and looked like something an ugly, goth, punk-rocker might wear. She'd smeared her makeup all over her face, and rubbed it and some sort of red stain in her blond hair, and on her face, arms, dress and stockings, and she'd frizzed the hair out so it no longer hung in lovely, little curls. It took a moment to realize that the red stains were blood. Blood!

As he looked on, she grimaced, her face a mask of anger and fury. She tugged at a spot on the dress just below her left breast and opened another tear.

"No," he shouted.

He had deactivated and destroyed the compulsion charm. He lifted the new charm to his mouth and blew on it. Her face slackened, her hands dropped down to her sides, and she sat staring straight ahead in a lifeless stupor.

He broke the circle, unlocked the office door, threw it open and rushed in. Standing over her, he pleaded, "What have you done? You were such a perfect Alice, and now look at you."

The will-sapping spell prevented her from responding.

Even if it took several hours, he had to fix this. He could strip her down, clean her up, and put one of the other Alice outfits on her. They were larger in size, so none of them would fit her as nicely, but she'd at least look like his Alice again.

Nooo, the voice said. *The time is now. You must act now. I care not if she is Alice.*

For the first time he considered defying his master. What difference would a few hours make?

If you defy me in this, your reward will be most unpleasant.

That was the key: obey, or destroy the careful rapport they had built up. He tried to calm his jangled nerves. It would be distasteful to take the soul of an Alice so ugly and defamed, even worse than the disgusting prostitutes. But afterward, they'd control the necromancer, and there'd be many more Alices to feed his need.

"Come, my Alice," he said, his voice trembling with disappointment. "My master waits."

Tonight his master would allow him to have this Alice, for once the necromancer was bound, there would be no more need for her. Like the young man, the spell that sapped her will left her completely languid and unable to function on her own. He had to help her stand, and when he told her to walk or turn, she did, but he was still forced to grip both her shoulders from behind and guide her. He led her out of the office and into the other small circle next to the one in which he'd entrapped the young man. The two circles were separated by about ten feet, so they'd easily see each other.

He sat her down in the middle of the circle on the concrete floor next to the dark mirror, then walked across the warehouse to his workbench and retrieved the bucket in which he'd broken a few panes of glass. Returning to her circle, he sprinkled a thin layer of glass shards around her so she wouldn't discard the shoes. Then he stepped out of the circle and set it, locking her within it. The two circles were identical in that he could enter or leave them, but they and his master could not. However, he had constructed them with one difference: sound could exit the witch's circle, but not enter it. She'd not hear the young wizard if he called out to her, which would help to increase her fear and terror. But the necromancer would easily hear her screams as she died most horribly, which would fuel his desperation.

He placed a simple wooden stool to one side of the two circles and sat down, then lifted the charm to his mouth and blew on it, bringing his Alice and the necromancer out of their stupors.

Time to summon his master. If only his Alice didn't look like a disgusting, goth, punk-rock prostitute.

••••

Colleen, McGowan and Salisteen took a cab back to his house to retrieve his car. Because of the presence of the cabbie no one spoke until they'd paid the man and climbed into the old wizard's car, with McGowan driving, Colleen beside him in the passenger seat, and Salisteen in back. While he drove them back to Paul's building McGowan said, "I need to call in some help."

He pulled out his cell phone and speed dialed a number. The two women could only hear his side of the conversation.

"Clark, it's Walter McGowan."

As McGowan explained the situation, Salisteen asked Colleen. "Who is Clark?"

Colleen recalled the gun shop owner. "Clark Devoe," she said. "A rather weak practitioner, but a dangerous man nonetheless. It'll be good to have him with us."

Still speaking into his cell phone, McGowan said, "Ya, come prepared for anything. But Karpov's bringing in his young thugs, so I need you to ride herd on those idiots as well."

McGowan listened for a moment, then said, "Just head up the peninsula. As we make progress tracking the son-of-a-bitch, we'll call and update you on our position."

When McGowan put the cell phone away, Salisteen said, "I don't understand how Amen is going to track this Primus caste. I don't believe *I* could do it."

That thought had bothered Colleen as well. "I know I couldn't."

"Nor I," McGowan said. "But Amen has demonstrated unusual abilities before, so we just have to go with it."

Another issue also bothered Colleen. "And if we have a Primus caste on the Mortal Plane, I'm certain we would know about it."

"Yes," Salisteen said. "What happened to Armageddon?"

As McGowan turned the car onto Paul's street he said, "Amen told me a Primus can exercise considerable control over a thrall without manifesting, can work from the

Netherworld almost as effectively as a Secundus that has crossed over. And like a Secundus it gains strength by feeding on human souls."

Up ahead, Stowicz, Karpov and Amen had been joined by three younger men, all of them standing next to two dark sedans. Colleen recognized the Slav with acne scars, and long, stringy, greasy-blonde hair. Paul called him Boris. Next to him stood the one Paul called Joe Stalin, with a bushy mustache, and bristly, short hair. Behind them stood the tall, skinny one named Mikhail.

"Who are the younger men?" Salisteen asked.

"Karpov's muscle," McGowan said. "All of them weak practitioners. The skinny fellow is the only one with any brains. If you have to go up against him, remember he's a knife guy, and he carries a rather large one with him at all times."

As McGowan parked his car next to the others, Salisteen spoke the thought that had occurred to Colleen. "The Primus needs Paul to help it manifest, doesn't it?"

"Yes," McGowan said. "And we have to stop it any way we can."

They decided Amen would ride with McGowan and the two women, while Stowicz rode with the Russians. As they sorted that out, Colleen leaned close to McGowan and whispered, "I won't let you kill Paul. You'll have to find another way to stop the Primus."

The old man grumbled, "I don't want to kill him any more than you. But we can't allow him to bring on the end of civilization."

••••

Katherine hadn't been unconscious, so she didn't *regain* consciousness. She recalled the fellow's hands on her shoulders as he led her out of the little room into a much larger space. Then he helped her walk into a circle and pentagram, and guided her to sit down on a concrete floor, her legs crossed beneath her. She remembered the events, and yet it felt as if it had happened to another person, and she'd merely observed their actions like watching a show on television. Then there came a moment when self-awareness returned, and with nothing but the slutty outfit's panties to insulate her butt, the damn concrete floor was just plain cold.

She took in her surroundings, saw Paul seated on the same floor about ten feet away from her, his head lowered, his eyes staring at the floor. Lines of white powder— probably salt, if she had to guess—in the shape of a circle and pentagram enclosed them both. The look on his face mirrored the way she felt, and she guessed he was emerging from a similar spell-induced stupor, though it appeared she was a little ahead of him on that.

She stood and wobbled a little on the platform Mary Janes. The bastard had sprinkled broken glass inside her circle, so she couldn't kick them off. The broken shards crunched beneath her feet as she walked to the nearest line of salt and carefully extended a hand. It encountered the solid, invisible wall of a strong, well-formed circle.

"Paul," she called.

His head snapped up and he looked her way. He frowned, gave her the oddest look, shook his head and squinted at her for a second. If they got out of this alive, she was going to have a lot of explaining to do regarding the ripped and torn slutty outfit with smeared makeup and blood.

Paul jumped to his feet and started toward her, but bounced painfully off the invisible wall of his circle, smacking his face in the process. He grimaced and grabbed his cheek. She saw his lips moving, probably letting go with a string of curses, but no sound reached her ears. He looked her way and clearly called out to her, but again she heard nothing.

To one side she saw a man seated on a simple wooden stool. He had light brown hair and looked to be older than her by fifteen or twenty years. His lips moved steadily in what she guessed was a chant of some sort, and she wondered what arcane forces he was attempting to summon.

She sensed something corrupt and malevolent in the circle with her. She turned about and saw a framed mirror supported in a cheap wooden stand. Its surface was shinny and bright, and when she looked into it she saw her face reflected there, with blood-red goat-slitted eyes.

••••

"Paul."

Katherine's shout yanked Paul out of his stupor. He looked toward her and saw her standing just a few paces away. She wore some sort of costume: black platform, stiletto-heeled shoes, white stockings to mid-thigh, a tiny little skirt that flared out like a ballerina's tutu, a plunging neckline with lots of cleavage, and a frizzy, blond wig with a disarray of curls and ringlets. The outfit had been torn and ripped in a dozen places, with red and dark streaks of something in her hair and on her arms, legs and the dress. She looked like a punk-rock, goth, Alice-in-Wonderland prostitute, and it was so not her style.

He jumped to his feet and started her way, but bounced off something invisible. It felt like someone punched him in the face, and he stood there for a moment holding his cheek and swearing. "Dammit, dammit, dammit!" He'd probably end up with a nice shiner.

"Dark master of mine, I humbly summon thee into my presence."

Paul turned toward the sound of the voice, saw the fellow he'd run into on the sidewalk outside Jessie's. The map on the hood of the car, the flashlight, it all came back to him in a flash of recollection, and he realized he was dealing with a rogue wizard, a summoner of demons.

"Circle and circle," the fellow said, "Witch and wizard, sustenance and power, come forth for a feast of fear and terror."

Paul tried to summon power, but something blocked him. "Who are you? What are you doing?"

The fellow ignored him. "I implore thee to grace me with thy power and malevolence, and to allow me to bask in thine own glory and hatred, and I grant thee the bounty of their souls, man and woman, sorcerer and sorceress."

Paul felt that sideways slippage in reality he'd experienced going to and from the Netherworld. He'd sensed it again when he and McGowan had summoned the demon in the old man's workshop. He looked over his shoulder and saw the dark mirror, and realized the maniac was opening up a portal to the Netherworld.

The fellow continued his chant. "I bid thee, I pray thee, I beg thee to come forth, my Lord and Master Abrasax."

Abrasax! Paul had heard that name before. The demon he and McGowan had summoned had said, ". . . Call for Abrasax when next you want to speak with me."

As the rogue wizard repeated the summons Paul shouted, "Abrasax, what do you want?"

I want you, necromancer, a voice said, sliding across Paul's soul like the foulness at the bottom of a cesspool. *I want your power.*

"Never," Paul shouted.

••••

At the sight of her own face contorted in demonic hatred, Katherine staggered back from the mirror. Only then did she realize who had abducted them; serial-killer-guy from Dallas had followed them to San Francisco. He'd hunted them down, and while he probably had nothing more than simple aspirations at revenge, the demon would want to cross over. As serial-killer-guy repeated the chant again, she sensed the monster in the mirror coalescing into a place between the Netherworld and the Mortal Plane, not fully in one, and not in the other.

She recalled Cassius, the Secundus Paul had destroyed, but this horror was far more powerful than that.

She spun about and shouted, "Paul, he's working with a Primus caste demon. It'll try to use you to cross over. Don't listen to anything it says. And we have to stop serial-killer-guy before he completes the thirteenth repetition."

She turned back to the mirror. Somehow she had to break the damn thing before serial-killer-guy completed the thirteenth repetition of the chant. She looked around for some sort of tool, thought of her shoes, but the splinters of glass crunching beneath her soles reminded her she couldn't take them off without shredding her feet. She'd do that if necessary, but that would be her last resort.

Her fist!

She could break the mirror with her fist. It would hurt, probably break her hand, and if she succeeded the shards of the broken mirror would undoubtedly cut it badly. But she had no choice.

She stepped up to the mirror, curled her hand into a fist and steeled herself against the pain. She drew her fist back, hesitated for an instant, then drove it toward the mirror with all her strength. But a few inches from the glass her hand slowed as it encountered an oily black cloud erupting from the mirror's surface, an unclean thing that smelled of sewage and death. Then her fist stopped completely.

She tried to pull it back, but the cloud wrapped around her wrist, then crawled up her arm. She recalled the remnant of the demon in the little Mexican boy doing the same to her ex-husband Eric when he tried his own spell on it. She staggered back, but it continued to crawl up her arm, and when it reached her chest she felt a hint of the cold, malignant, never-ending death that awaited her.

She screamed.

••••

Paul watched an unclean, black mist envelop Katherine, and the terror and fear in her scream frightened him more than any demon.

If you want to save her, the voice said, *then help me.*

"That's a great choice," he shouted. "Save her and bring on the end of civilization."

If he was going to help her, he had to find a way out of the damn circle. Everyone believed he could break a circle from within because they thought he'd done so in Faerie when he killed Simuth. He'd never told anyone that all he'd done was to turn their own spell against them, a spell designed to amplify his and Katherine's desires a thousand-fold. The Unseelie mages powering the circle that entrapped them had intended the spell to amplify their physical desire for each other, and turn them into a pornographic show to humiliate them. But he'd focused on his desire for vengeance, his desire for Simuth's death, his desire to break the circle, his desire for revenge on the entire Unseelie Court, and he let them amplify that. It was their own power that had broken that circle.

Open yourself to me and I'll give you untold power.

"Fuck you."

Without the contorted logic that had turned the Unseelie mages' power against them, he couldn't break this circle. But then he realized that maybe he didn't need to *break* it. The leprechauns had helped him escape the circle in the Seelie Court by flushing him and themselves down the shower drain. Maybe all he needed was some sort of hole in the circle, some flaw, some imperfection like . . .

. . . like a portal into the Netherworld.

Yes, come to me, embrace me, worship me.

He felt the formation of that sideways slippage in reality, and he thought he might step into it in the same way he walked the halls of Sidhe by stepping into the spiral slippage that took him to Faerie. He'd be a fool to go there, to walk right into the domain of the monster he sensed in the dark mirror.

Katherine screamed again.

"Fuck it," Paul said, and mentally stepped into the portal.

30

Two to Bear the Sword

"YOU SHOULD HAVE turned there," Amen said, pointing to the right as they passed the onramp to Highway 101.

Seated in the back seat of McGowan's car with Salisteen, Colleen continued to wonder at Amen's unusual abilities. Since she lived just outside of Dublin and he in Cairo, she didn't meet him often, but when their paths did cross, he always surprised her.

McGowan said, "I'll swing around the block and come back."

"I'm sorry," Amen said. "But I can't sense the next turn until we're actually upon it."

"Highway 101," Salisteen said. "Doesn't that go south down the peninsula?"

"That it does," McGowan said.

Several times now they'd backtracked or swung around the block to catch a missed turn. It was a start and stop process that had them all a bit frustrated.

McGowan's cell phone rang and he answered it. "What do you want, Vasily?"

Colleen looked over her shoulder through the back window of the car at the two dark sedans following them. She listened to McGowan explain why they had trouble simply following the demon in a straight-forward manner. The repeated missed turns had apparently upset Karpov.

When McGowan put his cell phone away, Colleen asked Amen, "How do you track this demon? What is it you sense that none of us can?"

Seated in the passenger seat next to McGowan, Amen turned his head and looked over his shoulder at her. "I sense its power, raw and deadly, and I think I have a more sensitive nose for that than most." He smiled at her, which sent a shiver up her spine.

McGowan circled the car around and got it back to the onramp, and they headed south on 101. They rode in silence for about ten minutes, and then Amen said, "Again, I must apologize, but you should have taken that exit ramp."

"That's South San Francisco," McGowan said. "I'll take the next exit and back-track. Colleen, please call Clark and give him the exit number."

••••

Paul landed on his side in the dirt, slamming his shoulder painfully into the ground. He rolled onto his back and groaned. A hot wind howled overhead in a dirty brown sky lit by a sun Paul had seen once before. The wind blew reddish-brown grit into his eyes, hair, and clothing. Thankfully, he'd managed to keep hold of the sword.

Sword!

He had to keep moving, so he rolled over and got to his hands and knees. In his right hand he held the sword he'd dreamed about. It had a straight, flat, double-edged blade, with a hilt long enough for a two-handed grip, and a simple cross brace. On the end of the hilt sat a cast, metal dragon, with two tiny rubies for eyes that shown an unnatural red, and the dragon's tail coiled about the hilt in an endless spiral. A patchwork of runes ran the length of the steel blade, and in it he sensed mortal power.

He climbed to his feet. He was standing on the side of a hill and could see for quite a distance, though clouds of sulfurous, yellow smoke obscured everything. Below him stretched a landscape of unending destruction, covered with blasted and torn buildings, some no more than piles of broken concrete and masonry. In the distance he spotted an open expanse of tarmac with the skeletal bones of destroyed airplanes scattered about it, the Netherworld equivalent of San Francisco International. Beyond that the steaming cauldron of San Francisco Bay emitted plumes of strange gasses, its shoreline a stretch of boiling mudflats.

Behind him something shrieked out an ungodly cry. He spun about as one of those bat-like monsters charged at him on clawed feet. It built up momentum, and a dozen paces before it reached him it spread its leathery wings and lifted off, gliding toward him just above the ground. It shrieked again, exposing a snouted mouth filled with razor-sharp teeth.

He swung the sword in a two-handed grip, swung it overhead like a baseball bat with none of the finesse Anogh had tried to teach him. He slammed the edge of the blade into the monster's head just as it plowed into him. A blinding flash erupted from the point of contact and a deafening thunderclap slapped him to the ground. The bat-like demon disappeared, and a rain of ash settled down over him like gray-brown snowflakes.

Coal-black Dayandalous and blood-red Mierfendoplay stood over him, and next to them stood a woman with bright, lemon-yellow skin. She smiled, "We haven't yet met, Paul. I'm Kellmarishmae. It's a shame we don't have time for proper introductions, but you must get to Katherine immediately. And remember, you are each most powerful when working in unison."

Paul struggled back to his feet and looked at the sword in his hands. "Get to Katherine," he said. Once again he stood alone on the side of the hill and he couldn't understand why he had dreamt of strange people with wildly colored skin.

He sensed the portals the rogue wizard had opened in the two circles, both made of that sideways slippage in reality. In one he sensed nothing, but the stench of the Primus caste permeated the other, which meant he'd find Katherine there.

He stepped into that slippage and materialized in the circle only a step away from her and a couple feet above the floor. The black, oily cloud had enveloped her entire right arm and half her chest. Paul hit the floor with a lot of momentum and had no time to think through any plan of action. He staggered, slammed into her, and wrapped his arms around her as they both bounced off the invisible wall of the circle. Paul landed on the floor on his back with Katherine on top of him, his arms still wrapped around her, the sword still clutched in his right hand. His right arm and part of the sword were hidden in the unclean black cloud wrapped around Katherine, and it felt so intensely cold he feared she might die.

••••

The monster shrieked, and Paul thought he heard fear and pain in its cry. The sickly, dark fog rose up off Katherine, so Paul rolled away from it, still clutching her in his arms, and came up against the wall of the circle. He let go of her and scrambled to his feet, stood facing the monster with the sword in his hand, Katherine behind him. As it flowed along the boundary of the circle, he heard Katherine struggling to her feet, breathing heavily.

"Are you okay?" he asked.

"I'll live," she said between gasps, her voice trembling, her teeth chattering as if they stood on a snow-covered landscape in the middle of the arctic.

The black cloud flowed up the far wall of the circle, then flowed toward them. Paul forgot all the lessons Anogh and Sabreatha had taught him about sword fighting, gripped the hilt of the sword with both hands and swung it back and forth.

The monster shrieked again and backed away, and this time Paul was certain he heard fear in its cry.

"It's afraid of the sword," he said.

Katherine said, "I'm glad it's afraid of something."

Behind the oily, black cloud the rogue wizard still sat on his stool several feet outside the circle, his lips moving, though now Paul could hear none of his words. Other than their own heavy breathing, the circle was filled with an eerie silence.

Katherine said, "We have to stop that son-of-a-bitch from completing the thirteenth repetition."

"But how do we do that?"

"I don't know. Maybe the sword."

It was worth a try. Paul swung the sword and slammed the blade into the wall of the circle. The invisible barrier shimmered and erupted with a shower of sparks. It crackled like bacon in a frying pan and wavered, but then it stabilized and remained intact. Outside the circle the rogue wizard stood up with a look of alarm on his face.

Katherine said, "Try again."

Paul raised the sword to strike the circle again, but the demon cloud flowed toward him, forcing him to keep the sword between them and it. The rogue wizard continued chanting, but now with a smile on his face.

Paul tried again to strike the wall of the circle, and again the demon cloud blocked him by putting him on the defensive. He realized the rogue must be close to the thirteenth repetition.

The sharp cry of a hunting hawk broke the silence.

Paul asked, "Did you hear that?"

"Ya," Katherine said. "But why? I can't hear anything else from outside the circle, so why that?"

Paul felt the strength of the demon growing, and realized the rogue must have reached the beginning of the thirteenth repetition. He had only seconds to stop the man, but how?

The cry of the hawk sounded again. Paul looked up and saw a shadow flitting through the rafters of the warehouse. The rogue wizard raised his eyes toward the ceiling as the shadow circled, descending slowly. He clearly hadn't spotted it because he didn't turn as it swung around behind him. The shadow leveled off at shoulder height far back in the warehouse, and Paul recognized the massive hawk-form of Sabreatha. She shot straight toward the back of the rogue, and at the last instant extended her claws and slammed into his back.

He staggered forward and stumbled into the circle of salt, scattering and breaking several lines. The circle broke and disappeared as the rogue's momentum carried him into the center of the circle where he plowed into the unclean demon mist. He shrieked out an earsplitting cry of terror and fear. The ground shook as the concrete floor of the warehouse cracked and split. The demon cried out joyfully, wrapped itself around the rogue and completely enveloped him.

The rogue's eyes turned blood-red and goat-slitted as he screamed, "Please. No." He didn't fall, appeared to be held up by the embrace of the demon as he writhed and struggled.

With Katherine behind him, one hand on his shoulder, Paul held the sword between them and the demon as they backed away from it. Blood poured out of the rogue wizard's eyes, ears, nose and mouth. "Please," he pleaded, spitting gobbets of blood as he spoke, "I am your servant. Take them, not me."

More cracks raced across the floor of the warehouse, and a block of concrete the size of a car shifted upward a couple of feet. The rogue's blood continued to flow without letup, and yet none of it dripped to the floor, while the oily cloud grew and expanded with power. Still backing away from the monster, Katherine grunted as Paul ran into her. He looked over his shoulder and realized they had backed into a corner up against the outer wall of the warehouse.

"Shit!" Paul said.

"Exactly," Katherine said

The rogue's cries dwindled to piteous sobs as his blood continued to flow.

"Let's edge along the wall," Paul said, "try to work our way around it and get out of here."

Katherine's eyes were wide with fear, and framed by smears of blood and makeup. "I certainly don't have a better idea."

She grabbed his arm in a painfully tight grip as they slid their backs along the wall, trying to keep as much distance as they could between them and the monster. Working their way out of a corner meant each step took them a little closer to the demon, even as it continued to swell and grow.

The rogue wizard now emitted only faint, incoherent whimpers, barely audible above the gunshot cracks of splitting concrete and the groaning steel of the building's structure. Paul and Katherine edged farther out of the corner and closer to the demon.

The rogue's groans dwindled to just a moan and a whimper, then he went silent and closed his eyes. Paul and Katherine froze as he stopped struggling. He hung in the air, no blood visible anywhere. His skin had taken on the texture of cracked, wrinkled leather, with the sickly, grayish cast of infected and corrupt flesh.

A block of concrete split with the sound of a gunshot. Paul and Katherine stumbled as the floor dropped a couple of feet. Paul could barely hear Katherine above the snapping of steel and concrete as she shouted in his ear, "Let's get out of here."

The rogue wizard opened his blood-red, goat-slitted eyes. "Not so fast," he said, as the greasy mist disappeared and he dropped to the floor to stand blocking their way. Far behind him the walls of some sort of office structure collapsed as he walked toward them.

The hawk dropped out of the rafters, transformed into the seven-foot-tall crazy woman and landed in front of the rogue monster, both hands gripping the hilt of her broadsword. She lunged forward and plunged the point into his chest. They both froze, and he slowly lowered his eyes to look at the blade that bisected his sternum. No blood flowed from the wound.

He raised his eyes, looked at Sabreatha and laughed. Then he lunged forward, ignoring the sword piercing his heart and forcing the blade even deeper into his chest. He extended his hands to wrap them around her throat, but an instant before he reached her she transformed into the hawk and flew away, taking the sword with her. The rogue turned toward Paul and Katherine and smiled hungrily.

"Guess he's not afraid of her sword," Paul said.

"Guess not," Katherine agreed.

"This is a Primus caste?" he asked.

"Yes, a prince of hell."

"And it's on the Mortal Plane?"

"No," she said. "It's haunting the body of that mummy corpse through the portal."

Paul looked into Katherine's eyes, and she looked the way he felt: scared shitless. They both had the same thought and spoke in unison. "The dark mirror."

It was only a few paces away. Paul spun toward it and dove, the sword held out in front of him. But the demon shifted from the mummy corpse into the oily black cloud, flowed toward him and slammed into him. In an instant it had enveloped him, and he felt it hungering after his power. He could resist it, but he couldn't fight back, couldn't overcome it.

••••

After turning around and heading back up 101, when they took the off-ramp Amen again picked up the track of whatever arcane scent he was following. On the surface streets of South San Francisco they returned to the frustrating process of missing turns and backtracking, but they'd only been at it for a few minutes when Colleen felt an un-warded shift in the arcane forces of the Mortal Plane.

"What was that?" she asked.

The others had clearly felt it as well. McGowan said, "Someone opened a portal to the Netherworld without containing it in a circle."

Amen said, "Or they contained it, but broke the circle before closing the portal."

Salisteen said, "And something very bad just showed up. We need to speed this up and get there now."

Several blocks away a bolt of lightning shot upward from a building and the ground shook.

McGowan said, "I think we just found out where we need to go."

••••

A pit had opened in the center of the warehouse, swallowing up blocks of broken con-crete and twisted steel, its diameter expanding slowly toward their position near the outer wall. Katherine guessed they only had a minute or two before the entire building collapsed into what had become a massive sink-hole. Paul lay on the floor, the black cloud enveloping every bit of him but his right arm and the sword. The demon had feared something about the sword.

Paul's eyes were open, his jaw muscles bunched. Somehow he was fighting the thing, but clearly not winning, though the monster didn't seem to be winning either. A stalemate!

Through clenched teeth, Paul said, "The . . . sword . . . mirror."

Paul had the monster preoccupied and Katherine realized he was giving her the chance she needed.

She crossed the floor to the sword, the damn platform high heels crunching on the broken glass around the mirror. A piece of the unclean, greasy cloud swirled up and away from Paul toward her. Katherine cringed back, but Paul growled, "No . . . fucking way . . . you . . . ass-hole."

He tensed visibly, his entire body rigid, and the swirl of cloud retreated.

Katherine bent down and gripped his right hand. It was locked so tightly about the hilt of the sword she couldn't pry his fingers loose. But she thought his arm and sword together were just long enough reach the dark mirror. She bent over with her ass in the air and grunted as she pulled on his wrist. His muscles were locked up in a rigid struggle against the demon, forcing her to fight against them. But little by little she edged the sword around until its tip lay on the floor just beneath the mirror. Paul was so preoccupied with fighting the demon he didn't know the tip needed to be lifted a few inches to the mirror's glass.

Another swirl of black cloud erupted from the demon and wrapped around her ankles, trapping her. Her feet went numb with bitter cold.

Damn the shards of glass, she thought and dove forward, extending her body to its full length. She landed on her stomach as the demon cloud began climbing up her legs, her fingers just a few inches short of the mirror. The black cloud reached mid-thigh just as she got her fingers around the blade near its tip and lifted it. She didn't have the strength to push it or thrust it, so she simply laid the tip against the dark mirror's glass.

An enormous thunderclap sent her senses reeling.

31

The Cat's Persistence

THE SOUND OF groaning steel and breaking concrete was deafening as Paul sat up. A large pit had opened up in the center of the warehouse, blocking any path to the door. It grew larger with each second as it swallowed the broken blocks of concrete that had once been the floor. Paul heard an earsplitting crack above him, and he looked up in time to see a block of concrete about three feet across falling straight toward him. He didn't stop to think how useless it was when he instinctively threw out an arm to protect his head; a two-ton block of concrete wasn't going to be too intimidated by his forearm. But when it slammed into him he knocked it aside as if it was made of Styrofoam.

When he'd fed on Cassius the Secundus he'd gained enormous strength from it. And now he'd fought off the Primus by feeding on it, using its own power against it. He realized that some of its strength still remained, though he'd learned that using it expended it quickly.

Katherine lay next to him. She rolled over onto her back and groaned, blinking her eyes in a daze.

Paul jumped to his feet, leaned down and picked her up as if she weighed nothing. With their escape blocked by the widening pit in the center of the warehouse, he carried her to the outer wall, the strength he'd taken from the demon dissipating with each step. "Can you stand?" he asked.

"I . . . I think so," she said.

She still seemed a little unsteady, so he put her down on her feet next a steel post and wrapped her hands around it. "Hold onto this."

He ran back out into the warehouse and picked up a thick steel bar that had fallen from the rafters. On his way back a metal girder bounced off his shoulders and his demon strength diminished further. He stopped next to Katherine and said, "Watch out."

He picked a spot on the outer wall about ten feet away, and swung the steel bar against it. The wall was nothing more than insulated sheet metal, but he'd used up most of the demon strength and he only dented it. He swung again and again, and by the time he'd punched a small hole through it he could barely raise the bar for another swing.

"Stand aside, mortal," a voice behind him said, sounding like the whisper of a soft wind brushing across his soul.

He spun around; Sabreatha stood there holding her broadsword. He stepped aside, she stepped in and punched the tip of the blade through the wall. She pulled it out and swung it overhead. It sliced a gash in the sheet metal about twice her height. Using her sword like a giant can opener, she pried, stabbed, sliced and hammered away until she'd opened a hole large enough for them to escape. Then she transformed into the hawk and flew through it, disappearing into the night.

Paul didn't have any demon strength left, but he had plenty of adrenaline working for him. He didn't ask Katherine's permission as he picked her up and carried her out through the makeshift doorway.

"Golly gee whiz, Conklin," she said as he carried her across an empty parking lot. "You're quite the heroic figure. Just makes a girl all atwitter."

He set her down on her feet at the far end of the parking lot just as the headlights of four cars swept over them. In the distance the building continued to collapse in on itself. An explosion erupted and a fireball lit up the night sky. A continuous stream of flame shot upward with a deafening roar and Paul guessed a natural gas line had just ruptured.

"Are you okay?" he asked.

She looked at the front of the torn-up, little dress, then down at her legs. "A few little splinters of glass," she said, clearly surprised, "and a few bruises, but that's all."

Paul guessed she'd gotten some strength from the demon through him, and that had protected her.

"Hold still," she said. "There's one thing I have to do."

She put a hand on his shoulder, lifted one foot, removed the platform shoe and tossed it aside. But when she put her foot down on the tarmac, she said, "Owe," and lifted it again.

"That hurt," she said. "There's little stones and bits of gravel all over the place."

"You're going to have to wear something," he said, "at least until you get home."

He picked up the shoe she'd discarded and handed it to her. She gave it an angry look as if she was about to have an argument with it. Then she gripped the body of the shoe in her right hand, the stiletto heel in her left, and yanked hard, grunting as she did so and snapping off the heel. She repeated the process with the other shoe, though on that one the heel didn't snap off cleanly and she had to worry it back and forth for a few seconds. When she finished, about a two-inch stub of heel remained on that one shoe. She still wobbled as she walked, probably because a couple of inches of platform sole remained beneath the toes.

The cars skidded to a stop nearby. The senior practitioners spilled out of them, accompanied by some of Karpov's thugs. Clark Devoe stepped out of one.

Boris and Joe Stalin marched up to Paul and Katherine and pulled out their howitzers. Katherine put her fists on her hips and said, "Guns! Really! Put the fucking things away, you morons."

Behind them Clark Devoe lifted a double-barreled, sawed-off shotgun.

Karpov snarled, "Do what she says, you idiots."

Salisteen asked, "Are you hurt?"

Paul said, "No, just minor scrapes and bruises."

McGowan demanded, "What the hell happened here?"

Katherine said, "Serial-killer-guy from Dallas summoned a Primus caste."

"We figured out that much," McGowan said. "Where are they?"

Paul said, "The Primus killed serial-killer-guy."

Katherine added, "And Paul closed off the portal he made, so the Primus is gone."

The building emitted a series of cracking, snapping sounds as the last of its walls collapsed. The sinkhole swallowed it completely and produced a gush of flame that rose up into the night sky.

"I hope that's going to stop," Paul said.

McGowan said, "It'll stop when the power that leaked over from the Netherworld is used up, though I wouldn't be surprised if it eats a few more buildings in the process."

Amen said, "We should leave before the authorities arrive."

Paul and Katherine joined McGowan and Colleen in his car. As the old man pulled out onto Highway 101 headed north, Paul watched Katherine pull off the blond wig, toss it out the window and shake out her own auburn hair. He asked McGowan, "What's going to happen with the authorities?"

The old man said, "The others are going to stay and plant a few suggestion spells around the periphery. You know, earthquake, soil liquefaction and the resulting sinkhole, fire from broken gas lines, stuff that basically fits the physical evidence. They'd probably come to that conclusion on their own, but it doesn't hurt to nudge them in the right direction."

Paul couldn't believe anyone would be that gullible. "They'll actually buy into that?"

The old man shrugged. "They have to make it fit within their own belief system, and *we* don't exist. There's always a few who think something's fishy, but more often than not they come up with a conspiracy theory involving a vast government cover-up, and no one takes them seriously. If they come even close to the truth and start talking about wizards and demons, they'll be written off as fringe whackos."

McGowan let them out on the sidewalk in front of his place before parking his car in the narrow little garage. As they stood there waiting for him, Colleen leaned close to Katherine and spoke softly, though loud enough for Paul to hear. "Dear, I'm sure you're already aware of this, but whatever possessed you to put on such an outfit? The slutty, punk-rock thing is just not you."

The older woman clearly had trouble hiding a smirk, and it took every bit of will-power Paul had to keep a straight face. Katherine looked at him and her eyes widened in anger. "Don't you say a word."

Just then McGowan walked up to them. "Nice outfit, Katherine. It's sooo you."

"That's it," Katherine said. "I'm going home and get out of this thing."

McGowan said, "Come on in and have—"

"No," Katherine snapped.

Colleen said, "You can't very well wander around dressed like that."

Paul said, "I'll hail a cab and get her home."

••••

Katherine seethed as she and Paul waited for the cab. She'd been about to kick off the stupid shoes, then Colleen made that snotty remark. And it looked like some drunk had urinated on the sidewalk in front of her father's house. She wasn't about to walk in that in her stocking feet, so she decided, *to hell with them all.* She'd wear the damn things all the way home.

The cab arrived, and when they climbed into it the cabbie took one look at her and smirked. He obviously thought Paul had picked up a goth, punk-rock hooker and was taking her back to his place.

They rode in silence as the cabbie constantly looked at her through the rear-view mirror and smiled knowingly, nodding his head while doing so. Paul struggled to suppress a grin, and only barely succeeded, which angered her even further. By the time they reached her place, her temper had risen to a solid boil.

••••

Katherine showed Paul where she kept a key in a phony rock in the garden near the front door. He tried to keep the look on his face neutral as he retrieved it, opened the door, and held it for her. Standing on her front porch, she turned around and kicked the shoes off, sending them flying one by one across her front yard.

Madge was waiting for them in the living room. She sauntered up to Paul, wrapped her tail around his ankle and said, "And you doubted I could deliver, eh hotshot?"

Katherine turned and looked at the little cat, her eyes sharp with anger. "And what are you supposed to deliver?"

Madge said, "I promised to help him score with you."

The little cat looked at Paul. "And you doubted me."

Katherine rounded on Paul. "You asked her to help you score with me?"

"No, I didn't ask her."

"You made her promise."

"No I didn't. She just volunteered."

"So you need help scoring with me?"

"No, I don't need help."

"So, no help needed. I'm that easy. Just snap your fingers and I'll spread my legs for you."

"No, I'm not trying to score with you."

She hesitated, frowned, and her anger grew. "You're not? That's not a very nice thing to say. I'm awfully damn good looking and you should be trying your best."

That almost sounded like an invitation, so he reached out, put an arm around her waist and pulled her against him. "How about if I start trying right now?"

She raised an eyebrow, but her anger dissipated and she spoke softly. "What?" she asked. "Are you into slutty, goth, punk-rock hookers now? That's kind of kinky, you know."

He couldn't resist. "I did like the view from the rear. You know, the carefully exposed butt-cheeks—"

"Don't even go there, Conklin," she snapped, then her voice calmed and she continued. "I am so not a butt-cheeks girl. And a thong! He put me in a thong! I should tie you up and strap you in a thong so you know what it feels like. I don't do thongs, Conklin. And I don't do slutty."

"I thought you said it was okay to be slutty."

"It's not okay to look slutty. It's okay to *be* slutty, as long as you look elegant while doing it, like maybe a Michael Kors outfit, with David Yurman accessories, a dynamite pair of Pradas, and the matching purse."

He said, "A thong, huh?"

"Don't push it," she said. "So what, you like your women slutty looking?"

"No, I just like you."

"So you like slutty Katherine McGowan, huh?"

He hesitated, then decided to plow forward. "No. I like Katherine McGowan any way she chooses to be."

"I didn't choose to look slutty."

He shrugged. "Well, I do like slutty Katherine."

Her eyes flashed with anger.

"I also like prissy Katherine, business Katherine, snotty Katherine, smart Katherine, and angry Katherine. Every one of them is gorgeous. I even like *Doctor* Katherine McGowan, and I bet I wouldn't mind kinky Katherine as well."

She frowned. "You know, Conklin, you're being rather nice. But I really do need to get out of this slutty, punk-rock, hooker outfit. It is so not me. And I need a shower, and some food."

"I could help," he said.

"Okay, while I'm in the shower you whip up something to eat."

He put a hand behind her head and she didn't resist as he pulled her makeup-smeared face closer to his. He brushed his lips lightly across hers. "I was thinking more along the lines of helping you out of the slutty outfit."

She frowned and pulled her head away slightly. He brushed his lips across the swell of her breasts above the push-up bra, and she inhaled suddenly, almost a gasp. "In fact, if you let me take care of the whole thing, I'll have to undress you very slowly, one piece at a time, and it just might take all night long."

Pressed together, face to face, body to body, he felt her heart beating rapidly. She'd calmed down, but her breathing had increased. Again, he brushed his lips across hers, and her tongue darted out as he did so, wetting his lower lip. He slid a hand down her back, reached further down and ran a finger lightly along the exposed edge of her butt-cheek.

"Stop that," she said, though she didn't sound like she meant it.

"Darn," he whispered. "I was kind of enjoying it."

She smiled, brushed her lips against his ear and said, "I sort of enjoyed it too, a bit, but just a little."

He said, "All you have to do is say yes, and you won't be able to keep that outfit on."

He was definitely having an effect on her. She looked thoughtful for a moment, then said, "No."

He knew he didn't do a good job of hiding his disappointment.

She grinned. "No, I'm not going to wear this thing, or even pieces of it, all night long. You're going to have to get this outfit off me much faster than that. After it's off, you can help me with the shower as well. Then . . . you can take all night long."

He couldn't hide a grin. "Help you with the shower?"

"Ya," she said. "You can soap my back."

"It's not your back I'm thinking of soaping."

She cocked her head and lifted an eyebrow. "Well, you can soap the other bits too."

She kissed him, and as their tongues danced back and forth, he realized she'd gained the upper hand again, and he suspected she always would. He didn't mind.

She pulled her lips away from his and looked at him. "By the way, I'm never prissy or snotty."

He decided to give it one last shot. "About the slutty outfit . . ."

"Ya, what about it?"

"You sure you don't want to hang on to it for a while? We could—"

She shut him up with a kiss.

The slutty outfit didn't last long, but the kisses continued well into the night.

Epilogue:

Mixed Blood

"I LIED TO the practitioners," he said. "He *does* have both demon and fey blood in his veins, though only trace amounts."

Then he is a true merlin?

After six thousand years their relationship had become more of a partnership, very unlike the master-thrall bond most possessed practitioners suffered. "He could be."

Then he could bring a Primus caste over.

"Yes, he could, and such a creature would dominate us. We'd lose all freedom."

Then we must kill him.

"Or possess him."

Yes, that would be better.

"And the woman too."

Yes, we'll take them both.

Notes From the Author

No Apologies, Leo

I HOPE LEV Nikolayevich (Leo) Tolstoy will forgive me for making liberal use of his story, and probably butchering it in a few places. I make no apologies for that, because unless it suited their purposes, Magreth and Cadilus would care nothing for historical accuracy, or for accurately portraying Tolstoy's characters. Of course, in *War and Peace* there were no such characters as Pavel Andreyevich Konklinov and Katerina Valtrovna Magovana, so it might appear that I deviated from the original story somewhat. But like wise practitioners everywhere, Pavel and Katerina would have preferred to keep a low profile, and gone out of their way to stay unnoticed. So as peripheral characters who didn't contribute to Tolstoy's plot, he simply decided not to mention them in the book, but they were there nevertheless. All good authors must sometimes be ruthless when it comes to excluding unnecessary information and characters, and Tolstoy was no exception.

I did make every effort to be historically accurate. Tolstoy wrote *War and Peace* more than fifty years after the Napoleonic wars. He was reputed to have done quite a bit of research to ensure accuracy in his story, but some scholars do believe he made a few minor mistakes. I myself did not find any, though I confess I wasn't looking for such errors. But since Pavel and Katerina are characters in Tolstoy's book, I always deferred to his version of events.

Language of the Imperial Russian Court

CATHERINE THE GREAT made French the official language of the Russian Court, and by the time of the Napoleonic wars in 1805, most, if not all, Russian aristocrats spoke fluent French. In fact, some were so poorly versed in Russian they needed to take lessons in their native language to converse with their more common countrymen.

Russian Names

MOST RUSSIAN SURNAMES have a variant that depends on the gender of the person. For male surnames that end with a "v" or "n", the female form is usually constructed by adding an "a" to the end of it, while male surnames that end in "y" are frequently converted to female by adding an "aya" to the end. For example, Count Rostov's wife is Countess Rostova, and Anatole Kuragin's sister is Helene Kuragina.

A Russian's middle name is a patronymic derived from the name of the person's father with the addition of a gender-specific ending. Male patronymics usually end in "ovich" or "evich", while female patronymics most often end with "ovna" or "evna". So Lev Nikolayevich Tolstoy's middle name basically means *son of Nikolay*.

First names are *given* names, and they usually have a variety of forms. In Russian, the name Maria has more than 10 variants. Maria is the formal name used for official purposes and by people of limited acquaintance. But there are diminutives that vary from the short form (Masha) to the intimate (Marusya), which itself has several forms. The situation is further complicated in that the same diminutive can be used for more than one formal name.

In formal situations, it is common to use the patronymic in combination with the given name, even in direct address. That's why, when Katerina first meets Pavel, she frequently thinks of him as *Pavel Andreyevich*, and when Dolokhov recognizes Pavel on the street, he says, "Pavel Andreyevich, is that you, old friend?"

Regarding Madge, the Potty-Mouth Cat

TILDA, OUR LITTLE black-and-white cat, was the inspiration for Natasha in the short story *Natasha Knows*. In turn, Natasha was the inspiration for Madge, the potty-mouth cat in this story. Madge got her talkativeness from Tilda who is frequently quite vocal, though Tilda is not a potty-mouth. However, she is often very direct and outspoken. Tilda was also the model who posed for both the cover on this book, and the short story *Natasha Knows*.

Acknowledgements

I'D LIKE TO thank Karen for both supporting my dream and being my most valuable critic, Tilda for being the inspiration for Madge the cat, Steve Himes, and the team at Telemachus, for their support for the the last several years, and for putting out a great product.

Books by J. L. Doty

Series: The Treasons Cycle
Of Treasons Born
A Choice of Treasons

Stand Alone Novel
The Thirteenth Man

Series: The Gods Within
Child of the Sword
The SteelMaster of Indwallin
The Heart of the Sands
The Name of the Sword

Series: The Dead Among Us
When Dead Ain't Dead Enough
Still Not Dead Enough
Never Dead Enough

Series: The Blacksword Regiment
A Hymn for the Dying
A Dirge for the Damned
A Prayer for the Fallen
A Requiem for the Forsaken

About the Author

JIM IS A full-time SF&F writer, scientist and laser geek (Ph.D. Electrical Engineering, specialty laser physics), and former running-dog-lackey for the bourgeois capitalist establishment. He's been writing for over 30 years, with 15 published books. His first success came through self-publishing when his books went word-of-mouth viral, and sold enough that he was able to quit his day-job, start working for himself and write full time—his new boss is a real jerk. That led to contracts with traditional publishers like Open Road Media and Harper Collins Voyager, and his books are now a mix of traditional and self-published.

The four novels in his new hard science fiction series, *The Blacksword Regiment*, were released in July 2020. Right now he's fleshing out ideas for the next book in *The Dead Among Us*, he's writing another episode in *The Treasons Cycle*, and he's working on a new fantasy series *The Deck of Chaos*.

Jim was born in Seattle, but he's lived most of his life in California, though he did live on the east coast and in Europe for a while. He now resides in Arizona with his wife Karen and three little beings who claim to be cats: Tilda, Julia and Natasha. But Jim is certain they're really extra-terrestrial aliens in disguise.

Visit the author's website at http://www.jldoty.com
Contact the author at jld@jldoty.com